Drunk in the Warm Glow

Drunk in the Warm Glow

A novel by D.W. Anderson

Creators Publishing
Hermosa Beach, CA

DRUNK IN THE WARM GLOW
Copyright © 2017 D.W. Anderson

Cover art by Peter Kaminski

CREATORS PUBLISHING
737 3rd St
Hermosa Beach, CA 90254
310-337-7003

Library of Congress Control Number: 2017938501
ISBN (print): 978-1-946630-55-2
ISBN (ebook): 978-1-945630-54-5

First Edition
Printed in the United States of America
10 9 8 7 6 5 4 3 2 1

"The unhappy person is one who has his ideal . . . in some manner outside himself. The unhappy one is absent." Soren Kierkegaard

~ ~ ~

"You have to be always drunk. That's all there is to it—it's the only way. So as not to feel the horrible burden of time that breaks your back and bends you to the earth, you have to be continually drunk." Charles Baudelaire

PART 1

Chapter One

It Sparks

Once in a stupor, I imagined a shadowy man in a black trench coat approaching me. He made an offer in a low rasp: "Do whatever I tell you, and you will become an observer of life. An onlooker. No longer will you dread mundane chitchat. No longer will the tension and burden of exchanging social pleasantries be upon you. No longer will you feel the burden of existence. No longer . . .

"Instead, you'll be invisible. Forever, you will be an observer. A face in the theater."

I said yes.

Then I blacked out and woke cotton-mouthed, red-eyed, and pantless on this couch in my living room. Since this man is gone—lost in a drunken memory—I am stuck here while my best friend creeps through the dark crevices of the Internet.

On the wall, the mustache clock ticks.

"I don't get it. What's the appeal of looking at this?" I ask Steven Bradley III, or Trey, as we've always called him. He's plopped in a computer chair inches from our 55" TV monitor. The webpage display reads "Get Revenge On Your Ex!" In a collage of clickable thumbnails are selfies of girls, all colors and ages. Most of them are tattooed and overweight. A few nude-dude selfies hide in the thumbnail collage. Like little hidden Waldos.

"Most those people," I say, "I'd never want to see naked in real life." I'm lying on the couch, my mixed-drink glass balancing on my chest as Toki the Cat is curled at my feet.

"Ty, I'm gonna find someone I recognize one day, and then the search will all be worth it," Trey says. "I'm a lot like a treasure hunter. Ya know, like Nic Cage in *National Treasure,* but sexier." He lets his out ponytail and shakes out his hair like a model. He clicks on a thumbnail of a shirtless woman with Popeye forearms. The page loads and the title reads "Cheating, Lying Mother of Two. Freak in the Sack." He leaves the computer chair and walks around the room with his long lighter, lighting candles throughout our duplex. His ritual, Trey lights the candles before smoking.

"Plus," he says, "I like knowing other people's secrets. Most these shitheads don't even know their exes from Texas posted nudies for everyone to see. But *I* know. And information can be powerful." He laughs maniacally, and the first candle smells like Funfetti birthday cake.

The mustache clock ticks, so I sip my vodka. It tastes like the smell, iced Funfetti cake. "You're a creep. You *do* know that, right?"

"No, no. Not a creep." He's shaking his head and lighting a second candle. Cinnamon. "I have an active imagination, my friend. Least that's what Mrs. Lemke said."

"Lemke? As in our fourth-grade teacher?"

He nods, lighting another candle. Lavender. "Yeah. Gotta hold onto those compliments." He snatches at a wisp of smoke dancing above a candle.

Over the years, I've seen Trey looking at the most absurd and obscure pornography, but he's never sexually interested. He studies porn as if Animal Planet is running a documentary about bonobo chimps.

"It's fascinating, man," he says. "Humans and who they decide to mash their genitals against. For example, who looked at *this* woman," he points at the monitor with the lighter, "and thought, 'Mmhmm, I need me some of *that.*'"

The stretch-marked mother on the TV-monitor stares at me. Her vulnerable expression forces me to imagine her as she might've been as a kid—what *she* was like in fourth grade. Once a person, she's now objectified as an arrangement of pixels in a stranger's living room.

Trey's blonde hair sways as he moves around the living room. The last candle smells like chocolate and the smells clash, overwhelming my senses. Too much. The mustache clock grows louder and my stomach to tenses; the burden of the first day of a new semester builds.

"You want a hit?" Trey says, sitting back in his computer chair. He lights a bong shaped like R2D2. The water bubbles.

"Nah." I sit up. Toki the Cat runs off and I head for the bathroom. "Class in a few."

"College." He shakes his head. "Just a waste of money, man. Got all that info right here," he says, holding the smoke in his lungs. He pats the computer tower. "All the info you'll ever need." He exhales.

In the bathroom I grab my bottle of lorazepam, my anti-anxiety pills. The start of a new semester means the start of the barrage of information, ideas, professors, people, choices—all of it, sources of anxiety. All of it, sparks for a fire.

1.

I sit in the back of the classroom at a table next to a dude-bro I recognize from last semester. The guy's a stock frat boy: a crew-cut; a sleeveless tee with a beer pong scene on it; grey sweatpants; a drawstring bag to hold his basketball shoes; a notebook filled with crude doodles.

Professor Nelson rambles about classroom rules as he paces with his hands tucked behind his back. He's wearing his signature argyle sweater that barely reaches his belt. Typically, he drops his favorite purple marker four or five times per class. He'll bend over, half his asscrack flashing the class. Like a plumber with a doctorate. In unison the class's heads turn away. Usually one person, a new student to Nelson, groans, mumbles to another student, *ugh.*

Nelson's reading off the class roster for attendance, out of order, commenting on every single last name. Everything Nelson says ends with a guttural, mumbled *riiight*, like Mr. Mackey from *South Park*. The class fidgets through his ritual. *Oh, is that a New Zealand-origin last name? I once knew a Clement back in college. Interesting fellow, riiight. Simmons?*

I despise attendance. Name by name, my tension builds. The anticipation of having to simply say "Here" causes my chest to tighten and my breathing to cut short. Short panicked breaths.

Logically, I know taking attendance requires no performance ability, but my body is preparing for saying "Here" like I'm preparing for battle. The anxiety starts as physiological reactions: shortened breaths, tightened stomach, and eyes blinking too much. I need to swallow way too much. I think about it, believing that *every person in the room* can hear me swallowing, as if my *gulp* echoes through a megaphone, and everyone is annoyed by it: *Fucking gross. Did you hear that?*

The cold sweat beads down my armpit, down my back, and my shirt sticks to the plastic chair.

Then the anxiety switches from physical to mental. *Everyone* sees me sweating, like I'm a fat dude who started with a light-gray shirt that he sweated into black. I wonder if my sweat smells like a concoction of rotting onions, corn-chip sweaty socks, and rotting fish. My illogical reptile brain dominates me and I'm helpless to respond. Fight or flight. Completely fear-dominated.

"Tyler Linley," Nelson calls. His right eye twitches at me. I take a deep breath—in through the nose, out through the mouth. The silent pressure of the room builds on me. Stomach contracting, I'm getting fidgety, so it's time to think through things. Let reason calm my illogical reactions.

See, I'd like to be cool, calm, unpredictable, quick with comeback, smart and in-depth, like a lead character in a book or a movie. Matthew McConaughey. Ryan Gosling. But externally, I'm boring and dull. In my mind I see it all perfectly. Problem is, when you're imagining it, everyone around you just sees your blank expression and the spittle collecting on your chin. You're just boring. Too stuck in your head.

But I'm here in the moment, I try to remember. Touch the cold, hard chair. Feel the fibers of my shirt. See the panels linked together on the dusty wooden floor.

Professor Nelson's big owl eyes are staring at me through his oval glasses. Christ. I never answered him.

"Uh, here," I say, waving at him after two or fifty-two minutes.

He runs through the rest of the list and I'm relieved. Almost proud. The sweat stains under my pits are visible in my peripheral, and, goddamnit, everyone is going to notice that. I've found acknowledging it first is the best route.

"Jesus, it's hot in here," I whisper to the frat boy. His name is C.J. or B.J the Frat Boy.

"No joke, man," he says, nodding his head to his music, one ear bud dangling, the other crammed in his ear.

I inventory the room. A few yoga pants girls; a few "I Heart Pink" sweats (which to me just reads "I Heart Young Vagina"); an older guy in a dress shirt and khakis; a few gals and guys in sweatpants and U of Ashgrove sweatshirts.

A girl busts into the classroom as Professor Nelson says, "Anyone I didn't read off?"

"Olivia McDermott," the girl says. She flashes a white smile at the professor. "I'm really sorry I'm late." She takes a seat in front of me. A whoosh of air and the smell of coconut shampoo fill my bubble of personal space. As she pulls out a notebook from her backpack, she turns slightly back and catches my eye. She smiles, holding eye contact for a second or an hour.

The name. The face. So familiar. After a moment of vague recognition, like an itch you can't locate, I remember. Jordan McDermott's kid sister. Not a kid anymore, though. Her grade school yearbook photo flashes in my mind, superimposed over her adult face like a before-and-after comparison. The tiny slanted teeth I remember are now straightened into a solid white smile, model-like. The stringy, matted brown hair now has volume and curl slightly around her tan face. The bangs are gone, her high cheekbones and little button nose no longer something to be hidden.

My third-grade teacher/mom once bought me this "How to Draw" book that broke down face shapes. Olivia's would be considered "heart-shaped," which I used to think was the prettiest. The tight blue t-shirt has a tiny pocket on the chest, and it silhouettes her curved figure. I'm suddenly awake down under the table. I have no choice, like the first wild and untamable boners that arise like zombies at the onset of puberty. Although I don't want to think this, I bet that B.J. the Frat Boy next to me is checking her out, too, and I'm angered by that; like, I knew her first, so back off, which, I realize, is ridiculous and primal to think. Should I bang my chest and roar, ape-like?

As I run through her changes, I get the urge to leave class right now and hit the gym. Work up some six-pack, washboard abs. *Hey, Olivia-girl, wanna wash that blue t-shirt on these?* I'd lift my shirt and she'd coo and—of course—I'd wash her clothes on my washboard abs. Then we'd make sweet *sweet* love. Maybe on top of the clean clothes I just washboard-ab-cleaned.

I realize Professor Nelson has been talking about Nietzsche for a while now.

"A magical movie," he's saying. "Each of us, a star in our own. But when you think of someone else as the star of their own movie, you realize you're just a minor role in theirs. You're just an object in their reality. You might be 'Boring Stoner at Party # 3' on their credits list, and nothing more. *Riiight.*" He rambles on, mentioning *No Exit, The Sickness Unto Death,* and other materials we'll broach. Despite my clawing need to pay attention to such ideas—*if I don't, I'll fail and miss everything essential*—I lose track of what he says. Instead, I'm staring at the back of Olivia McDermott's head, half terrified, half excited that she'll turn around again.

2.

Trey and I—our duplex is our haven. Each wall is lined with shelves that contain DVD box sets, video games (Commodore 64 to PlayStation 4), Betamax, VHS, Blu-rays, books, *New Yorkers,* and comics. Every inch of the wall, including the vaulted ceiling, is covered with magazine clippings and promotional posters. We each have our own room (!) and near the bathroom, we've set up a sound-proof(ish) movie room, called "The Dungeon of Love." In it, there are two leather recliners with drink holders.

Trey and I watch more movies than most movie critics (*which are a dime a dozen,* Trey says. *It's easier to critique than create something*). Despite his disdain for critics, Trey writes reviews every day on his blog, which I doubt anyone reads. As he types, he'll break away to click through porn websites and helicopter-blade decapitation pictures. That and his successful eBay store, which focuses on rare media collectables. I'm usually lying on the couch, my ancient laptop burning on my chest. I make a few bucks as an editor for a low-grade local newspaper, and I tutor college dude-bros. Most of this I'm able to do from home rather than dealing in-person with reporters writing about local high school sports or the local man who's been eating Big Macs since the '80s.

Trey rocks back and forth in his gaming chair. His hands are wrapped around the joysticks built into the armrests. Candles flicker, and the TV flashes as he shoots, jumps, and runs on-screen. Puffy headphones cover half his head. Standing next to him, I write in Sharpie on a notebook page. I hold it to up to him like a mute Looney Tunes character.

Remember Olivia McDermott?

He nods. "Friends with her on Facebook. She's a dime piece now." He yells this because of his sound-cancelling headphones.

I write on the notebook page again.

Sat in front of me in Phi 402. Gorgeous.

He nods and yells, "I know. I just said, I have her on Facebook." He gets louder. "Seen her bikini pics. Gorgeous. Very, very *noice!*" he says in a horrible Chinese-ish accent. "Now let me get back to biz*nass!*" He unpauses the game and starts jerking around in the chair, biting his bottom lip.

I try to read Nelson's assignment for next class, but the words don't register. I go over the same sentence again and again: "Face the facts of being what you are, for that is what changes what you are."

But nothing sinks in, because bouncing around in my head is that image of Olivia McDermott turning and smiling at me in slow motion like a *Baywatch* episode.

Maybe Trey has a piña colada-scented candle.

3.

It's amazing how quickly routine takes over. Every day on the way to class, I chew Big Red gum because it makes me sneeze (one of the best things ever). I chew a bit, glance at the sun, and bam: three powerful, eighth-of-an-orgasm sneezes. As I'm walking along, two thoughts fill my head as cinnamon Big Red burns my taste buds.

One: Olivia must sit in front of me again because I'm feeling loose today. I'm calmer (and sleepier) because of a double dose of razzy-pam. Feeling like this—anxiety temporary dulled—this is the time to talk to her. I'm not worried about much; I'm not worried that I'm wasting every moment of my life doing insignificant tasks. I'm not worried that I'm failing to succeed academically, socially, monetarily, intellectually, or romantically. Instead, I'm dulled. And this is the closest to normal I can get. I want to get to class before her, so I'll be sitting at my spot like I'm a principal at my desk when she comes to my office; it'll feel like home-court advantage. I'll be reacting to everything she says. I want to feel comfortable and at home so I can somehow—I don't know how—make an impression on her. Trick her? No. I'll be Ryan Gosling and at least make her notice me and remember my name. If only college life were like grade school. *Hi, I'm Tyler. I'm older than you. You're pretty. Wanna play?*

Two: this weekend is the Packers' first game. I love-hate this time of year because football starts (awesome), but so does school, which means anxiety and winter. Eight months of shoveling, bitch-slapping cold wind, and muddy snow.

Packers' kickoff, my favorite part of the week, is at noon this Sunday. As the Big Red cinnamon flavor disappears, I imagine myself as a punter on fourth down. The crowd stirring, the d-line rushing at me, I spit the red gum wad into the air. As it falls, I kick it as hard as I can. I stare into the bright sky, squinting. I can't track where the red gum is in the bright blueness.

"Oh, my God," a girl's voice says ahead of me. I focus ahead at her. "Oh, my God!" she says again. It's Olivia. She's digging in her hair. A girl in yoga pants stops with her.

"What's wrong?" the yoga-pants girl says.

"There's gum in my hair," Olivia says as she's rifling through her curls, trying but unable to see.

"Okay, okay. Hold still," Yoga Pants says.

I approach, and—fuck it—I'm loose.

Here goes.

"I'm so, so, so sorry. I didn't know you were ahead of me, and I punt my gum like every day. I didn't think it'd go this far or ever hit anyone or land in someone's hair so I—"

"Why would you throw gum into the air?" Yoga Pants says.

Well, I punted it, I don't say. She's parting Olivia's hair and picking at the red clump like a chimp. Olivia's head is tilted down, and I think she's almost crying. I want to help, but I'm just standing here like an idiot. I scan my memory for tips to get gum out of hair. Cut it out? No. Peanut butter and lemons? *The Simpsons* did it.

"Don't worry, Livi," Yoga Pants says. "It's not matted in there. Only caught in a few hairs. We'll run to the bathroom. I'll try to work it out." Yoga Pants death-stares at me.

"Okay, that's good," Olivia says, relieved. She takes an audible breath and looks at me. Her green eyes hold palpable energy. She wears no makeup, and the moisture collected around her eyes gleams, and I feel physically weak. Wobbly knees.

"You're Tyler Linley," Olivia says as I walk with her and Yoga Pants toward the restroom. "Remember me?" She wasn't almost crying, because she looks and sounds upbeat and perky, despite my chewed up gum gooing-up her 'do.

"Yeah. I knew I recognized you yesterday. Your brother's Jordan. Graduated eighth grade with me," I say in one breath. "He and I used to be at each other's throats all the time in grade school."
She nods. "He hasn't changed a bit. He's a Marine now, and, well—" She points to the restroom. "We'll be right back," Olivia says, smiling. They disappear behind the closing door.

I lean against the wall outside Stuart Hall's girls' restroom as students pass by. I probably look like a Fonz-like pervert loitering outside the women's restroom, but the double-dose of lorazepam makes me indifferent. I'm excited like a schoolboy that Olivia remembers me.

I'm a year older, so I guess it makes sense in grade school years; older kids were cooler simply because they were older and had more experience, like with making out or poking a vagina or yanking a penis. I hope she has a memory of me being cool, a positive image. Like the times I beat Jordan in schoolyard fights. Or my former basketball ability—impressive then, not so now. Something about being a 5'10" white guy with skinny legs who can't jump doesn't mesh with collegiate basketball. Then again, age doesn't matter in college years and beyond. A meathead idiot can be awesome in high school if he can call kids fags and fat-asses and be tall. But once he's out of the caged world of grade and middle school, it doesn't matter. Money, power, looks, intelligence, success—these things impress people. I lean against the cold brick wall, trying to look cool and non-perverted.

I glance at the ticking clock, but I'm able to ignore it.

Olivia flips her hair as she exits the bathroom. It's a *Baywatch* moment again. I stand there stupidly staring at her coming toward me. *Close your mouth, you dolt.*

Yoga Pants disappears down the hallway after Olivia thanks her.

"Got it out," Olivia says.

I give a double thumbs up.

Her head's tipped to the side, and she's eyeing me up and down. She says, "I'm wondering something, 'cause I've never had someone spit gum in my hair. Is this like back in middle school when you liked someone, so you had to be mean to them to show you liked them? Like, you'd hit a girl or tell everyone a guy was ugly and stupid and had a pizza-face."

Now I'm short on breath, my heart spazzing Neil Peart drum solo, and the clock's suddenly booming a bass drum—but I remember the lorazepam, and it relaxes me. The drug is inside me. Part of me. I just need to method act; I need to pretend I'm the person I want to be.

Channeling George Clooney.

Deep breath. "Well, technically, I *punted* the gum into your hair, not spat. Spitting would be rude and dickish. I'm a nice guy," I say, shrugging my shoulders and smiling like a romantic-comedy actor might. Not Clooney.

Channeling Ryan Gosling.

She says, "I mean, really, *punting* gum into a girl's hair to get her attention. Wow. I'm not sure if I'm impressed or if I think it's pathetic." She starts walking toward our class. I forget to walk. "Are you coming?" She laughs, a quiet little exhale of air from her nose.

"Yeah, yeah. I'm-a comin'." I walk next to her. The air is filled with her shampoo. Piña colada.

She asks me if I did the reading, which I did (early this morning) and always do. I ask the same. She did the reading and always does, usually early in the morning. Lots of notes, we both say. I don't mention how she distracted me last night while I tried to read. Gosling would never do that.

"I love challenging ideas and testing them against others," she says. "It's . . . it's like a freeing process, because if you have a way of thinking that is oppressing you or making you miserable, you can challenge it. You can overrule it because you control your way of thinking. No one can take that from you. You can change your thinking so you can think in a way that makes most sense to you. Then you can be your happiest." She's bouncing slightly as she walks, light on her feet like a ballerina. I expect her to break into a pirouette. I doubt she ever has a heavy day that seems to drag along.

I nod. Just like in class, I have something I want to say, but I hold it back, keep it chained in my head. The less I say, the less chance I'll look stupid.

"So," I say. "Young Olivia McDermott has turned into a philosopher."

"I wouldn't say so. I just like to explore new things. Every day's a possibility. I know that's cliché and cheesy." She shrugs. "I don't care. I just try to learn a new thing every day. And how am I *young*, Mr. Linley?"

I feign confidence, puffing out my chest. "It's just that I've seen so much, done so much in my one year more of experience. I could write a book about all I've learned. Like my times back in 'Nam."

"That so, Mr. Linley?"

"Indeed. You're even calling me Mr. Linley because you know I'm right."

"Maybe so." She pauses to think for a moment. "You know, it's crazy that I'd run into you after all these years, in a different city. Of all the classes to take, we take the same class, the same hour in the same semester. I almost dropped this class last week. Then we'd never have run into each other. And if I'd have been late again today, you never would have spit gum in my hair."

"Punted. I punted the gum," I pantomime punting a football.

"I don't say this to all guys who 'punt' gum in my hair. But do you wanna get coffee? Just sit down, catch up. It's been so long."

My head's nodding before I say anything. Fuck yes, is what I want to say. "I'd love that" is what I do say. A nice guy, that's who I am. Gosling. *The Notebook. I'll build you a house, Olivia.*

I'm caught in a daydream of what to say next when I walk right past the classroom as Olivia stops and turns in. "Tyler?" I turn around.

"Yeah, sorry. I'm a little out of it today."

She smiles and sits next to me, her leg brushing mine every few minutes. Everything Nelson says, Olivia is ready with a comment, usually representing the more optimistic view in opposition to Nelson's and my pessimistic viewpoint. I glance at her notes. I'm impressed by the color-coded organization, the round bubbly letters fitting perfectly inside the blue lines. In the margin she's drawn a smiley face, completely with eyelashes and lips. My notes are written in mismatched capital and lowercase letters, some slanting like backslashes, some straight as a pole. Zero consistency. It takes me a few minutes to decipher what I meant to signify with each jumble of chicken scratch. I say nothing in discussion, as usual, and I debate Olivia and Nelson in my mind.

Last time I faced speaking in front of class—I had to present last semester on the colonization of the blah-blah-blah—I chose another route. Rather than stand in front of my classmates and present my well-researched argument, I drove around campus with a plastic cup filled with box wine, in full-on panic mode. I had asked, via email, Professor Nelson if I could skip the presentation part of the argument. He emailed back:

"Guess who said this: 'Fear has its use, but cowardice has none'? Time's up. Gandhi. Which is to say, *no*, you can't skip the presentation part. See you soon."

That was the first class I'd skipped. Every time he mentioned me presenting again, I skipped the next class, cruising around campus, biting my nails, sipping my cheap wine, gnawing at the skin around my fingernails. Even now, my index finger, which grips my pen, has dried blood caked along the cuticle.

Toward the end of class, the lorazepam starts to wear off like an evaporating cloak, and I thank sweet baby Jesus when Nelson lets us out early, because I could feel my antagonistic brain about to start worrying about the inferiority of my notes, how I need to update them—all my notes ever taken. My brain runs wild about how my breath probably smells like a cat's butthole, how Olivia is just being a normal person by asking me to catch up, not showing actual interest in me romantically.

Brain, fuck you. Genetics, fuck you. Tyler, fuck you.

Before I stand to leave, she hands me a torn slip of notebook paper. In curly pink numbers are seven digits. Behind the digits, a smiling heart with curly lashes stares at me.

"Text me tomorrow morning, and we'll figure out a time to meet up."

I want to jump into the air and freeze frame like the end of *Breakfast Club*, but I don't. I play it cool. Smile and coolly drift away.

Gosling out.

4.

That night I walk in the front door and try to look at our duplex through a girl's eyes. I imagine Olivia and me walking in together. Holding hands. A girl probably wouldn't love the Budweiser bikini girl cutout or the 55" porn displayed on the TV. A cool girl *would* appreciate the George Carlin special collection DVDs set on a cardboard shelf in the shape of his body. But the *Metal Gear Solid* action figures lining the walls, the cartoon and video game character action figures, the video game chairs with old-school joysticks built in, the freakish sex toys Trey's collected over the last few years—this all might not make a girl drop moisture bombs. I'm a bit embarrassed by it. Maybe she'll be into games and pop culture? If so, adding her into the duplex mix wouldn't give me a reason to leave it and venture out into the world. Trey never does—other than to restock his drug pile or slough through the Lion's Den for new sex toys he'll never use with a live person. Oddly, his action figure collection is no different than his collected sex toys: unopened and in mint condition.

As always, the candles are lit, cinnamon's scent reaching my nose first, joined soon after by . . . ugh.

"Trey, is that pickle juice?"

"Yeah, man. I tried making my own candle scent. Behold my new creation: Dill Pickle Juice. Get it? Like *Rugrats*." Trey's lying on the couch, his head to the side watching *Blade Runner.*

"It smells horrible." I put out the flame with my thumb and index finger.

"Don't hate on my creativity, *buddy*." He pauses *Blade Runner.* "And I was just getting into this when you came home. The best scene—you know the one—was just about to come on. Ruining my life, man. Just out to ruin my life." He's shaking his head.

"Seriously, I'm going to puke."

"Quit being so dramatic," he says, swinging his body to stand up. "Oh, by the way, your dad called. Whoa. Blood rush to the head." He braces himself on the back of the couch.

I scowl at Trey. "And?"

"He wants you to call him back."

"Why?"

"I don't know. He didn't say."

"You answered my phone?"

"No, dumbshit. He called mine, not yours."

I drop my bag to the wood floor.

"Eh, fuck him," I say as I drop my books in my room. "He won't call me, but he calls you. He won't . . . ." I know this isn't worth having an aneurysm over, so I change my train of thought—a suggestion every therapist and self-help book tells someone with issues.

"I got a date with Olivia McDermott."

"A date?" Trey is incredulous, his voice and body curling into a question mark.

"Well, we're getting coffee." I now wonder. "Is that a date?" My voice matches Trey's.

"No. That's just catching up. Coffee? My mom and I get coffee and talk about who's died recently in Dad's church. My grandma and I get coffee and play Old Maid. Not a date. Besides, she's too hot for you. No offence."

"Screw you, Tubs."

"Hey."

"Sorry. *Ahem.* Steven Bradley III."

"Steven Bradley, *ahem*, is my father's name."

"And his father's too."

"I'd appreciate you leaving Pastor Bradley out of this. He is, I say, he is too holy of a man to be discussed in this sin-engorged domicile of the Devil," Trey says, mocking his father in a southern accent. "I just don't think Olivia would say yes to a date."
"She asked *me.*"

"Weird. From her Facebook profile, I gather she's the go-getter type of a gal. A real flapper." Trey adopts an advertiser's voice: "*The lady of the future who's up for anything,* I suppose—anything, including asking a loser who was kind of cool in middle school. Sort of cool. Not really cool, but people would admit, 'he's okay,' if asked."

Trey lights his bong, which always seems to materialize whenever he summons it. Poof, and it's in front of the couch-dwelling meat-bag. He lights, inhales, and says, "I seen most the girls you bring back here, all drunk." He exhales, coughing between every few words. "And, yeah, I will concede you've brought back some good lookin' ladies. But you can't build a relationship. I mean, you did well in high school, but you've gotten so much worse. I'm not trying to be a dick, but I live with you. I know you can't, and—

hell—you shouldn't try, either. We can't have some girl come in here and PMS the place up with Toto posters and sequined throw pillows and Build-a-Bears. Besides, all that'll happen is you'll build some relationship up into this pretty, lovely thing that exists only in your mind. Then it'll just collapse like a Sichuan school building."

"A Sichuan school building?" I ask.

"I say, you know I'm right," he says, raising his palms to the sky like a prophet.

"Relax. Just getting coffee. Two adults getting coffee. *Sip, sip, hmm, that's a good Guatemalan blend.*" I'm nodding and smiling.

"Good. Keep it that way." Trey thumbs the lighter and watches the flame dance. "I'm saying, yeah, bring her back here if you need to. Diddle her bean and motorboat her skin flaps, whatever you people do. But don't let it grow. Roundup-kill that weed of a relationship before it grows. I'm just looking out for your own good. Nothing good'll come of a relationship. Just remember high school. You and I, we've got what we need here."

"Just getting coffee. That's all."

5.

Trey and I've been friends since before I had memories. The first recollection I have, I was jumping on a bed, naked. The room dark, my little-boy penis bounced and slapped against my little pale thighs. I was shaking my little teacup buttcheeks and singing a nonsensical song about dog bones and grave-digging. A young blonde girl giggled hysterically in the corner. Trey was rolling around on the ground next to her, out of breath from laughing so hard. Pastor Bradley's paintings hung from the wall. One painting, styled in cool colors, depicted white Jesus reaching down to pat a child who held a fish in one hand and a slice of bread in the other. Pastor Bradley is an excellent painter like my mom, and they got along so well for so long. They painted together and had a chemistry like they were married more than my dad and mom.

As I bounced, giggling uncontrollably, a squirt of yellow pee arched across the room. Trey's dad busted through the door and went insane, spewing things I didn't understand. He dragged me by my arm into the bathroom. I felt the rug burn along my entire right side. Still naked, I curled into the fetal position on the cold white bathroom floor. Pastor Bradley turned on the shower and dropped me in the tub, the whiteness blinding. I couldn't catch my breath under the falling ice water, so I peed and shat in the tub. Pastor Bradley was yelling at me, crossing his hands across his chest. As I first learned what fear is, little Trey popped into the bathroom, the heavy wood door slamming against the wall. Two of Pastor Bradley paintings crashed into the white linoleum, their corners denting. Trey pushed his dad's leg. "Stop it!" Trey screeched. His dad picked him up with one hand by the collar, like a bully, and disappeared into another room. I heard a slap. Another. Then Trey crying.

Trey and I've grown parallel to each other. The world's developed before us as if we shared one eye. He's the closest thing to family I have; well, I'd say he *is* my family, which is sad. (Now, understand that I'd never say any of this to him because he'd give me shit until the day I die. It's more of a shared knowledge neither of us ever acknowledges, like after walking in on parents slapping uglies.)

We've built our duplex into The Sanctuary, borrowing the term from one of Pastor Bradley's paintings he hung above the toilet. The works of art within The Sanctuary allow for an escape from anything; reality is formed by each of us in our minds, but so much of my reality is left to chance and other people's whims. I'm steered by anxiety except in our home. In The Santuary, in The Dungeon, I can select who manipulates my emotions.

You want to feel something? You find the movie, the song, the TV show, the novel, the book—whatever you need. We've been collecting it all, and it's a bit like Bubble Boy for Trey; he's relegated himself to The Sanctuary (only Trey and I are allowed to call it this, by the way). I want to venture out, to live a life like those found in movies. I know I could be so many things with focus and time and lorazepam. But sometimes I fail. Usually, I fail. And it *is* reassuring to come home to a place of control with a person who understands the world the same as I do, at least most of the time. At least part of it.

We're the same but different. I've got all the nonstop anxiety all that comes with it; he's got all the nonstop being overweight and hermit-y and all that comes with it. He says it is genetics. Big-boned. I'm convinced it has something to do with his routine: gorging a twelve pack of jelly-glazed throughout the morning while surfing free porn and playing *Elder Scrolls* and *Call of Duty* with ten-year-olds online. He wasn't like this in high school; then, he was calm, insightful, caring, and thin. Now—not so much. His weight didn't come from his mommy or daddy, that's for sure. I'd say Sharon Bradley is pretty hot underneath the bags and lines on her face, and all the Christian de-sexualization she's gone through over the years. I've definitely thought about it.

I wouldn't tell Trey that, either.

Ask Trey to describe himself and he'll say something about being a simple man of the mind. One night he got blitzed or hammered or somehow inhibition-manipulated. He showed me these comics he's been drawing starring himself as "The Wond'ring Turtle." The Wond'ring Turtle—complete with anime-style blonde ponytail—searches for and expounds upon the knowledge of the truth. He (slowly) wanders the lands, running into troublesome individuals, helping them with knowledge and insight. Somehow The Wond'ring Turtle has a six pack and big biceps and is always turning down sexual advances from other turtles—usually sexy turtles with colorful shells and tight hourglass bodies. When I saw the comic, I, for the first time in my life, thought of turtle sex.

Then I Googled it.

We cling so tightly to our fantasies as the stars of our own movies.

Chapter Two

A Connection

I'm staring at the ceiling fan trying to shut off my brain, but there's no switch. Without the aid of sleeping pills or muscle relaxers or alcohol or some sort of benzodiazepine, attempting to fall asleep is just inviting the circus to town. Every question, every possible thought must be explored. *I wonder what'd happen if . . .* And inevitably, I think of something brilliant (or so I'm deluded to think) that must be written down. *Yes, a solar-powered hat that charges your phone would be a best-seller.* So I think about writing it down, pulling me out of sleep somewhat, but I'm too tired and comfy in my *Space Jam* bed sheets to roll over and jot it down on the matching *Space Jam* notebook.

And yes, I'm twenty-three and have *Space Jam* covers. Nostalgic.

Lying here, I feel my stomach coil into tightness from not writing these brilliant, million-dollar-making ideas down in my notebook. If I fall asleep, I'll know I'll wake up with a sore stomach like I've just worked out.

Some say orgasms help sleep. I believe they do for most people. But that just means I lose interest in sex for a while—the refractory period, science calls it—which is like removing the best part of the circus (*no more monkeys?*). And the ringleader—my brain—he's bored and starts talking about killing himself (*that's like sleep*), using family members who've done the same as a model. I just want to exit my head, but I can't. Overall, trying to sleep is just an unpleasant experience.

It's got to be close to sunrise—birds chirping, a lawn mower starting—when I give up.

Maybe no sleep will make me tired, relaxed, and calm for my coffee kinda-maybe-date with a pretty girl. In a moment of sleep-deprived insight, I realize the fantasy world in which I live is a waste of a life. But I don't roll over to jot this down, so I forget it.

drift off a few minutes before *Kill Bill*'s whistle wakes me.

1.

In the kitchen Trey is pouring tea for me into my *Mad Men* SCP mug.

"You ready for your coffee date?" Trey hands me the mug.

"Don't start. Didn't sleep a lick last night." I usually appreciate Trey making my tea for me like we're an old married couple. I set it on the table and sit down.

"I read this morning that Robin Williams hung himself," Trey says. "So I pulled out all the Williams movies for us to marathon." He points to the circular table next to the couch where two tall stacks of plastic cases hold hours of Robin William movies and stand-up comedy. I'm too tired to react how I normally would: devastated.

"Trey, you ever think about shit?"

"Can you be more specific, please?"

"I mean, you ever sit wide-eyed at night and think about reality. 'Cause, here it is: If I don't find a girl soon, college will end. I'll drift into a job surrounded by married or divorced women with several kids and regrettable tattoos and stretch marks and cottage cheese legs twice the size of mine. Maybe we hook up because there's nothing else available. I mean, where do you meet girls after school ends? The gym? Grocery stores? In a park? Maybe in a movie, but not in real life. So I hook up with a gelatinous blob of a woman, maybe I marry her, and every time I make love with her, I'm just reminded that I need to pick up cottage cheese next trip to Piggly Wiggly."

I pull down a plastic bottle of bottom-shelf vodka from the top of the fridge.

"And honestly," I continue. "Today isn't a big thing, but it could be. If I don't do well today, my mind is telling me, I'll never do well in the future and no one will want me. What's there to want? Christ, what'll I say after I graduate? 'Hey, baby. I've got a bachelor's degree in Englishing. I make the same per year as a motel maid.' That'll give her a crazy wettie, no doubt. It's like, I might as well just stick with watching reruns of *The Office*, relive Pam and Jim's scripted relationship roller coaster as if it's my own. And ten years down the line, where will I be? Clacking away in a five-by-five cubicle, stuck in the doldrums with an albatross weighing down my neck? Soon enough, I'll—"

I'm rambling, breathless, over-tired, over-anxious.

I mix the vodka with pink lemonade and swallow the drink as a shot, coughing as I continue. Toki the Cat gazes at me with sleepy eyes. He's calm. I point at him. He subtly smiles like happy house cats do.

"The cat that licks his own butthole is more assured and relaxed than me. I'm smarter but more incapable of basic things. And for some reason I think a successful catching-up with Olivia McDermott—the younger sister of some guy I went to middle school with—that this rendezvous like a Facebook chat will somehow change everything for me." My heart's a-racing and I pull open the drawer with my pills in them.

Trey says, "Come on. Deep breath, man. You're over-thinking this whole thing. You're a good-looking guy, I hate to say. She's a lot better looking, but you just gotta—I don't know—play the part. Pretend you're awesome. Tyler with balls of steel." He pats me on the shoulder. He wraps an arm around me and half-hugs me. My hands are shaking, so he opens the orange pill bottle for me. Like an old married couple.

Will you open the pickle jar for me?

Did you remember to take your pills?

"But to answer your question," he says. "No, I never think like that."

"At some point last night a thought occurred to me. I need something, man. I need something." I wash three pills down with another flamboyant pink drink before showering and putting on a tight green V-neck with worn jeans that hug my legs and drape over my top of my blue Vans.

2.

Olivia and I meet at New Moon cafe, a hip, coffee grower-friendly cafe on Main Street. She's sitting cross-legged at a tiny corner table reading a book. An orange scarf is wrapped around her neck, her curled brown hair flowing over the top of it. Her dress is dark blue with white dots and no straps over her shoulders, which are tan and smooth and, wow.

Wow.

"Whatcha reading?" I say as I sit across from her in the rigid metal chair.

"It's this book about a guy who loses his Eleanor right away, and it rewinds how he lost her. You'd like it."

How would she know I'd like it?

A server with her hair piled on top of her head comes to the table. She asks what we'd like.

Olivia orders vanilla latte and smiles at the waitress.

The server smiles at me. "And you?" A spiderweb is tattooed on her elbow and over her arms are random sketches of skulls wearing makeup and birds flying from a tree that winds around her forearm.

"I'm not a coffee drinker. So I'm not sure," I say, distracted by the tattoos. They remind me of high school parties when someone passes out and everyone draws penises and *I love penis* on the drunk's face and lower back.

"Try something fancy. I'm buying, so go nuts," Olivia says.

"You are so not buying. I'll try a—" I'm looking at the chalkboard menu on the wall, written in all caps surrounded by elaborate waves. I'm jealous of the beautiful handwriting. "I'll have a whatever. Anything ending in '-chino' sounds good to me. Frapp, cap, Al Pa. I'm not picky."

"He'll have a vanilla mocha with a few squirts of strawberry." Olivia smiles and the server laughs and shakes her head, her gauged earlobes dangling like Dumbo's.

"I see who's got the power in the relationship, huh?" the server says.

"We're not—" I start to say, but Olivia interrupts.

"Got that right." She nods her head like a tough guy, pursing her lips. I try to hold back a smile, but Olivia's smile is contagious like a yawn. I smile big and goofy. A doofus.

Olivia waits until the server walks away. She leans across the table and says, "Her tattoos are so interesting. I wonder what stories they tell." I can smell she's been chewing spearmint gum.

"They're probably just random drawings some college artist did. She's probably got some Chinese symbol on her bum and a flower that reminds her of a dead Grandma Gertrude."

"I don't think so," Olivia says, shaking her foot back and forth. "I think tattoos are a permanent expression of an emotion or something essential to a person's life."

"So what could a spiderweb on a chick's elbow mean?" I tip my head to the side, showing my disbelief. Like Owen Wilson might. My voice even has a sprinkle of Owen Wilson in it.

"Could mean anything. That's the point. It's personal and intimate. You can't judge it because it doesn't mean the same to you as it does to the tattooed person."

"I can tell you for certain, Mike Tyson's facial tramp-stamp is stupid. I'm gonna go ahead and judge that one right away." She laughs, and we hush as the waitress approaches and sets our drinks on the tabletop.

"Need anything else, let me know," the server says. She spins on her heel and walks away.

"Look at her other elbow," Olivia says, leaning over the square table again. "Looks like a heart, but how hearts actually look, all veiny and fist-like."

"Kind of gross. No offense, body," I say, resting my hand on my chest.

"I like it. The tattoo is honest and real."

"A heart on an elbow? Yeah, *real* honest."

"I mean it," she says. "Showing something how it really is, not trying to hide behind some round, fluffy idea of something. Guess it reminds me of what the book I was reading was talking about." She pulls the book out of her purse and sets it on the table. "There's a lot of great stuff in here. Last chapter I was reading when you meandered in here—late, I might add—"

"I wasn't late, I was—"

"Lombardi said fifteen minutes before is on time," Olivia says in an I-Told-You-So voice. "So this book is talking about love, the idea of it, and its different forms. And as I was reading, I saw you meander in here—you do know you *meander*, right? Like you're kind of lost and not really sure where you're going?" She laughs. "Not in a mean way. It's cute. Innocent in a unique way." She looks down at her coffee and her long tan fingers spin the cup on the table. I look at the silver ring on her ring finger. It's two hands wrapped around her finger holding a heart.

The few vodkas and pills begin circulating my blood stream. My limbs loosen. My muscles relax and settle into the chair like the chair and I are becoming one object. I point to the ring and say, "Is that one of those Irish love-ring-things? Starts with a 'claw—'"

She laughs and holds up her hand. "A claddagh."

"Yeah, one of those." I smile as smoothly as I can.

Channeling Ryan Gosling. Six pack abs.

"My mom used to have a claddagh." I sip my coffee. It's not too hot, and the strawberry squirts are delicious. I think of my mom and try to remember how she wore the ring. "If the heart is pointing in, that means you're taken, right? I think that's how my mom wore it for a while."

Olivia nods. "Yup. And the heart pointing out," she says, pointing to her ring. "That means the wearer is single."

And looking? I almost ask.

"Hearts. Love. Relationships. This book," she says, tapping with her long tan finger on the crinkled book cover near the library barcode. "There's this part where the girl says, 'I don't like you. Sometimes I think I live for you.' I really like it. I enjoy other people's ideas. And I'm curious about your ideas. Hearts. Love. Relationships."

I take a long sip of coffee, and my intestines gurgle like Trey's R2D2 bong. Coffee has two effects on me: energizing and bowel-loosening.

"I don't really have much concept of love." I hesitate. Trey is the closest to love that I feel for someone. And thinking that just now made me uncomfortable. "My dad kind of raised me to think love was a gay thing. We weren't comfortable expressing things. If one of us tried, it was uncomfortable—almost inappropriate. 'Love' was connected, in some loose way, to gayness for Dad. Like guys— manly men who love being manly with mustaches—they can't love things or other people without jamming something up someone's ass." I'm pantomiming shoving a stick into my hand when I realize that I shouldn't be talking like this. I'm not talking with Trey, so I check for her reaction. She smiles even though I'm being vulgar and inappropriate.

Again I get the feeling she's hard to shock or catch off-guard. I sip my coffee, and Olivia is cupping hers with both hands. My mind takes a mental snapshot of her.

I say, "If you do love something or someone, you better not say it. Dad's an ultra manly-man Marine. A guy that's probably uncomfortable when medics do mouth-to-mouth. Least that's how I remember him always being." I imagine his gravestone one day. Depending on the cost of each letter, I think I'd like it to read *Bruce Linley, Father, Son, Marine Who Loved Women and Not Men 'Cause, Gross, That's Gay. Semper Fi.*

"So he's not the talkative type?" Olivia says.

"I tend to talk with him around Christmas, maybe around my birthday. He'll call to make sure I'm not dead. Then he'll give me updates on people we used to know."

"You don't get to see him much?"

"Get to? I avoid him as much as possible. He's off valiantly fighting terrorism and protecting freedom, stationed on the beaches of Cali. He's an engineer for the Marines. He remarried some chick with fake tits. Sherry or Cherry or Candy or Cookie. I don't know. They had a kid together a few years back, before they got married. I met the new wife at their wedding. I've never seen a dress so low cut in a church. She sends postcards from their base, the picture always of some beach in the foreground, the Golden Gate in the background. Sometimes, Lombard or Haight Street will be in the background. Tourist stuff. She signs her name and Dad's and the kid's."

Olivia doesn't need to know this now, but it all changed five years ago. Mom stayed here, in Wisconsin, near her family and friends. Dad relocated to the West Coast. He threw his hands up helplessly—*Semper Fi*—and told Mom he had no say in being relocated. But later I found out he requested the transfer so he could do his glorified engineering in a nice vacation climate instead the persistent cold bitch-slap of Wisconsin. Mom, the selfless art teacher—she knew the details before I did.

A man with a Packers Clay Matthews jersey enters the cafe, and a scene flashes: I was sitting on the carpet in front of the small TV screen as Dad rocked in his chair behind me in his Favre jersey.

He'd rest his feet on my shoulders, and I'd wear my Edgar Bennett jersey. After Sunday lunch at Benny's, we'd watch three straight games of football, high-fiving after scores, jumping to our feet after an interception. We'd even talk about players, offering critiques about cornerbacks' athleticism or field awareness. It was good. But that was the exception, not the rule.

"I'm sorry," Olivia says. "It sucks not having a dad there for you. I know the feeling." She looks out the window to her right and watches people load onto a bus. "What about your mom? I remember seeing her short curly orange hair, all perky and bobbing when she walked. I always wanted hair like that when I was in middle school."

I want things to stay light, happy. I don't want Olivia to see me and have a Pavlovian reaction to feel sorry for me, so I lie. "Freak car accident after the divorce. Coroner said she felt no pain," I say, maybe too detached. So I add: "I miss her every day."

I close my eyes for a few seconds, one Mississippi, two Mississippi, three, Mississippi. That's good. Method act, to pretend to be a person worth being around. Gosling. Six-pack abs. Emotional. "I don't want to dump all my bummer stories on you, Olivia." I search her face for a single blemish, and all I see is a small scar above her eyebrow, the skin slightly lighter than the tan around it. The rest of her face, masked by no makeup, is smooth and soft.

"I'm so sorry," she says. "I didn't mean to bring up sad events. It's just been so long, and—I had no clue." In her green eyes, I can see true empathy. Actual human feeling for another person's pain. It's almost shocking to see it authentically displayed on a live, real beautiful girl in front of me instead of an actress being paid to feign sadness on a screen. "Not to keep the bummer train chuggin' along," she says, "but I lost my dad. His, uh, death was drawn out to the point where at the end, we were glad he wasn't suffering anymore. You know, when someone's been sick for so long they aren't even themselves anymore. Like a molted shell of themselves."

"What happened?" I ask, my voice soft and tender—Owen Wilson. I even squint my eyes a bit and purse my lips to feel more like him. I sip the coffee, and my insides are gurgling so I cough to cover it.

"He never smoked a day in his life but got cancer. One of those inexplicable things."

Like *Breaking Bad,* I can't help but think. My brain wonders if he tried selling meth to make them money. Not a lot of meth, just a little.

Jesus Christ, I need to focus on her.

"I'm sorry," I say. What else can you say? In the movies, the server should walk up right now to divert the attention, but the server is outside now by the dumpster, smoking a cigarette and leaning against the window.

Olivia McDermott nods her head a bit. An awkward moment.

I ask what her brother is doing now.

"Jordan joined the Marines, like your dad."

I roll my eyes. "Ah, right. Doesn't surprise me."

She laughs. "I remember you two fighting one day during recess. It was over something ridiculous, like tetherball or something. You two were rolling around on the ground."

It was foursquare, I don't say. Instead: "I won the fight. Jordan started crying and your mom called my dad about it. My dad gave me a high five and let me stay up late watching WWF. He didn't tell my mom, either. One of the proud moments he had."

"I thought you were a jerk after the fight. Jordan kept saying you kept pinching him, that's why you won."

"Pinching him? No way. I'm way too manly for that. I gave him a Stone Cold Stunner and then the People's Elbow. The rest is history." I punch the air in front of me.

"That's not how *I* remember it," she says, her voice crescendoing to a high pitch.

"You know what *I* remember about *you* from grade school?"

"Oh, God. I was such a dork."

"Not my last year there. You were starting to grow a pair. I mean, like, you were getting confident. I bet you don't even remember this."

She braces herself, crossing her arms over her chest.

"I was hanging out with older kids. Cooler kids in high school," I say. "Kids from public school."

"Evil public school kids," she says, mocking shock and disapproval. "Always doing drugs and worshipping Satan."

"Well, yeah, most us Lutheran school kids didn't know about them. But you walked up to me while I was playing foursquare with Trey. A few of your friends trailed behind you, like your entourage.

You stood there waiting for me to pay attention to you. You said, 'Tyler, I heard you were hanging out with *Nikki Johnson*,' you said to me."

I mock imitate a high-pitch girl voice. "You said, 'Nikki Johnson's a whore. You probably have *the* AIDS.' And then a few of your entourage girls were like, 'Yeah, the AIDS,' snapping their heads back and forth. Then you all turned, your hair whipping behind you, and you walked off into the sunset."

"Oh, God," she says, bashful but smiling.

"I knew AIDS was bad, but all I knew about it was Magic Johnson had it. So I encyclopedia'd AIDS—'cause they never taught us that in school—and I thought I was gonna die. I wrote up a will, giving my N64 to Trey, all my possessions out to different people I thought worthy. I thought I was gonna die," I say, laughing.

"You did not."

"Honestly. Thought I was gonna die. Ah, yes," I say, leaning my head back as if reflecting on the long-gone past. "That was the first time I thought I had 'the AIDS.'"

"The first time?"

"Yeah." I pause and look down. "Now I actually have 'the AIDS.'"

"Shut up."

"Okay. HIV, as of now."

"Shut up."

"It was an orgy and, you know, it happens."

"Someone invited *you* to an orgy?" She laughs and shakes her head. "I can't believe that."

"Pfft. I would totally get invited to an orgy. You're crazy."

I finish my coffee and gravity seems to be pulling on everything in my intestines. I scan the cafe for a restroom, but the old building doesn't have one. So I hold it. Freud's infantile anal stage.

Olivia and I relay what we're doing. I'm TA-ing for an English class, tutoring at the college, editing for the local paper. She's into environmental activism ("environmental science"—as she says) and taking philosophy classes for fun.

We talk about books, music, classes, and careers. Several times, I pull the conversation toward TV shows and movies, but she's clueless in that regard, which strikes me as irregular and crazy, bordering on Amish. "I grew up without cable," she says. "We were outside all day, riding horses and fishing and running around. Why waste time watching fake reality when you can go experience the real thing?" I'm offended, but I'm not sure why.

I tell her someday I'd like to tell jokes and perform, but I struggl*ed* with anxiety. I feel comfortable telling her this, as if she's completely neutral. My reservations peel away in layers until I'm talking with her like I would with Trey. I'm not worried about what she'll think because she is relaxing me. She lulls me into trusting her, like a counselor. It isn't a logical thing, but a visceral feeling.

I tell her if I can't muster up courage to tell stories on stage, I'll shave my head and start a four-piece band called Foreskin. All bald, we'll play covers of famous songs like "I Know What Boys Like," "Sweet Child o' Mine," and "Tube Snake Boogie" on flutes. Olivia and I alternate between joking and being serious, a delicate but seemingly natural teeter-totter balancing act that when we tip too far to one side, the other pushes the conversation back toward central balance. When we joke, it seems to magnify the more serious bits. Laughter among the dreary.

However, the thought that we are fundamentally different never leaves my mind. And this difference appeals to me; she is different than me in a better way. Somewhere in me, the thought of a positive change lingers. At one point, she talks about her relationship with her mom and grandparents, how her family is her strength and her weakness. I realize in that moment what I want. I want a strong family. Her mentioning it just finally highlighted that I don't have it. I've never had it.

I forget my surroundings and I lose my basic urge to use the restroom when the server approaches us.

"Sorry to interrupt," the server says, the smell of stale smoke emanating from her body like stink lines. "We closed ten minutes ago." Olivia and I look at each other then at the massive clock hanging from the wall. 9:10 p.m. Through the window I see red taillights of cars passing by, glowing in the dark beneath white streetlights. A smoker's cigarette pulsates a dim red as he inhales.

I grab my Styrofoam cup and realize I've picked and chewed it into pieces that I've piled inside the nub of a base that remains intact. Collapsed like a house built upon sand. Her ceramic cup remains stoic, untouched like a house build upon rock. Did she notice me picking at the cup? Did I seem like a nervous wreck? Because now I want to tell her I'm more relaxed than I've been in forever.

She makes a joke, but I don't hear it, so I match her laugh and smile. I read somewhere that mirroring someone's movements and gestures makes them more likely to be attracted to you.

We walk outside toward her car, a maroon Chrysler Lebaron.

"You drive the same car as George Costanza and Jon Voight," I say, laughing.

She's shrugs her shoulders. "I don't know who those people are."

"Oh, man, Olivia. You've never seen *Seinfeld*? Every American's seen it. It's un-American to not have knowledge of *Seinfeld*."

"Yeah, I don't know who George Custansia is or the other guy. I'm not a nerd who watches movies and TV shows all day."

"Ouch, hit me right in the pride."

"And show some respect to Lucille. She's a classy lady, except when I take the top down and she goes topless in the summer."

The name makes me think of Lucille Bluth from *Arrested Development*, but I don't say this.

"Ah, Lucille LeBaron, the Chrysler. Nice." I point to my car a few empty stalls away, the only other car in the square parking lot. "Betsy."

"Also a classic lady. Bet she has a wild side, too."

"Mmhmm. In a minute she'll let me inside her, which is a daily thing. But sometimes she lets a few people slide inside her at the same time."

Olivia fake-gasps. "What a wanton woman. Look at us, making jokes like fifth-graders."

In a hoarse old-man voice, I say, "Damn whippersnappers."

She opens her arms for a hug. "I'm glad we did this," she says.

Wrapping my arms around her, I realize how small she is. I pick her up so her feet are off the ground. Thoughts from the morning run through my head: the dread of a future with no family, no partner. The fear of a future loneliness takes hold, fight or flight almost. I kiss her on the side of the head. Coconut shampoo. I set her down and break the hug.

Bashful, she laughs.

"You're a lot of—" I'm saying when she steps on my Vans. She leans onto her tiptoes, bringing her to my height. She kisses me— pop—right on the lips. Vanilla with faint spearmint.

She pulls her head back after a second. "You still have my number in your phone, right?"

I nod.

"Good. I hope I hear from you later," she says. "Like when you get home. None of this *I'll-wait-three-days* stuff. Okay?"

I smile and turn away toward my car. I'm not going to look back.

I slide inside Betsy and stick the key in her. Sitting there I realize the shit I had to take has disappeared, which makes me worry where it went. But I'll never know, and I'm sure Science has a simple answer. But I don't care, because making a human connection and the winning lottery feel the same to me.

Chapter Three

Kennedy at Ghetto Gas

I'm not that drunk.

It's usually said by someone who's too drunk but doesn't want to admit it. You know the guy. He's spilling drinks over girls' tops, bumping into circles of friends, flashing cash and offering to buy drinks for people who wear a shirt in a color he likes. *Blue is da bomb, yo. Lemme, lemme buy you a drink. On me, man. Great shirt, awesome shirt.* Maybe he's spinning his key lanyard around his finger and telling people how he's driving home, drawing the attention of all in the area.

I'm not that drunk.

It's a Sunday, a free day, a day of rest—the Lord's direct orders. I can't relax, though, unless I've got some help. So I've been mixing screwballs all day, lying on the couch, marathoning Netflix. Trey went tubing down the Tiger River with a few friends from high school. I feel my successful coffee date allows me a day to myself. I'm skipping the lorazepam today, mainly because I'm out, but that still makes me proud, as if not abusing a drug for one day is an achievement.

Driving in Betsy the Buick, I'm off to meet a guy I had a biology lab with. He never did the work, but he traded me pills, so I just did his labs. We both aced the class, and I made an acquaintance I've been relying on for a few years. We always meet at Ghetto Gas, which is a station where the cashiers sell smokes to kids and booze to anyone with a card that looks like an ID. (I once saw a cashier sell a thirty pack after checking a library card.) I've never seen a cop within five miles of this side of town, so I'm never worried at this point in my drinking routine.

I'm cruising down Parkway Avenue at five miles an hour because of the road's sporadic potholes, which feels like driving through the aftereffects of a detonated mine field. I pull into the dark parking lot where a few teens skateboard, trying to board-slide on a bike rack. I'm sitting in my idling Buick with my glass wedged between my legs as NPR classical piano flutters through my speakers. Kennedy is a white kid with a blonde afro tucked under a straight-brimmed hat. He pulls up next to my window on his bike.

"Linley. How've you been, man?" he says, handing me a three Tic-Tac bottles filled with pills, each a different flavor.

"Good. Good." I raise my glass. He laughs.

"Can't believe you do that, man. It's stupid. You're gonna get it one day. Accident or the fuzz."

I shake my head and scrunch up my face. "Still living at home?"

He nods. "Until I move outta there, away from that crazy woman, we'll be meeting here. Only takes me five minutes to ride down here. You know she brought back three dudes last week? Different dudes. Just, ugh. That's Mom, you know? Be glad you don't hafta worry about that."

I nod as I watch a teen try to board slide on the bike rack, but he slips and lands on his tailbone. "I'd much rather have my situation than be dealing with that," I say, not meaning it in the slightest. Truth is, I'd give anything to have Mom back, even if she was gettin' friendly with all the townspeople like Ken's ma.

"Yeah, yeah," he says. I hand him cash. He rifles through it. Shaking his head, he says, "It's $210 now." He hands it back. "Recount it, add some more, my man."

"You're kidding. Fifty bucks' increase? I can't afford that."

"Sorry. Been hard lately." He looks away. His foot's tapping on the tar holding cement chunks together. He's lying. He pays for nothing. He's bragged about this a million times. The government gives him an EBT card. They pay for his college—grants, scholarships, loan forgiveness. His ghost of a father writes him checks each month that appear in the mailbox.

The three Tic-Tac bottles sit in my lap, wrapped in a plastic bag next to the glass between my legs. In my drunken mind, I picture peeling out, leaving him and his idiot bike in a cloud of dust and exhaust. He pokes his head into the car, leaning on the open window inches from me. Balancing on his bike, he says, "Sorry, bro. Just the way it is. Pay it." He puts his hand out.

Behind Kennedy, I see the shadowy man in a black trench coat. I make eye contact with him, and without saying a word, the man reminds me. *What would you do to be an observer? Would you kill? Steal? Here's your chance. These pills—they're easing you into a state of observance. They're getting you closer. They'll do wonders. Wonders.*

"That's bullshit, man," I say, my head swimming in alcohol and spite. He's trying to pull this on me. Only me. "You're upping again? I'm out from now on." I don't think this through. I'm not thinking straight, but on the radio, Sarasate plays; his beautiful, happy, carefree violins dance and prance on my speakers. I want my car to move as light as the violins.

An urge rather than a thought makes me push his head away from my car. He loses balance on the bike. I crank the wheel and shift to drive. I accelerate into the street, Betsy bottoming out as I crank the wheel. On the pedal I put my whole weight. The car jerks forward, roaring. But it feels more like an accelerating boat. I crank the music and the speakers are crackling when I see police lights flashing red-blue, red-blue, tiny as ants in the squinting distance of my rearview.

I turn right onto a residential street and hit mute on the radio. People sit smoking and drinking on their porches where music plays; one porch blares Toby Keith, another thumps ODB. I hear the sirens mix with the music through my rolled-down windows. Curbside, I shut off my lights as the flashing police lights and siren blast down the street behind me. My heart's racing, and I've spilled the screwball between my legs, so my pinstripe shorts are soaked. The car smells like cheap vodka. I imagine Kennedy cursing under his breath in a forced street dialect he's never used in class or at home where his mother is probably reverse-cowgirling some dive-bar skullet-headed drunk.

But Kennedy's college is paid for; his vanished father benefitted him. His mother's regretful motherhood led to the government laying down a green carpet of cash. For some reason these few years of spite finally hit a breaking point as he tried to squeeze money from a drunk student looking to avoid the cost of insurance. Here I'm dog-paddling each year on five thousand a year while Kennedy skips classes, asks me to write essays, and demands more money for what he gets for free. To those who gave me life, my life's been an inconvenience, too—but I haven't been paid for it.

As I drive home, hands at ten and two, the radio silent, my left foot hovering above the break, guilt settles in my gut. I'm disgusted by my bitching and moaning and my whines: *It's not fair.* But I know after a few more screwballs it won't matter until the regretful morning of what-ifs and whys.

Chapter Four

In Bloom

1.

Toki the Cat is curled on my lap as I'm reclining in the Dungeon. My phone rests atop his back. Ice cubes float in pink Brisk mixed with vodka in a glass in the armrest cup holder. The dark room's projection screen loops the menu images and music for *American Psycho.* The calm piano music plays from the seven speakers mounted on the four black walls; on the carpet, the two subwoofers rumble, lumbering bass notes so it feels like a thunderstorm engulfs me. My eyes are closed, and I've no idea what time (or day) it is. The sun is irrelevant in this room.

I try to avoid my tendency to ramble as I text Olivia. I think of possible greetings to send her, most of them rugged and terse, like a youthful Hemingway . . . or like an insecure twenty-something afraid of appearing to try too hard. I realize how ridiculous this over-thought, edited and filtered form of communication is, so I just send her a random fact.

Donald Duck comics were banned from Finland because he doesn't wear any pants.

Which makes sense. Once I woke up wearing only my shirt. Looking in a body-length mirror, I realized how odd it is to wear only a shirt but nothing below the waist. If a kid tried that, he wouldn't fit in so well in school. Or maybe he'd be the coolest kid. If I had another life to live, I'd find out.

Olivia responds:

I guess Donald and I have something in common right now . . .

I don't know how to respond to that, so I wait. A response from me will no doubt be perverted, or at least awkward, so nothing is the thing to say. The rumbling speakers repeat the menu music. Toki the Cat paws the air in his sleep—a kitty dream. Adorable.

The phone vibrates and I see the text. Not from Olivia but from Kennedy:

U steal from me, ur fucked, man. Better beware 24/7.

I ignore the text and try to think of Olivia naked from the waist down, but all that pops in my head is a female Donald Duck-esque cartoon version of Olivia with furry white legs. It's still sexy but in a weird way.

Olivia's text pops up:

I'm kidding. Or am I . . . Here's my fact: In 14th century France, a pig was hung for murdering a child.

Kennedy's text pops up:

U R a coward, man. I'll find where U R livin. I will. U will C.

Olivia and I toss facts back and forth until she says:

Don't call me Olivia. Call me Liv. I like Livi, too. Or get creative . . .

Naturally, I think of *Jay and Silent Bob Strike Back* and the pet name "Boo-Boo Kitty Fuck." But I don't think she'll appreciate or get the reference. Plus, it's not exactly romantic.

I like that she types out entire words and uses punctuation, an attention to detail that shows care and focus, unlike the near-illiterate Kennedy.

I like and hate that she uses ellipses (. . .) because it changes a lot in texting conversation. Even the most innocent things followed by three dots will add a mysterious and sometimes coy or flirty quality to the statement. For example:

Sneaking in the back door late at night—I've never done that before . . .

The section of my brain in charge of scatological and dick humor lights up (which is to say my whole brain) as if Livi's constant ellipses indicates some double-entendre or deeper meaning.

At one point she messages me something about meeting later, followed quickly by: "Sorry, wrong person." By then, I'm too sauced to bother thinking about it. I'm just feeling the menu music rumble the dark room, the two-minute chunk of music ingrained in my brain from the few hours of repetition.

As it gets later, maybe five a.m. or midnight—I have no clue—we call it a night.

Olivia: *Remember: Livi or Liv. Or get creative.*

Me: *Otay.*

Liv: *Good.*

Me: *Indeed.*

Liv: *Quite.*

Me: *Indubitably*

Liv: *Mmmhmm*

When I tell Trey that Liv kissed me, he calls bullshit and shows me the Facebook bikini pictures on the 55 inch.

"That girl, there, next to the tan guy with washboard abs, *she* would never be into you. No way, man. I mean, look at her," Trey says. His jaw drops and he points at the screen to stress his point.

"I *am* looking at her, you shallow twat." My eye is drawn to the shirtless guy next to her, presumably her old boyfriend.

Trey pokes the screen, causing the pixels to smudge.

"I heard he was hung like a—"

"Trey," I say. "Shut the fuck up. Where do you even hear something like that? Don't answer that. But can't you just be like, *Right on, Ty, that'a boy*, or something supportive. Shit."

"Sorry. I just want you to see the truth." He shrugs his shoulders, and I see Trey the Wond'ring Turtle, traveling the lands offering wise advice and suggestions in search of the truth.

2.

I'm sitting in the back of the classroom, where I usually try to hide so I don't need to speak in class. I'm early, and my phone vibrates:

Save me a seat!

Livi shows up as class starts and sits next to me. C.J. the Frat Bro sits on the other side of Livi and he's sneaking peeks of her, clearly trying to see down her tank top as class begins. Professor Nelson's brown and red argyle sweater seems to have shrunk because when he bends over to pick up his purple marker, half his back shows, leading all the way down to his crack.

"Oh, baby, that's what I'm talkin' 'bout," Livi whispers under her breath, biting her bottom lip. I hold back a laugh because it's silent in the classroom except for Nelson's strained groans.

He starts discussion of the reading, an essay by Kierkegaard. Right on schedule, Olivia's perking up and offering her thoughts on the reading. Again I glance at her color-coded notes, purple and pink and black and blue with a few bubbly smiley faces in the notebook margin. Faces with rounded cheeks and flipping eyelashes. The attention she draws from Professor Nelson and the class is directed dangerously close to me. No matter what position I sit in, I feel awkward and uncomfortable. I lean back in the chair. I rotate the chair so my left arm rests on the backrest. I lean forward with my elbows on the table like a rude dinner guest. No matter what, it's all uncomfortable under the scrutiny of the entire class's attention.

I'm not listening to what Livi is saying when Nelson looks at me.

"What do you think, Mr. Linley?" he says. "Your colleague here is dominating the floor."

"I agree with," my voice falters like I'm mid-stride puberty, so I cough as if I needed to clear my throat. "I agree with Livi." My breath is gone. I've been hit in the gut and the air is gone.

Nelson stares at me with disappointment. "What a contribution," he says dryly. "At least I hope you'll deliver on the essay, like usual." I nod my head as the class's gaze heats me like a sunray through a magnifying glass. I am an ant.

Ten minutes before class ends, everyone starts packing up, running zippers back and forth, slamming shut huge textbooks from different classes, fidgeting in their seats—anything to signal the approaching end of class. T.J. the Frat Boy even yawns using his vocal chords, which is louder than Professor Nelson's drone.

"You guys can fuss all you want, we're here 'til the clock hits the six," he says, pointing a sausage finger at the ticking analog clock, which hangs next to a simplified digital clock (installed because we young people can't read analog clocks).

When the clock does hit the six, Livi says, "Why don't you ever say anything in class? I see your notes. I know you've got *something* going on up here." She points to my head.

I hush my voice so no one hears me explain because it's illogical.

"Most of these people are idiots," I whisper, nodding my head toward T.J. the Frat Boy, who slides Dre Beats onto his nodding head. "But there's always a few brilliant people peppered in a class. I don't feel like sticking my neck out so they can chop me up and make fun of me later if I say something stupid."

She looks at me, her mouth confused, but her eyes soft and concerned.

"You realize you're not the center of the world, right?" she says gently, as if suggesting sobering up to a raging drunk.

"I know." I'm taken back. Maybe a little offended. "I don't think I am. How egocentric do you think I am?"

I look away from her as I sling my backpack over my shoulder. In my mind, I have a set order of how the world should be. When I'm in my control, I'm calmer, like at home where I'm surrounded by structured realities. Out here, in class, or anywhere else, anything I imagine is powerless because the world is out of my control. It's chaos and random. No one cares about details, ideas or ideals. It's all a chaotic free-for-all. It's hell. Satre was right.

Livi and I are walking down the bright white hallway where students sit against the floor waiting for their next class to begin. Some peck at laptops, some poke at menu-sized cell phones, others stare blankly ahead.

After minutes or an hour, she says, "But—" she pauses, choosing her words. "Why would you think they'd be so concerned? People say stupid things all the time." She leans in and whispers to me, her breath against my ear. Wintermint. "Remember when that frat kid said his dad drove a 1970s Chevy P.O.S?" The frat kid is walking ahead of us in the hallway, nodding his head to contrived hip-hop. "And he thought that was an actual model?"

I do. So does Livi. Clearly, people remember when people say stupid shit.

"No one laughed," she says. "Plus, you'd never say anything nearly that stupid. Unless you tried. Most people, I'm pretty sure, do stupid things all the time. I'd say most human lives are a string of dumb things followed by stupid things and stupid thoughts, but no one really cares because they're caught up in the stupid things they're doing and saying."

I nod and shrug. "You're right." I'd never thought of that. Maybe people are just bumbling one moment to the next, trying not to make a huge mistake.

"Of course I'm right," she laughs and pushes me a bit. "We're in college to learn something. I figure it should be a little uncomfortable, don't you think?"

No pain, no gain, I think. And I feel like punching myself when I say it aloud.

"Exactly," she says. "You've got it, Schwarzenegger."

3.

After tutoring, class, and my readings, I hole up in the Dungeon with the last drops of my vodka in front of the projector. Per Livi's suggestion, a documentary rolls on about the costs of corporate supermarkets on local business, its workers, the environment, and so on. Halfway through, I pause it and drive to the local supercenter—a massive warehouse monolith plopped between two boarded-up stores. One store was formerly a barber shop ran by a guy named Chet where Dad took me to get buzz cuts against my will: "You look handsome with a crew cut," Dad'd say. "Trust me, I know handsome," and he'd laugh and run his hand over his cut.

The other building was formerly a small grocery store where Mom used to shop. She'd set me next to the cashier at the checkout lanes—a personal favor from the store—and I'd play with toys at the cashier's feet while she checked customers out. Between sales, the cashier would squat down and drive Matchbox cars in circles with me and drop me little Tootsie Rolls like feeding an animal at a zoo; I pretended to be a baby lion, roaring and pawing at her leg. Simba from *The Lion King*.

All of it is gone.

Inside the supercenter I push a cart and in the cup holder I set my empty *SpongeBob* coffee tumbler. My big cargo shorts pockets on the sides of my legs are unbuttoned, and my long-sleeve windbreaker covers most of my hands. I toss a few plastic handles of Barton vodka into the cart, add some bottles of vermouth and O.J. and pink lemonade. In an aisle with no cameras in sight, I drop a phone charger into my cargo pocket. And another. I screw the top off the tumbler and drop a couple small bags of cat treats in. I screw it back on and walk to the register. I self-checkout my booze, the employee watching the section comes to me when the red light glows. Out of breath from walking fifteen feet, she asks for my ID. I hand it to her and make the same smile and brush my hair the way it is in the photo.

She laughs and says, "You haven't aged a day since this was taken. Have a good day, sir." I smile and pay. I wish I could help her in some vague way, but not in any real way.

My pockets weighed down by the unpaid merchandise in them, I leave the store, the elderly woman smiling vacantly and waving. No alarm goes off, no one notices me. I'm numb, walking in the parking lot with my $60 worth of vodka and a few bucks worth of garbage in my pockets and tumbler. My head's whirling and swimming. Sitting in my car, my mind fills with thousands of things I need to do, but I'm unable to focus on anything in particular. I mix a drink into my coffee tumbler and try to control my breathing.

Driving home, I stop at a red light. A few teenagers sit on the curb, texting. I roll down my window.
"Guys like free stuff?"

They look at each other, then to me. They nod.

"Good. Here." I hand the plastic bag to them, and they dig through the electronics and thank me.

In through the nose, out through the mouth. Just breathe.

4.

I wake with a rare vodka hangover, which tells me I went overboard. I tell myself I'll take a break from alcohol. Detox. This means the Tic-Tac bottles will be of use.

Trey hands me my morning tea. As he's lighting a candle that smells like strawberry, he tells me it's Olivia's birthday this weekend.

"How do you know that?"

"Do you ever listen to anyone? Like ever? At all? We're friends on Facebook." He points to his phone. "It reminds you so you don't have to ever remember anything about people you don't care about but would like to *appear to care*," he says, like explaining to a child.

"Nice heads up. What do girls do on their birthdays?" I ask.

"Hmm."

"I think Google might help here."

"Or you could just ask her. She'll be impressed you even remembered, especially considering you have no way to have known in the first place. You could just make a Facebook profile, you know."

I shake my head.

The strawberry candle's flame flickers and elongates into an orange tail.

~ ~ ~

I'm lying on the couch with Toki the Cat on my chest, his tail resting across my lip like a bushy gray mustache. My finger's hovering over Livi's name in my phonebook. Do people still call each other for something like this? Or does this mean I'm like a parent calling?

I ask Trey. He says, "Just do it," and makes a check-mark swoosh in the air. He's casually cruising Porn4U like clicking through cable channels.

She picks up on the first ring. Her voice carries a perkiness and energy that makes me sit up, then stand, sending Toki the Cat running off, all bushy-tailed.

After pleasantries I ask if she's doing anything for her birthday tomorrow. The energy in her voice somehow gets higher.

"Tomorrow I'm turning 21, but everyone is working," she says.

"We *could* go out to celebrate," I say. My voice shoots up an octave with each word.

She loves the idea. "We could play bags, or cornhole, or, *oh, my God*, beer pong. There's no one better at beer pong. This'll be great. I'm gonna kick your ass," she says.

I guess I won't be taking a break from the alcohol.

She asks how I knew it was her birthday.

"I have my ways."

"You don't have Facebook, right? I checked the other day—not being, like, a creep or anything. But you weren't listed."

"You stalker, you," I say.

"I was just—yeah. I was stalking you. Unsuccessfully, I should add."

"I don't have a Facebook. I don't like Facebooking or Twittering or Instatweetergrimguring." I mumble that last portmanteau. I'm not sure she understood me.

"Hmm. Interesting," she says.

"Quite."

"Indeed."

"Indubitably."

"Mmmhmm."

5.

In the morning, I pace myself. I mix orange juice, vodka, and vermouth before tutoring for a few hours. (A few graduate students working on their MLA and APA formatting. One regular tutee gave me $7 to show his appreciation. I'm like Jay-Z.)

When I return, Trey is sitting in his gaming chair, his headphones engulfing his fat blonde head. I wave and jump like a puppet from *Team America*, but he doesn't see or hear me. At the kitchen island I make a tall drink, five or six worth into one glass so I won't have to refill for a while. I duck into the Dungeon and recline.

Toki the Cat settles in on my stomach. Via remote, I set Radiohead's *Kid A* on repeat. As the strings harmonize in "How To Disappear Completely," my phone atop Toki the Cat lights up. The grad student who tipped me asks me to join a pickup basketball game at the campus gym. After I ignore him, I'm able to settle back in and block out everything not in my Dungeon.

My eyes closed, I fly over three-dimensional landscapes, zipping past Tim Burton-like towers whose tops disappear into dark clouds, electric bolts jutting across the sky with sparks. Toki the Cat kneads my legs and everything feels right. The alarm wakes me. If it weren't for the phone display showing the time, I'd have no clue what time, day or night, or even which day it is. *Kid A* is now on "Everything's In Its Right Place."

"Treefingers" orchestrated a lucid dream in which I floated through the day as a confident, carefree figure who ebbed and flowed—body elongating and fluttering—with rhythms of those around me. I'm disappointed when I wake as myself; it's the immediate feeling after finishing a movie wherein you remember who you are. For a few minutes I'm bummed I exist as me. Then I remember the night I'm supposed to have.

Driving with the tall glass between my legs, I pull into Gunslingers and park next to C.J. the Frat Boy's bullet-like Camaro.

He's leaning on his hood as he smokes. His Chicago Bulls straight-brim is skewed on his head. He flashes a "W" with his left hand toward me as his right hand grabs his crotch through his basketball shorts. I don't know what that means, so I just nod.

Livi lives in apartments behind the bar. She appears around the corner as I near the bar door, which is a swinging door like in an old gunslingin' western. She's wearing a blue and gold dress with no shoulder straps. Around her tight stomach is a gold belt that gives her that model hourglass shape.

Breathe in, breathe out.

She walks toward me and steps on my blue Vans and kisses me.

"Have you been drinking?" she asks.

"Yes, many times."

"Ha. I've only heard that one a billion times."

I think to clarify. "My roommate and I had a few drinks at our place. We play this drinking game to *Slingblade*." She's never seen *Slingblade*, I already know.

She gives me a blank look.

"I know. You haven't seen it." I smile and explain. "Billy Bob Thornton plays this big-time special-ed fella who says *Mmmhmm* after everything. Like how Professor Nelson does his 'riiight' thing. We drink every time Billy Bob *Mmmhmms*."

"I wanna play sometime."

"*Mmmhmm.* We will."

"You shouldn't drink and drive," she says, almost nagging, which is a thing I've heard Trey repeat in many different locations and many different outfits in many different tones. I should compile a scrapbook of all the times I'm told it. But I appreciate the thought.

We sign up to play in the beer pong tournament. Pairs of chest-bumping dudebros dress in matching colors with Sharpie-drawn doodles and team names on the backs. Names like "Spankbank" and "Chodehead." I'm in a blue V-neck, which I hate, but it compliments a wide-shoulder frame. Her sundress matches, so I feel like we're a team.

I order drinks—vodka and whatever—and she gets something pink and fruity. After seeing Livi's ID, the female bartender offers the birthday drink.

"The three wise men," the bartender explains. Judging from the pink fruity drink Livi ordered, she'll hate taking shots named after men, each followed by another liquor chaser.

Livi raises her eyebrows at me. "Load 'em up, barkeep," she says like an old cowboy. She raps her knuckles on the wooden bar top. A couple bartenders huddle around and cheer as she takes the shots like a champ, her face not wincing. A female bartender drops a paper crown on Livi's head. It reads *Happy Birthday, Pardner, From Gunslingers.*

"Pretty good. Pretty, pretty good," I imitate Larry David.

"I could tell you doubted me."

"I did. But you showed me."

She sips delicately from her pink drink.

"That was disgusting, though," she says. "But I can cross that off the ol' bucket list."

A song by Lil Yo Something ends. The DJ calls our names for beer pong over the speakers. Surrounded by four other pong tables, we stand on one side of the beer pong table. The overhead lights glow blue, switch to pink, then to red. The DJ calls our opponents. A thick-necked bald bro stands across the table next to C.J. the Frat Boy. To decide who shoots first, C.J. the Frat Bro and I stare at each other and shoot. I make it, front cup. His shot hits Livi, and she catches the ball against her chest. Livi and I shoot. We miss. Livi, pink drink in hand, tries to distract the opponent by waving her hands above the cups, making noise which is drowned out by the thump of the subwoofer.

"Yeah, Liv," C.J. the Frat Boy says. "Lemme see what I know you got."

He shoots and hits Livi again, aiming for her chest. She catches it and almost spills her drink.

It being her birthday, she's in a good mood. She laughs it off. I don't.

We make our shots in the same cup. Balls back. I hit another and another and I'm on fire. I finish my drink and the thick-necked bro is aiming to shoot.

"Damn, girl, I can't shoot witchoo behind there," he says. "Shit, Liv," C.J. the Frat Boy says. At the same time, the two toss the balls at Livi again, overshooting the table by a foot.

"Typical," she says, now irritated. "He's always been like this."

I nod and focus on the shot. She misses, but I hit the back cup. It spills onto the thick-neck's untied Air Jordans.

"Whoa, man. No need to be shooting so hard," he says, throwing his hands up.

They shoot, both miss. I hit the next few shots and we're done. The opponents come over and shake hands. C.J. takes Livi's hand and tries to kiss it like she's royalty. She pulls away.

"Uh, no thanks, not like that," she says and yanks her hand away. She walks off, unaffected by the two. She quickly changes the topic. "You're pretty damn good, Tyler. Like the honky Kobe of alcoholism." She smiles. I mirror the smile with my mouth, but my eyes are watching C.J. He struts to another girl who stands talking to a guy wearing sparkly jeans, a black dress shirt, and a loose tie. C.J. plants his arm against the wall between the guy and the girl.

"You know him already?" I ask, still looking at C.J.

She waits to respond. "He, I, uh, knew him from a few classes." She gulps from her pink drink, and my lip rises in reflex disgust.

"I'll be back, Livi, in just a minute." I grab and hold her hand. "I gotta grab something from my car. Will you grab me another drink? Just use my tab." I'm drunk enough for confidence, so I kiss the top of her head—piña colada shampoo—while still looking in C.J.'s direction. He's clueless I'm seeing him.

My phone buzzes. It's Kennedy. I don't bother reading it as I climb inside Betsy and dig in the center console. My knife is buried beneath receipts and napkins and charger cables. Elbow deep, I find it; my finger runs along the smooth wooden handle.

Walking back toward the bar, I stroll past C.J.'s car. I jab the knife into his front right tire and pull out quickly. The air hisses out. I'm surprised the knife is sharp enough, and I'm relieved the tire didn't explode like I'd imagined.

I drop the pocket knife in the trash outside the door. I nod to another college student I tutor. That's the first time I've ever needed the pocket knife, and it fulfilled its ten-dollar cost. The colleague who I tutor approaches and praises me.

"I got an A, man. Been since grade school since I got an A. Let me buy you a drink," he says.

I shake him off. "I gotta meet someone inside, man. I'm sorry. It's a gal, believe it or not, so I can't keep her waiting. Gorgeous, she is." The guy pats me on the shoulder. He's genuinely happy for me, but I'm preoccupied. He says, "You in for basketball next time?" I nod and turn away from him. I'm at the swinging doors when I notice I'm scowling and clenching my teeth. My jaw is sore and tired.

~ ~ ~

It was when Mom died that I stopped buying into karma. After that I knew it couldn't be real. It was a liberating thought, same as drifting from Christ and the religious team of super friends. Buddha—at least in my doltish rudimentary understanding—he's less about the gas-guzzling Hummers and backyard pools and flat screen TVs. He's more about releasing into oblivion. Disappearing completely.

If I believe something is wrong, that something is unjust, I act on that impulse. Sometimes, I realize minutes or days or years later that I was entirely wrong, but at least I'm acting on a feeling sparked from a real moment. It's the only real-time thing I engage in. Otherwise, I run my life with a remote that starts, pauses, fast-forwards, and rewinds any collection of events.

All the events I watch are carefully structured and edited, unlike my rambling, incoherent reality. I once overheard my Dad tell his wife—while I stood in the next room during their wedding reception—that I'm an "idealist who should live in the real world, not some imaginary world some nerd made up."

In a shitty way, I feel better as I'm entering the bar again. C.J. the Frat Boy is eyeing Livi and nodding his head, licking his thin lips. He's talking to the thick-neck guy, whose head resembles a fat thumb. They both ogle Livi.

My Livi.

Cue clip of a chest-banging ape.

At the smooth wooden bar, I order a double and tip the barkeep to add a third and fourth. I'm running my hand over the smooth countertop as my brain orchestrates thoughts of that frat boy and Livi naked. I can't stop it or censor it. It's just a film running in my mind, my eyes taped open like *A Clockwork Orange,* which Livi probably hasn't seen (but should since it's a staple of American culture).

My circus is now filling my mind at anytime, not just when I'm trying to sleep.

Livi runs up to me and throws her body weight into my chest. Behind her is the drink she ordered for me.

"I was worried where you went," she says, blinking her eyes rapidly. "Where did you go?" Her head's swaying. Alcohol's flowing through her. My urge is to be cold to her, shake her off. But I'm in no position to do so. I can do nothing about her past. Plus, who am I? We're just here celebrating her birthday.

"Just said hi to a friend who was out smoking." I say. "By the freakin' way, happy anniversary of your birthing!" I'm method acting. I am Owen Wilson.

She hugs me, says thank you, and pulls my arm as "Play Hard" by David Guetta plays over the speakers.

"Lou, let's go dance," she says.

"What?"

"Oh, God, I'm sorry. The ex . . . it just fell out. I'm drunk, and—it's been a habit over time." Her palm hits her in the forehead. "Can we just pretend that didn't happen?"

Half of me is about to flip a pong table over, stand on another and flip off the entire bar. *Fuck all of you.* The other half knows to look past and be unaffected—*censor yourself and you'll be glad later*. It's this latter half that breathes in the nose, out the mouth, and smiles—eyes *and* mouth.

Channeling Ryan Gosling.

"It's okay, a mistake," I say. *Freudian slip,* I don't say.

"Thank you. I'm so sorry. Let's go."

She pulls me onto the dance floor. We leg-kick. I dance like Borat. I try to do the John Travolta-Uma Thurman dance part from *Pulp Fiction,* which doesn't work if only one person does it and the other doesn't know what you're doing. But she's smiling. She's drunk-white-girl dancing, her hands messing up her hair, her head pointed down. A mess—yet still sexy somehow. A bowel-rumbling thumper of a song plays. She positions her legs on one of mine, her arm around the back of my neck. Halfway through the song she turns and pushes her ass against me. She pulls my head between her hand and head.

After a song's worth of grinding my jeans zipper into my nether-regions, she pulls me off the dance floor by my arm.

"Let's go," she says. We weave through the crowd, which is packed butts-to-nuts. I can't see her in the crowd, but she's still pulling my arm like we're two people connected by rope in the dark.

Outside we walk to Betsy the Buick. I glance at C.J.'s car tire, which rests on its rim. Livi and I are sitting right next to each other, my car having no divider between passengers other than a retractable armrest, which she moves out of the way. I'm driving off when Livi lies down, curled up, and rests the side of her head on my lap.

"You gonna be sick, Liv?" I say.

"No. I'm okay," she says, giggling.

She's unzipping my pants when I realize my car lights are off. I switch them on, and Livi's wiggling my pants down as I sit in them, which is an awkward and difficult process. MGMT's "Electric Feel" is on the radio. Olivia's moving her hips to the beat, her ass shaking in the air, and *this is great*. I've always loved driving, a pleasure in and of itself. I've also always loved what she's doing, and multitasking like this is overwhelming because I want to pay full attention to both things, not to mention I love the song on the radio. An overload of three wonderful things.

I brush her hair out of the way and whisper to her when in my peripheral I see a cop car turn onto the street. I grab the wheel, 10 and 2. I turn down the radio, as if the cop would pull me over for listening to music at an audible volume. I turn right at my first chance. So does the cop. I tap Olivia on the head and whisper, "Cop's following me, and I'm, uh, too drunk to get pulled over."

She whips her head up and turns around and flips off the cop.

"Jesus Christ, Livi. Turn around and face forward. Like we're in school."

I pull to the curb, and my front tire rests atop it. I shut the car off. The cop slows down, idling past. His round face scans the license plate. He cruises past, and I turn to Livi.

"Let's just walk home. It's not too far from here."

"But—" she complains, pointing to my crotch, which is such a gross term for a groin, which is also a bad name for the genital-area. "I wanna—" she points again in the crotchal region.

"Let's get back to my place," I say. "We can run." I feel a bit like I'm encouraging a kid something is fun when it isn't.

"I'm too tired," she says, her hair disheveled but still flowing in layers like a shampoo commercial.

"Hop on my back. I'll give you a piggy-back ride."

She jumps on my back, wrapping her thin soft arms around my neck. As I carry her, I imagine C.J. the Frat Boy trying to drive off with some blonde girl when his rim starts scraping the cement. The circular rim crushing into an oval. Maybe he's drunk and walks home alone instead of getting into a drunken accident, in which case, I've done a good thing.

Rationalization, what would I do without you?

After half a block, my calves and back are burning, but she says, "I like Tyler-back rides." She kisses the side of my neck, so my calves and back quiet down.

6.

I set Livi down inside the duplex where the lights are off. The candles and TV light the room. Trey's sitting in his computer chair, bathing in the TV's glow. Over his ears are headphones, so he doesn't hear us.

Olivia points at the screen and puts her hand over her mouth to cover a bursting laugh.

"Is he watching porn?"

"It's a thing he does."

"But," she says, confused. "He's not, you know." She pantomimes stroking a zucchini.

"Yeah, I know. He surfs porn like we'd flip through Nat Geo. Like he studies porn. It's weird, not even sexual. More like curiosity—studying an animal like a visitor at a zoo. *Hmm. Interesting how he spills his seed on her face, which serves no useful reproductive purpose.*"

"Gross." She pushes me.

"Sometimes he'll smoke this old-school wooden pipe with his glasses on like he's a porn professor flipping through new work."

"What if I scare him?" she says.

"I'd love that. But he can't hear you. Sound-cancelling headphones."

Livi tiptoes across the room like Pink Panther, looking back and me every few steps and making a *shhh* face with her finger over her mouth. She barrel rolls until she's behind Trey's chair. After crouching behind Trey for a moment, she jumps up, screams, and grabs Trey's chest, which is to say she grabbed two handfuls of manboob.

Trey screams and throws his arms in the air. His full weight tips backward in his chair, and he thuds against the floor. From the ground on his back, he puts his hands up in a feminine bear's *rawr* clawing position, as if that'd ward off any robbery or attack.

Olivia falls flat on her ass, laughing. Trey scowls over at me and gets up.

"What the fuck. I shit my pants," he says, shaking his head and flipping both of us off.

"Trey, this is Livi," I say. "You guys are friends on Facebook, so you probably already know each other intimately."

Livi sticks one hand out, the other covering her mouth as she laughs. She lifts her back leg behind her and curtseys as she says with a bounce, "Pleasure to meet you."

"Uh, yeah. You too." Trey hesitates to shake her hand, as if he's worried she thinks there might be some goo or lubricant on his hand not fit for hand-shaking. He puts his hand into a fist and fists her open palm.

"Ah, the turkey. And a fan of the knucks. That's cool, that's cool, too," she says, as if trying to be tough for some reason. "I scared the shit out of you, didn't I?" She's laughing again, and Trey is walking toward the bathroom.

"Yes. I'm going to check how bad it is," he says completely serious and monotone. "I legitimately shit myself," he mumbles.

~ ~ ~

In the living room, Livi's looking around at the walls, the cardboard cutouts, the walls of movies and books.

She walks up to a cardboard cutout of Kate Beckinsale from *Underworld.*

"Who's *this* sexy lady?"

"Kate Beckinsale," I say expecting confusion as a response.

She grabs Kate by the shoulders and dances with her, cardboard-Kate tipping left and right.

"You're such a babe," Livi says to Kate. "Wanna go back to my place?" she whispers in cardboard Kate's ear. "You were wonderful in *Pearl Harbor.*"

"And holy shit, Liv knows a movie *and* an actress. Praise Jesus, Muhammad, Snorlax, and whatever the Scientology guy is."

"Xenu, the dictator of the Galactic Confederacy," she says, changing her voice to a movie trailer narrator. "He who brought billions of people to Teegeeack—or earth—and stashed them in volcanoes and killed them."

"You know *that,* but don't know who Billy Bob Thornton is?"

She rubs her chin. "He works at the Kwik Trip on South Main."

Livi looks at the ceiling-high shelving unit filled with movies and TV box sets.

"This is insane," she says, running her finger down the DVDs and Blu-Rays. "Are these in alpha-freaking-betic order?"

Trey appears out of the bathroom in new shorts, now plaid and white.

"All better," he says, his hair now hanging over his shoulders, wet and stringy from an apparently quick shower. "Happy birthday, by the way."

She smiles and curtsies, "Why thank you, Professor Porn."

"No problem, Olivia the Ogre."

~ ~ ~

Livi is checking out the shelves, where action figure memorabilia pose. There are action figures from *Shawshank Redemption, Pulp Fiction, The Godfather,* and a complete set of Mario-related characters.

"These toys are awesome." She grabs a *Metal Gear Solid* Big Boss posable figure and pretends to shoot at me.

"Pew pew pew."

"Oh, ho-ho, these are not toys," I say, feeling like I'm in *Toy Story* when Woody tries to explain to Buzz he is *a child's plaything*.

"Action figures they are," Trey adds in his masterful Yoda voice. "Collectable they are. Unopened, they are worth some cash, especially in my bedroom stash." He's nodding, like *aww yeah, baby, action figures*. I roll my eyes because he's bragging, as if girls care, especially drunk girls. Especially drunk, horny, beautiful, intelligent girls.

Right. Horny.

"Livi," I say. "We should, uh, check out my room."

That's the best I've got.

"Wait a freaking fucking goddamn minute," she says. She grabs a Chewbacca cutout out from the corner. "I seriously love *Star Wars.*"

My heart sinks because I hate *Star Wars.* The one thing I don't watch, Olivia's into. *Star Wars* is Trey's thing, so Olivia and Trey talk about ships and hairy creatures and gay robots while I get tired and antsy, my total hours of drinking closing in on seventeen.

She's telling Trey how impressive the organization of the media is. He tells her numbers: five thousand movies, four hundred TV shows, too many CDs to count, but we're converting them to MP3, not ACC, and digital formatting offers more . . . . He just drones on.

Olivia sniffs the air around her. "Is that vanilla strawberry . . . with a hint of . . . lavender?" she asks Trey.

"Why, yes, it is," Trey says. "My own candle mix. I like to try out new smells, keep this place smelling bitchin', you know?"

The two gab on about candles and *Star Wars.* I'm staring at the 55" display of interracial midget porn, and I'm amazed no one has said anything about this.

"Hey, Livi," I say. "Let's let Trey get back to his . . . research." I point to the screen.

"It was lovely meeting someone with such great taste," Livi says. I nearly drag her away from my roommate.

In my room, she comments again on my toys.

"Action figures," I say.

She laughs. "You're cute," she says and tries poking my nose, making a *boop* noise. Instead, she pokes me in the eye. This makes me laugh like Pillsbury dough boy. I'm not as drunk as her, although I am still quite loose. I'm positive—despite my animal instinct—I don't want to "get some" like some frat-boy-dude-bro fist-pumping-sleeveless-shirt fuckshit who'll knucks some protein-shaking jack off the next day, claiming he didn't even know her name.

I want more from this.

So I make no moves.

She pulls down toys—er, action figures—and plays with them. It's clear now how drunk she is. She messes up everything, which normally drives me insane. My urge for order and perfection arises, but I suppress it. I'll fix it in the morning after she leaves.

I lie down on the bed, and she crawls under my arm, her big green eyes looking up at me.

"You know something?" she says.

I shake my head. "I don't know anything."

"I think you're beautiful, but you don't know to show it." She pokes my nose and is on the mark this time. "You just don't know how to be normal."

I'm not sure how to respond, because I don't know if that's a compliment or a slight. If it's a compliment, I've never gotten used to receiving them. So I divert her attention to something else. I'm about to ask about her brother when my phone vibrates.

Kennedy: *I got your addy now. I know where u livin.*

I shake it off. By himself, he is harmless. But a part of me is bothered because of the people he hangs around with. They are not harmless.

"Who was that? Your *girlfriend?*" Livi says, trying to peek at my phone.

"Not exactly. Just a guy who—" I think for a moment whether to tell her the truth or not, but she's so open and, now, drunk. "It's a guy who sells me pills for my anxiety." I leave out the other pills he's sold me—Adderall, hydrocodone, others I'm too tired to remember.

"Oh. So, not your girlfriend?"

"Nope. He's mostly a boy, with a wiener. Definitely not a girl or a friend or a girlfriend."

She smiles. "Well, I think it's crazy you don't have a girlfriend."

"Yeah, I'm such a catch."

"Shh." She presses her tiny finger over my lips. "You know, we're not boyfriend and girlfriend. You have to ask." She smiles.

"Like in grade school?"

She nods. "And it should be sweet."

I shake my head. "I gotta be creative, don't I?"

She nods. "At least you should try. Especially since you didn't think of a creative nickname name for me."

"Boo Boo Kitty Fuck?" I say.

"Try again another day," she says.

She talks about how her mom and dad met, at a gym: how sweet he was, how she felt when he died.

"Every day," Livi says. "On Facebook, on the streets, wherever, people say things like 'End cancer' and 'Save the tatas!' And it had never bothered me until cancer was close to me. Then all those people wearing cancer T-shirts seemed so superficial to me. What does wearing a T-shirt do for cancer? They raised $10? That's nothing. And if you 'Like' a message on Facebook, so what? Spreading awareness changed nothing in my dad's case. Or in anyone's case."

"Might as well pray for someone," I say, unaware of her religious views.

"Yes. A lot like praying."

"Same as saying, 'I'll be doing nothing to help you.' But I will, however, feel good about myself. Hints of empathy over compassion. It's the American way."

"And it's bullshit," she says, showing anger for the first time. "I should do something, anything, to actually try and change *something*. I don't care how much I make or how prestigious my job is because it doesn't matter. Change is good. Helping people is good. What I've been involved with so far, it hasn't done anything for anyone." She takes a deep breath. Selflessly, she flips back to talking about my anxiety. Instead of following up on her thoughts, I am so comfortable talking with her, I allow the shift in conversation.

"Why don't you just go to the doctor?" she asks.

"No insurance." I shrug.

"You're not on your dad's?"

"He dumped me after Mom died. Said, 'I'm sorry, son. You're on your own,' and that was that. Well, first we had a fight."

"A fight?"

I nod. "Physical fight." I punch at the air. "Might've been my fault, but it needed to happen. It had been building up for so long that it was inevitable."

I've told myself this again and again.

Her hand goes over her mouth. She's still under my arm, looking up at me, her eyes bright and glossy. Blinking a lot, she says, "Do you hate him?"

I almost say yes, but I don't. "Not hate. I blame him. Especially—" I think of Mom, but now isn't the time. "Especially about the divorce. He went out to Cali; my Mom stayed here in Wisconsin. Dad was sleeping with this young waitress with a thing for military types. Like straight out of a shitty novel. And 'sleeping with'—what the hell does 'sleeping with' even mean? He was fucking her. That's how his Cali-lover got knocked up. Bam—they had a kid. I didn't even find out about it until after my mom died. Semper fi, always loyal."

She looks softly at me, nodding her head as if to say, *Keep going, I'm listening.* I feel guilty for talking so much, but she invites me to continue in every way, apparent that she cares.

"Dad's other kid . . . he's my brother. But a different Mom."

"Do you know him at all? Your half-brother?"

"His name is Christopher. They call him Toph. He's . . . five now? That's about it. He never signs the postcards Sherry sends, so I have no clue what he's up to."

"And no Facebook to check."

"Sometimes I wonder what it's like for him growing up," I say. "Before the divorce, I had it made. At least I thought. I'd stay over at friends for entire weeks, not even checking in at home. Not even a call. They'd never check in on me, like they didn't know how to be parents, which makes sense. Who teaches you how to? But people figure it out. Or at least they try to. Ma and Pa didn't. Holidays, Christmas get-togethers, I was free while every other kid got dragged to Easter sunrise service and second-cousin's graduations in some podunk town drowning in draft beer."

She's resting her chin on my chest. It's painful but a good pain— a feeling of being present in this moment.

"I had a family that dragged me to everything," she says, kissing my chest. "Sometimes I missed out on things friends were doing. But once college came around, those friends disappeared. Moved somewhere or got knocked up or worse—married."

"But your family's still there," I say.

Tracing the outline of my chest, she nods.

"One summer," I say, partially amazed she's not bored with my complaints. "I stayed with a girlfriend. Entire summer, between freshman and sophomore year of high school. Got my own makeshift room with a futon and everything. They *wanted* me there. They had breakfast and dinner every night. Lunch on the weekends. Jokes, they had fucking inside jokes and supported each other and encouraged each other. For that summer, I was part of the inside jokes, part of the encouragement and support. Her dad taught me how to ride a fucking unicycle. Seriously. I'd wear this pinwheel hat and cross my eyes like Jerry Lewis and whistle show tunes. Let me teach you how. It's awesome."

She smiles. "I've got balance like a teeter-totter." She blinks a million times. "You would have traded anything to have that in your family, wouldn't you?"

I nod and brush the fallen hair from her face like Gosling might. Gosling to Rachel McAdams. I almost say something romantic, but hold off at the last moment.

"Every time I went home, seeing Mom and Dad was a reminder I didn't have that."

Olivia props her head up on her hand, her elbow digging into my pillow-top bed.

"A rolling stone," I say. "That's what Mom was like. Sorry, Bob Dylan and other rich famous people, but Mom just wanted to travel. But a kid—me—that meant having a certain groundedness she couldn't handle. It just sent her into a downward spiral." I whistle like a bomb descending before it explodes. "One time, Dad was drunk, a full day of football and a pile of empty sixteen-ounce Spotted Cows. He said Mom had postpartum depression after I was born. Really bad. Dad said she never really snapped out of it. Permanent depression because of me. I changed her life for the worse. Not in an 'Oh, pity me' way, but in a 'This is the truth, deal with it' sense."

I pause and take a drink of the screwball sweating on my nightstand.

I say, "It's just a bad feeling to have in the core of your gut, you know? No one asked me if I wanted to crawl out her vagina like a gooey cave spelunker. And when she died, part of that guilt had to be laid on me, in one way or another."

"How can a car accident be your fault?" she asks.

I'm thrown at first. Then I remember. I don't correct the lie.

"I guess 'inconvenience' would be how to describe life to this point. I just complicated things in a bad way." After I realize I've said all this, I feel stupid, exposed, and I can't look her at her anymore. I'm being dramatic. Lifetime movie. My vision blurs, and I stare off at a Solid Snake action figure and try to distract myself.

As I sense her stare into my straying eyes, I feel heavier, like it's not just me anymore.

"I want you," she says. "I want you now. Because somewhere in there," she points to my chest, "there's a nugget. A golden nugget."

My eyes bulge involuntarily, rather than roll. I shake my head. Holy shit. She's drunk. Beautiful and intelligent and caring, but drunk. The two critters on my shoulders bicker, the demon and angel, but before they begin to whisper in my ear, I've made my decision. Beyond her, I see the shadowy man. He shakes his bald skull. He whispers, *Being with her will never allow you escape reality. She's going to pin you to this hell all around you. Don't let her in. Do not.*

I blink until the vision of the man dissipates. I distract Livi with questions and conversation until she falls asleep. I figure I'll make a move in the morning. Be a kind-of good guy and still maybe make happy-time in the a.m.

She falls asleep with her arms wrapped around my *Kung Fu Panda* stuffed animal, her head on my chest. I don't sleep a tick. I lie there and appreciate her. Her piña colada hair tickles my nose, draped like a mustache over my lip. My circus comes to town, but they bring only snapshot memories I haven't visited in years.

Chapter Five

Night Terror

Age nine, I drift off watching *Ed, Edd n Eddy* on my 13-inch TV in my dark bedroom. In a dream, my fourth-grade teacher hogties me, and I'm wriggling like a fish out of water while she digs a hole, as Ed often says. *Dig a hole, dig a hole.* My teacher is burying me alive, dirt falling from her shovel into my mouth as I try to scream. She's finished piling the dirt atop me when my breathing gets shallow and my legs spasm.

I shoot like a torpedo underground, pushing dirt up like Bugs Bunny. I wake up, screaming and my arms shaking, my legs giving out a few times as I stand from bed. My familiar room is different, like through a Beastie Boys fisheye lens. The room fluctuates, huge then tiny, huge then tiny. I'm screaming with every breath, and I feel that I'll be dead any second, so I run up and down the hallway. Mom and Dad are awake in the living room. I'm awake, but I'm still pulled half to the dream, half to the distorted room.

Dad cuts me off halfway down the hallway, and he's panicked, yelling, too.

"What's wrong, what's wrong?" His eyes are two suns, pupilless. I'm still in the dream.

"I can't believe they're killing me. I can't believe they're killing me," I'm screaming like a broken record.

Dad's yelling almost as loud. "Who? What?" He grabs me in his arms and carries me like a baby—a sack of potatoes, like nothing—to the couch where Mom lies, her eyebrows scowling. She's pressing the remote so the TV grows louder. Dad holds me on his lap. He's rubbing his huge hand against my back, and I rest my head on his warm shoulder. I'm terrified because I will be dead soon. Something is killing me, and I can't be fixed.

When I tuck my face into his warm shoulder, I sense him tense and almost recoil, but he doesn't. Instead, he rubs my back and holds my head there like I'm a child. I scream into his ear until I calm to a sob. My tears wet his strong shoulder, staining his gray T-shirt into a darker, blacker gray. Mom watches us blankly, her mind distant in the world of the movies. The TV set blares as if I were still screaming. But I wasn't screaming. No. Dad had pulled me above ground and calmed me until the world became okay again, if only for that night.

~ ~ ~

Olivia wakes up and, since I'm already awake—unable to sleep with this precious beauty sleeping on my chest—I pretend to wake up, complete with big yawn and arm-stretching. After we brush our teeth, as Kung Fu Panda and Toki the Cat watch, we do everything health class told me makes a baby. I feel love, but know I'm an idiot.

Chapter Six

I Choo-Choo Choose You

At work, the gym, or in class, no one likes the smelly guy. You know the one. The rancid-onions BO guy with green stink lines dashing from his pits. He's clueless, unaware of the singed nose hairs that carry his stank all day. I suppose the female equivalent is the woman who swan dives into a tub of perfume before going anywhere, always keeping a bottle in her purse holster to spray every time someone shifts the airflow of the room. No one's digging that person.

I'm hyper aware of stinking around Liv. I don't want any trace of those smell-extremes. According to an article I read explaining How To Be A Sexy Man, everyone has a unique scent, and your deodorant and cologne, if you wear them, should align appropriately. If you find the right match, you might even make women "chemically addicted to you." That sounds too good to be true, but it can't hurt to try.

After a cocktail of medicine, I go to Kohl's. I ask the first clerk to help me "find my scent," which I can't say without laughing and waving my hands in the air. Mandy—college hipster wearing a Kohl's nametag—sprays me with scents by Toby Keith and Ryan Reynolds and other handsome-smelling men. As a team, she and I find a good smell. She says while laughing, "Yes, it'll probably make a woman addicted to you."

I say, "Good. Take all my money. All five of it."

Mandy helps me find the perfect briefs. In passing Olivia mentioned that she prefers the smaller, tighter briefs than boxers. (A drunken Livi: "They give me a wettie!" Duly noted.) Mandy gives me suggestions where I can buy card-making materials. At the hobby store, I grab construction paper, glue, glitter, colored markers. It's like forty dollars in kindergarten materials by the time I'm back at the Sanctuary in front of my computer.

Next, according to Google, I need to make sure my breath is always vagina-wettingly fresh. The key: a tongue scraper, which is exactly what it sounds like. Scrape the goo off your tongue, and you'll have orgasmic breath; keep gum and mints always nearby in case said orgasmic breath sours after eating a mountain of garlic cheese.

I'm texting Olivia as I continue my quest to Be A Sexy Man. We play this game: She names two actors or actresses, and I must connect them through the movies and TV shows they've been involved with. I nail it every time. She claims I'm looking it up, so I call her. We do it live, voice-to-voice, with no help from Google. *Live here from Tyler's bedroom. Livi thinks she can stump this machine. We'll see if she can, up next, Adam Sandler and . . . .*

She's impressed, as indicated by her saying, "That's amazing. I'm impressed."

I say, "Yes, yes it is amazing," because confidence is another way to Be A Sexy Man.

We hang up via the awkward "Who's Gonna Hang Up First" bit new couples in sixth grade do. Then my phone buzzes.

Kennedy: *Just Pay it and I'll Let it Be. Else You'll get it s00n.*

I text Olivia: *What's the best smell in the world?*

Olivia: *Lavender.*

According to How To Be A Sexy Man, lavender is not a smell I should wear; that's a relaxing bath smell. I should smell like a man oozing testosterone.

I ask: *Second best smell?*

The phone vibrates:

Kennedy: 323 Hemlock Ave. Got U, man.

Now I'm irritated. I stole prescription medicine from him. Okay. A terrible thing to do. But let it go. Nagging me will not get him his money, because I don't have it. Plus, most of the medicine is gone.

I'm waiting for Livi to respond, so I have some free time. Here's what I know about Kenneth Dennis Williams:

His dad's a drunk. Drifted to North Dakota after he found out about the pregnancy. Kenneth's cousin, Ka (real name Karl), tried finding Ken's dad via court websites and public records. Never had any luck. In high school, Kenneth found out his dad killed some old lady named Gertrude or Mildred in a convenience-store robbery. His dad wanted cold meds for the pseudoephedrine (for making meth—you know, like *Breaking Bad*). In prison, the dad might've hanged himself—they don't know for sure; he just disappeared. The government started funding Kenneth's necessities. His cousin became like a father to him, started calling him Kennedy instead of Kenneth because "people would hate him like they hate the Kennedys." And people do hate him because of the façade he puts on, but Kennedy's alright. He tries hard to be gangster, but it comes off as one of those MTV-manufactured rappers. There's nothing threatening about a six-foot, hundred-fifty pound white kid that looks like D.J. Qualls. We live in a town of 70,000 in which the worst parts of the city need to be repainted. We also have potholes, yo.

There are no gangsters here.

~ ~ ~

During my tutoring session, the grad student asks why I didn't play ball with him the other day.

"I fell asleep and totally forgot to respond. I'm sorry, man. Next time, I'm in." I don't believe myself, but he seems to.

"We want you there, man. Games aren't the same when you're skipping out."

I almost ask him if I smell manly.

1.

Sunday, the Packers play the Seahawks. Trey, Livi, and I scrunch together on the couch. Sandwiched between us, Livi sits on her tucked legs. My Clay Matthews jersey hangs down to her knees, and her hair is braided over her shoulder. Trey's close friend—Caleb, dressed in a sleeveless Packers tee—rocks back and forth in Trey's video game chair. Throughout the game, Caleb mashes the buttons built into the chair, jerking left and right as if he's playing a game of Madden. This makes Trey laugh like a giddy child.

Even though she knows plenty about football, Livi's asking questions throughout the game: Why does the kicker even wear a helmet? Why do running backs wear diamond earrings under their helmets? Why is that running back sucking on a nookie? Where is the line drawn for ass-slaps? Is a pinch-squeeze okay or not? Cup or no-cup?

Caleb and Trey answer her, and she plays along with them, making them laugh. It's like they've been friends for years. She has no problem opening up to these new people. She's confident. Personable. It's daunting to listen to them poke fun of each other after such a short time knowing each other. I'm nowhere as compatible with them as Livi. As they all laugh, the mustache clock catches me eye, and it will not stop ticking.

Who am I and what is wrong with me? Why am I not like this with my friends? My friends can sense how well-rounded she is. They latch to her.

I write a note to myself and tuck it my wallet: *Figure out what's wrong with you.*

After the game, I glance at her claddagh, which is still pointing out. She catches me glancing.

"Are you ever going to ask me to be your girlfriend?"

The next morning, I'm cutting construction paper, tracing the fat 3-D letters (always running out of room for the last few letters), and sprinkling glitter on top of glue. My letters are deformed and lopsided, and glitter's sticking to everything. Toki the Cat struts around looking like a bedazzled hood ornament. Stuffed Kung Fu Panda's bum is glittery. No matter how much I vacuum, I can't clean this. As Demetri Martin once said, glitter is truly the herpes of craft supplies. When I finish my card, formally asking Livi to be my lady friend, Trey walks in my room and laughs at me. He points and *haw-haws* like Nelson Muntz for a day or two.

"You can't seriously be giving that to her," he says, his finger pointing at my official letter of courtship, stamped and sealed in glitter.

"Fuck off. I'm giving it to her."

"But Tyler," he says, eyes glistening, "you're not in the third grade."

"Well, obviously," I say, having no good come back. "*I'm* twenty-three." I poke both my thumbs into my chest to stress my confidence in this fact.

"And if you were in third grade, Jesus H. Christ, your mother would not approve." He picks up the square card and examines it from all angles. Glitter falls like helicopter maple leaves. They pepper the carpet. "It's like Kesha had an orgy in here with a bunch of other deformed Keshas."

"That card took forever, man. I'm giving it to her. I don't care." I'm frustrated with my own shitty crafting ability.

"Good luck. But if I've learned anything from being alive today, you don't do things like this." He holds the card out like a dirty diaper. "Unless you're being sarcastic or ironic. You can't be vulnerable or honest anymore. It's obvious to anyone paying attention."

Maybe I'm not paying close enough attention.

2.

Livi wants to go ice skating. Every romantic movie has an ice skating scene. The dude is always a clumsy Bambi, and the girl is a graceful swan (or vice versa), and it's just *oh-so-totes-adorbs*. But I'm up for it. I pack a backpack of necessities: a few handfuls of airplane-sized vodkas; my preferred assortment of pills in a baggie stuffed in my wallet; and the card asking her to be my boyfriend. I avoid thinking about the card, because I'm embarrassed by it, for good reason. It's horrible. *And* I spent like forty dollars on materials. I can hear Trey's Nelson Muntz laugh in my head as Livi pulls up to my duplex.

My first time inside Lucille, her Chrysler LeBaron, Livi drives us to the skating rink across town. Her radio's set to NPR, and African drum music plays. The pills in me want to dance in the car seat, shaking my ass and pantomiming maracas in my hands, but I hold back the urge and tap my foot instead. *Just be a normal human being.*

She takes a sharp turn, and metal dog tags swing from the rearview mirror. I glance at them when they settle. Lou's tags. What a stupid fucking name. Out of nowhere, I want to tear the rearview mirror off and pummel the dashboard until the airbag deploys and knock me unconscious. Deep breaths. I scale it back like pulling a dog's leash.

In the nose, long exhale out the mouth. Deep in, long out. Here in the moment, not the past.

"Livi. I'm just asking." I'm calm. Not bothered. I'm not even officially in a relationship with this girl. "But why would you still have these?" I backhand the handles, the ID tags for someone who'll never see combat but will accept praise and adoration. A fella first in line for free shit on military appreciation days.

She eyes them and shuts her eyes for a moment.

"I completely forgot they were there," she says, hands on ten and two. "I'm an airhead. I'm sorry."

"Isn't it kind weird to keep them right in front of your face? And now my face? I mean . . . ." My stomach tightens and I find comfort in knowing my Tic-Tac bottle is in my backpack, my medicine in my wallet.

"You're right," she says.

She yanks on the dog tags and the rearview mirror falls off the windshield.

"God damn it," she says. Trying to untangle the dog tags from the rearview mirror, she says, "I'll get rid of them right now." After a struggle of untangling and driving with her knees, she whips the tags out the window.

"That make you happy?"

It does.

I say, "You didn't have to do that. I just—"

I want to say I'm sorry, but now that the dog tags are in the street, it's over. The military will think Lou got killed fighting for freedom here on Johnson Street. You know, murdering arbitrarily labeled terrorists, slaying evildoers with America's throbbing cocksword. They'll praise him on the news. He'll be lauded for his selfless sacrifice day after day. He'll live on as a martyr eternally remembered on a marble wall somewhere. They'll build a statue of him fixing telephone wires, and a day will be dedicated to his sacrifice. Then they'll find him at home playing *Call of Duty*. I can't help but channel my frustration with Dad, another military man. Dad and this ex-boyfriend military fella—these two synecdoches of my idea of the military as a whole.

Think of the future, of the now, not the irrelevant past.

I'm clenching my fits, grinding my teeth. "I'm sorry, it's just—" I slam my palm down on the dashboard ahead of me. Before I begin to apologize for being such an anger-prone ass, the glove compartment drops open. Proof of insurance peeks out from a messy stack of photos of the ex-boyfriend and Olivia.

She looks down at them, and palms her forehead.

"Jesus," she says. "I am so sorry."

She reaches over and slams the glove compartment shut.

"I'm—it's just that we were together for so long," she says. "All through high school and college. Six years. Bits of the relationship are tucked and scattered everywhere, in cracks and under things. So, I'm sorry."

I stare out the window and imagine shooting out tires of passing cars. My stupid homemade card sits in my backpack. I'm a dolt for making the card. It's unlikely Lou ever made her something as dopey as a knockoff Hallmark card. Military guys don't ask girls via homemade cards to be their lady friends. Fuckwads like me do. Maybe it's best to burn it so no one in the post-apocalyptic future ever finds it among a pile of diapers and used condoms, wondering why someone would make a card asking to be someone's boyfriend. *Is this the third grade? Will you be my Valentine? Will you choo-choo choose me?* Even Mom would be laughing at me.

We arrive at the rink. I get out and head to the bathroom. The shitter door is ripped off, so I sit down on the toilet and dig through my wallet and take a pill. Calm down. Shake it off like a wet dog. But even after I shake, I'm not dry.

So it's time to method act. Fulfill the role. Fake it until I make it.

Channeling Ryan Gosling.

I pay for the skate rentals and break the silence with a playful comment about her tiny feet. "You know what they say about girls with tiny feet, right?"

That makes her smile.

So we're skating, my feet deep drifting off in opposite directions—*oh no. I'm a cliché.*

She's graceful and fluid, like Jesus gliding over water.

"I'm athletic," I'm saying to anyone that will listen. "I promise. Just awkward on skates. Bad ankles, crackly knees." Livi's whipping around the rink; I'm waddling like a toddler with a full diaper. "Dad has 'em, too—bad knees, ankles."

After a few times of flying past me, she stops behind me and wraps her arms around my chest, resting her head on my back. Piña colada shampoo.

She tries not to laugh when she says, "You've got Bambi legs." She shoots off away from me and I feel the calmness circulating my bloodstream, lulling me into normalcy like a rocking chair. For the moment, the past seems far away and silly, unlike in the car when it was screaming in my face. The ball of anxiety in my gut drops and splatters onto the ice, and I'm feeling light.

Pushing off the rink walls, I glide after her and little kid pro skaters whiz past me, arching ice. My ankles burn. She's skating backward, blowing kisses at me. I want to lasso her and pull her close so I can give her my stupid card.

Sitting outside the rink, blowing glitter into the air, I hand it to her. I brace myself for laughter; I even imagine what Liv's Nelson Muntz laugh will sound like. I'm looking away, watching a kid struggle out of his skates. Instead of laughing and crumpling my card, Livi holds it to her chest—glitter globbing onto her coat. She clenches her eyes tight and nuzzles her face in my chest.

3.

I'm reading an essay by Professor Nelson. I read the line, "People fall into routines, and those routines define them." I lie on the couch with Toki the Cat on my stomach. He's purring. A glass of vodka—four-fingers and O.J.—sweats in the armrest holder. Trey walks into the living room around noon, his eyes puffy and red.

"She liked it, you asshat," I say.

"What?"

"My card."

"Oh, right. Good for you." Missing the first time, he pats me on the shoulder.

He plops into his computer chair and clicks to wake the TV monitor. He opens a browser and starts flipping through images on ExRevenge4U.com. After half hour, he snaps out of his daze. Turning to me, he says, "I'm just reminding you, as a warning. Don't forget about Samantha. Don't forget about Marla. Don't let it happen again with Olivia." He turns on Nazareth's version of "Love Hurts" over the surround sound. He sings along in a falsetto voice with his eyes closed, his open-palmed hands reaching out to me.

He doesn't need to remind me. In high school, Sammie was seventeen. I was fifteen. I clung to her like a puppy. She dazzled me with big boobs, experience, money, and a family who welcomed me like a son they'd never had. I pounded my ape chest and everything I did mirrored Samantha. If she went swimming, I swam. If Samantha was working, I was a puppy scratching at the door until she finished work. As a high school boy, a girlfriend offered much more than any of my guy friends could. Shane, Trey, Caleb, Carlos—they paled in comparison. Sammie was hilarious, fun, and smart. She was like Trey except she had boobs. Girl boobs. Plus, her dad liked having me around, even when Sammie wasn't there. We'd hang out and talk music—Neil Young, CCR, ELO, Allman Brothers—and old movies. He'd buy me beer and booze, and we'd sit on the porch talking. This is when I discovered vodka's limited hangover effects.

Sammie's family had a pool in the backyard, and we'd skinny dip when the family was gone. I'd do "the tuck" or pretend to be a naked dolphin jumping in the water. One day her neighbor came over while we swam. A few years older than Sammie—nineteen or twenty—this guy came over in his swimsuit, his shirt off. I didn't once look him in the eyes because he had these giant pepperoni nipples. He chatted with Sammie as she and I treaded water, our kibbles and bits floating beneath the surface. Above, the moon was shaped like Jay Leno's chin. They talked about people they knew, some party a while back, and he left. Sammie climbed atop me, and we did what unsupervised naked teenagers do.

A few months later, Sammie started crying during breakfast, saying she's sorry, that's all, she's just sorry. That's all she can say, and it's over. She said, "I'm seeing someone else."

Not "We should break up." Not "We're done." No, she was informing me that she was currently "seeing someone else." And, oh, how we love harmless euphemisms like "seeing someone" or "sleeping with someone" rather than "mashing genitals together." Cheating is cheating; I played the gullible flunky who waited at her parents' house for her to finish work when she was with this guy, doing what teenagers do. I couldn't kick the image from my mind. Again, my eyes were taped open to watch this imagined scene. *A Clockwork Orange.* And the imagined scene is always worse than the actual scene. But after she told me she was done, I was on my own again.

That was that. I packed my three changes of clothes in my duffle bag and Sammie's dad took me home in his Sebring. After giving Sammie's dad a hug, after him saying, "You're welcome to hang out with me anytime, just chill," I went home where my parents were watching TV in the living room. I walked in. They said nothing. As if I hadn't been gone all summer, occasionally coming home to grab a pair of boxers or a movie.

Iron Man was on FX, so, I don't really blame them.

Pepperoni Nipples (or Peppi Nip-Stocking between Trey and me) was the guy, and that night he had come over to meet Sammie, not knowing I was with her. Had I not been with her, he would have been the naked fella in the over-chlorinated water, risking a UTI for a little tickle.

Even without Trey's constant prompting, the past always glimmers faintly in my peripheral. I feel the vague uneasiness from a memory, and I hold onto pain like it means something to me; like it's something I can't let go of. Sometimes when I'm feeling bland— ennui, *poor me*—I just think of painful events. I clench them until I squeeze emotion out of the past. Then I throw a pity party for myself, complete with a cornucopia of pills and vodka mixes and structured realities acted by paid professionals. Even though I reject the past and the future in philosophical terms, I can't escape the ever-present past casting a shadow over everything. I can't help but picture Sammie and Peppi Nip-Stocking mashing naughty bits together like high-fives behind my back.

I do feel for Mom on some level.

Dad. My dad, a baby-daddy with some big-tit Hooters girl. How many guys was *she* sleeping with when Dad knocked her up? Dad was out in California, being praised by family for endless sacrifices for his country. But really? He was out cheating on his wife who stayed behind to keep her job; to avoid what she knew was going on across the country. Mom knew about the Hooters girl before I did, and I found out one night when Mom flatly told me. During a three-minute commercial break, she said, her face glowing from the TV: "Your dad is going to be a father again. Not with me." *A Knight's Tale* returned from commercial, and she was sucked back into a false reality.

~ ~ ~

Last time I saw Mom, three flickering candles lit the dark bathroom. Water overflowed the tub ledge. Little rivers of water leaked onto the floor. Half her body draped over the tub's ledge. Chunky brown puddled below her mouth. Her index finger was wet with vomit. I held her cold wrist and stood there, without thought. On the wall hung a few of her students' drawings: a seal I drew; some of Pastor Bradley's religious paintings; a third drawing, by Pastor Bradley, lay on the ground, wet and crumpled, edges bent forever.

blew out the candles. Dialing 911 in the dark, my face was lit by the phone's glow. Besides the pulsing numbness, my first instinct was to do something to Dad. Revenge. A knee-jerk reaction. A reaction to her action, her reaction to his actions. Dominoes falling. But he was across the country, lounging out in the sun next to his upgraded girlfriend—both with Coronas, their toes wiggling in the sand. A little bastard growing inside her chicken-wing-filled stomach. Someone was to blame and something needed to be done. My latent anxiety woke, like some genetic material's hibernation ceased. Everything in my life appeared to be marred by an ominous tinge, like someone's aiming a gun at you. Your eyes are closed and you know the shot is coming, but the anticipation is what kills you.

Chapter Seven

We Need a Montage

1.

Growing a skill or a relationship takes time. It isn't like the movies with a two-minute montage and then everything is awesome. Growth and improvement is in the daily routine. The movie montages give us the impression that it's easy, and it's imprinted in our minds, altering our expectations. According to Hollywood, to be a championship boxer, you drink raw eggs and run immediately after while music plays. Then you punch people while screaming like Howard Dean. Movies skip the part about vomiting raw eggs, icing shin splints, and the hours of training in solitude. They skip the post-fighting brain damage—CTE. Same goes for relationships. Movies don't have moments where a guy brings a chicken salad lunch to the gal or when they wait in line at the bank. You find no dead-end conversations that end with, *oh, okay;* there's no quiet car rides with bugs splattering the windshield. You'll find no quiet moments where both people enjoy the silence. Yet all those moments contribute to what the relationship becomes.

Olivia and I "see each other" a few months, frequently "sleeping together." We say this, do that, and learn things about each other. (Example: Olivia has a fake tooth where a horse kicked her; she can do the splits; she once had twin albino hamsters as pets; she never wears makeup, except for weddings; she thought the ancient wartime chant was "rake and pillage." So, for years, when she cleaned the leaves in the yard, she'd yell, "I'm off to rake and pillage!")

Often, days are mundane and unremarkable, but we fuse together like conjoined twins. Well, something like that, but more romantic. It's day by day that I settle into the reality of having something and someone I've always wanted. Around Livi, I'm less anxious and more balanced, which means I'm drinking less and washing down fewer pills (relatively speaking). My swollen liver shrinks and heals each day. I'm more energetic. But I know the high of being around her is a phase—an unsustainable chemical high. I've read books, watched movies, and heard old people cram advice into youngsters: *That poon dries up like a raisin, and she'll stop fellatiatin' your throbbin' doodle. And after a while, your doodle don't throb, either.* Passion and novelty fades, I know. But right now, it's yet to fade, and I'm going to bathe in it while I can.

A meathead football coach once barked at me, *Fake it till you make it, bitchtits.* And I've remembered it since but never practiced it until Livi. Method acting is how I see it, like Daniel Day-Lewis would. The stack of books and movies I've consumed come in handy, like I'm an alien who's digested enough media to have a filtered Hollywood understanding of the human race. Half the time I'm just acting out scenes I've seen before. I avoid saying what I'm thinking, which is usually pessimistic, dickish, and glib. Instead, I act like a normal person. I recite what an actor would. And *voila*! Things are smooth like a baby's butt (which I touch for the first time when I change Livi's cousin's fat baby—think mini-Michelin man in a poopy diaper).

Everything we do together has been done in real life, in movies, in novels, in songs. The variables switch. An X and a Y. An A and a B. A cousin and a nephew. A mom and a daughter. It's all repeated. Ultimately, it's not unique or new. But to me, right now in real life, this all is new. If I were stronger mentally, I'd forget or block all media I've seen so I can experience this without relating and comparing it to some form of media.

But I can't.

2.

Like a rom-com montage:
We visit an aquarium, which I only relate to *SpongeBob*.

"Oh, look at this starfish," she says.

"Like Patrick. Where do they have the underwater squirrels?"

We have a picnic at the park.

"It's such a nice day. Let's eat at the park across the street," she says. The picnic table, normally red, is painted white with bird shit. Seagulls shriek and surround us. They're communicating—*Mine! Mine!*—squawking directions to seize our gluten-free wheat bread. Livi grabs my BLS sweatshirt, puts it down on the bench and sits on it.

"What the hell?" I say.

"Well," she says, "I didn't want to sit on bird poop. It's everywhere." She smiles—a smile that earns forgiveness no matter the wrong.

I sit on the bench. Some of the bird poop is dried and crusty, some is squishy. Flies land on me, my pants, and my food. Every second, a heap of flies land and take off my sandwich.

"They shit when they land, you know," I say.

She shrugs her shoulders, says, "You did forget condiments."

Swear to god, not a single fly buzzes near her. She says, "Shoo fly, don't bother me," and they comply. I windshield-wiper swarms off of me until my arms tire, and I throw the ham sandwich to the seagulls.

Like a Nicholas Sparks movie, we sneak into a family pond out in the country. Swinging from a rope, we dive into scummy water and kiss as a cow moos in the background. Livi's makeup doesn't run because she's not wearing any.

Like silly lovers, I pile on top of Livi as she lies in my bed. Then Caleb's shih tzu piles on, followed by Toki the Cat. The animals perch atop of us, and I yell, "Livi pile!"

Laughing, she says, "I can't breathe!"

She wakes me up one morning, pinning me down, insulting all my favorite TV shows, video games, and movies, saying how they're all made-up and ridiculous. When I rebel, she pushes her armpit into my face.

"No!" I say.

"Admit they're stupid, or smell my armpit!"

"Never!"

"Then smell my armpit!" she says.

"No!"

She mashes her hairless armpit into my face. It doesn't smell, but I pretend to faint. We play "ragdoll," and she tries dragging me off the bed.

Like *Mystery Science Theatre 3000*, we watch muted movies and improvise the dialogue, mine always being sexual, Livi's always being polite inquiries about the location of facilities.

Livi shows me her drawings, the sketches she's created of her ideal wedding, with lines drawn through names of attendees. She shows me drawings of her perfect home, with solar panels and geothermal energy, complete with a terrier named Shiloh. I brag about one drawing from third grade.

"My seal I drew, it was *amazing.*"

"I bet. You have it?"

"Nah. Dad tossed it."

"I'm sorry."

"Don't be."

Through flurries and snowdrifts, we cruise in Betsy and Lucille. We pass the crowded coats waiting at bus stops. We drift down Main Street where families window shop like a 1950s painting. Their breath clouds near their heads, and they point at snowmen built in front of small craft shops. Idling through suburbs, we ogle the Christmas lights that glint along gutters. Rat-pack Christmas music sauntering on the radio, we share our past holidays as we watch people through our fogged windows. She blows hot air on the window. With her slender finger, she writes *Livi + Tyler = heart.*

Like every relationship ever depicted, at Wal-Mart we stroll and people-watch, inventing their back-stories. We name shoppers who zoom in rascal scooters. *Jelly-Glazed Felonious Monk. Cletus Chevy Jones IV. George Custansia IX, driver of Chrysler Lebarons, wearer of sleeveless flannels, proud-displayer of side-boob.*

Like the past refusing to die, the ex boyfriend calls, and they chat. Livi laughs in the other room. She shakes it off. *It's nothing*—but it festers in me, a growing sore. I know this: there will always be someone there before you, and there's no changing it. I don't say anything when he calls because censoring myself has been a good thing up to this point. Deep breath in, exhale out. Ignore the ticking clock—ignore it and breathe. When I forget this, I play Flaming Lips' "All We Have Is Now," and I'm lulled into comfort.

Like brushing away layers of dust, I tell Liv mundane details of my dull life. The way Dad went out with friends most nights. Golfing in warm months, playing basketball and racquetball during cold months. Shooting at the gun club range when he couldn't do anything else. I tell her the way Mom relayed how life used to be before family life tied her down: backpacking through Europe; sketching Shakespeare's Globe Theater; seeing the Louvre; climbing through Anne Frank's house. How all the rest of the glorious past was relegated to faint memory when I was born.

I tell Livi about Mom's everlasting postpartum depression. How according to Dad, it never left her. I burden Livi with my sense of guilt. A guilt for existing, a visceral feeling that I've weighed my parents' lives down by roping them to the routine and predictability that arrive with a baby. And every few weeks, I realize I dump information on her as though I'm trying to figure something out by talking through it. I cut back on what I say, but like I imagine a shrink would be, she welcomes the back-story and my thoughts. She asks questions. I open until I say things I didn't pay thought to before. Before, whenever an inkling of a feeling or thought would spark, I'd divert attention to an album, a film, a TV show, or a novel. I'd analyze the characters there, as if that somehow improved my standing in life. It didn't. It never would. It is an escape—nothing more. How can one be in their twenties and not realize it? But Livi listens, and I dump the tedium on her. She values it, and somehow, I start to.

Like a changing character, I scale back my assholery, bit by bit.

Sheryl Crow once sang that a little change can do you good.

3.

The week of finals is here. Snow falls light and white, then spinning tires dirty it into soggy black.

As with every semester, Trey joins me to help prepare for finals. Livi, Trey, and I are sitting around a table at New Moon. Livi lectures us about the Great Pacific garbage patch and how it affects the marine life and our own consumption. She explains how exfoliating face wash has tiny bits of plastic that fish swallow and we find it in our food; she explains how water filtration systems can't catch the tiny beads. Trey jots notes and draws doodles on a napkin. I nod, impressed by the fluidity of her explanation as if she were a professor. Also, I'm impressed by the sexiness of her everything, like the way she gets worked up because she cares about things and stuff—in that order.

Trey sips from his vanilla latte, Livi from her chocolate mocha latte, and me, I gulp from my coffee tumbler filled with rum and Dr. Pepper. The open mic performer provides background music—solo covers of Bon Iver and The National—while Trey's pen scratches on the mahogany. Livi uses her hands to speak. She ties her curly hair into a bun as I begin to fade into a calm blackout—a comforting nothingness.

4.

Liv and I are sitting in the back of the classroom, far from C.J. the Frat Boy. Professor Nelson is reading from Dostoevsky's *White Nights*:

You do grow up, outgrow your ideals, which turn to dust and ashes, which are shattered into fragments; and if you have no other life, you just have to build one up out of these fragments. And all the time your soul is craving and longing for something else. And in vain does the dreamer rummage about in his old dreams, raking them over as though they were a heap of cinders, looking in these cinders for some spark, however tiny, to fan it into a flame so as to warm his chilled blood by it and revive in it all that he held so dear before, all that touched his heart, that made his blood course through his veins, that drew tears from his eyes, and that so splendidly deceived him.

As Nelson drops and picks up his purple marker—flashing his asscrack to the class—Livi leans and whispers in my ear: "If you talk in class today," her warm breath is wintergreen. "I'll do you a little . . . favor." She rubs her hand up my leg. "Think we've got a deal?"

I nod, my head swimming and blurred.

"You speak up, and I'll—" and she whispers close to my ear. Without thinking I offer my glib opinions on Dostoevsky's view of guilt, his understanding of the fragmented past. After my spiel, I have no idea what I've said, as if I was the Hulk blacking out and coming to. *Where am I? What happened? And where is my shirt?*

C.J. the Frat Boy looks at me. He points at me, his face twisted in surprise. He pantomimes talking with his hand. He mouths "Holy shit, you spoke" before going back to poking at his phone.

After my Hulk moment, anxiety spreads like a delayed chill, but I'm done talking, and every time Professor Nelson refers to my comment during the rest of the class, my heart jumps. But I can deal with it because Livi owes me a favor later. At some point while digging through my briefs, either Livi or I found a pair of balls dangling there.

Chapter Eight

Cruisin'

After a suggestion made by Olivia, I watch *Forrest Gump*. I get up six times to refill my glass, and by the end of the movie I'm in the mood to cruise—*drive, Tyler, drive*. I toss the empty vodka bottle under my bed and grab my keys. In the living room, Trey's headphones block out reality. The screen flashes as he twitches in his gaming chair. His ponytail bobs left and right. On the carpet, a speck of glitter catches my eye.

I mix a roadie with three floating icebergs, and a burst of energy sends me to Betsy the Buick. I cruise the dark neighborhood, observing everything like a drive-by camera shot. One house has a fish mailbox where the bills and ads go into the fish's mouth; one yard is with scattered toys: a tricycle, a Nerf football, a red wagon with a toy red Power Ranger inside; a giant inflatable Green Bay Packers bear wearing a cheese head. All of this peppered with light snowfall. Like a scene from a post-apocalyptic movie in which all that remains of a neighbor are the possessions scattered about. The scene is vaguely lonely. As I imagine the kids playing with their dad, a squirrel darts in front of my car. I slam the brakes. Seconds after the squirrel, a young golden retriever trots across the street, apparently having lost the squirrel's trail. I shut off the radio in the middle of NPR's African drumbeats. I pull to the side of the road.

Setting my sloshing glass on the roof of the car, I slam my door and approach the dog who wears a blue collar.

"Hey, little Air Bud. Whatcha doing out here?"

Little Air Bud trots to me and sets his front paws in my crotch, and I scratch behind his ear.

"Where do you live?" I, not the dog, say.

I pull him close by his collar. Only his name and an illegible phone number are listed. I open my car door and call for the dog to come. Responding to "Air Bud," it leaps into the backseat. I start the car, and I'm about to hit the gas.

"Can't forget my drink." I grab the glass from the rooftop and let the car cruise down the street. In the rearview mirror the dog slobbers on himself, looking back and forth out the window. He's clueless to what could happen to him right now. He blindly trusts me, entirely domesticated and opposite in instincts of a wild cousin. Patrick Bateman of *American Psycho* comes to mind and I see the mutilation that'd develop in his mind. But I also picture a worried owner running down a street yelling, "Air Bud" or "Clifford the Slobbering Dog." Maybe a misshapen boy with a wooden leg named Timmy is blubbering, facing the loss of his best friend. Maybe he's screaming muffled curses upon Santa and white Jesus into his Spiderman pillow. But soon he'll regret those curses.

Air Bud sticks his head out the window and slobbers long thick strings of saliva all along the back of the car, and I barely hold back the urge to do the same. We arrive at the monolithic supercenter, and I run in to get dog food. The good chow costs more than my diet of tuna, noodles, bread, and hot sauce. In my empty glass, I pour dog food and set it on the seat in the back. Air Bud spills it and licks off the seat. The refrain of "Who Let the Dogs Out" sticks in my head on repeat. He slobbers over the faux-leather as I apparently drive us to the Humane Society where Betsy sits until the sun rises. I'm confused and lost when the Humane Society employee wakes me from my stupor with a knock on my window. She asks me if everything is all right. Air Bud barks, and I don't know what to say.

Chapter Nine

With Two Eyes Made of Coal

Olivia is sitting hip-to-hip with me in my car. My arm is around her, and I can't help but kiss her head every few miles. (It's puke-worthy, I know.) We're on the way to spend the day with her mother, Keri, at the mall. The mall, with people peddling cheap plastic shit down the walkway. The mall, with the lingerie stores decorated with overpriced boobie-holders made with strands of thirty-cent fabric. The mall, where the headset-wearing employees meander around a fifty-square-foot store asking, "Are you finding pants okay?" But I go because Livi is going, and she wants me to spend time with her mom. Spending time with them is worth dealing with the empty promises of the mall.

On the radio, an ad plays. The voice is cartoony and exaggerated like the wacky morning DJ Tommy Tought-Nuts.

"Sick of that gut-feeling of dread and nervousness? Tired of nonstop anxious thoughts running through your mind? Call 800-854-0261 to try our brand-new, exclusively patented anxiety medication that promises to end that crippling anxiety that holds you back from being the person you know you truly are."

Livi pulls out a pen and jots the number on a crumpled napkin she grabs from the floor.

"What are you doing?" I ask.

"I know you get built up about the smallest things, so I figured, I don't know . . . it's worth a shot," she says.

"I'm not going on some daily pills just so I can get dependent on them long-term," I say.

"I've see you take pills a bunch of times."

"Whatchoo talkin' 'bout, Livi?" I say, assuming she won't get the *Diff'rent Strokes* reference.

"Those pills you take from the Tic-Tac container. They're like a really small button." She runs her thumb over a button on her pants.

"I don't take those every day. They're just for when I really need them. Like a take-as-needed emergency prescription." I'm backpedaling, trying to avoid this dreaded conversation.

"Then why are they in a Tic-Tac bottle?" she asks, her voice stern.

"It doesn't matter. I just don't want to take anything every day. Doctors put these pills in kids all the time. The kids are still growing, their brains still developing. Their brain grows with its chemistry being altered by these pills. And if you take away a pill that altered chemicals in the brain as a kid grew up, something bad is bound to happen. It's not natural or healthy. And I don't want to be part of it."

"And it's healthy to drink every day? Your brain won't stop growing 'til you're, like, twenty-five. Yet you still drink and take whatever those pills are. Isn't that a little . . . hypocritical?"

I stop and wonder how many times she could have seen me take the pills. Maybe five or six times, max. And I avoid heavy drinking around Livi because I know she doesn't like it. A beer or two, sure, but nothing strong. How can she be saying I drink a lot? Unless Trey and Livi are talking together about me, she's likely exaggerating to make a point.

"Yeah, you *are* a hypocrite," she says, growing momentum. "You hate on the kids and doctors for the medicines, but your pills and booze do just as much damage, even if it isn't *that* much booze and pills. You're no different, but you think you are. You think you're above them."

"No. I just . . . ." I've got nothing. I stare out the window at the open field where horses stand. A young horse trots to an older one and nuzzles his head against the elder's neck.

There's silence. Then she says, "I just want to help you, even if your anxiousness isn't a big deal. I want you to always be happy, and I figure help couldn't hurt, right? Tyler." She's holding my hand. "All I want is to help you."

Hanging above the highway is a flashing LED sign. It reads: "Traffic Deaths This Year: 457." Construction workers line both sides of the road. A sign reads: "Fines doubled in work zones."

I look at her for a long time as I drive. Longer than is safe. Her hair runs over her right shoulder in a braid, a fake yellow flower is tucked behind her ear, and the way she looks at me suddenly weighs a ton. I feel an Acme anvil dropped on my head, and as the cartoon red bump grows on my head, I see real, live compassion. I feel it, painfully weighted and daunting, but novel and fresh and real. I've seen this scene acted out by Julia Roberts and Ellen Page and Emma Stone, but hearing her say my name, having her look at me and say something sweet, showing her concern even though no one else is watching—it is overwhelming. Like a burst of something inside me. Her compassion shown to me chokes my throat, and I can just stare at her, that's all.

As I'm staring, she laughs. "What are you staring at? 'Cause the road's that-a-way."

"It's all better than the movies."

~ ~ ~

We drive on for a while with the radio turned high. Iron & Wine's *Shepherd's Dog* playing.

"I was thinking that I'd really like something. And my mom agrees."

"What's that?"

"Would you like to join my family for Christmas?"

As I nod and smile at her, scenes from previous Christmases roll in my mind's theatre.

~ ~ ~

Year twelve, Christmas Eve: Dad's gone for the weekend for military training. He goes monthly. Mom calls it his "Military Menstrual Cycle." She invites her brother and the cousins, but no one shows up. She makes eggnog and after a few glasses, she introduces me to her "special ingredient," which she dumps into the carton. After she passes out in her recliner, still in her blue robe, I take the carton from under her arm and finish it. Neither of us wakes up in time for the Christmas service, our yearly church attendance day. In the morning, she says she's going to paint at her friend's house, a thing she does regularly. When she doesn't come home by five, I walk to Trey's house and stay there for the night. Trey's mom runs to Walgreens and buys me a rabbit's foot, a last-minute Christmas gift for me. It still dangles from my backpack today.

Years thirteen through seventeen, Christmas: According to my mental historical records, these years blend into one marathon of *A Christmas Story* watched on my bedroom TV while I studied fantasy football magazines surrounded by my action figures standing on shelves running along my walls, which were adorned with *My Little Pony* wallpaper—wallpaper my parents bought when they thought they were having a girl.

Year eighteen, Christmas: Pastor Bradley, Trey's father, invites me to Christmas with his family. At dinner, I pass on saying grace when Pastor Bradley asks me. This unravels into an argument in which I do not censor myself. My words prove to Pastor Bradley that I'm a "vulgar, immature, barbarous idiot with no respect or sense where a boy belongs in the world." I start to filter myself when Trey's mom tells me she used to think I was so bright and respectful and well-put together—none of which are true.

Year nineteen, Christmas: I attended a Packers game against the Cowboys with a college kid named Luke whom I tutored. His rich parents gave him tickets so we could go together—as a thank you. Beer was $8. My fake ID worked, and $112 later, I was out of money. The game was over (Packers 45, Cowboys 28, Sportscenter said the next day), and I was feeling warm, so I stripped down to my boxers and took pictures with random people trudging through the snow to their cars. The pictures bring back some of what happened, including a lot of air guitar and hip-thrusting, but mainly I remember the flurries were only visible falling like feathers when the camera flash lit the area.

Year twenty, Christmas: I had the place to myself since Trey visited his parents'. Watched *A Christmas Story* five times with my special eggnog. Drove buzzed through the streets gazing stupidly at flashing Christmas lights. I practiced Onanism three or four times to the same video Trey left on the 55-inch monitor when he left. I woke up shaking and dry-heaving with an empty box of donuts and some sort of glazed goo on my forearms. I promise myself I'll never drink again. On Christmas, at least.

Year twenty-one, Christmas Eve: I make good on my promise not to drink again (on Christmas), but I spiral down into the pits of a panic attack when I drive past the houses with families gathered inside, the flashing lights outside their houses. I imagine what someone would see looking into my window, and now I only think of Robin Williams at his end. I realize a future awaits me in which I'm alone and afraid of everything without good reason.

Chapter Ten

Christmas With the Higgins and McDermotts

1.

For the car ride to Olivia's mother's house, I prepare a few CDs of music she loves. Cruising through light flurries atop a highway beneath a sunny sky, we sing a CD's worth of Simon and Garfunkel in falsettos. After months of forcing Livi to watch *The Simpsons,* we try to master the voices of characters, from Homer to Uter to Groundskeeper Willy. All of our impressions are horrible. She raps word-for-word to Biggie Smalls' greatest hits in a low voice, moving her hands like a rapper. She makes me play a game in which we go through the alphabet naming words that start with each letter, then repeating the previous ones and adding a new one. I'm not a fan. It goes:

Livi: A, Alphabet.
Tyler: Alphabet. B, Boobies.
Livi: Alphabet, boobies. C, Coral.
Tyler: Alphabet, boobies, coral. D, Dingleberry.
Livi: Alphabet, boobies, coral, dingleberry. E, Elephantitis.
Tyler: Like what I have with my you-know-what?
Livi: Why can't you just play a game I want to play?
Tyler: Fine. Alphabet, boobies, coral, dingleberry, elephantitis. F, Fart.

She tells me about her Dad's dying process—oxygen tank and wheelchair and wheezing—how it changed the way she lived.

"He'd been everywhere, done so much, and I've done none of it. I've never made a difference. I haven't seen Greece or Italy or Brazil. Nothing. I'm too limited. When he died, I decided to change that about myself."

I actively listen—like a Google search said—by making consistent eye contact, nodding my head, and showing empathy through little comments and adjustments of my face. Her travel-talk tightens my stomach, like she'll be doing these things without me, and I'll be left behind. But I breathe in and out and remember what Ryan Gosling would do: WWRGD. I should buy Livi a bracelet. Livi . . . my Rachel McAdams. She wouldn't just ditch me; yeah, we'll do these things together.

Olivia's resting her head on my shoulder as I drive down the long dirt driveway leading to her mom's house. The house is a small wooden cabin surrounded by a small grass field on each side. Each field has a path that leads into a wall of thick trees. In the backyard, you can follow a narrow trail. Avoiding eye-high tree branches and shin-high poison ivy, you'll reach an open field with a river flowing through it. All along the river is a trail where Wisconsinites ride ATVs, snowmobiles, horses, and anything else you can manage to saddle.

Keri, Livi's mom, said once when she was little, she was casting and reeling, catching zero fish. Then a shirtless old man rode past on a saddled donkey. The old man wore a straw hat and spoke in old English, like Chaucer. Beyond that path, beyond those thick trees, it's like a new world, a Narnia.

My car's temperature gauge displays *10 degrees*, so I shove my hands in my coat pockets where a baggie holds emergency pills in case. I open Livi's car door for her 'cause Keri loves that chivalrous shit. We step out into a gust of icy wind that flips Livi's curled hair to the other side of her head.

"Hubba, hubba," I say. "Stick with that style, and I'll never leave you alone."

She's fixing her hair when we hear the rumble of a motorcycle. Livi's brother, Jordan, appears on the dirt driveway. His hands rest on the high handlebars. He looks like a little kid riding a Big Wheel. Revving the engine right next to us, he salutes as he dismounts.

"Sup, Sis? So this is what Tyler Linley turned into since back when, huh?" He sticks his hand out, his leather jacket creaking like in an SNL skit. I grab his hand, and he squeezes with all his forearm muscle, which I was prepared for, so it's like half a minute of one of those Grip Tester machines where it rates you from Wet Noodle to Strong Man in a Singlet. We both tie at Strong Man. We exchange small talk, Jordan using terse, Hemingway-esque statements to explain everything as he runs his hand over his smooth head.

"Should get a haircut, hippie," he says.

"I'd rather keep the shaggy 'do than look like a shiny bowling ball."

He ignores me. "Ranked up last month. PFC. Planned to up another soon."

I nod like I know what the hell he's talking about. Livi is watching me, curious to see if I say anything negative.

"Been training with some live M2HBs, M40s, you know? Hoping to aim for gunnery," he says.

I nod, say, "Oh, yeah, nice, man. WD40s. Impressive."

Per Livi's request, I don't say anything bad about the military. The one thing she asked of me: "Don't say anything about military stuff. Nothing. Please. Promise me." And I did promise. But I said "plomise"—to be fair.

"Then you'll fly to the Middle East and do some work?" I say.

"That's the plan. Fly over and blast some sand niggers."

Livi slaps him on the shoulder and says, "Don't say that."

Jordan laughs. "They've got what's coming to 'em. You threaten our freedom, we'll fuck you."

Livi glares at him. "Just shush with all that today. Please."

"Whatever, Sis. But Ty-guy here knows what I'm saying, right?" He nudges my shoulder.

I literally bite my tongue, teeth sinking in. I want to rant, but when I meet Livi's green eyes, I just shrug.

Another gust of wind bitch-slaps us, so I head inside where we greet Keri, the cousins, the nephews, the uncles, and the pets. One nephew runs up to me and punches me in the nads. He yells, "Bam!" I bend over and catch my breath and apparently no one sees this because Livi and Jordan continue greeting everyone as I hope my kibbles and bits aren't knocked up into my stomach.

Keri hugs Livi and fixes some messy hair strands stuck to Livi's face from the wind. Keri's hair is shorter than before, now a bob cut. The bangs swoop over her face, covering part of her eye until she brushes it away. She's wearing an orange dress with gray spandex underneath and fluffy slippers.

"Ty-dye, come with me for the grand tour," Keri says, spinning like a ballerina. She floats through the house, stopping to explain the significance of the few items in it. The living room is compact and intimate, perfect for a minimalist style of life, as Livi's grandparents lived. A neutral rug is placed in the middle of a couch, a loveseat, two recliners, and a cushioned rocking chair where I plan to relax. A tiny tube TV hides in the corner beneath a plant's hanging leaves, which strikes me as nearly Amish or of the settlers' day of fireside stories. The Christmas tree is covered in ornaments and fake snow. The fireplace crackles, and the house smells like firewood and smoked jerky. In Keri's bedroom, there is a table in the corner packed with every imaginable lotion, cream, makeup, product, toothpaste I could imagine. Under the table are stacks of unopened boxes of products.

"Hot damn," I say, "You could turn me into a pretty woman with all this, Mrs. McDermott."

She glares at me.

"Keri. I mean Keri." I smile and wink, imagining myself handsome and charming. "You've got a beauty salon in here. Really, wowzas."

"A woman's got to stay at the top of her game," she says, flipping her hair out of her face.

Cousins and nephews, Keri, Livi, Jordan and I sit in a circle around the rug, catching up on the details of life. Keri offers me a plate of snacks, but I decline, feeling out of place like an oozing pimple on a face.

"Don't mind me, Keri. Pretend I'm not here."

"You're our guest, so *shh*." She places her finger over my mouth. "Seriously, I'll be just a fly on the wall."

Livi shakes her head and says, "You're not watching. You're here with us. You're family." She brings me a glass plate with slices of cheese, crackers, chunks of sausage and a beer. My stomach warms up and expands like it's about to burst. As I chew, I'm aware of how loud I'm swallowing, and it dawns on me that everyone near me can hear me swallowing, even though they're laughing and talking, and I'm disgusting, and all I can think of is my swallowing when the entire room's energy and eyes turns like a laser to me. I imagine my face is just a question mark that makes that guttural sound from the intro of *Home Improvement.*

"Well, Mr. Tyler, what do you think?" an uncle says, his mouth hidden in a bushy red beard. The boy who rung my southern bell—the man's son—runs over and sits cross-legged by my feet.

Under the pressure of the room's gaze, my body temperature heats inside my Livi-picked argyle sweater. My armpits start crying. I'm about to whistle like a boiling teapot, when Livi steps in, sensing my infant-like inability to function as a normal human being.

"Tyler's a bit out of it—burnt out from the long week. Finals wrapped up and his tutoring sessions were getting intense with panicked grad students and twitchy undergrads worried about grades."

Red Beard nods. "I remember the good ol' college days." He rubs his belly and looks to Jordan. "By college, I mean boot camp." He belly-laughs and Jordan smirks. "College has never been a thing for us Higgins. Generations of Marines who love this country. Livi's the first to bother with *college.*"

"And I love it," she says. "Much better than getting screamed at all day and being reprogrammed into Yes-Woman."

Jordan says, "Hey, you've got to sacrifice to serve and protect. And I'm no Yes-Man."

I bite my tongue. My mouth tastes of metallic blood.

"I just prefer to think for myself, form my own opinions," Livi says.

"So do I," Jordan says. "I just know what's important: the country. And our orders are always to help you civilians."

Dad barges into my mind, and I bite harder on my tongue and the metallic taste gets stronger. He's off fixing an axle on some city truck used for transporting guns right now. Protecting America.

"Plus," Red Beard says. "What do you need to know philosophy for? Doesn't serve any good in real life. Just book stuff, nothing real. You're not learning anything, really. Might as well go play video games and live in a made-up world."

Livi exhales. "I'm studying environmental studies, not philosophy."

Red Beard and Jordan laugh. Keri tries to say something to mend the argument, but Jordan speaks louder.

"Hippie shit. Tree-huggers and people like that just get in the way. I love you, Sis, but, c'mon, what good is conserving a few trees? We're here to dominate and manage nature and the world."

"That's not at all what it's like. You're being reductive and simplifying what—"

Red Beard interrupts, holding his hand up. He says, "You can't explain what you guys *do*, because you don't *do* anything. You're like teachers. You just read and talk about ideas and chat about doing things. Who cares about protecting wild Antarctic do-do birds and retard wobblin' penguins?"

The red-haired boy by my feet stands up and waddles around the room with his arms pinned to his sides, repeating, "Penguin, ka-kaw, ka-kaw" to laughter from the whole room.

"Don't say retard," Keri says. "And I think there is value in both sides here. The military protects the civilians so we can engage in more recreational things, like books and games, and I think—"

"Are you joking?" Livi says. "You've got to be joking. You're reducing what *everyone* does who *isn't* toting a gun in the name of the government."

"Nah, government ain't got nothing to do with military," Red Beard says as he drinks from his American-flag Budweiser. "Two different entities. Government just plays high school politics, but we—" he points to Jordan and two uncles sitting in the kitchen playing cards—"We get it done. We take care of business."

Livi looks at me for help, but I shake my head lightly. In that look she knows I'm saying, "It's best I shut up."

Jordan looks at me. "Ty-guy, you don't have anything to say?"

"I'm staying out of this one."

Red Beard and Jordan laugh.

Red Beard says, "Liv, i'n't your old boy-toy a military man? Not Marines, Air Force or something. Thought he was gonna be a pilot, something like that. Nice guy."

Livi gets a little red beneath her tan skin. My jaw clenches and I look around the room, diverting my attention and blocking out whatever Livi's response is.

"Used to give Lucky Louie so much shit for joining Air Force instead of the Marines." Red Beard laughs. "Some can't cut it."

Deer mounts clutter one brown-carpeted wall. On another is a collage of pictures, and I'm scanning through, redirecting my focus. Hanging there is Keri with her deceased husband, a man who had a strong jaw, black gelled hair with roots graying. He had a thin-lipped smile in which he showed no teeth, like a Clint Eastwood grin. "Handsome" is accurate. A clutter of military outfits hang near the photos, and smack in the middle of the wall I see Keri, Olivia, and Lou, all three in swimsuits with a white beach and blue sea behind them. His arms are wrapped around both women, and their heads are resting on his shoulders. The same Facebook photo Trey showed me on his 55-inch TV. Lou, "the Air Force pilot." The ex. Lucky Louie the Hero from the past who echoes through every moment Livi and I are together. The memory doesn't fade. It's a sinking feeling trying to escape something when it's attached to you. Like trying to escape a shadow.

I'm forcing a pleasant appearance, but I want to rip an antler off a dead deer and stab Red Beard and burn the photo and memory of Lou the Ex, the Air Force pilot who's a great man for serving his country and being so selfless. And being in the past, relegated to a polished memory, he's even gotten more wonderful. Flaws fade in memory when the relationship ends on a harmonious note. Everybody loves the 1920s and 1950s because no one focuses on the negatives. We love the roaring upward momentum, but forget all the flaws. Instead, we just flip through the flashback montage moments. Snapshot. Snapshot. Snapshot. Beautiful and perfect.

A small shelf with a few war movies stacked reminds me: perform. It's all a performance. Each of us is an actor with his own role to fulfill, like Billy Shakespeare said. I glance at Keri who's saying something to the room, probably something soothing so everyone stops discussing uncomfortable things. Would she fit in a movie? What role would she play? Yeah, I can see her being a mother to McAdams or another dime piece. Acting—just play the role until I make the role.

"Excuse me," I say, interrupting what Keri was saying.

She smiles and says, "Of course."

I walk to the bathroom and lock the door. I take a pill from the baggie, turn the faucet on, and suck water as I swallow the pill. Staring at myself in the mirror, I prepare.

"Funny Tyler. Carefree Tyler. Entertaining Tyler. Playful Tyler. Ryan Gosling Tyler. WWRGD."

I flush the toilet without using it and join the circle again. A new sweating beer sits on the table next to my cushioned rocking chair. Livi looks over and smiles. Her smile says: *Drink that beer so you don't rip an antler off a mounted deer and stab my military family to death.* And I'm impressed she knew that's what I was thinking, and that a beer would help deter me from turning this into a Christmas Day massacre featured on *Podunk Times'* front page.

The red-haired boy is now untying my blue Vans and trying to tie them together. Jordan and Red Beard still argue with Livi, but I've removed myself from that world. Now I just see this little red-haired midget who socked my boys.

"Don't you know how to tie shoes?" I ask, as the adult conversation grows louder.

"Nope. I have Velcro." He points to his Spiderman Velcro shoes.

"Spiderman sucks. You know that, right?"

"Nuh-uh. He's the best."

"The Dark Knight is the best."

"Not uh."

"Because Batman trained and earned his success. Spiderman's a freak, just like you." I smile and wink.

His face contorts into a frown, a pre-wailing, cry-frown, and I poke him in the side, hoping he's ticklish.

He is.

"Tee-he-he, sop dat," he says, kicking his feet. For a second, I'm worried about all the connotations and implications of tickling a kid I met, like, an hour ago, but I take the risk of being labeled a child molester instead of blowing my top taking part in the military-cock-stroking conversation.

"Sop what? I'm not doing anything." I poke him in the belly. He giggles like the Pillsbury Doughboy. In the armpit, in the back, I keep poking him until he's giggling and kicking, and Red Beard looks over at us.

"Well, Livi, least it looks like your new boy-toy is good with kids."

"Stop saying boy-toy."

I stop tickling the kid, and he looks at me.

"Why'd you sop?"

I shrug, and he stands up to me.

"I'm Tywer," the boy says.

"But I'm Tyler," I say to him.

"So we're both Tywers." He climbs onto my lap, so I adjust him away from my sore junk onto my leg. He sits there playing with a plastic Spiderman action figure that looks nearly identical to one Trey has on a shelf at home.

2.

Twenty minutes later, I'm outside rolling a snowball with Little Tyler. My snow boots are Livi's deceased father's and the gloves are his, too; they're tight on my wrists. The family joins us outside, standing in coats, with gloved hands holding beers. The snow near the fire is melted. Two young nephews join little Tyler and me by mashing mittens full of snow onto our growing snowball. The adults chat about overtime, military trainings, and other dull things, until Red Beard introduces himself as Steve, offering a gloved handshake. He asks about my life, and we fill the air with dating-site information: hobbies, jobs, careers, sports, music tastes, and preferred deodorants.

Steve: Old Spice.

Me: None; Livi says the aluminum zirconium is bad for humans. Promotes Alzheimer's.

Steve: You two are hippies.

I say, "Yeah, in the last few years I've been doing odd work, mostly boring, like tutoring, fixing TVs, giving guitar lessons—I'm all over the place. A while back I was a paperboy." My head raised tall, I feign pride.

"Yeah? How was that?" Steve asks.

"I was awesome at it. Started as a paperboy, ended as a paperman."

When I finish a beer, little Tyler runs inside and fetches me another Spotted Cow, slid in a sock-koozie. I teach him to crack it open with the bottle opener, and he's impressed with himself.

The snowball grows as tall as a doorframe. I picture rolling it down a tall mountain with Jordan in its path when Little Tyler grabs a handful of good packing snow and mashes it in my face, yelling, "Wash your face. Wash your face."

Picking him up with both arms, I cradle him and rock him back and forth. "Rock-a-bye baby in the—" I sing.

"I'm not a baby!" he says.

"Then why are you being cradled like one?" I say. The other two nephews are staring at me. One is blond with sporadic teeth; the other is the real-life version of Eric Cartman.

"'Cause you awe bigger than me."

"Rock-a-bye bay-bee in the—"

"I'm not a baby!" he's screaming in my face. "I'm a big boy."

The other two nephews grab handfuls of snow and attack my legs, so I set little Tyler on my shoulders and fight off the two with my hands. I stiff-arm both their faces—Marshawn Lynch-style. Little Tyler is giggling on my shoulders, wrapping his arms around my head so I can't see. His fingers cling and claw at my eyeballs. Nephew Cartman packs a tight snowball, and it splatters on my face. I laugh through the snow. The blond nephew clings to my leg like a koala to a eucalyptus tree. We're laughing, and Steve is laughing and urging his son to poke my eyes out, which I don't appreciate. Keri is taking flash photos.

Then my back feels wet. Little Tyler stops laughing.

"I want to get down now," he says, now quiet and shy. "Uncle Tywer, I want to get down now, please."

I lift him off my shoulders and, holding him in the air above my head, I see yellow dripping off his boots and dark wetness all around his bum and front. He runs to Steve and hugs his leg.

"I need help in the bathroom, Daddy," he says, and the pee soaks through the coat and onto my back. The air around my face smells like Toki the Cat's litter box mixed with a farm. Steve picks little Ty up and says, "You're gonna want to shower up, Ty. This boom-boom's a wet one." He's gut-laughing *and* trying to make his son feel better.

Inside, Livi and Keri grab me a towel. Livi pulls me aside. She whispers, "You are so fucking cute with those kids. I love seeing you like this." She kisses me hard, and almost hugs me until she breathes in the pee-poo witch concoction wafting from my clothes.

She pushes me away. "Phew. You smell like Trey's bedroom," she says.

Ah, yes. The rare and sought-after girlfriend burn.

The shower is scorching my shoulders, but I barely notice because getting pooped on never felt so right. I get out and change into Livi's dad's old clothes: a tight blue sweater with thumb holes in the sleeves; jeans worn at the knees with bottoms that widen to fit over work boots. I free-ball it because pee dripped down my back onto my grey briefs. Free-balling in my girlfriend's deceased dad's jeans might be the weirdest thing I've done in a long while.

3.

Later, Keri asks the two non-pants-pooping nephews to grab firewood from the garage. They look at each other and say, in offbeat unison: "We want Uncle Tyler to help."

I'm officially Uncle Tyler now.

Grabbing the wood, we play swords, and they both ask for Tyler-back rides, which I give until I'm dripping sweat despite the blasts of ice air and snow they mash down my shirt.

Inside, they hand me a book to read. Story time. It's titled "Pigs," and on the cover is a smiling cartoon pig.

"Oh, that's my favorite," I tell them.

"Mine, too!" the blond nephew says.

"Have you read the sequel, 'Bacon'?" I ask.

"I love bacon," Nephew Cartman says.

I'm not fat, guy. Just big-boned.

~ ~ ~

At dinner, we sit at a massive wooden table. After Uncle Steve says his version of grace, Keri announces a game we'll play at the table, which is less a game and more a question.

"Livi, my princess, where do you see yourself in five years?"

Steve (Red Beard) speaks first, "Married to a girthy tree, I'll betchya." He looks to Jordan and they high-five with their eye contact.

"Shh, Steven Michael Higgins. Learn to shut your mouth sometimes," Keri says.

Olivia looks at me for a second, and then sips from her wine glass. I gulp from my Spotted Cow and look to Nephew Cartman and tap my bottle. Nodding, he shoots off and returns with a fresh beer. Out of breath, he sets it on the table and nods, as if confirming his mission is complete. I salute him and he salutes back.

Livi says, "I guess I'm torn. It depends on the day, but five years from now? I'd like to be married," she smiles, bashful, her cheeks a tinge of red. "A baby boy and maybe thinking about a second one."

My genes mixed with hers. If it happened, I hope all my genes would be recessive. To pass on my basket of psychological laundry would be cruel and unusual punishment.

"But, I've also been thinking," Livi says. "I want to travel. Like Dad. So I see myself somewhere new, far away where people live differently than what I'm used to. Hopefully, I'll be helping people."

Keri is smiling and nodding, and it reminds me to show active listening. Red Beard—er, Steve—perks up.

"Okinawa, Livi. Now there's a place to see. Back in '83 we were down there and we—" Steve rambles about Marine things like going to a whore house—he quickly adds while looking at his frumpy wife, "I just went 'cause the guys went." He follows with gun stories and "how crazy-nuts them people are."

Keri turns the question to me, and the eyes hovering above the tables all aim at me like red sniper lasers, but I've got to be half a case in, plus my self-medication. I'm dulled enough. I'm barely even here; I'm absent, just watching—my thoughts are being acted out by someone else.

"Five years? Depending how wild I get, probably dead," I say, deadpan. No one laughs except Steve, whose gut explodes with *hwah-hwahs*.

He slaps his knee and mumbles, "Dead. Hah! Classic."

I say, "Otherwise, grad school, teaching, telling jokes to people. I don't know. Something like that."

"Jokes?" Jordan says. "You don't seem funny. Tell me a joke right now."

"Uh—"

Little Tyler jumps in.

"Knock, knock."

"Who's there?" Jordan says.

"Your face," Little Tyler says.

"Your face who?"

Little Tyler smiles, and starts to laugh. "Your face is ugly as a butt!"

"I'm stealing that one."

We laugh. Keri asks, "What about travel?"

"Haven't really traveled much. Only time I travel is in basketball."

Steve slaps his knee and points at Jordan. "Now there's a joke!"

"What about family?" Keri says.

"Yeah. Out of everything in the world, that's the one thing I'd want. But I can't see it. I can't imagine having what you guys have." Awkward silence.

I add: "You guys are great, is what I'm saying. And I'm grateful to even be here." As I say this, Little Tyler sets his Spiderman action figure on the table next to my plate and sits back at the kids' round table.

"We're glad you're here," Keri says.

Steve nods, says, "That kid never lets anyone touch that stupid toy."

Livi says, "Action figure, not a toy."

4.

They all chat, but I pull away like a camera backing from the scene. From a distance, I can appreciate this. I drift back into my seat, and my head is swilling with poisons that allow me to just watch. I'm almost disappearing, or so it feels. I see the shadowy man lingering outside in the dark. I know what he wants: drink up; pop another pill. You're *this* close to escaping and just fully disappearing.

But I don't. I just watch.

It's so foreign to engage this family for the entire day. They interact with each other, and no one runs off to their bedroom to escape and watch a movie or TV show. This family, with their tiny, nearly absent TV, they have almost no escapist books. No XB1 or Wii or PS4. They live in reality, together, as a family. It's foreign to me, like watching aliens copulate with arms and forceps and weird dangly phalanges that drip with goo. The family interacts as if it's normal for them, like they don't have to try. They, a family. Me, beers flowing through me, benzo pills, all just so I can feel and act normal. I'm the alien. I'm not truly here. They're the normal, well-adjusted people. Livi never had cable growing up. You don't need it if you have this.

After goodbyes, I hand Little Tyler his Spiderman action figure. Shaking his head, he pushes it back into my chest.

"I want to you have him. You'll start to like Spiderman the more you play with him. I promise." I picture the unopened action figures lining the walls of the duplex. Untouched. Pristine. Unloved. This one? So unlike what lines the duplex, what lines my life.

Jordan gives me a gruff goodbye with a forearm-flexing handshake. Steve apologizes while laughing for me getting poo-peed upon. In the car, Livi rests her head on my shoulder as I drive home. The farther we get from Keri's, the more it seems this little vacation is over. The film is over. This glimpse into what life could be like. Each mile closer to home, I feel and remember who I am, and the feeling of disappointment is leaking into me. Eventually, it will flood. But Little Tywer pooping on my shoulders seems to mark a moment of admission and acceptance into a periodic holiday vacation where I visit the family as an honorary guest. A guest who kids can play with and poop upon. I set Spiderman on the dashboard against the cool window, and I am calm driving through the dancing snow flurries.

We get home to Livi's place. Before unpacking, she pulls me into her bedroom and pushes me against the wall, knocking a picture frame of her family to the ground.

"You'd make such a hot dad," she says, which is the weirdest dirty talk I've ever heard.

"And you'd make such a sexy mom, with your mom dance and mom butt and mini-van," I say.

"I'd be the sexiest mom ever, and I'd never," she yanks my belt out through the loops. "Ever," she pushes me onto the bed. "Dance like a mom or have a mom-butt." On top of me she's grinding into my groin and hits the spot that's sore thanks to Little Tyler, but it's a good pain, like after exercising. I pull her as close as possible and end a perfect day.

5.

The next morning, I walk home because I wake up fresh and bright; the sun's warm, the air brisk. As Livi leaves for work, I'm excited to go home where I'll whistle when I walk in the door, and Toki the Cat will run to me, rub his face all over, meowing because I'm back. We'll get to chill in the dark room, his furry gray body curled on my chest. We'll watch a new episode of *Boardwalk Empire*. I'll check the mail for my new box set of *Arrested*

Development; maybe I'll see what Trey's up to for the day. I'm in one of those moods that I'd like to calm down and disperse over time so it lasts longer rather than blowing it all at once for an hour of extreme happiness and optimism—it's kind of like the emotional equivalent of premature ejaculation, followed by a deep low. Nearly manic-depressive. I want to skip, so I look around and see an old woman in a robe grabbing her morning paper. Who gives a shit. I skip down the sidewalk. I skip in the light flurries on the snow-glazed sidewalk like a schoolgirl in pigtails just after a first kiss by the jungle gym. I skip and I'm high, like a runner's high; yet, I'm sober. No pills or alcohol in this sun-drenched morning air. I'm mid-skip when I see our duplex and I stop. I stand. My pigtails come undone and my skirt is blasted with a gust of frozen air. My mind blinks until it goes blank. There in front of me, the flames dance into the sky. The smoke billows and tumbles out shattered windows as my entire life burns.

PART 2

Chapter Eleven

Wave Goodbye

Trey and I are back at Livi's apartment where I've let us in using the key she gave me. Head in my hands, I'm sitting on the dusty hardwood floor.

"Can't believe it," Trey says, poking at his glowing cell phone. He takes off his backpack and unzips it. He flips through his backpack, pulling out a few comics. "Guess I'm glad I wasn't in there, right? Plus, I didn't lose my best comics, like Spiderman's first appearance in *Amazing Fantasy*."

I haven't spoke to him or even looked at him since he strolled up to the burning house, returning from a run to the gas station with a bag of Cheetos and a can of Monster in a smiley-face plastic bag.

"You okay, man? You haven't said anything," he says. "It's freaking me out."

Rubbing my eyes like I'm tired with my thumb and a finger, my contacts blur. The pictures of Liv and her mom around the room look cloudy and distant. Nothing is real right now—just a fiction. My worldly possessions' burning is surreal. Unreality. My stack of terabyte hard drives filled with meticulously organized music, digital movies, television shows, and memories. The hidden porn deep in folders within folders—all gone. Everything I've collected and organized. The reality I've forged. Poof. The Packers 1996 Super Bowl DVD Dad gave me, his prized possession for years: the DVD he watched when he was depressed about how long the boring summer baseball season felt. Now it's just a shriveled clump of black plastic among black ashes and burnt skeletons of furniture.

I picture Toki the Cat, not found by firefighters or neighbors. Probably caught in flames during a nap in the dark room while he waited for me. Maybe kneading my recliner, sniffing the spot where I'd lie. His loud meows directed to me. Pawing at everything, claws clinging to curtains, his tail bushy and—

"How are you not pissed off?" I say.

"I am, but, seriously, what's getting pissed about it going to do? It's over and there's nothing I can do to change it."

"But doesn't it just—just make you fucking nuts? Thousands of dollars, countless hours poured into collecting, organizing, just gone, like *that*."

"I know, man. I'm sorry. Thank God for insurance, right?" he says.

"Insurance?"

"Yeah, got to have it on a collection like that."

"I don't have fucking insurance."

He fiddles with his backpack straps. I stand up and look him. His eyes are red and he smells like weed.

"You're telling me you insured all that shit, all your action figures, the posters, the weird collectible sex toys?"

"Yes. I did," he says, looking away.

"And I'm just shit out of luck, huh?"

He doesn't answer. He just gazes out the window.

"Trey." I grab his ponytail and force him to make eye contact with me inches from his face. "Were you high when you left for the grocery store?"

"Nah, man. Nah." His nose scrunches up toward his eyes. "Well, I guess a little."

"And did you have your candles burning when you left?" I say.

"Nah. No way. Pretty sure I put 'em out after you left, 'cause, you know, I only burn them for you because I know you aren't a fan. You know. Of the weed."

Deep breath. I say, "Are you sure?"

He pauses. "Not really. I don't remember, to be honest."

"You don't remember?"

"No."

"So you burnt the house down and killed my cat."

"I said I don't remember."

"You fucking idiot," I say, slapping the back of his head. "You piece of shit stoner." I backhand the back of his head.

Trey stands up, rubbing the back of his head.

"Ow. Dude, settle down."

"God damn it," I say. "You better run for your life."

"Run?"

I slap the back of his head again and push him. He loses his footing, but holds himself up with a stiff arm. Once he gets his footing set, he darts from the living room, knocking over a tree-shaped lamp, bumbling over the couch toward the door where he whips it open. In socks and short-sleeve tee, I run after him in the snow. My feet sink into the snow, deep above my ankles.

"You fucking idiot-stoner-shithead bitch-titted chode-chomper," I yell as I chase Trey.

"Settle down, settle down, man," he's saying, between breaths, his asthma likely wrapping its hands around his throat, choking him.

"I never got to say goodbye to my—" I tackle him into a pile of dirty snow near the road. His head is stuck in my headlock, and it's about to pop off like a champagne bottle cork.

"Stop man, stop man, I can't breathe," Trey says, his face red. His bulging forehead vein about to burst, I loosen my headlock on him.

I say, "I never said goodbye to my shit, man. Like, like my *Mad Men* collection, or *Metal Gear* action figures. Or my, my—" I hear myself and feel pathetic. "I'll never see my . . . ." The air in my voice is gone. "I'll never see my . . . Solid Snake action figure again," I say, my voice weakening to a whisper. "I'll never see your terabytes of rare midget amputee interracial animal porn. I'll never–"

I let go of Trey and slump into the snow as pathetically as possible to make sure he feels sorry for me. Me, playing the role. Finally, the emptiness is clear.

"It's just stuff, you know?" Trey says. "It can be replaced."

"Not the cat."

"No, not the cat," the wise Wond'ring Turtle says.

Chapter Twelve

Up in Smoke

1.

Spring birds chirp as Trey and I are sitting in the new apartment living room. Trey's been using the insurance money to gather up replacements of his old stuff, such as his limited-edition double-edge Darth Maul saber dildo. My room sits empty but for a bed set on the carpet. On top of it is a comforter bunched in a ball. I haven't bothered to put the sheets on yet, so the discount pillow-top is visible. The nightstand holds whatever book I'm reading and a lamp like from the beginning of Pixar movies. Nothing else. I don't have the cash to do much, so I'm keeping things bare. When Livi stays over, which is less frequent as of late, her duffle bag of essentials—toiletries, thongs, socks—take over the room. It looks like she's moved in and I'm now the guest. A guest in my own life. Lately, I've been crashing at Livi's a lot, learning how to cook, like grilled zucchini. Shit's delicious.

A few months back, I'd just bought the mattress, so I was driving with it on the roof. I held one side with my hand out the window. Trey, with his orange Cheetos-fingers, held the other side. I was laughing and giggling, drunk as a skunk, half hoping the mattress flung into the air and landed like big slice of bread on the Mustang riding my ass.

"What's the point of collecting shit?" I said to Trey. "Things wear and break. They burn. They just fucking disappear into smoke. Nice moments—they just disappear into nothing. Memory tries to keep them, but it all just fades. Things fade. People change. Nothing's constant. Why keep trying to build something up? It seems like being comfortable and seeking pleasure and immediate gratification is the best thing to pursue. The *only* things to pursue." I steered with my knees as I took a drink. "I busted my ass for years. Stressed out. Yet it made no difference. Of it gone. Up in smoke. People I will work with for ten years will leave one day for a new job, and then I'll never see them again. As if they died. Or never existed except in some fictional memory. No different than a memory of a movie. No different than Michael Scott or Walter White. What's the point? Co-workers and I, we only knew each other because we were both trying to make money to stay alive longer. Artificial relationships. Meaningless as watching some actor pretend to be a warrior or have Down syndrome. It all makes no sense. It's all a waste of time. It's all—"

"Man, take a chill pill," Trey said. "You're just worked up over the fire. Loss hurts, man. I know."

I wish I had a chill pill.

"Shouldn't have burnt your bridges with that Ken fella," Trey says.

I stare at him.

"Sorry. Poor word choice."

2.

I haven't scooped shit and piss out of a litter box for so long that I get the urge to attract a feral outdoor cat. The rear entrance of our first-floor apartment gives us access to a small patio with a cruddy grill caked with black gunk. It's here I set a spaghetti-stained Tupperware of water and a small plastic Brewer's helmet holding cat food. First night, the food disappears, as it does the next few nights. But I never see a cat munch at it. Dreams of what might be taking the food pop into my sleep bubbles: A raccoon; Sly Cooper; a homeless man who scratches on the back screen door, mumbling, "Feed me." *Bad Carl,* I'd tell the homeless man, and I'd spray him with the hose. He'd mope away with a wet, dripping beard. Dreams are all that's interesting for a handful of months.

I stay away from too much TV, although I do order a new copy of the Packers DVD, but on Blu-ray, upgraded. For a split second, it seems like it's a good thing to come of this. It is my chance to start rebuilding my empire, my perfect world of humor and art and pretty music (and hidden porn).

But without my shows or my movies, days are directionless and uninspired—like I'm missing a way to center myself on something solid, fixed, and permanent. Favorite characters who have inspired portions of my personality fade from memory. With the memory, that part of my personality fades. I'm a collage of scenes and characters. Bits of me dissipate like cigarette smoke. I'm not sure who to be or how to act. I become more dull and generic. There is no one who'll tell me who to be—how to act—outside of the realm of religion. I can see myself playing any role: maybe I become a lumberjack with a scraggly beard grown over my mouth, long plaid sleeves hiding hairy arms, terse in expression but carrying a big stick. Maybe I live in an electricity-free cabin and roast rotating dead squirrels over a fire.

I'm confident of this: given a few days with a certain personality type, I can fulfill any role. Say, I could take on the role of funny guy at the office who takes life with a laugh, a joke always on-deck when a melancholy moment hits the water cooler discussion. I can be whoever I can mirror. I am Ryan Gosling. I am George Clooney. I am no one.

The lens that filters my world isn't set. It never has been. This separation from my media world leaves me abandoned and vulnerable like a motherless infant. Me, without my motherly glass teat. Me, vulnerable to being swept along in the daily routine until calendar pages fall like leaves to the carpet. Then, one day, I'll realize how much time has passed. *What happened to those months?* I know it'll eventually be *What happened to those years?*

When I had my heavenly media, whatever film or show I consumed switched the lens through which I saw the world, like at the eye doctor. *One or two? Two or three?* A comedy made me see the world with levity and a smile. A drama directed my energy to the poignant moments in a day; a drama flipped my disposition to more pensive and thoughtful. When I switched media, the lens changed. *Which is better, three or four?* And to me, they all looked clear and correct. I couldn't decide.

So I'm here now, naked, clueless.

Livi has been showing me environmental documentaries, which means I'm inclined to filter the world in that way. *Which is better, four or five?* She takes notes on a yellow pad as we watch a documentary on wolves in which two "hunters" ride their snowmobiles. They follow a wolf until the wolf tires out. The hunters shoot to wound it, and torture it because "wolves kill our way of life"; that "way of life" being the wholesale slaughter of cows for dollar burger meat. Out loud to Livi, I suggest bringing back medieval death penalties. I get the urge to go out and do something, and I'm standing in the living room with my fists ready to fight before I realize it. A month ago, I didn't give a shit about wolves. Fuck wolves. Wasn't *Balto* about wolves? And didn't Kevin Costner dance with wolves? I guess I liked *Balto*. But before this hour snapshot of a documentary, I didn't know a thing. But show me an hour's worth of a documentary, and I'm ready to go out and kill some wolf-hunters. I'm a goddamn environmentalist. At least until the novelty wears off.

Like a chameleon, my morals fluctuate with my surroundings, and in the absence of my dark room of escape, I'm ready to be washed along with whatever momentary feeling that flows through me. Nurture is what makes me; I have no defined nature.

In an effort to express something—to fake it 'til I make it—I wrote this little note to Livi on college-ruled loose-leaf paper in my all-caps, slanted handwriting. I debated for days if I should give it to her. Here's what my sappy letter reads:

In Symposium, *Plato speaks about how once all humans were whole hermaphrodite beings with four hands, four legs, two faces, four ears, and both sets of naughty bits. These beings tried to overthrow the gods. Zeus (like the Mt. Olympus ride) got pissed and split them into man and woman, and created in male and female an innate desire for one another—the desire to feel whole again.*

That feeling of whole "again" . . . it's a wonderful feeling.

I believe what I wrote, I think.

3.

I can't stop thinking about it. If Trey burnt the house down by mistake—the result of being a worthless spoiled stoner—then I'm living with the person I need get even with. His dad, a pastor, would disown him if he knew the porn collection Trey had backed up on a cloud server. Maybe Pastor Bradley would accidentally stumble upon it. Maybe Trey's weed stash in his car would be visible to a cop when pulled over after a taillight is seen smashed in.

If Kennedy burnt the place, then I'll need to get closer to him, somehow. But I can't see it; he isn't a bad guy. His cousin, Ka, though, is a basket case. The one piece of evidence pointing toward Kennedy was the text he sent:

Kennedy: Saw the flames a-burrrnin yer place to ashhes. Comes around goes around. Justice, bud.

When I can't sleep at night, when my circus comes to town—the monkey juggling unanswerable questions and posing unlikely scenarios—scenes pop into my head of their own volition. Scene after scene of revenge on Trey and Kennedy play out, as if I'm not sure who deserves it, so both deserve it. Revenge is needed, because somehow the balance needs to be tipped back in my favor. The world shouldn't work like this; if a bad thing happens, it should be corrected in some way. If the random events don't happen, I should make them happen. There should be a balance in the world, and most times it doesn't balance out on its own. Not like in the movies. So I try to help.

Sometimes, I pace the living room like a madman, but Livi settles me down. Her attitude is contagious. When with her, I'm optimistic. I'm functioning. I tip waitresses. I smile when people say hi. But alone, I'm just a curmudgeon.

I'm bitching to Livi about government taxes and misappropriation of funds when she suggests we go camping.

"Why?" I ask as I sit on a stool, biting my fingernails.

"It's fun to get out into nature," she says as she stirs eggs at the kitchen counter. "Live like people used to."

"Camping is stupid."

"You're stupid," she says, pouring the eggs into a wok. "I'm sorry. No you're not. But how is camping stupid? *Everyone* loves camping."

"It's stupid and illogical, but I'm just going to hold back my opinions so I don't rant."

"No, tell me." She stops cooking and looks at me, her head tipped forward in preparation for my cynical rant.

"I'm not getting into it."

"Fine. But, sure, everything is going to be illogical and stupid if you sit and think about it for five hours." She turns back to the stove, dropping green peppers and spinach into the wok.

"Don't need to talk about it for five hours to know camping is stupid."

"Why can't you just enjoy it? It's time we get to spend together. I don't see why you have to impose your pseudo-intellectual ideas on everyone. Go and relax. Have fun. And I want to invite Trey."

I laugh. "He won't leave his dungeon."

"I want to get to know him better. He's your best friend, so, he should come with us." The thought of bringing Trey with brings a gut reaction of repulsion.

"He'll hate it. He's what we call 'indoorsy.'"

"We'll break him out of his shell."

Like a turtle.

"He's going to agree with me. Camping's stupid and a waste of time."

"Oh, my God, just back off the criticism. Spending time with important people in your life isn't a waste of time."

She's right. "Well, if we're going to camp, I'm going to grow my facial hair out. Not just that—all my hair, even downstairs. That'll make me manlier just like camping will. Out in the rugged outdoors, we—"

She waves the wooden spatula in the air. "Here comes another long-winded rant with no point."

"Oh, come on. My *opinions* always have a good point, like the one about how musicals inherently make no damn sense. *I'm not gonna pay the rent! La-la-da-da-dee-daah.*"

She ducks out of the conversation and walks into her bedroom. I stare at her caboose and follow her, planning to put the moves on her despite my asshole behavior. My disconnection between sex and conversation is apparent to me, but I ignore it like everything else. I kiss her in the bedroom and offer empty apologizes. I admit I'm an idiot and I'm too cynical.

She walks back to finish cooking, and I change the subject to insignificant chatter. She's laughing and smiling, and I feel I won the camping argument.

There's no way she'll make me go camping.

Chapter Thirteen

Camping

1.

Light rain falls all day from the sunny sky as Trey, his friend Caleb, Livi, and I glide down the zip line near our campsite. I scream, "Wee!" and Livi, zipping close behind, yells, "Ner!" and we successfully act like weird children all morning. As we put up the tent and spark logs into fire, I can't help but sing mock country songs about being wearing jeans and drinking cold beer on a Friday night. After sweating and collecting all the dirt of the entire camp on my body, I shower under a freezing drizzling faucet and yell to Livi: "It's so cold! My pee-pee went from an outie to innie!"

From outside the phone-booth-like shower, I hear Livi scream, "Noo!" and assume she is on her knees, shaking her fists at the sky. The entire camp, no doubt, can hear us, and I'm loose enough to not care. I feel like making out with the first person I see, male or female. I imagine doing exactly that, Livi seeing it, and a spontaneous three-way erupting like a long-dormant volcano.

Maybe it's the outdoors. Maybe it's the Old Fashioneds. Maybe it's happiness. I don't know what, but I'm light and loose and glad to be here.

Maybe camping's not so bad.

Livi is growing on Trey and Caleb. Throughout the day she develops a sarcastic, semi-flirtatious rapport with both friends.

Because Livi's relationship with the two is immediately better than mine, I pour a rum and coke, a vodka and pink Brisk, a seven and seven, and set them around me like a protective wall.

We're sitting around the smoking wood fire. Betsy the Buick's windows are down, and Iron & Wine plays on her speakers. At first when Livi burnt me the CD, I disregarded the band as a band that a tree-hugger would listen to while cooking a veggie burger. However, Sam Beam's voice has grown on me, and I find myself imitating him in the shower. In the throes of a panic attack, his voice rushes over me like calamine lotion.

"She was like a cat pawing at a vacuum cleaner hose," Caleb is saying. "Like, her head was tipped to the side, confused but intrigued. She stared at it, like, *Is this what it's supposed to look like?*"

We laugh and the circle turns to me. Livi smiles, hiding a sense of curiousness. "What about your first time, Ty?"

"Well, let's see." I debate sharing my lost virginity at age thirteen to a sixteen-year-old. I leave the age out. "We were on a lumpy brown couch in my parents' basement. I was on top, and we were naked, and I literally asked her, 'Is it in yet?' because I had no idea if it was. I was afraid to look down in case her hole snapped at me like a snapping turtle. Big-eyed like a kid caught with her hand in the cookie jar, she nodded her head. After that, I just remember a mess. It was like—like a red version of getting slimed on Nickelodeon. And I'm sorry I just said that out loud. I should have just kept that detail suppressed until I die. Sorry 'bout that."

I'm especially sorry since Livi missed the Nickelodeon reference. I don't look at her right away because we never talk about previous experiences. To me, it's something that lingers on the edge of my mind at all times: her previous experiences—my lover being dominated in some primal way, and my knowledge of it is a constant insult to any sense of pride or alpha-maleness. Hearing about her experiences, no matter how long ago, makes them real and immediate, like they're happening now. The movie plays in my mind—*A Clockwork Orange*—while someone stabs me with hot irons.

Caleb shakes his head, "You sure *she* didn't ask if it was in yet?"

They laugh and I look to Livi for some representation, a little comeback of defense—a *No, no, she'd never be able to ask that*—

but she just laughs away, her hand covering her mouth as she snorts just enough to catch our attention.

Leaving me out to dry, Livi? Really?

"Miss Piggy over there, what about you?" Caleb says. Livi stops laughing and gives him a stern but playful stare. I'm a bit jealous, which isn't a good feeling to have as your girlfriend is about to tell you and two of your friends about the first time she got nailed.

"Well, Lou and I were together a long time," she says, looking at me. "And I want to be honest with you fellas, but it wasn't anything all that funny. He loves camping, so we used to go all the time with my mom and dad, before Dad passed."

And now I have to love camping or else I'm an inferior boyfriend. I should join the military, too. I can't escape the echo of the first explorer. A hovering mosquito buzzes by my ear, and the metal of my belt rubs against my lower stomach, so I scratch it like a dog and swat at the mosquito.

She says, "Anyways, Mom and Dad went off on a kayak trip. Lou and I were left alone at the campground, and we snuck a little bit of wine and a few Mike's Hard Lemonades—really badass stuff. We tucked ourselves into the tent. And I'm sorry it wasn't funny or anything, but it was close to what I'd hoped for."

Trey, who's been quiet, as he's the self-proclaimed virgin here, says, "Well, what about that awkward finishing move, though?" Without a doubt, he's seeing this painful romantic scene as a porno, with the ultra-romantic money shot ruining a young gal's makeup and maybe giving her a lazy eye.

I'm breathing in and out, trying not to be bothered, and because we're in front of Trey and Caleb, I play it off. *Doesn't bother me. I'm above petty jealousy. I'm not an envious person.* I mean, who gives a shit if Olivia lost her virginity to an asshole Air Force prick who can't be a man without joining the military so he automatically gets the praise and *thank yous* and rounds of applause of all Americans. He can't just earn it on his own?

Nah. It doesn't bother me at all.

I don't know what she says next, because the circus enters my head. Images of tent-sex pop up like Internet ads, and the sound of grinding teeth is all my ears pick up. Like fish hooks, the images pull my gut down through my skinny ass, and I'm bummed out from the past again, as if sprayed by a magical Monsanto product: *Insta-*

Bummed! When you're having a great time and your girlfriend mentions how awesome her ex was and how he poked her sexy-hole first. Order now and you'll never forget that fact.

2.

Livi and I are lying in the tent on top of our sticky sleeping bag. The scene keeps running through my mind, a scene in a tent just like this one: the cicadas outside, distant laughing and clinking of bottles, the orange flickering of a fire illuminating the wall of the tent to a Gumby-green glow.

I do my best to think of the funny moments around the campfire:

Livi insulting Trey's hobbit feet.

"You don't know even L-O-T-R, Olivia Something McDermott," Trey had said.

"Bullshit I do," she said, lying.

"Name one thing," Trey said. "No. Actually, you know what. Look at your feet. You got long monkey toes."

"Better than hobbit feet," she said.

"Grab me another poker stick," Trey said. "With your monkey feet, though."

"Trey," Livi said, "can you grab a marshmallow I dropped in the fire? You can probably just walk right in the fire with those callused hobbit feet and those sausage toes."

"I *could* because I'm manly. Not 'cause of my hobbit feet. But I won't because the fire would singe my foot hair. So I'll pass right now, you monkey-footed, tree-humpin' hippie."

They both smiled, flipped each other off, joking that a foot wrestling competition was in order, at which point Caleb pointed out how disgusting this all was.

"I think it's kind of hot," Livi joked.

Trey said, "I concur. And fuck off, Caleb. Also, camping sucks. I have one billion 'squito bites on places I didn't even know I had."

Breaking my memory, a mosquito buzzes around my head as Livi is talking to me.

"I'd wish you'd open more about your family. I mean, what if we have a family someday? Wouldn't it be best to avoid all the bad stuff we've gone through?"

"If *we* had a kid," I say—and I think of the process of making the kid more than the kid—"we'd actually want him or her. We'd change the way we live for the kid. My parents, they didn't. It's not worth talking about."

"But I'd really like it. I've been thinking that, if I travel, I want to plan it with you," she says, hesitating and saying each word deliberately, as if afraid of my reaction. "And I just feel like opening up is a way to, I don't know, like grow and feel more connected."

I just shake my head.

"Fine," she says. "I'll back off."

"I guess the biggest thing for me," I say, "is when you have a family, it's easier to put yourself out there, take risks and be yourself. Who gives a shit if people reject you? You've got family to return to. You might as well go on an adventure 'cause when you come home, your family is all still waiting for you."

"Well, it's not all waiting for me. I've lost, too. But . . . you've never had that family part. I understand." Her chin is resting on my chest, and she's looking up at me, as if she adores me, which causes me to instinctively look away.

I say, "Talking to Dad about anything was too awkward, like if an emotion worked its way into a conversation, suddenly we'd burst into flaming dudes in spandex and roller skates, tweaking our nipples and whining for cock. Just sports—that's all we talked about. And Mom didn't break her gaze from the TV. That or she was working on some painting that she'd never finish. She was always in a daze, off somewhere else. But her students loved her. Students love a teacher who lets everything slide."

"And you loved her, too. No matter what, you loved her, right?"

I hear a truck engine roar outside our tent, and it breaks the silence surrounding us. I remember Trey and Caleb in the tent next to us. They might be within ear-shot, so I just roll my eyes, shake my head.

"Tyler, honestly, you can't be such a cynic all the time," Liv says, looking up at me with those big green eyes. "It's got to be exhausting."

The grasshoppers and cicadas drone around us, and I see the tent next to us is glowing in two small orbs. Caleb and Trey brought their PS Vitas along. Video games on a camping trip. My mind is wandering off, wondering which games they're playing, whether there's Wi-Fi here or if the Vitas can connect using 4G or not.

"We should visit your dad in California," she says softly until she gets to "California," which she says in a horrible Arnold Schwarzenegger voice.

"No. You don't get it. He's a piece of shit. He's military. He hides behind honor and duty so he can be a coward."

"He couldn't be *that* bad, sweetie," she says. She reaches toward my face and kisses me.

"He's a fuck. A coward who puts his shriveled up military chode before his family," and out of nowhere I'm choking up, because Mom's face is popping up in my head. I've been great at pushing her out, but she's demanding my attention now like a roadside freak show.

"Tyler, are you okay?"

A deep breath. I keep my eyes wide open to not allow any collection of wetness.

"I'll be right back." I get up, she rolls off me, and I walk barefoot across the pointy twigs and rocks to Betsy the Buick. In the glove compartment I swallow my last lorazepam—just a weak drug addict—and I feel better. Before the actual pill hits my brain, I get immediate placebo comfort.

When I come back, she says, "Can you tell me what that was all about? You never act like that," she says, concerned. She's genuine, and I'm softened by this—still not used to it after months. Her concern for me is still a novelty, and sometimes I just gaze at her when she's worried, as if she's a foreign object, something outside the realm of language that can only be gazed upon like a shiny object by a bonobo chimpanzee who just wants to hump everything with a thumping heart.

And I'm comfortable. And I don't have any hesitation.

I tell her about Mom, plainly, like a reporter. Told not shown. Mom never wanted a kid. She resented having me, having to give up on all she wanted to do. Her loose adherence to her religion kept her from an abortion. Dad told me this after she died.

"What did she give up?" she asks, gently, not wanting the eggshells to crack.

"Being an artist. Drawing these cartoon strips. That and traveling. She wanted to paint and draw and travel. Bohemian, you know?

The fire crackles outside the tent and I yawn, so she yawns and my eyes water, so I dry them.

"What if you just . . . try talking to your dad?"

"Waste of time."

"It can't be that bad."

I look at her and reach near the entrance flap and grab my phone. Two bars glow like white towers. I dial 768 plus Dad's number. It starts ringing. I press the speakerphone button, and the phone's light casts shadows on the tent walls. Phone rings twice, then to voicemail.

I say, "Two rings means—"

"He rejected it," she says.

Rubbing her hand against my back, she says, "I'm sorry. Maybe he's just busy."

Normally, I'd push her away: *Don't feel sorry for me. Don't worry about it. Just the way it is.*

But I let her.

"What if you just believe that you can change the relationship? Just work at it. Really work at it. It takes work to make a relationship work."

"But I don't want that relationship. I want *this* one."

"Why couldn't you work on both?"

"I only want what you have," I say.

She stares at me for what seems forever while rubbing my leg. Climbing on top of me, she pulls my head toward her, straining my neck. She kisses me hard, grinding her warm body against me. I cover her mouth with my hand so Trey and Tony don't hear.

~ ~ ~

Later, Olivia says, "I brought up the traveling stuff at Christmas for a reason. And I'm sorry I didn't mention it again. But I need to do more. I need to get out there. There are these trips coming up, one in July, one in late August, and—" she pauses. "I've really been meaning to tell you."

"That's great. How long?" I ask, expecting to dismiss this quickly. *Quick trip? No biggie.*

"First one, a few weeks. The second one's a bit longer." She's tentative again.

"How long we talking?"

She winces and hesitates. "All semester."

"All the semester? Three months?"

"It actually ends up being about four . . . I'm sorry, but no matter how I look at it, I can't turn down the opportunity."

She doesn't invite me or mention the possibility. Feeling like a guy no one invited to a party, I ask if I can travel with.

"If you were allowed to, I'd love that. I even asked the trip director. But only environmental studies students can do the semester-long travel," she says, avoiding eye contact. Her eyes trace my chest. Just minutes after being as close to her as possible, I'm nowhere near her anymore. She's overseas; I'm lying here on the dirt, scratching a mosquito bite.

"In essence, you'll be gone—probably no contact—for a chunk of a year," I say.

"Well, yes . . ." She wraps my hands around hers. "I want to do this, and the opportunity came. You can do stuff like this, too. And once this trip is over, we'll do it together."

"I don't want to do anything like that. I don't know. I guess I don't feel all that adventurous for saving trees and stuff." My voice is running. "It seems hopeless to fight an entire industry with the government on their side. I can't buy into that."

"Then find something else. You can't always wait for me to pull you around. I feel like I make all the decisions. You just wait around until things happen to you. You're just along for the ride."

And I'm silent because she's right.

3.

At first thought, four months seems long—especially so early in a relationship. But it isn't, right? Instead of looking at months, I need to think in terms of day by day, hour by hour, minute by minute, second by second. I repeat this to myself until time seems less overwhelming as broken-down units. Looking at things all at once is overwhelming. For example, you learn you must take a lifesaving medication for the rest of your life. But if you think of it as a simple daily thing, it's not as bad. Day by day. Then it adds up to something bigger, better, if you plan well. Someone once told me: You'd be amazed at what a person can accomplish one drop at a time at regular intervals over a length of time. If I take this day by day, maybe these four months will fly.

Livi's reading under a bookworm light. It's a chilly night, so she's wearing a slouchy white beanie over her curly hair and drowning in my Packers sweatshirt.

"What're you reading?"

"A Bill McKibben book".

"Read to me a bit," I say. My head is resting on her stomach, rising and falling with her breaths.

After reading aloud to me for a while, she stops. "What do you think so far?"

I'm not sure if she means the writing or her reading, but I haven't been listening to the words. Her voice—I'm just letting its pitch and inflection flow over me like lulling classical music.

"You should keep reading."

She reads aloud to me and I'm relaxed to the point where I could piss myself and not care. I'm almost asleep, twilight images floating in front of my eyes, when she says, "I love you," and I fall asleep with my head resting on her stomach.

Chapter Fourteen

Narc

Sitting on the can at my naked apartment, I read the back of *The Breakfast Club* Blu-ray case:

When Saturday detention started, they were simply the Jock, the Princess, the Brain, the Criminal and the Basket Case. But by that afternoon they had become closer than any of them could have imagined.

A year ago Toki the Cat would be curled atop my feet. Instead, my feet are freezing, and I'm staring at the pink cover of the case where the posed actors pretend to be people; they pretend to feel emotions, and I'm not sure if there's a difference between love and need. When Livi's gone, I don't know what I'll do. Without my media collection, she's what I turn to for direction. She shows me how to act. What to value. But love? That's a thing I'm familiar with in terms of romantic comedies, insincere Hallmark cards, and that Haddaway song.

If love and need are synonymous, then I loved my movie and book collection. Like a family, it told me who I should be each day. It told me what I should value—that it was okay to act any way as long as there was a reason behind it. Flawed actions are okay in movies and TV shows and novels. I loved that. When I came home, I had my escapes for support. Livi is now who I turn to. But love—that cliché—I don't know. I can say it. I can fake it until I portray all the elements of love, as demonstrated by all the actors before me, the Goslings, the Orlando Blooms, the Bogarts, the Gables.

Maybe using Olivia as a replacement, I could completely wean myself off the glass teat. From my porcelain crown, I toss the Blu-ray case like a Frisbee into the trash across the white tiled floor. It hits the back of the tin, rattles, and falls gently on used tissues and TP.

"Nice shot, me," I say.

I stare at it for a minute.

That was too dramatic. I waddle to the tin can, my pants round my ankles, and fish the case out, trying not to touch crusty rolled up balls of TP.

"Trey," I yell, "want a copy of *The Breakfast Club*?"

He can have it. He isn't changing.

~ ~ ~

Vibrations from my car speakers alter my mood. All day my stomach has been tensed like I was bracing for a punch, but the drinks have relaxed it. I crawl into my Buick, crank the head deck knob, and Tool's music hotboxes me into a general sense of aggression and pigheadedness. I had to leave the emptiness of my apartment, of my room, and surround myself with the mobile room that is Betsy the Buick. The setting outside of this mobile room can always be changed. I can cruise outside a farm, the calm moos of spotted cows that graze. Maybe I drive past a dilapidated school, feeling nostalgic about those days of four square and tetherball. But now, with my eyes closed, the alcohol amplifying the music's energy, I can only think of my duplex burning, red flames slithering into the sky like thick snakes, the ceiling collapsing like a king of spades atop a house of cards, the melting snow revealing pale grass around the house like a green moat. Preventable. Avoidable. Unjust. I did nothing to deserve it.

Tool's symbols crash over the speakers are a signal for me like a gunshot for a sprinter. I'm going to act, going to do something, but how I'm going to act, what I'm going to do—these things are vague.

Kennedy's mom will be out tonight. She'll be bouncing around like a pinball between dive bars. Her son will be at Stevie's, a local college bar where frat boys, dude-bros, and protein-shaking muscle-bound meatheads sling themselves at packs of dyed-blonde college girls. Kennedy will be hunched over the electronic blackjack game, losing again and again until he's just about to quit. Then he'll win that handful of cash that'll keep him playing all night. His dog, during these spring months, will be tied to the clothesline running up and down the backyard. Don't know its name, but it's a black slobbering pit bull with a white stripe running down its chest. When I used to pick up at his house—nights his mom wasn't coming home—that dog would dive headlong into the side of my car door. Thump. Kennedy would smack it with a backhand. The image of that dog dead materializes in my mind. Tongue out, drool collecting on the cement, its white stripe splotched red.

~ ~ ~

The route Kennedy walks home passes the cop shop, the college, and the basketball courts. Weekend nights, a few officers patrol the campus area, watching for drunks. Kennedy doesn't drink much because he sells right from the blackjack game. His post.

I open my eyes, slam my fist on the dashboard with the sound of a clashing cymbal over the speakers and drive toward campus as I play air drums. On both sides of me, clumps of college kids walk past, a straggler here and there crossing the street. They expect me to stop without them even paying a look to my oncoming car. The Tool album reaches the last track and starts from the beginning, its first song building in volume, the bass rolling down a scale. Three or four sleeveless guys strut out into the road right in front of my car. I slam on the brakes, but in my mind I plow through them, and they scatter like bowling pins, and I drive on, celebrating a strike.

My legs are now soaked with the drink that I had tucked between my legs. The smell of vodka and my strawberry air freshener make me wish I had a mixed drink with those two ingredients. A cruise isn't the same without a drink tucked between your thighs.

A tan frat boy with Chinese symbols running down his arm slams his palms on the hood of my car. He slams his foot on my hood and flips me off with both hands. "Fuck you, faggot," I hear through the windshield. I don't see his face, but instead I see Livi's ex-boyfriend's face. I see Kennedy's spoiled, freeloading apparition. I see Dad saluting the flag. I roll down the window while the rest of the guys with him all keep walking across the street, waving for him to come with. I hit the gas and jerk forward. His body is thrown forward, and I slam on the brakes. He flops forward like a sack of sand—his full body weight onto his shoulder. Before he can get up, I swerve around him and rifle my empty glass toward him, and I've accelerated past by the time I hear the glass shatter and a guttural yell.

The engine's crescendo matches the song's drum freak-out, and I play air drums on the steering wheel and scream the lyrics along with Maynard James Keenan's voice. The red speedometer dial hits fifty-five and the campus library blurs by. Little red dots of cigarettes hanging from mouths blur by like zigzagging laser pointers. I see Stevie's blue neon sign above the two-story campus housing, and I ease on the brake, realizing my lights have been off his whole time. My dark car zipping through the night, unseen but heard because of its music. Outside Stevie's, I park in the handicapped spot, leaving my car running. I flash my ID like a copper and enter the bar. The dance floor flashes the colors of the rainbow in a seizure-inducing sequence. The strobe light makes me feel like Charlie Chaplin in an old silent film, so I dance a little with my feet, pretending to be the actor.

I've blocked out all people in the room; they register in my vision, but are as relevant as cardboard cutouts in my mind. The only sentient being I register is the hooded body slouched over the blackjack game, his face lit blue from the screen's glow. He pounds his fist into the screen. He lost that round. I stare at him just long enough to make sure it's him. I buy a drink from a cardboard cutout. A vodka and something—it tastes like strawberry—and I walk out with the glass in my hand. The thick-necked bouncer cutout says something to stop me, but I keep walking. I sit there in my car sipping my drink until Kennedy leaves.

I switch to the radio and each song throws me into different states of thought and emotion. I wax toward wanting to kill him during the solo of Metallica's "One." I wane when a Doobie Brothers song plays. I want to talk it out, explain my frustrations, and ask him if he burnt my house. I wax; I wane. I'll kill; I'll concede. I'm just a reflection of the music now. When Kennedy appears below the red neon exit sign of Stevie's, shaking hands with the bouncer, giving knucks to a guy sucking on a shrinking cigarette, I'm unsure what to do. All the anxiety is brought to life. Whatever action comes next I'm afraid will be a knee-jerk reaction. He cuts through a few yards, and I trail slowly on the side of the road. A perfect distance. Like a gumshoe. Fuckin' *L.A. Noire.* Philip Marlowe. Between two houses, he stops and a fat silhouetted figure hands him something. They exchange a bottle or a bag and Kennedy's got something on him. I reach for my phone and dial.

"I have to report a drug-related interaction near campus," I say into the receiver, sipping my vodka. I'm pulled to the side of the road, watching as Kennedy walks through the cop shop parking lot, past the empty striped squad cars as if it's an act of defiance. I give information to the lady's voice on my phone and hang up. A song later, a squad car pulls up next to Kennedy's black figure and two officers exit the vehicle. They lean him against the car, his hands on the roof, and I realize how close I am to the scene. I sip my drink and Kennedy looks over toward me, so I sink into my seat. I only allow my eyes to peek through the steering wheel over the dashboard.

There's no doubt he sees me.

Chapter Fifteen

Horse-Riding With My Love

My mattress lies on the carpet. I'm face down in my pillow, barely able to breathe. In my sleep, my subconscious tried to suffocate me in my own pillow, but my genetic drive to survive fights sleep-suicide off valiantly.

The phone on my nightstand—which is to say the floor—vibrates. I roll over to it and realize I'm wearing only a white t-shirt, nothing else. Donald Duck morning attire. Cotton mouth, thumping pulse in my temple, aching muscles—they're part of the normal morning. The message is from Livi. I tap the screen and the phone explains it's retrieving the data, which means it's a photo. As I wait, I stare at the bare white ceiling, blurry without my contacts. Panning around the room, I see only the blurry white. The white closet door hides my few shirts, mostly white t-shirts from Target, so around me is just white wall and comfy white carpet. White like purgatory. Simple and empty.

I check back to the phone and expect it to be a picture of some five-legged wildlife creature that's been genetically modified by radioactive sludge—like Teenage Mutant Ninja Turtles. Instead of something I don't care about, it's a picture of Livi. One that makes my brain blood rush south. She's wearing a black lace thong, a Hooters top (*where did she get this?*), and heels that make her calves pop. She's leaning up against her bedroom wall like a cop's about to frisk her. Like Kennedy last night. I laugh out loud, a bursting gut-laugh. What a lovely way to start the morning. The best thing about waking up is not Folgers in my cup.

~ ~ ~

The car ride to the ranch is long, so I've put together a master playlist of upbeat jams. The Waitresses' "I Know What Boys Like" starts things off, followed by The Doors' "Peace Frogs," some Beck, and Vampire Weekend. For an hour or so, we both sing along, mouthing the words, playing air guitar. She plays air piano on my driving leg, slapping my relaxed calf and watching it jiggle to the beat of Billy Squier's "Stroke It." Her brown hair is braided over her tan shoulder, and her big eyes glisten like water. Her tight t-shirt says something about ending lung cancer, and on the back are the names of a few local bars and insurance companies.

She has endless energy. After the hours' worth of gettin' jiggy wit it, *nah, nah, nah, nah, nah, nah,* I'm ready to clamp on headphones and escape into the world of George Carlin or the moody rumblings of Tom Waits. But she bounces the whole trip, wanting to engage with me. Although I adore her every action, I teeter between extreme tiredness and irritated and anxious for no plausible reason. I pull into the horse ranch's dirt parking lot, and the lot is packed with SUVs, a Hummer, and a few soccer mom mini-vans. One spot is open. I gun it.

"Jesus, Ty, slow down," Livi says, overreacting in her best Bo Peep impression, hands flailing in the air until she accidentally slaps my rearview mirror, and it falls off the windshield onto the dashboard.

"God *damn it*," I say as a raised Ford F-150 with knee-high rims roars into my parking spot, cutting in front of me. The truck is spotless. A confederate flag flaps from a pole sticking up in the truck bed. The driver wears a cowboy hat. I sense Livi worrying I'm mad about the stupid rearview. "That sonovabitch Toby Keith horse-fucking racist cowboy wannabe asshole," I mutter in a Popeye voice, shaking my fist.

"Settle down, sweetie," Livi says, putting the rearview in the backseat as subtly as possible, but I don't care about the mirror.
"No. Fuck Keith Urban," I say.

"We'll just find another spot."

I shake my head and take note of how well potatoes would fit into Keith Urban's dual exhaust pipes. Or hay chunks. Or horse doo-doo. The baseball bat in my trunk would be perfect for cramming it deep into the pipes to make sure they didn't fall out.

I let sexy Betsy the Buick idle behind the truck as leather cowboy boots step down from the Ford truck. Toby Keith has a dip bulging in his bottom lip, which is harboring a pube-like soul patch, and he's sportin' a sleeveless Larry the Cable Guy T-shirt. I'm trying to make him implode like a nova star with my hate-stare. Despite my effort, he has no problem sticking a Marlboro Red in his mouth and lighting up as his kids and wife crawl out of the tank-truck fueled by Native American tears and bald-eagle feathers.

"You ready to play cowboy, my Ty-guy?" Livi says with a smile. "There's a snake in my boot!" she says, quoting my favorite movie, and I want to squeeze her and smooch her. When I make eye contact with her, I'm softened, liquidized. I avoid eye contact with her so I can stay pissed at this pseudo-cowboy.

We park six hundred miles away, and Livi and I dress in our riding gear, which is to say she dresses me—like a mommy might—in her brother's horse riding gear. "Hold your arms up," she says, and I bite my tongue so I don't say anything to taint our day together. Only positive thoughts and comments, I repeat to myself like a sacred Hail Mary. My teeth plunge into my tongue and my mouth tastes metallic when Livi says, "Jordan hasn't fit into these since, God, like grade school."

I say, "Take that, Tyler's self-esteem."

After we change, we wait in line behind Conway Twitty and his crew-cut rug rats. The riding supervisor asks Conway a few basic questions but Conway is on his cell phone, and he puts a finger in the air as if to say, "Just a moment, buck-o, I'm on the phone." My teeth plunge deeper into my tongue until I feel solid teeth-on-teeth contact through my tongue and an intense metallic tastes spreads as my teeth touch.

In the bathroom, I squeeze Ora-gel benzocaine over my split tongue to numb the pain.

I return to line. As I'm waiting, my phone buzzes, though I usually don't get service this far north.

Kennedy: Remember yer burnin' cat? Told you u got comin 2 u.

A few seconds later:

Kennedy: Saw u the other night. U narc-in' Judass. Revenge, itll cum. It'll cum again.

I hold the power button until the phone shuts off. I glare at the wanna-be cowboy as he interrupts the riding supervisor again and again, insisting he could tame a wild horse.

Livi is laughing as her horse's thick wiggling tongue slobbers over her hands. She wipes her hands on me. I grab her and throw her over my shoulder and spin her in circles.

"Stop," she says between gasping laughs, "I'm gonna pee. I'm gonna pee." Her braid is whipping against my back, and she bites my shoulder while growling. I set her to the dried dirt and she kicks up at me. "You little shit," she says. Her braid is frizzled at the top of her head, the little baby hairs static and shooting in different directions.

"I'm your massive napkin, aren't I?" I say.

"Yup," she says, jumping onto my back and kissing my neck. The horse stares blankly at us. "Just remember," she says, "don't go behind the horse." She taps with her blue-painted fingernail on her fake front tooth. "They'll kick at you, and you'll get a quarter from the tooth fairy before you know what hit you."

On horseback, we follow through the woods path behind the guide. My horse keeps veering to the right. My ass bones rub raw against the saddle, my weight shifting to each ass bone with every horse step. My feet feel constricted in the stirrups. Half an hour ago, the horse trainer walked me through saddling the horse like an adult showing a child how to tie shoes. As I struggled, Livi stood a few feet away running her hand down her horse's neck, stroking its nose until it ceased doing that lip fluttering noise horses do. She soothed her horse. My horse shat onto the dirt while giving me the stink eye.

As the pile steamed, I watched Livi bond instantly with this creature like it was the natural thing to happen. Jealousy flared up—just like when she became closer with my friends in two minutes than I've ever been in my entire life. Something amiable about her allows even wild creatures to bond naturally with her, while I remain detached from the thing I've mounted.

The longer we ride, the younger I feel. The less tense my stomach and neck feel, as if each trot shook tension out of the hole in my ass. Like Woody riding Bullseye, I trot along freely and happily, with no minutiae to deal with. I just enjoy a simple horseback ride next to Livi.

This is the third time she's taken me riding and I'm still clumsy like a thumbless troglodyte with an iPhone. The trainer pulls a good football field ahead of us as the narrow path opens into a field of knee-high grass that bobs with the wind like tired head-bangers at a metal concert. Livi pulls on the reins and slows to a meander. Her horse's head is straight and tall. Mine is cocked to the right like it's trying to see if it has a tail.

"Jordan wrote me about what he's doing for work, and I've been thinking a lot," she says. She pulls her horse to stay alongside mine regardless of how erratic my movement. "I need to do something. Something to make a difference, like he is. Soon." The rhythm of the hoofs beating the dirt punctuates her words. Like two coconuts together. *Monty Python and the Holy Grail.*

"What do you mean? Making a difference?" I say.

"Like going and fighting for a cause."

"Just like your brother?"

"Yeah. But less . . . forceful," she says.

"And what cause is your brother fighting for?" I ask.

"Oh, come on. Don't get started on this again."

"I mean it. He's caught up in the illusion of making a difference. By signing up for the Marines, he thinks he's done some great service to mankind, and now we must all thank him endlessly for his tireless battle against the tyranny of terrorism." I point at a tree in the distance. "Holy shit! Look out, Liv! Terror! I see terror over there."

"Oh, my God, just let me talk."

"Fine."

"I feel like everything we do on a daily basis is so insignificant. Most of what we decide isn't going to impact anyone. It's all trivial. Yet there's a ton of people who need help with basic things like food, clothes, and water. I could help these people."

"And your brother made you want to do this?"

"Partially. He encouraged me to in the last e-mail he wrote. I just think I'm wasting my time and effort dinking-and-dunkin' around here."

"He has access to e-mail? Where's he stationed now?"

"Told me the location was classified."

I laugh. "Top-secret information, huh?"

"If I just focus on putting my energy into something bigger than myself, I know I can help change something."

I take a deep breath and try to be understanding. I realize how much of an ass I'm being, and it's partly because I despise the existence of her ex-boyfriend and his military status. It's partly because Jordan and Dad have that macho, respect-me-because-I'm-military attitude. Plus, we all love the illusion of doing something.

"Okay, sweet-cheeks," I say with a smile. "What were you thinking?"

"Well, of course, the two trips I told you about. And anything else I can find. I thought about Greenpeace and some nonprofit cancer-research benefit organizations, but I'm not really sure what direction I'd—" she continues on, but all I notice is Toby Keith in his sleeveless t-shirt with his cowboy family trotting from an adjoining path into the open field. He's clamping his heels into the horse's side repeatedly with force so the horse is reacting with jerking movements and groans.

"I could even see doing something with lung-cancer organizations," Livi says. I glance at her anti-cancer shirt, then to the military-looking boys following behind Toby.

"I don't know," I say.

"You don't know what?" There's irritation in her voice.

"What good does fundraising for cancer research really do? Or even worse, spreading awareness of something? Cancer research takes millions of dollars being poured in regularly just to keep the process going. And there's no guarantee they'll make any progress. To make actual progress, we'd need the government or some private corporation to be routing cash into a research fund. Raising a few hundred dollars at a five-K run doesn't do anything. It's drop in a dry lake when the sun is scorching."

She exhales like air being let out of a balloon. "Just once, couldn't you look on the positive side of things?"

"I usually do. I know how it *should* be. I just would rather see things realistically. Not through some dreamy cloud world where running for half an hour makes cancer disappear. I can yell '*end childhood hunger*' through the streets all I want, but that doesn't mean I've done anything. I just get to feel good about myself at the end of the day. It's more about people feeling good about themselves."

"You mean *me* feeling good about myself."

"No," I say. "I mean, like, in general. People in general. It's like, people giving money to their church and the church buys some new HD projector to display the monthly newsletter program. That donator feels good but did nothing."

The cowboy dad and his kids blaze in front of our horses, kicking up clumps of mud and what might be horse shit.

"What the hell," Livi says as they pass, chunks of dirt pegging her face and chest. "What an asshole."

~ ~ ~

We ride the snaking trail past ponds where ducks trudge through water caked with green algae and floating plastic water bottles. She tells me more of her plans to explore and help the world. Every so often I hear a distant "Waa-hoo" or "Yee-haw" usually followed by a more youthful version, likely from the Toby Keith's kids. We arrive back at the ranch.

"You go wash up, Livi my lady," I say. This will give me a few free moments.

I sprint the six hundred miles in my riding gear to Betsy the Buick. I pop the trunk and grab my aluminum bat and an old pair of emergency boxers. I hop in my car and cruise closer to the main building on the ranch. I let my car idle in park and run toward the Ford F-One-Tough-Nuts. Nearby is a small mountain of horse dung. I scoop it up with my hand, which is covered by my old plaid boxers like when you scoop dog shit. I run in a crouched position behind the huge truck and mash the gushy dung into the tailpipe. I run back and grab another handful. Mash. Another handful. Mash. Some oozes onto my riding pants, so I brush my body against the truck bumper and it globs onto a bumper sticker reading "'Merica: You Don't Like It, You Can Get the Eff Out."

Once I've mushed in as much shit as I can, I plunge the handle end of the bat into the tailpipe until it's compact and tight. I cram a jagged rock in behind. Then I toss the bat and shitty plaid boxers into the sparkling bed of the truck. I wipe my hands on the grass and hop in my car, driving with my knees to the main building where I'll wash my shitty hands and my shitty arms and then I'll ride home with my intelligent, environmental idealist girlfriend who somehow loves me.

At least parts of me.

Chapter Sixteen

Fourth of July: Fuck Yeah, America

Out my front window I see tiny red-white-and-blue flags fluttering in unison near curbside mailboxes. Trey is talking at me from his computer chair, but I'm blocking him out and running through the string of dreams from the night before; my mind plays a collage of clips in which I do bunch of small asshole-ish (but justified!) actions. I saw each of them through a shimmering wave, I guess to symbolize shaky reasons for my behavior or something. The most recent dream involved exhaust pipes exploding, little horse turds flying through the air like brown confetti . . . even though I know all that happened to Toby Keith's truck was, at worst, the car engine stalled and wouldn't start. I wake with that feeling that today I should be a decent human being, no matter what urge stirs up like gurgling indigestion. I look at my baggy eyes in the mirror—almost looking black and blue, my nose a little crooked, my skin paler than normal, blond hair on one side of my head flipped out from sleeping on it—and I promise myself to behave and be a normal, respectable citizen of the world. I cross my fingers, hope to die, stick a needle in my eye.

God, I look like shit.

Trey helped me out big-time. He's got insurance under his dad's plan, which is paid for by his church because he's a pastor. Trey went to a shrink and unloaded a bunch of symptoms I listed for him, plus his own symptoms, which he collected from WebMD. This scored me a prescription for Adderall and lorazepam. He fills the script, and I pay him the ten-dollar copay. I've got thirty anti-anxiety pills. Illegal, yes, but no more illegal than before, right?

It's been months since my last razzy-pam, so I'm just on cloud nine as Livi drives to her mom's house. I keep asking myself how I ever survived without these pills. For once in months, I'm not imagining anticipated conversations, my responses, my standing position, my hand positions, whether to be sarcastic, self-deprecating, sincere, or to mirror the person with whom I'm talking. It's like the medicine triggers the real person inside this exoskeleton of shuddering anxiety and fear and cowardice.

But *shit*, with the medical aid to balance my brain, I'm golden. Just golden, and I couldn't be more excited to spend time with the family—even though Jordan, with his salute-greetings and trigger-finger personality, will be there. To me, he's become like that uncle that no one really wants to show up, but he's always there, so you just make the best of it. And I plan to make the best of it. I enjoy fucking with him. I'm sure he enjoys picturing choking me out in a Marines wrestling singlet while sporting a half-mast chubby.

"I'm seriously pumped to see your mom," I tell Livi in the car over the beautiful layered harmonies and punctuated drum thumps of a Grizzly Bear song. This medication is making me love everything, including these amazing speakers, these amazing ridges along the volume knob, the amazing architecture of the smooth roads on which we glide. "I've never been excited for a family get-together."

She laughs. "I love that you call them family."

"It's weird. Maybe I'm just in a good mood or something"—probably the pills—"but I feel like I'm a part of the fam. No joke. It's making me feel all warm and fuzzy inside." I take another sip from my coffee tumbler, which is not filled with anus-tasting coffee, but with off-brand grape soda and bottom-shelf vodka. BOGO on vodka last week at Tillman's. *Ah, America.*

She's smiling as big as possible, like a good version of a Glasgow smile. I feel the day rising like a roller coaster inching to its peak. The worst part of today has been the metal of my belt rubbing against my upper-crotchal region, giving me the impulse to scratch it until it's red, bumpy, and burning.

As we near the family's house, a sign hangs over the highway. It reads: *73 Traffic Deaths This Year. Drive Carefully and Help Prevent Wisconsin Auto Deaths.* Last year's death total of 457 was wiped out. The dead body count was reset, as if the people never existed.

1.

"Grandpa, this is Tyler," Livi says as I extend a hand to him. "Tyler, this is Grandpa Higgins." Keri, Livi, Grandpa, and I are standing in Keri's open backyard, which expands for a few acres until the forest begins. To our left, the neighbors' yard begins. It is immaculate, with towering flags flapping. Vines run down the wooden house.

"Nice to meet you, kid. You look different," Grandpa Higgins says. His thick and smooth hand smothers my hand. He towers over me, and his rumbling voice sets me weirdly on edge. I scratch at my belt rash as a man from the neighbor's immaculate yard limps toward us. His left arm ends at the elbow. Huge fisherman sunglasses mask much of his face. Following behind him is a white border collie who wears a red-white-and-blue shirt over his little body.

"What do you mean, 'I look different'?" I ask.

"Oh, Grandpa means nothing by it," Livi says.

"No," Grandpa Higgins says. "He looks a lot different. Hair's shaggier. Skin's paler. I thought you joined the—"

"Dad," Keri interrupts. "You're confused." She turns to me. "Don't pay it any attention, Ty."

"What do you mean?" I say again to Grandpa Higgins, and he pulls a pack of Pall Malls from his red flannel pocket, slides out a smoke, and sets it in his mouth.

"Always fucking with my head, you women. Always," he says. He grabs a camouflage lighter from his other shirt pocket and lights the cigarette with one hand. "Just playing your little games. Like your mother."

I know little of Grandma Higgins except that she is dead.

"Hey, you've got some of the sexy-hot Higgins crew rounded up again," the backyard neighbor says with a cackle as he joins us. He coughs, hollow and productive. He spits whatever he coughed up onto the grass near my blue Vans. "Where's our Marine boy?"

On cue, Jordan's motorcycle growls down the dirt path, and I see Grandpa Higgins's thick caterpillar eyebrow scrunch up. His crusty lips slide around, tight on his teeth, like an angry Clint Eastwood. I can't hear him over the engine's roar. Jordan parks. Before shutting off the engine, he cranks the handlebar and the engine roars again, even though he still looks like a little kid riding a big wheel with his hands on those high handlebars.

"Turn that damn shit off. Jesus shit Christ, you asshat," Grandpa Higgins says, grumbling toward Jordan.

"Sorry, Gramps. Marine way of doing things," Jordan says with a good-hearted smile and shrug.

"Ah, yes. There he is," the neighbor says. Jordan struts to him and they shake hands, and hug. The neighbor, who Jordan calls Mr. Buehl, steps back and holds Jordan's shoulder as he takes a look over him.

"Mr. B., how you been?" Jordan says after the two salute each other.

"Just living the life. Been creating my Garden of Eden." He points to his yard where a grid of flowers colored yellow, orange, red, is punctuated by purple bushes that sit beneath full-headed willow trees.

The two catch up, trading military jokes. Mr. Buehl makes self-deprecating references to his absent arm. It strikes me as odd that Grandpa Higgins and Jordan say nothing to each other, and at times, Higgins scowls behind his thick square glasses as he finishes cigarettes and drops the butts to the matted grass at his massive feet.

"I hope yer all ready for the show tonight," Mr. Buehl says.

"We just can't fucking wait," Grandpa Higgins says flatly out the side of his mouth as he turns and trudges back to Keri's cabin.

2.

Keri, Livi, and I are in the living room when Jordan breaks through the door, its knob smashing into the wall.

"Jordan, relax in the house," Keri says, like a mother to a child.

"Sorry, Ma. I'm just happy to be back with you all." He smiles at Livi and Keri. He stares at me with a scowl. "But this guy? Can't believe you're still with him. I mean, shit, you went from Air Force to *this?*" He points at me.

"Jordan, language," Keri says.

"Whoa, man," I say. I bite my tongue. *Method act, Linley. Method act*. I say, "Don't forget the time I beat you up."

"In grade school," he says."

"Yeah. I'm 1-0. Undefeated," I say. "The King. Muhammad Ali, George Foreman, Manny Pacquiao, Tyler Linley. Fists of fury. The main event. Unstoppable." I'm throwing my fists in the air, flexing in various bodybuilder poses. I punch the air above my head. "Crushing Marine after Marine." I punch my open palm. "The military fears and—"

"Oh, my God, Tyler. Stop," Livi says.

"No, let him keep going," Jordan says. "He's got to take any pride he can get. Not everyone is able to sacrifice and be selfless."

"Oh, c'mon, bub," I say. "You've got to be joking. What, they have you fixing phone lines or doing mechanic work? That's not military work. That's glorified blue-collar work in a pretty uniform."

"All part in the fight against terror."

"My God," I scream. "Look over there!" I point out the window toward Mr. Buehl's yard.

Keri and Livi look with sincerity. Jordan just stares at me.

"Terror! There! In the bushes. Oh, God!" I point to the spinning ceiling fan. "Terror! Get it for me, Mr. Marine! Ahh!" I dive to the ground and roll under the coffee table, smacking my knee against the glass underside.

"Tyler, please—" Livi says.

"Sis, your boyfriend is just jealous that he can't serve something bigger than himself. He's insecure. He's weak. He's selfish."

"Nuh-uh," I say from beneath the table. I feel drunk, and it's like I'm watching myself be an ass. I crawl out from under the table and flex my arms like Hulk Hogan and squat down into a sumo-wrestler pose.

"This here," I gesture to myself, "destroyed you back in grade school. This machine." I flex my arms by my stomach in a U shape. "This machine is a monster," I flex above my shoulders. "And truly—I'm honestly wondering—did you see any terror today?" I say "terror" like George Dub-yuh Bush would. I approach Jordan in a wrestler's stance.

"No," Jordan says. "But I see you dressed yourself, so I'm sure that's considered a pretty productive day for you, huh?" He moves closer to me, also in a crouched wrestler's stance.

Keri and Livi leave the room. They roll their eyes and slam the door behind them.

"Yeah, your sister put 'em on me, like a pro, bro." I pound my chest, and we're two feet from each other. "Your smoking hot, tight-assed sister." I stick my arm out, and he does the same. "That nice, tight—"

He grabs my arms. "And now, to show a bitch how to—" he struggles to speak as we grapple for position— "wrestle like a real man."

I get lower than him and grab his left leg and yank on it. He loses his balance and pulls the back of my shirt over my head as he falls onto his back with a thud. A deer head mounted on the wall falls onto the room's couch. We both stop for a split second to look, like two dogs hearing a high-pitch whistle. We start again. He's underneath me, and I'm trying to pin his arms above his head, but he keeps thrusting his waist up into the air, throwing me off balance as I mount him. (Heterosexual mount, I mean—in case my dad or the church is wondering.)

After a few thrusts, he bounces me off him, and he turns the tables. He's got both my arms pinned above my head.

"Ha! You little bitch." He says this with his face centimeters from my face. It's so close I feel his prickly hairs against my freshly shaven face. I smell the faint mint from Grizzly chew on his breath.
"Eh, I'm just tired. Lucky this time," I say, strained. I'm unable to fully breathe with his knees pinning my shoulders to the ground and his arms pinning mine together above my head. *Claustrophobic, claustrophobic, claustrophobic. Get the fuck off me.*

"You know, Livi told me something," Jordan says. "And normally, I'd never try anything this faggy, but . . . it's a special occasion."

He starts tickling my armpits and my sides, and I start screaming and flopping around like a fish out of water until Keri and Livi fly into the room, following by Mr. Buehl and Grandpa Higgins. As soon as Jordan sees Buehl, he jumps to his feet and acts calm and collected. Jordan folds his arms behind his back. I'm still in the fetal position on the ground, my dress shirt untucked, my tie wrapped around my neck, and half my tummy and back exposed. I'm recovering from a fit of uncontrolled giggling.

"You youngsters are something else. Something else I don't want to know," Buehl says, shaking his head, but letting out a hollow chuckle.

"A Marine playing gay-boy tickle-tummy with an Air Force chump. Never thought I'd see that," Grandpa Higgins says, a cigarette hanging out the side of his mouth. "Military chodes." For the first time in my life, I hear an old man use the word "chode."
Check that off the bucket list.

In Keri's bedroom, Livi straightens out my purple tie and adjusts the collar on my black dress shirt. Livi stands behind me, and we both look into the full-body mirror. She kisses my neck, and Keri joins us in her bedroom, which is stacked with oils, spa treatments, topical creams, conditioners, shampoos, lotions, and anything else a woman needs to retain her youthful beauty. It's a Bed, Bath and Beyond.

"Ty-guy, you look so handsome," Keri says. Livi adjusts from the front as Keri enters the mirror's reflection.

"Why, thank you, Keri-berry," I say, playing cutesy.

"Black tie with the purple shirt and your blue eyes and the blond 'do—it works for you," she says. "Seriously, if I were twenty years younger . . ."

I make an O with my mouth, raise my eyebrows above my head, and put my hands to my cheeks.

"You know, Keri. Age is just a number," I say.

"Ty," Livi shouts into my face, and playfully slaps my cheek.

"What? I'm just telling the truth. You're mother looks beautiful and appears much younger than her age. She's simply *gorgeous*," I say in my best Boston accent.

"Jesus Christ," Livi says as she yanks my tie tight, choking me.

"Yes?" I say.

Keri and I laugh, and Livi slaps the side of my head.

"Livi, you need to be gentle with such a delicate and . . . sexy face," Keri says. She and I burst out laughing. Livi gets red and slaps both of our shoulders and walks out of the room.

"You guys are assholes," she says.

"Keri, now that she's gone," I say.

Keri looks left then right. "I think I hear my dad and big leathery Mr. Buehl a'comin'. We'll have to wait for the right moment," she says with a sardonic smile.

3.

In the living room, we sit at a long table: Jordan, Mr. Buehl, his short plump plum of a wife, Grandpa Higgins, Livi, and me. Keri and Livi serve the food on the scarred table. The fireplace crackles faintly; Keri burnt some wood for the smell, even though it's a humid seventy-five-degree day.

Grandpa Higgins eats nothing all meal but keeps sliding the Pall Malls into his mouth, lighting them with one hand. He stares for long spells at Mr. Buehl, his caterpillar eyebrow scrunched in anger and focus; I imagine a laser beaming from Grandpa Higgins's eyes and melting Buehl, like in a plastic army man under a magnifying glass. Every time I say something to G-paw Higgins, he seems bothered and confused, like I'm a stranger asking him if I can borrow a pair of undies. I eventually stop talking to him, as do all in attendance. He becomes the ignored elephant-sized man in the room. He mashes cigarette after cigarette into the corner of his plate while peering around the table like a poker player behind those thick magnifying spectacles.

The conversation darts between topics of Jordan's military work—top secret, undisclosed, not at liberty to discuss—to Olivia's plans for travel in the near future. Something about her discussion of traveling makes me feel like I'll be abandoned for all the more appealing things (and people) to be found in the world yet unknown to such an adventurous and adaptable girl. But I suppress the feeling when the focus comes to me. My anxiety mounts, the lorazepam having worn off since this morning. I look at Livi, and she seems to sense this. So she disappears and returns with a six-pack of Spotted Cow, "for whoever wants one." I grab one right away and pop the top off. And that placebo of alcohol at hand relaxes me back into a more normal and balanced person who doesn't freak out over simple queries, like *What're you planning to do after graduation? Do you have the time? Pass the 'taters?*

After I field a few of these polite questions, Grandpa Higgins smashes a Pall Mall into his plate, which sends a cloud of ash in my direction.

"Wait," Grandpa Higgins says.

"What?" Keri says.

"Just wait, damn it," he says.

"What's wrong, you old crabby coot?" Mr. Buehl says, adjusting his huge sunglasses.

"Shut your face, you nub-arm freak. I said wait," Higgins says.

"What did you call me?" Buehl says, pushing his chair away from the heavy wooden table. He struggles to stand.

"I said, wait, you ingrate pseudo-hero."

Holy shit, I mutter to myself. Grandpa Higgins insulted the man who lost an arm in a war. Vietnam, probably.

"Did I hear you right?" Buehl says, standing at the table above us all.

"Kid," Higgins says to me. "You said you was thinking about grad school? Thought you was an Air Force pawn."

"You," Buehl says to Grandpa Higgins. "You can't possibly be saying I'm a false hero." He now holds a steak knife in his hand. "I've lost parts of myself for this country. For freedom. For crabby incontinent ol' coots like you, *Higgins*."

"Yeah, G-paw," Jordan says, walking on eggshells. "Mr. B's a hero. He gave himself for *us*."

To me, Grandpa Higgins says, "I was stand-offish 'cause Livi said you was Air Force all these years, you know? I never knew you weren't. Shit, I'd-a been a nicer fella to you all these years if I'd-a known you weren't in the military. Fuck all these assholes signing up to garner respect before even doin' a thing."

"Grandpa, Tyler isn't the same person as you think. He's my boyfriend. He's not who you think he is. He's . . . new. You've seen pictures of him a few times already."

Jordan says, "G-paw, you're thinkin' of Lou, Livi's old boy-toy." Jordan stifles a laugh. "Louis was Air Force." Again, I feel the echoes of the past. Inescapable.

"God damn it, Higgins," Buehl says. "You listen to me, you lumbering idiot. I deserve respect for what I've done for you all." Buehl is pointing the steak knife at Grandpa Higgins.

"Ain't anything respectable about you, *Teddy*," Higgins says with a sneer as he exhales a cloud of smoke.

Keri has been sitting silently looking down at her plate, cutting her steak, potatoes, and green beans into perfect little squares before eating tiny bites. Her eyelashes are long and each calm blink strikes me like a butterfly flapping its wing. She seems to be mentally somewhere else.

"Look at this," Buehl says. He pulls off his sunglasses and picks at his left eye. He pulls a false eye from its socket. "You think I did this for nothing?" He's yelling now, and he sets the false eye on the table. It rolls down a crevice in the wood table until it clanks against a bowl of green beans.

"Jesus H. Christ, you shithead," Grandpa Higgins says. "Put that thing away. No one cares and no one wants to see that when they're eatin'." Higgins flings a lit cigarette across the table at Buehl, and Buehl slaps it down with his hand with impressive reaction time.

Buehl stabs the steak knife into the table. "You people can't handle seeing this?"

Livi stands up and leaves the table. "I'm sorry," she says, "but I need to use the restroom." Keri stays focused on her neat little cuts of food and seems oblivious of the eyeball situation.

Buehl says, "Is this what you want, old man? You want me, huh? Every year you get worse. You get older, more clueless, more stubborn. No wonder your wife poisoned herself."

"My wife's on vacation, Buehl, you ugly ape," Grandpa Higgins says.

"Mr. Buehl, please don't," Jordan says. "Just don't."

"Higgins, your wife is dead. My platoon is dead. But I lost them for a reason. You lost your wife 'cause you're a failure."

Buehl's plump wife watches blankly as they argue. She's disinterested, just waiting it out; she must've heard this bickering too many times to count.

"My wife. My wife. *My* wife," Grandpa Higgins repeats again and again as he stands up and lumbers toward Mr. Buehl. He towers over Buehl, his fists two cinder blocks. Higgins scrunches up his caterpillar eyebrow. He looks down at Buehl, whose false eye still rocks slightly on the table.

"I'm going to bed," Grandpa Higgins says, turning away from Buehl and lumbering down the hall to a guest room.

"Mr. B, you didn't need to do any of that," Jordan says.

Keri looks up. "It's all about you men, isn't it? Everything revolves around your lives and pissing contests." She stands up and leaves the room, leaving Jordan, Buehl, Buehl's plump wife, and me with the slabs of steak and mound of potatoes where a knife stands protruding from the table.

.

4.

"What the hell was that all about?" I ask Livi later in the backyard where Mr. Buehl's dog, an athletic border collie, is curled up at my feet. He reminds me of Toki the Cat curling at my feet.

"Just the routine," she says. "The mess of a family."

"Guess family has its messy side," I say.

"Buehl isn't family. He's just integrated like family."

"And? What was all that about?"

"Well," Livi says, "Buehl lived next to Poppy—er, Grandpa Higgins—forever. From like the sixties until a few years ago when Mom moved into the cabin. Poppy moved into an old folks home. Mr. Buehl and Poppy are like brothers who hate each other, but had to live near one another for forty-plus years. But one year, Buehl had an affair with Grandma Higgins. It went on and off for a few months until Poppy found out—walked in on it. Grandma was a lot younger then. Buehl told me all this. Mom never would. Poppy never forgave Grandma. He never let the past go. You know how that goes."

She pauses. I feel the shot she's taking at me. Frustrated from the day so far, I don't blame her.

"Grandpa just shut Grandma out of his life," she says. "Even though they still lived together, Poppy just shut down. Stone-faced. He stopped speaking with her. Silent treatment for years. After a few years of that impersonal marriage, Grandma drank strychnine."

"Strychnine."

"Poison for killing rats and rodents." Livi nods her head slowly. I know that I'm supposed to lean in and hug her, so I do.

As I hold her, it dawns on me that every family is skewed and skewered in some way. You think you're the only family with a suicide, but you're not. You think you're the only one who's walked in on a still-warm but dead mother; yet, you're not. We're utterly alone, but we're also not. Our experiences are never unique, new, or individualized. Someone somewhere sometime has shared the horrible experiences, whether we know it or not. While it depresses me sometimes that I'll never experience something new in this world—that all people have done it already—it is comforting to know our pain is shared. We're in a collective experience, even though we're disjointed, displaced, and off-kilter because of our physical limitations, like location, hunger needs, shelter needs, and basic survival essentials.

Without a doubt, I'm not the only one who is burdened by not knowing who the fuck I'm supposed to be, or what to do with every moment of the day. I'm not the first to panic every day. I'm not the first. I'm not the last. These drugs—lorazepam, diazepam, buspirone, fluoxetine—they exist because so many people share this experience that a business demographic exists. Yet, I feel I'm the only one. Isolated. And there's something wrong about that fact. There's only one person to blame for carrying this alone. Me.

I decide to finally tell her.

"My mom killed herself. Just like your Grandma."

"Tyler." She grabs my hands. "I'm so sorry." Her eyes soften, moisten. It's not Rachel McAdams or Sandra Bullock or Julia Roberts. This is real. I feel it like a punch to the gut. Real emotion.

I say, "I found her. But it happens. It's happened to so many people. All the time it happens. Right now, someone is probably killing himself or herself. And it's no big thing. It happens and that's it," I say but don't believe. I want to believe it isn't significant, but it is.

"Tyler. Come here." She hugs me tighter, and the smell of piña colada shampoo comforts me like home.

"I love you," she says.

I smile and nod and kiss her on her little button nose.

"How long ago did that happen?" I ask. "With your grandma?"

"Geez, sweetie. It was before I was born. I never met my grandma. Think she took her life fifteen, twenty years after the affair."

Fifteen, twenty year of holding onto a grudge. I can't help but think of how I've been with my dad.

5.

It's dark. Cicadas vibrate. Crickets do their thing. Mosquitoes nip at my ankles, elbows, neck, making me slap myself every few seconds until I become paranoid and start smacking my legs for phantom bites like phantom cell phone vibrations.

"Ten grand, my man," Buehl tells Jordan as he lights off the first firework, sending an explosion five-hundred plus feet into the air. "Each years, ten G's on these explosions in the sky. I gotta go all out to celebrate my nation." He lights another and salutes the sky as it booms and ignites into red, white, and blue streamers that fall softly into the dark sky.

Livi and I lie on her weaved Packers blanket. She rests her head on my chest, and I feel her smile. "Thank you for coming. This holiday means so much to my family."

I smile and nod my head, although it still seems odd given that her Grandpa hates military men.

"And I appreciate you putting up with so much today. They're—God. They're nuts."

"Honestly," I say, "I love it. I just fucking love it."

Keri joins Livi and me on the green and gold fleece. Keri lays her head on my stomach, looking up at the sky, as Livi rests her head on my chest. I've never felt more at home. My family resting on me. The flashing lights in the sky, representing something happening within me, whether it is the rapid succession of Spotted Cows or some change within, things feel okay. The border collie, named Burr (after dueler-politician Aaron Burr) even joins us and curls by my neck. In this moment, anxiety seems idiotic and foreign, as if that was a different life of a different person. Things are new now, and the past seems unacceptable. Here, I lie in a newfound home that renders all escapes illusory and shallow. All of it feels cut-out and cardboard. The hours, days, months I spent with my escapes seem such a waste knowing what could have been. But now, this is where I belong. This is my family. This is home. This is how I'll escape.

"This pup just loves you," Livi says. The dog licks my elbow for half an hour before it runs in circles near Buehl. He lifts the dog with one arm as if she was a sack of grain.

"My little Burr-boy," he says in children-babble. "Daddy loves you, doesn't he?" Burr slobbers over Buehl's face, and they both love it. Buehl's smile is goofy and his teeth jut in all directions—a dentist's nightmare. Yet, it's beautiful in its honesty and vulnerability.

Buehl's wife stands near our blanket sipping on a liter of Diet Coke, and she mumbles, "Loves that dog more than his wife."
Keri smiles at the plump woman, who returns the smile.

"Look who decided to watch the fireworks," Livi says, pointing toward the cabin. Grandpa Higgins stands across the yard. He's leaning against the wooden log siding, his hand resting nearly on the gutter of the roof. He puffs on a thick cigar, and the smoke slithers into the sky.

Jordan stands away from everyone. He's lighting Roman candles and hand-sized tanks that fire off a line of small white explosions. At one point he runs past us with a lit sparkler in his hand, saying, "Like I'm a ninja of the night," making quick and agile jabs and slashes in the cool night air. I imagine this is his one time to let loose and act like the child; in a few days, he'll be back in a military lineup where wrestling your sister's boyfriend is a punishable offense.

The fireworks boom and light the sky, and between the explosions of American flag colors, the stars dot the sky and I try to connect the dots. I'm about finishing connecting the dots in a shape of cat when I hear an unearthly howl, one that shudders down my spine. Keri and Livi's heads pop up, and I jerk up into the sitting position.

Behind us is a blurring line of orange running back and forth, the howling panicked and incessant like a fire alarm.

Mr. Buehl sprints with a limp toward the dog and tackles it onto the ground, patting Burr's tail with his bare hands. He screams for someone to get water. His face is sheer terror. Vulnerable fear and concern. His neck tendons pop through his leathery skin, his near sobbing breathing as he sprints the best he can manage. Keri runs over with a bottle of water and pours it on the dog's tail, smothering the flame with a sizzle. The smell of burnt fur is difficult to express, and I'm holding my breath when Buehl points toward the house.

"You fucker," he screams at Grandpa Higgins. Higgins now sits in a lawn chair puffing away at his nub of a cigar. He plays with a lighter in one hand, and his yellow-tooth smile glows in the dark. At his feet rests a tipped-over tin of lighter fluid.

Keri, Livi, Jordan, and jump between Buehl and Grandpa. Buehl charges Grandpa, who stands up slowly and stands tall, ready to react to whatever Buehl brings. As I stand next to Buehl's pear-shaped wife, I'm disgusted with Livi's grandpa. I'm ashamed by his inability to forget the past. I'm repulsed by his petty, misdirected act of revenge like it'd change anything about the reality of things.

Like Ebenezer Scrooge, I'm repulsed by who I see in that aged mirror.

Chapter Seventeen

Porn People

I lie on the couch with my legs crossed at the ankles. Less than year I've dated this girl, but somehow I have trouble conjuring what it was like before her. I know what Trey and I used to be like, but we're off now. I can't quite get us back to the same rhythm we once had. Interacting with him now feels like a chore, something I have to force and think about—almost plan out. Now we're more like co-workers who catch up when they pass in the hall:

How was your weekend?

Wish it wasn't raining.

Seen the Packer's game?

Yeah. How 'bout them Packers.

But it's worth it. I now have so many new scenes floating in my mind; they make it worth drifting away from a friend. Liv's head nuzzled on my shoulder, her green eyes looking up at me before falling asleep. The two of us dancing at weddings while lonely me— like Grandpa Higgins—sit at round tables, watching with a beer in hand. The way Livi wears my thick grey wool socks when her feel are cold, pulling them up to her tan knees. When she wears my beige Alice in Chains concert t-shirt around the house, clashing with some colorful underwear, maybe purple, maybe pink polka dots. Maybe her mismatched socks are pulled high.

A fading friendship is worth the early morning showers when I'm worn out, and she steps in and hugs me from behind, her hair wet against her back, the water beating down like calm, soothing rain. When I'm overwhelmed with work, classes or insignificant worries, she helps me manage. She helps me think it through by going on walks and runs. She helps me make lists to organize thoughts, and then we cross items off the list, one by one—the black ink spearing the words. She tries to include Trey in so much of what we do, and the way she meshes with him, the relationship they now have—their relationship replaces what Trey and I had. But I'm glad it's passed to someone closest to me. Sometimes I wonder if her desire to help people, to make a difference, is starting with me. By training me, she's easing herself into the role of helping the helpless. Tyler Linley, her first volunteer focus.

I roll off the couch and walk to Trey's room. I knock on the poster-covered door, directly on Jamie Foxx's face (*Django Unchained*).

"Yeah?" Trey says through the door.

"Can I come in?"

"Just a sec," he said, sounding strained.

The door unlatches and he opens it. He's wearing a too-tight *The Boondocks* shirt on which Huey's face is distorted on Trey's rounded gut.

"Sup, roommate?" He says as he gathers his hair and ties a hair tie behind his head.

"I don't know. We should do something," I say, looking into his room, which is chocked full of color: posters over every inch of the wall, collectables lining the shelves of the walls, the huge computer monitor displaying a background of a bikini-clad Kate Beckinsale standing next to a shirtless Hugh Jackman.

"Yeah. Okay. Alright, let's do something." He says this as if convincing himself more and more with each word. "But first, I gotta show you something. Or, I guess, I should probably just tell you."

"Uh, okay." He waves me into his room, and he plops into his black computer chair. I sit on the edge of his bed, my bare toes digging into the soft carpet. Trey spins back and forth as he speaks.

"Well, you know how I rummage through that one website sometimes."

"Which website?"

"The one with the, uh, ex's nudie pics," he says. His eyes dart everywhere in the room but at me.

"The revenge porn websites?" My chest is tense, waiting for what I can already feel.

"Yeah. Well, the other day I was looking through the newer stuff, like from the last year. And I was looking locally, 'cause you can search by state. And in the newer section of Wisconsin, I saw a thumbnail that looked familiar. I didn't look long. Just enough to see if it was her. I'm pretty positive it was." He stops talking and finally looks at me, hesitantly, as if eye contact would shatter me.

Nude revenge pictures posted on the Internet. For anyone to see.

I say, "Are you sure it was Livi?"

Trey nods slowly while looking at me. "There was a message from the guy who posted it, too. Message was pretty . . . harsh."

Lou. The ex boyfriend. The inescapable past. I lie back on his bed and close my eyes. *How do I react?* Depending on which person I'm going to be today, I could go one of two ways, and I have an oddly serene sense of control over it. One option: I flip out at Livi and this piece of shit Air Force fuck. Second option: I curl into the fetal position like a dying beetle and let the past barrage me. Whatever media I next approach will influence my reaction; I mirror the stimuli around me.

I nod my head and stand up. "Thanks, man. I appreciate you telling me."

"Yeah, Ty," Trey says, surprised at my calmness. He looks like he's about to get punched. "I'm really sorry," he says. "I promise I just glanced until I realized it was her. Then I left the page. I saw that there's an email listed if you want to get the pictures removed. I tried emailing, but haven't heard anything back, and I'm pretty sure that—"

Trey keeps talking as I walk out of his room and shut the door behind me. I feel like an ass for walking away from him. He was just being honest with me. All this time, he's been there for me, but I've turned him away. I've ignored and neglected him. He's been ready to return to our friendship, but I've let my indifference separate us. I've let my suspicions grow—my suspicions that he caused the fire that burnt all my supports, my media. I've let a petty mistake grow into something big and ugly, and I hold onto it like it means something to me.

I'm useless.

And he's a stoner. He's not motivated. But he's happy with who he is. He's just himself, and I've held that against him for so long. I should turn to him for help, but he's not what my thoughts revolve now.

I grab my keys from the elephant trunk hook on the wall that Livi gave me. I crank the key in the ignition and back out of the driveway. On the radio LED, 105.7 displays. Alternative rock station. A wacky-voiced DJ announces upcoming local shows, and then Soundgarden's "Rusty Cage" comes on. The harmonizing guitars, the upbeat drums—they have the same effect on me as cocaine. I'm driving fifty down the residential area. I fly past Kennedy's mom's house and continue over the Fox River bridge where the boats float beneath like tiny rubber duckies. Runners stride on both sides of the street, a few in just sports bras, and illogically, I wonder how many of them have seen Livi on that website. What if the picture is making its way through emails and photo-text messages? How many people have saved the images (and videos? *I hope there aren't videos*) to their hard drives, never to be deleted? The thought of Livi being exposed, naked to all these people panics me, as if she was cheating on me, in front of me. *Illogical*, I repeat to myself, but logic is helpless when emotion and fear runs wild. It's like Livi's taken her clothes off and can never put them back on again.

"Rusty Cage" ends as I take a turn going thirty, the half-empty water bottles and half-read books flying around in the backseat. I pull to the curb in front of her apartment complex. I don't know what to say. How does someone react to this? I haven't seen a precedent. I haven't seen it in a movie. I should've watched more movies, read more books.

I'm buzzing her apartment when her voice comes over the intercom.

"Who is it?" her voice says through the little holes on the box.

"It's me," I say. The door clicks open and I leaps up the stairs, three at a time. I'm out of breath when I reach her door. It's open, and she's drying dishes when I walk in.

"Hey, honey-buns," she says. "Why didn't you call? Is everything alright?"

"Well, I just found out something," I say, nearly yelling. A head pops up above the back of the couch.

"Hey, Tyler," Livi's roommate, Brianna, says.

Damnit. I reign myself in. I can't let myself be an ass in front of her. *Appearance. Fake it.*

"Hey, girl. How you been?" I say, poorly imitating a stereotypical black girl.

She answers about her job—yadda yadda yadda—her boss is overpaid; she's not paid enough. Vacation time, yadda, yadda, and she stands up. She's wearing a tight white tank top, and I notice how thin and soft her upper arms appear, and it calms me for some reason.

"Ty, what did you find out?" Liv says, drying her hands on a towel. She's wearing jean shorts that end just a few inches after they start; the pockets hang below where the shorts end. Her pink bra straps show over her shoulders.

Was she wearing that bra in any of the pictures?

"Uh, nothing. Wanna swing by Kerry's Cafe for a drink?" I know Livi will never turn down a latte or a cappuccino.

"You know the answer to that. Let me change into some jeans," she says. She walks to her room, and half her ass cheeks are visible out the bottom of the jean shorts.

In the car, Livi slides a CD into the head deck. A calm guitar arpeggio fills the car—Gustavo Santaolalla—and she looks at me.

"What's up, buttercup?"

"Why do you always say things like that?" I say, irritated by it.

"I'm just . . . I don't know."

I cut right to it: "Trey told me about something he found online."

"Oh, God. It's probably some perverted website I don't want to hear about," she says, laughing as she cranks the handle to roll the window down. "Midgets having sex with farm animals? Pterodactyl porn? Tentacle porn? Nursing porn? Am I warm or cold?"

"No. He found nudies of you on a revenge porn website. Probably posted by your ex boyfriend."

Her mood sobers, and she looks out the window, the breeze ruffling her hair. I drive in circles for a while in the local neighborhood for several songs. The weight of the air grows. She finally looks at me.

"I never thought someone would sink so low."

"Well, he did." I'm trying to be gentle, but the more I think, the more worked up I get. Luckily, the calm guitar arpeggios dictate my behavior, and I'm balanced and steady. Cruise control.

She says, "I don't know what you want me to say. He's a fucking asshole and I'm gonna rip him a new one."

"I don't want you to even talk to him. I want—" I want him to stop existing. I want the world to expunge him from history. This is what I want. I want Leo DiCaprio and Joseph Gordon Levitt and the *Inception* team to go in and erase all memories that this guy existed. I want some *Eternal Sunshine of the Spotless Mind* shit to happen. The harder I try not to imagine the two together, the more vivid the details, the more real it feels; the circus comes to my mind, and it's all Livi and Lou together. To combat the images and scenes, my mind conjures violent deaths to both—vultures plucking out his eyes and lions and tigers converging upon Liv. But my stomach sinks, and I'm repulsed that my brain presented such a thought. I could never wish harm on Livi. Yet, my brain does what it wants. I have no control. I feel sick. I am sick.

Emotionally, my gut says *fuck her fuck him fuck her fuck him*; rationally, I say it's not her fault. She used to see him as she now sees me. She's sent me pictures, and eventually she saw me as she once saw him. Unfair as it is, I'm pissed that she has a past and the past can never be removed from her. But before, at least it was not physical—it was abstract and unreal. Now, it's palpable. Visual. What bothered me is now physically manifested in these fucking pictures. And they're shared with anyone who stumbles on the website. It is not longer the past. It is captured and permanent and here. It is endless.

"How could you have given him those pictures?" I ask, well-aware I'm being a hypocrite.

"Tyler, we were together for so long."

"Which shows your taste in men," I say, immediately regretting it. "I just mean . . . what a fucking asshole. I just—" I'm not sure what to say, and she's not sure what to say, so we just sit in silence as the next song plays. Gustavo's stringed instruments harmonizes in a minor key.

I walk her to her apartment door, and she hugs me. "I'm sorry," she says. I just shrug my shoulders and feign a smile. She mirrors it. We kiss—a peck—and say goodnight. The past is gone, but still has too much impact. Is this my fault or hers?

No. It's not even a legitimate question.

~ ~ ~

I'm in the dark sitting on the ground typing on my laptop. My back leans against the wall, and I debate typing in the URL. The black bar blinks after the *.com,* and I work up the courage to hit enter. The website pops up. Ten rows of thumbnail photos run down the screen. Once you click on a thumbnail, all the pictures associated with that person are visible. Some have a dozen pictures, some only a few. Next to each person is a link that says, "Click here to remove your name." I don't see Livi on the first page, and I don't particularly want to sift through 968 pages, so I scroll down to the *Contact Us* link. There is an email listed, so I write:

Dear Porn-people,

Someone posted private pictures of my client on your website. I'm requesting that you take them down as soon as possible.

Sincerely, Craig Branson III, J.D.

I hit send. I figure using a fake name and adding the law degree will help make myself appear a little more threatening without outright saying it. Throughout the day, I'm checking my email on my phone. Each time, nothing. I get addicted, and I'm twitch-checking every few minutes—ghost vibrations. I make myself a deal; I can check it on the hour, every hour. No more than that.

Meanwhile, I turn on the living room TV, which was paid for with Trey's insurance reimbursement. On HBO, *Schindler's List* plays. I try to forget myself and how insignificant my situation is. I throw my consciousness fully into the movie, like I used to. At several points throughout the movie, I weaken and cry. My phone vibrates, and it's a text from Keri. I think of my mom, and even though I've just cried over a film, I feel dull and vague when I think of Maggie Linley.

Keri ends the text with an "I love you," and I can't bring myself to text it back. She loves me in the sense that I'm dating her daughter, but to bring myself to say it even in a text message is too foreign and uncomfortable. My presence in any situation taints the scene, and I distance myself because of my self-awareness, my self-consciousness. I'm in the movie and watching at the same time, and I'm keenly aware of the clichés, the mundane, and the absurdity of it all—so much so that I can't fully commit to the scene. I don't buy into what I'm feeling or what I'm seeing in myself. I may be incapable of feeling these things just as an actor is incapable of truly being who he feigns to be.

But an actual movie—where I'm fully removed and irrelevant—then I can buy into the fantasy. I fully buy into the false reality. Until it ends. Then I'm left alone with myself, exhausted from the escape, dried out and empty when the credits roll, and the black fills the screen reflecting my vacant image back at me.

Chapter Eighteen

Mistakes

The highway slips beneath my car like a treadmill. I'm sipping from a Dr. Pepper bottle. I gnaw with my molars on the plastic screw-top mouthpiece.

"You know," Olivia McDermott says, "Dr. Pepper is just high fructose corn syrup and artificial ingredients."

I stop gnawing and glance at the label. "But here on the label is says, 'Color'. That's gotta be healthy."

We're heading to Milwaukee, the General Mitchell International airport, where she's flying off to Peru. As the pre-trip meeting group explained to me a few days back—in upbeat unison—they're off "to build low-carbon emission stoves for the economically disadvantaged!"

Cue jumping high-fives.

Sitting in the passenger seat, Livi continues on about my unhealthy drink as if I hadn't said anything. I sense the onslaught of one of her diatribes about the evils of processed food and drinks. Here comes the routine, the facts, and the statistics I've heard it before. Aspartame, worse than sugar. HFCS, worse than AIDS. BPA, lining the plastic bottles (and sprouting man-boobs across 'Merica), and the near-indefinite lifespan of plastics floating in the oceans—the Great Pacific Garbage Patch.

"And," she says, "the aspartame is just sweet poison. It's been linked to blindness, knee problems, emotional problems, ADD, and a billion-zillion other things, which is downright bullshitty by these money grubbing corporate pigs."

"But . . ." I say, "a little risk is okay, right? Life isn't worth living without a little risk. I learned that from you, sugar-tits. I mean, your whole trip is a risk. An adventure. And since I'm too poor and lame—mostly poor—my risks and adventures are limited to in-town late-night cruises and drinking corn syrup and off-brand booze."

"Well, at least it's not diet soda," she says. She sips from her coffee tumbler. Behind her, I have my own coffee tumbler sitting in my backpack's bottle holder. Hers is filled with fair-trade organic Guatemalan or Nicaraguan dark roast. My tumbler is filled with distilled potatoes and grape soda.

"Yeah. Diet takes like ass," I say.

"You know what ass tastes like?" She adjusts the radio knob.

"I'd rather not talk about it. Prison. Rough times. Right after 'Nam." I take another sip, and I'm still drinking the top of the bottle where the Sailor Jerry rum floats unmixed. Livi doesn't know that before we left, I dumped out half the Dr. Pepper in the toilet—like I was pissing—and filled the other half with rum. I hate soda, and I almost shake it to mix it, but I stop before shaking the carbonated drink. *I'm in college. I'm S-M-R-T!*

At the group meeting the other night, Livi introduced me to the fair-trade coffee-guzzlers. Thin-beard types, ones who wear sagging beanies year-round, their twiggy legs shrink-wrapped in skinny jeans. Their T-shirts spout sayings like "Donation Delivered with Love" and "Proud Level-5 Vegan in the House" and the plunging V-necks reveal tattooed activists symbols inked on chests with black curly hairs. Every other dude wore a *reduce, reuse, recycle* symbol inked somewhere on his fake-baked tan. Clichés and blowhards, I'd told Livi. She'd begged me to be nice; these people are wonderful.

Livi smiles at me from the passenger seat, the belt running across her cleavage. A slight shake of her head and the braid over her shoulder falls between the top of her tan breasts. Little baby hairs are visible at her hairline because of the sunlight shining through the passenger side window. It strikes me as precious, and I want to capture this moment in time. A Kodak moment. My mind takes a snapshot.

"I'm really gonna miss you," I say, maybe a bit maudlin. Every day I've spend at least part of the day with Livi or someone in her family. Without her, the days ahead will be vague and directionless. A movie without a script or director.

She smiles again, repeats it back to me. That beautiful smile. Genuine. Another Kodak moment.

Her smile, it reminds me of Zeke's smile—this guy from last night. Zeke has dreadlocked blonde hair, and a goatee tied into two straw-like tails. His nose is pierced like a bull. In a circle around the punch bowl—which I'd spiked out of necessity—they chatted about plans after college. Some brown-ponytail hipster in a hemp sweater had sticks tattooed along his arms that read, "For the Fight Against Breast Cancer" and "Enough Rape!" He explained his plan:

"I'll open a cafe, right? And—I've been really thinking about this, guys—I'll buy a building, like historic, right? Keep it in the town. And we'll load the walls with local photographers and artists' work. We'll sell it, and really, truly, represent the little man. You know? And women. Sorry, ladies. Didn't mean to be sexist."

This Zeke fella next to me, he rolled his eyes, and I couldn't stop glancing at him. Something magnetic in his eyes. He piped up and said, "I don't want to live under any illusions. Just reality. I want to help people, but, really, it's *doing* that makes a difference." He glanced at the future cafe owner.

Zeke said, "Wearing some stickers or t-shirt doesn't do anything. Nothing." He shook his head, sipped from a mug.

Zeke said, "It's all an illusion. Am I right? Anyone see what I'm saying?"

1.

In the car, my phone vibrates on the dashboard and the Samsung jingle plays. I type in my password, 0815 (Livi's birthday, so I never forget), and the email pops up. The sender is listed as "RevengeCS." It takes me by surprise. I open it and read it while occasionally glancing up at the road ahead of me. It reads:

Dear Porn Fan,

Thank you for using our website. Please send a URL of the photos/videos you are referring to. Once you've done that, we have two questions about the pictures and videos (if applicable).

1. Was she under-aged when the photos were taken? If she was under the age of eighteen, we will remove it immediately. We have a zero tolerance policy for underage pictures.

2. Are you claiming ownership of these photos/videos? If so, do you have the copyright registration information? This is a number you received after registering the copywriter. If you do not have a registration number, then you have not registered, and you haven't the copyright for the photos; therefore, you have no claim to ownership. If this is the case, we will ignore any future emails.

Have a fine day.

With passion and grit, we'll take what we can get,

Revenge4You

"Whatcha readin', handsome?" Livi says. Apparently, she trusts my ability to text and drive (and drink).

"Uh, just an email," I say tossing the phone onto the dusty dashboard.

"Well, what kind of email?" Her voice jumps an octave as she says the question.

I take a deep breath and look out at the cornfields interrupted by fenced grass fields where cows graze and lie around near mounds of shit. Above us, an LED sign reads: *Driving Deaths this Year: 102.* Maybe one was Lou. It wouldn't be terrible, for me, at least—maybe it'd end the endless thoughts: I've dreamt of the ex-boyfriend and Olivia romping every night. Against my will, of course. The dream scenes degrade into more vivid and explicit images: a backseat BJ, the windows fogging, a rhythmic gagging; doggy style ass-slapping, red hand imprints fading on her tan ass while the muted TV flashes scenes of *Late Night with Jimmy Fallon*; topless reverse cowgirl, her red-tipped finger nails spreading asscheeks; her moans; her ponytail bouncing until strands unfurl in bunches until the black hair tie falls onto his chest; a money shot.

I do anything to numb my runaway imagination. Shots of rum, vodka. I repeat mantras. I slap my face, shower in frozen water— anything to break the evil scenes flowing through my head. I wake from sleep feeling like I've been cheated on. It takes an hour every morning to the push the super-ultra-uber-detailed dreams to the back of my head where all the other fucked up thoughts hangout like the part of hell where GG Allin and Euronymous and Elizabeth Bathory and Himmler and Ivan and Zedong and Eichmann and Pol Pot run around juggling flaming dildos and slinging strap-ons like lassos.

I say to my love: "I, uh, emailed the webmaster of that porn website where he—your fucktard ex—posted that stuff of you."

She says nothing for a bit. I've still yet to look at the pictures, so I have no clue what to expect. A prisoner of my own skull, I'm bound and shackled.

"Tyler, there's nothing that I can do. It happened and it's over," she says, exhaling like she's tired.

"But anyone can see the pictures. Anyone in the world with access. And people can save the images to the computers, tablets, phones, gaming systems, TV's. They can even print them. Then paint water color versions and post them in art galleries in Paris and France. And I don't get why you—"

"Tyler, I know. But, c'mon." She looks at me with disbelief. "Of all there is on the internet, especially in porn, the odds of anyone ever seeing anything are miniscule."

"Trey found it."

"Well, Trey's a lonely pervert."

I don't object. From the driver's seat, I watch a lifted green Ford with rusted siding pass us. The black-bearded college kid glances through aviators at Livi, and my gut tells me that he's seen the pictures. No doubt he's shown his co-workers who forwarded them to bowling and golf friends. The golf friends mention to their bosses the smoking hot, young local nude girl they snagged pics of. Suddenly, everyone I see seems suspect. Does that guy picking his nose and singing while driving his coupe have nude photos of my girlfriend on his phone? Printed and tucked in his glove compartment? Or worse, in his wallet? Perverts. That old man shuffling with his walker down the street, the fuzzy tennis balls sliding along concrete cracks. Shit, the city bus driver. The mayor. The governor. The president of the United States, clicking behind his maplewood desk in the oval office. Livi, a digital Monica Lewinsky. Everyone. Everywhere. She's everyone's.

My heart starts racing, and illogical thoughts flow like a rushing tide over the dry sand. I focus on the breathing like my doctor, Dr. WebMD, said. Deep breaths in through the nose, out through mouth. But what if your breath is bad? Then you're just blasting ass-breath into someone's face like an air conditioner that doesn't cool air but blasts shit-breath.

The sign above us updates: *Traffic Deaths this Year: 104*

"Livi, Livi," I say as if hordes of half-chubbed men surround the car like Cialis-injected zombie-retirees. "I want you to be mine, and just mine. Maybe that's selfish, but it's true. And those pictures and videos or whatever—they ruin that, that, intimacy." I'm wimpy and weak saying *intimacy*. My voice wilts like a dying flower. "I don't even know what's on the webpage, so it's just a nightmare. A wild, drunken imagination running wild, escaped from the zoo. Monkey's flinging poo at everyone that—"

"Well, what do you want me to do? Seriously? Show you the pictures?"

I shake my head.

"Do you want me to tell you everything? Everything we've done? In detail? Because I remember it all."

I shake my head.

She says, "Then, what? Do you plan on just bringing this up again and again until I'm beaten down, feeling worse than I already do?"

I shake my head and take a massive gulp while my left hand rests at twelve on the steering wheel. My fingers caressing the sticky pleather grooves, I notice how the rum's been hitting me hard the last few miles, the road starting to look glossy like a glazed Long John donut.

"Well . . . fuck. I'm sorry," she says. The swear sounds wrong from her mouth. "Is that what you want? An apology for what I can't change?"

"No."

"Then what?"

"I wish they were off the website."

What I should say: I wish I could change the past. But I don't say it.

"Well, they aren't," she says. "And if you're pissed because I sent naked pictures to *my boyfriend* at the time, then maybe I should be more careful sending pictures to you."

"No, no. That is not what I meant," I say. I try to settle her down, but she just keeps getting more worked up about the whole ordeal, saying how Lou has been texting her, messaging her on Facebook,

Twitter. Instagram, Tumblr (all these sites I don't use or understand). He even dropped by Keri's house to catch up.

"What the fuck," I say. "Why didn't you tell me?"

"Don't get pissed. It's not a big deal. I'm leaving the country, and I'm disabling my social media stuff for now."

"He's got your number still, right?"

"Yeah, he does."

"He'll keep bothering you, won't he? What's he trying to do? Win you back or some bullshit?"

"I don't know, Tyler." She's annoyed and tired of this, but her voice keeps flaring up with anger at random points. "I just can only put up with *so much bullshit*." She smacks the dashboard, and I've never seen her so angry. I didn't know she got angry.

I turn to look at her. Her face is red, barely showing at the top of her tan cheeks, and her eyes are wet. She blinks and a tear forms and runs down her cheek, taking with it a faint line of mascara; for once, she's wearing makeup. She starts to blubber with her head in her hands.

"Sweetie," I say, "I'm sorry." The words sound foreign in my voice; they aren't mine. "I didn't mean to make a big deal of it." I continue to try and comfort her, rubbing my hand on her thin leg, on her shoulder, and I pull up the center console so she can slide right next to me. I wrap my right arm around her. Her face buried in my shirt, I'm looking down at her, kissing the top of her head. Strawberry-vanilla shampoo. I'm telling her how much I love when she uses that shampoo.

She's crying, wiping her button nose on my shirt. Her rare makeup smears on my shirt. But I don't care. Once she's gone, my clothes will be filthy. I'll have no one to impress. I'll be a useless slob until she returns.

Then the thought pops into my head. Zeke again. Something about him struck me as he and I spoke. "Comedy's your thing, right?" he'd said to me. Something supportive oozed in his voice. So much so that I imagined myself into him. A knee-jerk thought, I tried to put myself in a physical homosexual situation with him—all the nitty-gritty details, but I couldn't stomach it. I'm attracted to him in every way but sexually. But something about him, his presence, it attracted me, and I instinctively thought of ways I could join the crew on their three-month Peru trip.

But I can't. I'm not like them. I'm not like other people.

There in the car, poking out of Livi's pants pocket is her cell phone, which glows and vibrates, and in my peripheral, I see his name pop up.

Lou.

The message reads: *It'll be weird not talking to you for so . . .*

I'm staring down at the phone and I'm saying, "What the hell, Livi? Why when we're together?" I'm saying, "Why can't you just fucking ignore his stupid douchey fucking asshole messages? Why is it that—"

A foursome of deer flashes out from behind a red barn to our right. In a single-file line they leap onto the road-treadmill. My feet don't react, but my left arm jerks the wheel to the right. The front left of Betsy the Buick crushes the last deer's legs, and it limps off into the bushes. The headlight glass litters the highway.

Heavy breathing. Silence. Calmness. I let Betsy continue under cruise control.

"Are we—are you okay?" I ask Livi. She's bracing the dashboard. I'm not touching the gas or the brake. Too shaky. I've spilt rum and Dr. Pepper all over myself.

She nods, looking at me helplessly. Her green eyes are massive. Anime-massive. Again, she rests her head on my shoulder. She's shaking.

"I'm sorry, Livi," I say. "You know . . . you are, without doubt, the most important thing in my life. I promise I'll get over this and stop bringing it up. I know it's not your fault. I'm immature." I continue on, kissing her head in between words. "And I just wish—"

Another deer darts out. My foot crushes the brake; my left arm cranks the wheel; the Buick spins. We're now inside the Gravitron. My loose cheeks are pulled against the headrest. The shattering glass is a blink—the windshield falls like confetti inside the car. A brown deer leg stabs through the shattered window where Livi had been sitting—in the passenger seat. Now her body is against mine, inches from the twitching leg. The car is covered in dissipating smoke; the smell of burnt rubber wafts. We've spun 360 degrees, ending in motionless silence, facing the road ahead.

I stare straight ahead and feel the silence. Heavy. The leg twitches then stops.

Just silence in the smoking car.

She's dead.

I can feel it.

Beneath my arm, she's dead.

My right arm wrapped around her head. Not love. Not comfort. Now, it's a headlock. The thought flashes with my blinks like a neon sign. Tucked under my right arm, I know she's dead. I sit there shaking, staring ahead at the yellow-lined blacktop that rises and disappears into the sunny horizon. I cannot look. I cannot breathe.

The deer leg kicks wildly until the he rolls off the hood and limps away, falling onto the road. It twitches, moans, bleats, and collapses into the roadside brush.

I stare straight ahead. I don't breathe until I hear silent sobs and the warmth under my arm. Feeling her heartbeat against my shoulder, we sit there shaking with the glass littering our laps like bloody confetti.

2.

From the tow truck's front seat I watch the deer try to scoot on its side off the road. His comrades ditched him. Livi cries into her cell phone. The tow-truck driver stares forward, his forearm resting on the steering wheel, feigning disinterest in my hysterical girlfriend who sits between him and me.

Tyler wasn't paying attention, she's telling her cell phone.

Tyler smells like booze, she's telling Keri.

Tyler and I, this can't work, she's telling her mother.

I'm afraid, and I almost died, she says through clenched teeth.

He drinks and drives and doesn't care about my safety or his own, she hisses.

I just want to get the fuck out of this country, she screams.

The driver and I both tense. He glances to me through his sunglasses, saying with his glance: *Settle her down. You got to comfort her, man. You can't guilt her for her past, bud. She isn't your girl; you don't own her. You don't deserve to, yo. You're an inhuman robot sometimes, and—shit—would it kill you to love? To just be supportive? Who gives a shit about past mistakes? You ever wonder why she don't talk to you about important stuff? Why she never says nothin' about her dead dad? About her past? Wonder why she only listens to you? It's a one-way relationship, dude. And, you, my man, you're the parasite. Keep at this, you're going to be part of her past, too.*

That tow driver's glance, I understand what he's trying to say to me.

Chapter Nineteen

College Graduation Party, August Something

This morning, a coconut sat in my mailbox.

Below the USPS stamp, in erratic black felt marker, it reads: "From your Livi-loo, I am so so so missing you. So is all the crew!" A sloppy mess of illegible Sharpie signatures are spattered on the underbelly of the desiccated coconut. A huge *Z*, like that of Zorro, overlaps part of Olivia's *ia*, including the heart that dots the *i*. The *Z* is followed by an *eke*.

Running my dry fingers over the coconut's ridges, I smile like a big, goofy, doofus. I almost say, "Aww, golly shucks," when I meet the eyes of a neighbor. His newspaper is in his hand, his slipper-feet shuffle along; his blue robe trails behind like a lame cape, and I get the knee-jerk urge to spike the coconut like a football. *I'm tough. I don't care.*

According to the ever-trustworthy Internet, you can send shit in the mail. Not literally. But stuff like a pillow, a potato, a brick, an inflated beach ball, or a coconut. Simply write an address, adhere postage, and let the USPS's magic elves work their underappreciated magic. So I learned a thing today, which puts me ahead of most in terms of daily success.

Cradling the coconut like a football, telling Keri about the coconut, I'm getting in her way while she cooks. In her kitchen, brussels sprouts steam on her stovetop. Tilapia and salmon sizzle in

side-by-side pans, bits of lemon pepper and red herbs peppered
throughout. A vanilla Funfetti cake bakes in the head-sized oven.
Ground turkey is sprinkled with yellow peppers. Miller Lite-soaked
brats bask in the outdoor grill's heat, the smell wafting in through
the open patio door. An animated odor finger curls, urging me to
come closer. Through the black lines of the oven door, my eyes read
the blue frosting, which reads "Congratulations! We Love You!
Summa cum laude!"

n my gut, my chest, a warmth grows, expanding like a balloon. I
see all Keri is doing: the streamers sagging between taped points on
the ceiling, the dunce cap paper party hats, the white smile she
beams as she works for me—this all expands the balloon within me,
and, like when you get too high, you freak out, you worry that it's all
too much. I want Keri to sit down, relax, sip some wine, and stop
spoiling me.

"Keri, you do too much. *Please,* can I help? At all?" I know I
can't. I can't cook. Can't clean. Can't do kitchen-y things. Outdoors,
Dad and Jordan and Uncle Steve, his red beard now down to his
tits—they all chop wood, grunting and talking about hunting like
cavemen. I can't do those things. Can't fulfill either gender
stereotype, so here I sip yet another seven and seven, doing the only
thing I'm good at. Boozing. Escaping. A feeling flows over me as I
sip the drink. Comfort. Easing into myself.

"You just relax. It's your special day," Keri says. She winks, an
emerald eye flashing at me. A glint. Her bangs curl like a cursive
"C" over her tan forehead. She wears a skin-tight long sleeve shirt,
like thermal underwear with ridges, and I refrain from running my
fingers over them. She brushes her sunburned button nose with the
back of her arm, and the apron moves with her arm, and even
through the apron, I can see her figure, sculpted each morning at the
gym: Stairmaster, elliptical, yoga, Kegels (probably?)—all the things
taught to Livi to keep her in shape.

I suggest I help with this and that—cooking-like things I can't
do. But we both know I can't. Cooking was neither valued nor
practiced by Mom or Dad or by their unfortunate offspring.

"Actually, these onions," she nods at the cutting board littered
with white onions. "You could chop these up." I almost approach
from behind, reach around her, but I wait until she clears out.

I'm sniffling, bringing down the handle of the knife over the onions, leaving the tip of the knife set on the board—just like Keri said—slamming the base of my palm into the knife handle, when I catch a whiff of her perfume over the onions. That spicy Jennifer Lopez fragrance line Kohl's and Wal-Mart have been pushing. *Emit the sexy!* Eighty bucks for six ounces. I think of Keri's bedroom; in it, her bed is surrounded by ointments, creams, lotions, bronzer, makeup, eyeliner, all brand-name . . . more than a single woman could use. On a single-mother budget, a mother working as a nutritionist freelancer, one without a college degree—it's all more than she could afford.

~ ~ ~

Yesterday, mid-seventies, she wore a thick coat. She explained: "I get cold easily. Poor blood circulation. Ask my father." The blinding fluorescent supercenter lights whitewashed the aisles filled with sweatpants-clad shoppers pushing brimming carts, yanking children's arms. "Go grab some tartar sauce," she said, popping the top off a coffee tumbler. I trotted off to fetch.

Like a good boy.

~ ~ ~

"Tyler, buddy, you helping with the graduation fixings?" Jordan says, turning his body sideways and sliding past the patio door. "Doin' your housework, like usual?"

"I was hoping," my dad says, his V-neck revealing too much of his chest. "*We* we're hoping you'd come join us, shoot some guns. Brought the '32 NYC police-issue revolver. Spick-and-span, ready to go." He finger-shoots at his new wife. Dad's brown eyes meet mine, widened and hopeful, like a kid. "I told Toph *you* had first dibs." Dad smiles, as if this would make me happy. "You know, you being the older bro and all." *Half-brother,* I want to say.

Dad's eyes soften as he smiles. His dimples indent, making his beard's grayness flicker a darker black. Something in his face makes me feel warm, yet disgusted at the same time. Dad hadn't told me he was flying in for my graduation party. In fact, Keri hadn't even told me I was having a graduation party until she drove me to the airport—*It's a surprise!*—to pick up Dad, Sherry, and Toph.

Sherry and the young boy follow behind Jordan and Dad. They slide the patio door open and step onto the scarred linoleum floor.

"These two were out there, Ty-guy," Jordan says. "A kiddo and a chick. But not you? Don't be a bitch." He steps toward me and crushes his bruised knuckles into my shoulder. "Even Bugsy-Babes here shot a few off." Jordan smiles, good-natured. The skin around his eyes loosens and pools—so odd to see him smile authentically. His black widow's peak recedes, and his gum-dominated smile flashes like a latent monkey-threat.

"I'm an awful shot," Sherry says, bashful, her head shaking. She wears a low-cut V-neck sundress, her freckled chest drawing my eye before I divert it. She's my stepmother, after all, despite this being the second time meeting her. My brother . . . half-brother . . . he stands there, staring wide-eyed at me.

I stare back at Toph, and he glances away. The kid is six, almost seven now, and he has my straight blonde hair. It's sticking straight up, naturally, as if it had rebelled against gravity. This kid has future in modeling. Easy money. He's got Sherry's eyes, almond and with flare, a coy wink; Toph has Dad's jaw, defined and set apart from his cheekbones, high and mighty. Like a goddamn action hero.

I answer my father's request. "Dad, I'd rather shit blood," I say, smiling with my mouth, staring with my eyes. Keri turns from the stovetop and looks at me like I've imagined a mother should.

"Tyler William Linley. Did I hear what I think I heard?" Her thin fists rest on her slender hip, on her hourglass body. I try fighting back a smile, all bashful. I'm proud on a visceral level of her motherliness. A thing we all pretend to not want. I want to be in trouble.

"Sorry, *Keri*," I say, wishing *mother* came out instead.

Dad takes a visible deep breath and plants his index finger and thumb in the pits of his eyes.

"Do you mind if we talk?" He says with his eyes clamped shut. "Just you. Just me. Outside. The two of us. It's been too long."

"Oh boy, I'd *love* that, Puppah!" I say, my mouth with a stupid smile and my fists waving in the air.

1.

Keri and I, we had met up in the cat-food aisle, near the stacked fish aquariums. Near lonely 69-cent betta fish. "Because it's in the middle of the store," she'd said. I returned to Keri, her cart nearly identical as before, but now with ground turkey ensnared in a seaweed-green package.

"No luck," she said, her coffee tumbler top twisted atop again. Her hair looked a bit frizzy, like she'd been in a high-moisture room. "But," she said, her eyes fluttering, confident in herself. "I did get a fill-up of some nice Peruvian dark blend from the cafe."

Livi's adventure popped into my mind; I wondered what, at this moment, she was doing. Like a true romantic, a docile idealist, I pictured a lime-green, sweat-stained T-shirt clung between her chest, her nipples subtly poking through. Her Neil Armstrong-esque stamina being tested. Livi's vague catchphrases of optimism were probably echoed by her American cohorts alongside the worn-thin Peruvians.

Then I wondered: this supercenter has a cafe?

~ ~ ~

Outside, under the dancing trees, the breeze whistling through them, "Ty," Dad says. "I'm sorry. You know that, right? I've always been sorry." He stares at me for long time. A few gray hairs sprout like a time-lapse video; his face changes expression; his eyebrows grey and furrow; they arch; his eyes plead, and, I swear, drops of moisture collect. He says some words in there. Generic. Cliché. Nicholas Sparks lines. Janet Evanovich bullshit. Romantic comedy. Bad Adam Sandler movie. Dad immediately ages and becomes frail in a sequence of snapshots.

Weak. That's how they'd describe it in military-land where terrorism lingers in the shadows cast by bearded men. It's weak to show that emotion. A bead runs down through his beard like water down a dried plant. It's laughable. Not pathos. Bathos, Pops. Learned those two words in college. Paid for by me, not the military. Pathetic, Puppah.

"I did everything I could," the coward says. "I couldn't control your mother—and me leaving, that was out of my control. I did what I thought was best. Your mother's paintings and her art directed her and what she did. It directed who she was drawn to." Dad's eyes are wet. Jordan might say, "Crying like a pussy, *hu-hehe*," while his gummy smile flashes. Maybe he might wait for a slap-high-five.

It's all weak. Pathetic and manipulative.

It's a father for you.

2.

"Let's get going, hun," Keri had said, pulling at my sleeve, her chest heaving. Monkey see, monkey do. My heart was racing, the pink Brisk and vodka flowing through me, letting the circus thoughts come to mind: I imagined her every position I'd seen Livi, beginning with crawling on all-fours, nipping at my lower lip. Keri, at that moment, was my Livi. Olivia McDermott, a girl gone.

There's no way Keri couldn't see my heart thumping like in the cartoons, but it was pounding away. *Thump, thump, thump*— speaking for me.

"Ty, you know something?" she said, her eyes lapping mine, I swear. Swear to God. To Buddha. Zenu. Anyone else. Name 'em, and I'll swear. Her eyes lapped mine.

"What?" I said, dumb, idiotic, shallow, gullible. Well, me.

"You are the best thing that's happened to my family." She brought herself close to me. Piña colada shampoo. And, I thought, faint honey-crisp apple. Maybe she ran out recently. Was it Livi's? Or Keri's?

She said, "Since I lost Thomas, things have been as you can imagine." The blood flows away from my peanut brain. "Take my cart, my card. Pay for this stuff while I grab a few more things. I'll just use my other card," she said, her wintergreen breath lingering on my face, replacing any smell in my hair follicles, my eyelashes, my tongue. It replaced my logic.

I nodded, and I was nodding as I paid her bills with the green EBT card, pin 1208, as she said. 12/08: my birthday. I smiled. I couldn't help it. Dumb, goofy smile. A dopey, aww, shucks smile. A shithead. Well, me.

Good thing, I thought as I slid the green card, she didn't see my heart jerking out of my chest at the sight of her. Thump, thump, thump . . . . What kind of guy eyes his gal's mom? What kind of cheap-shot shithead wants to be with a woman double his age? Double his wrinkles? Double his fucks? Triple? Quadruple? *What comes after quadruple?*

Keri was gone, off grabbing her things, and I waited by the automatic sliding door with a cart full of her groceries swathed in cloth bags. Groceries, swathed like baby Jesus, I stood there, thinking of lines to bring her to my apartment for a movie. These were drunken thoughts. Drunken lines to get the woman or idea I loved to spend more time with me. The woman I could never have. The idea I wanted.

3.

"Ty, look at me," Dad says. "Tyler William Linley," he says, trying to pull a Keri moment. "Look at your father."

I scowl at him. But I'm weak and softened by his familiar face. Nostalgia dilutes the liquor I've been guzzling like the Hulk with water after an anger binge.

"I cannot be held responsible," he says, carefully, each word tiptoeing over a landmine. "I cannot be held responsible for your mother. She did as she wanted." He stares at me, his hot gaze warming my face like a heat lamp. He gulps the drink glistening on the wooden chair near his thick denim leg. I recognize it. The smell. The look. Sailor Jerry and Dr. Pepper. Like father like son.

"She killed herself," he says, "because of her own actions, Tyler. She killed herself not because of what I've done, but she killed herself because—"

Like an inbred troglodyte, I bite down on my jaw. My canines scrape until one cracks. The jolt echoes up through my jaw into my ear canal like a crunching car crash. My spine, it shudders and curls. Cliché, Dad. Excuses, Dad.

"Because she couldn't live with a coward?" I mumble through cracked Clint Eastwood teeth.

"Because she couldn't live with *being* a coward," he says, his brown eyes burning through me, courageous and strong. My returned glance is weak and pathetic.

I throw my body at his. He braces like a sprinter, his hands in front of him, Mortal Kombat-style. His legs are planted, one ahead of the other. My hands squeeze at his prickly neck to see if can touch my fingertips to one another by squeezing until life stops spouting out his crew-cut head. Ten to fifteen seconds, and he'll be unconscious. Carotid artery will stop sending oxygen. I've read it again and again in an anger-induced research binge. He'll be out cold. Anything after that, it's all in my court.

Primitively, an American ape, I hope his brains gush out the top of his head like a popped pimple.

4.

"No, ma'am. We have it all," the white-haired manager had told Keri. His nametag greeted all shoppers: *Hi, My name is CRAIG*—as if he had no ability to introduce himself. "All of it, ma'am, I promise. It's captured on our closed-circuit system, which has been proven again and again to be perfectly accurate." CRAIG nodded, and nodded until his pale whiskers grew into a tattle-tale grin like a proud hall-monitor. The hip-adhered walkie confirmed, *Yes, a woman, curled brown or black locks, tanned, perhaps from south of the border, by the looks of her skin.* "Ma'am, you will need to join me in the back room," CRAIG said, reaching for her tanning-salon-brown arm.

"Get off me, you drone," she said, juking into a spin move, her leather purse wrapping around her thin waist. A waist my ape brain wished to grab.

5.

Dad's dry hand is stiff-arming my face, his fuck-you finger digging into my eye. It creates puddling blackness and shooting pain to the back of my skull. Dirt is in my mouth from his thumb, sand grains crunch between my teeth. He mumbles, strained, choking, something about Bradley. Pastor Bradley. Mom. Pastor. Mom. Pastor.

Jordan yells, "Hey," again, again, as he chokeholds me. "Hey, hey, hey," I'm hearing as the edges of my eyes darken.

"Can't blame the pastor," the voice says. The voice says, "I left to save what little we had left. She chose him, not me. I never wanted you to be angry with her," the voice says, as the blackness closes over my vision like a tube TV shutting off.

6.

In a dream, we're all mesmerized by Zeke, who is dressed like Zorro. Trey, Caleb, Keri, Livi, and I—everything Zeke says, everything he does, we follow and laugh. We wish we were him.

My head throbs when I wake. Like a hangover—something I haven't fully experienced in months. Maybe years. Maybe since the day after Trey and I took swigs in Ledgeview Lane's restroom stalls. If my dad knew of our early drinking, if Dad knew of my thoughts of

Zeke, what would he say? Nothing. He'd say it all with his eyes. That look.

Dad's gone when I come to, my contacts dried and blurry. In a foggy daze, I wander around the living room, my socks static-y with the carpet, electricity lingering on my finger, the smoked jerky smell curling into my nose. Keri waves me over to the island kitchen counter. On the wooden countertop a drawing sits. The corners slightly curled, the paper faintly yellow, a first-place blue ribbon is still pinned to the upper corner. It's a sketch of a seal, complete with faded grids and shading cast by a third-grade hand. A yellow Post-It note reads in all black caps, in Dad's writing: *THE SHADING IS BRILLIANT. STILL IMPRESSES ME TODAY.*

7.

My ass cheeks heated and sweating on Keri's leather seated Audi, Wal-Mart had disappeared in the rearview. Our slow getaway. "I'm so embarrassed," she had said. "That asshole employee, he got this all messed up."

Keri's a horrible actress. She has the looks, but not the acting ability.

I knew. I may be emotionally blind, selfish, detached—sure—but I can tell a cover-up. I know a bad acting job when I see one.

Keri picked, tucked, and pocketed anything to keep things even. Or maybe to tip things in her favor in a world of inequity.

Her husband, dead. Never smoked a day in his life. Inequity. Unjust.

She practiced petty theft. Little by little, she'd snag things to prolong her beauty. Lotions. Creams. Conditioners. You pay money for that stuff, and the second you use it, it's gone. It's evaporated. Money lit on fire. But free—that's worth the risk. Beauty prolonged without the cost. Wal-Mart, Target, all those big chain stores; after all, they do more harm than good, some might say. (Livi's documentaries would certainly say so.) Keri, stealing like a Robin Hood staring in the mirror watching herself age: the lines, the sagging, the yellowing, the inevitable downfall of it all.

And I knew. This made me feel comfortable in the Audi with her. I felt comfortable with her secret. Knowing her tendency for theft, I knew her better than Livi. I understood Keri. I felt it. It was a brief connection without words. A look—that's all we needed. She lied verbally, but she knew I saw through it. We had a wordless understanding.

People are fucked up. It's normal. It's human. And, Keri, accidentally sharing this embarrassing secret—it makes me love her. She with her secrets. Me with mine. Keri Leigh McDermott (née Higgins), the women who squeezed out a girl to whom I've said the words "I love you"—this is now the closest person to me.

Chapter Twenty

Night at O'Malley's

"This is hysterical," Keri says, "This song." She giggles, covering her Malibu-and-Sprite-filled mouth with the back of her hand. "I lost my V-card to its dumb rhythms." Keri slaps herself on the forehead. "Ugh, God, looking back it's just . . . hilarious." She laughs and bobs her head, standing and dancing a bit in front of the bar stool. She sways her hips.

On the eye-level stage, a dread-locked bassist thrusts his head back and forth like a rooster. The lanky pig-tailed lead singer gags herself on the microphone, the gurgling amplified in tune with the bald guitarist's simple, repetitive punk solo over the bass lines of a Clash song. Keri's curly bangs are bobby-pinned with the hair swoop framing her smile.

"Keri, you know I was worried today," I yell, fighting to be heard over the drone of the bass and the high-frequency tings and twangs of the guitar. "With my dad."

She winks at the bartender and points to her empty glass. He nods and mixes another pink drink.

"What do you mean?" she says.

"Worried that he'd, you know, try and hit on you. Get with you." I hesitate for a second, but the alcohol loosens the words and they fall out. An alcoholic laxative. I don't say I was preemptively jealous he'd get to be with you.

She laughs as the bartender set the V-shaped glass in front of her. The bartender plops a cherry pierced by a plastic sword.

"Bruce is married, honey. And even if he did, you think I'd just spread 'em wide, welcome *your dad* into the promised land? *You*, my handsome fella," she touches the tip of her index fingernail to my nose. "You never need to worry about me. *You* just need to worry about you." She giggles. "Yourself. You need to just worry about yourself, Ty-guy, you goof." She waves her hands at the bartender. The bartender hovers over. His jaw line is firm, set in stone. His face is that of business in the most un-businesslike setting. Maybe he's a young owner.

Keri says, "Barkeep, you spikin' these? Tryin'ta get a young girl white-girl wasted?" The bartender stares at her, the forty-five-year-old mother of two using phrases like "V-card" and "white-girl wasted" (whatever that means). The bartender glances at me, at her, and rolls his eyes. The spindly chest hairs poke above his blue V-neck like black weeds. *What is with all these fucking V-necks?*

"Ty-guy," Keri says, "whychon't you ever wear the V-neck *I* got *you* for *your* birthday? Your dad wore one today, too." Her fingernails grab and work their way in through the top of my collar, the tips scraping gently against my skin. "It looks so good on you, right *here*, on your neck." Like a lanky spider, she walks her fingers up my neck, her nail tips tickling me, until she grabs my earlobe between a thumb and finger. She starts rubbing for a bit with one hand, drinking with the other. I do all to fight off purring like a cat. I love ear rubs. A mother knows these types of things.

"Seeing your father today was . . . weird," she says. "You two look so alike. He's like a cleaned-up, gray-tipped version of you. Aged like good wine." Closing her eyes for moment, she yells, "Hey, barkeep," three times until he rigidly walks to us. Her pink drink sits untouched, the three ice cubes floating. "Gimme some good wine. Oldest, best aged you've got." That lanky finger, it's curling her hair, like a teenager curling a telephone wire while lying atop of a pink bed. That finger, I can't stop watching it move through the air.

Grabbing the round Leinenkugel's coaster from the wooden tabletop, Keri fans herself. "It's hot, Ty. It's seriously so hot in here." Undoing the top three buttons on her tight long sleeve, she turns away from me, staggering toward the jukebox, away from the band's drum solo. She staggers away from the neon Miller Lite signs, the red *O-P-E-N* that cycles through each letter, then flashes the whole thing. She walks away from the car lights zipping past the wall-sized window.

"Keri, don't waste your money," I say, following her as she digs in her purse for money to slide into the jukebox.

"I'm sick of this off-brand punk wanna-be jamming; I'm in the mood for some *jazz.*" She wiggles her finger in front of her face, and she dabs her fingernail on my nose again. "Boopsies," she says, rolling up her sleeves, undoing another button, her tan chest rising and falling with her rapid breaths. No doubt, a push-up bra is working wonders, but the image has a stunning effect on me. It would on you, too.

"Keri-berry," I say, all cutesy-like, hoping to catch her attention. "You can't play the jukebox right now. The bartender turned it off because of the band. You'll just be wasting your money, and I know you don't have—"

She cuts me off, those long fingernails sliding through the hair on the back of my head; those fingers pull me close to her, her eyes wide and emerald. Those lashes flower out toward mine like a sunflower to a sun.

Her wet open mouth, it vacuums onto mine. I taste the pink, the strawberry of her drinks. I feel the bumps of her tongue slipping into my mouth, running along my chipped canine tooth.

What the shit, my mind says, *what the damn shit,* it says again, and my heart is skipping across the sidewalk, avoiding all the cracks that'll break Mother's back.

There's a hint of mint, too. Wintergreen mint. And it floods over me like a shiver, and Livi is in front of my closed eyes. As fast as she pops into my black vision, she disappears. The tongue is gone from my mouth. I hear Keri's voice, high-pitched, then calmer after the first few words.

"*I'm sorry,*" she ekes "You, your dad," she exhales and grabs the Leinies coaster, fans her face, looks past me to the bartender, as if to check for judgment. "My God, Ty-guy, I've had a wee-bit too much to drink, couldn't we say that?" She says this in a sudden Irish accent, her eyes closed. The thin age lines run down her eyelids, partially masked by skin-toned mascara.

No, I want to say, you've had the right amount. You're in the mindset I've been in for so long—this cloudy drunken confusion where sober reality is a dull punctuation between pill-induced serenity and alcohol-filtered screenshots. Moments of poignancy, as I interpret it.

Reality, as it should be.

Her eyes closed, she says, "You know, your dad and I—" she nods slowly, much slower than the spastic flailing of The Clash cover band clattering throughout the room. "We, just the two of us, we went out back while you were out. Knocked out, or passed out, or . . . asleep. While you were sleeping." She puts her hands out, those long fingers, her palms raised up. She says, "He's a good man. I know you don't believe, or want to hear it, Ty-dye."

In my mind's eye, dye is spelled die, and I can't recall how else to spell it.

I'm shaking my head, my face scrunched together like how De Niro or Redford might play it. She says, "I know what you're thinking about him. But you're wrong, and you've *been* wrong. You've been wrong about him, and about mostly everything." Eyes blinking rapidly, fast as frames in a Charlie Chaplin silent film, she says, "He's better than you can imagine."

Looking at my reflection in the mirror behind the bar, the old scene pops into mind. I'm seeing myself in the bathroom mirror, my image fogged up from the dissipating bathtub heat. In the grand scheme of things, it was a common scene, really. A Lifetime Network movie scene: a pale, hairless arm slung over the tub edge; faint red diluted pink in tub water. A candle or two flickering, distorting shadows, making them dance like mocking demon ghosts. Something like that—my memory's been mixed and altered with fictional scenes. I'm not sure what's a movie scene or a novel scene and what's the scene I saw. The smell, though, I know that. They forget that part in movies, when they turn life into a two-dimensional reality; they miss part of it. The memories and feelings that linger on your nose hairs. The movies miss everything that pops into your body when a breeze carries a faintly familiar scent that brings a feeling rather than a thought. An urgent feeling of loss.

"He tried hiding all of it from you. That's the only reason he seemed so . . . ." Keri yawns, blinks her eyes. "You know what I mean."

I nod my head. Insensitive? Distant? "Dickish?"

She shrugs. "Sure." Eyes closed, she seems vulnerable, tired. Drunk. "But, Ty, my God, the things I'd do to get a man like your dad." Her lips pucker, a round pink hole. "They don't make men like him anymore," she says, opening her eyes, squinting, scanning the bar. She glances at the bartender with his gelled hair and the carefully manicured beard organized to appear careless. So calculated and vain.

"I have no fucking clue what you are talking about," I say, annoyed, and suddenly not drunk enough. I order a few shots dumped into orange juice. The bartender doesn't even watch the glass as he pours; instead, his eyes nod inside his head as he listens to a blonde bombshell. She wears yoga pants and a sinewy white scarf that highlights her store-bought tan.

Eyes closed again, Keri exhales, says, "Your mom, she was an art teacher, right?"

I nod. "Third grade."

"Religious school, right? With daily devotion and Jesus in math and science class?"

I nod.

"Yeah, she was getting with the Pastor Bradley. Real artsy guy." She's bobbing her head to the spastic drumbeat, her thin hand striking air cymbals. Her eyes pop open, big glassy emeralds. "Tyler, I'm sorry," she says, reeling, realizing, and wishing she could smack the rewind button.

But my eyes are blinking now, the silent Charlie Chaplin film reeling in front of my eyes. Her pink mouth moves, mouthing *sorry's*. Her lanky fingers run down my arm. The goosebumps rise, like a basketball's bumps.

Trey's dad, Pastor Bradley. The one who hosed me down in freezing water for jumping naked on a bed. The goose bumps, the shriveled penis, shivering hands cupped to cover my shame. God's representative who spoke of the law, the gospel. Pastor Bradley, now, the indirect murderer.

"He—your dad—called his supervisor, or whatever military people call them," Keri says. "And he asked to be moved. Err, relocated. Figured he could blame it on the military. If he left the area, your parents wouldn't have to divorce right away, and you'd hopefully never ever know what happened. He didn't want to hurt you or your mother. He just wanted you to get through high school without hating her. He figured: what better than to request a common Marine relocation? Just doing his duty for his country. And the divorce would seem more natural after the time spent apart." She sucks down on the straw, her eyes following me, the pink liquid sucked up, the straw lit pink, liquid disappearing.

"Don't shoot the messenger," she says. "I'm hazy on what he exactly told me, because he was all secret-y and whispery when he telled—told me—but I think the preacher and your mom both liked art or drawing or something artsy-fartsy." She shakes her head, waves the bartender over again, her pink drink gone, the pink-tinted ice cubes shrunken and withered. "Wow. I sounded really old there." She sips at her aged wine, tasting the gray hairs of a father. "Your pops, Ty, he was just hiding your mom being a who—" She stops, a deep breath in, deep breath out. The strawberry and winter mint smell fills my nose. "Your mom gave this priest-pastor guy an ultimatum, you know? Like, 'Leave your wife and be with me, or else we—we're done.' And this religious guy, obviously, he picked his wife, leaving your mom out in the cold. Your mom didn't take it so well. She'd already lost her hubby. Your dad wanted you to finish high school without too much problems, you know? He left for you. He took the blame so you could be clueless for a bit. And once your dad was gone, she also lost her pastor-lover-boy. She musta figured she was too old to pursue her art or travel anymore. Not enough money, not enough time . . . all of those excuses. And I'm *so sorry that it happened*!" She looks at me, suddenly realizing the information she's dumping on me. She wrings her wrists, and sips the wine, clanging the glass against the smooth wood tabletop. "But Bruce said the Pastor-guy didn't want to tear apart his own family, his church. Scandals are never good for religion."

God doesn't like the bad PR.

PART 3

Chapter Twenty-One

Riding a Downward-Spiraling Double Helix

The morning light tints my bedroom a dark blue as I pull the cap off a new Sharpie with my teeth. On my worn-out flip flop, the big toe bit out long ago by a neighbor's yapping Yorkie, I finish my love letter. Drawing the letters in all caps, I sign it, *Your best friend, your studly stud-muffin-sexy-buns, Tyler William Linley the IV.*

The fourth added just because it sounds fancy.

In my letter, written on my USPS-stamped, foot-fungus flip-flop, I tell Livi how I miss her. How I miss that piña colada shampoo, her horrible impressions of me (*I'm Tywer, and I don't wike bugs*). I write how I miss her lazy back massages. God I miss them—a Matchbox car driven all across my back, up and over my shoulder blades, down the ridges of my spine, over my *lil butt* (her words), until tickling my feet. I tell her in capitalized Sharpie letters that I can barely wait to see her face, hear her voice, and feel her hug—all those things that'll hopefully make me remember her again. To remember her more than just little lovey things we do together and places we've gone side-by-side. I tell her as much as I can fit on my corn-chip-smelly flip-flop. The flip-flop makes the USPS postal worker named Carrie giggle, her chins jiggling as I slap a few dollars on the counter.

To Livi, my love, my soul mate, my better half, I leave out the part about her mom kissing me.

I leave out all my ape-brain, drunkenly animated fantasies.
I tell her I love her.
It's better than sending a Hallmark card.

1.

I steal a movie from Trey's room this morning because the pressure of silence builds, and my heart is thumping in my ears, waiting for a break from reality. I do all to not think of Trey's father.

I cry while watching *Eternal Sunshine of the Spotless Mind.* Full-on blubbering: watery snot drips down my blonde mustache. It trickles into my chin-hair, which has sprouted into a weed-like, inch-long beard. I catch a glimpse of myself superimposed in my bedroom window that looks out onto our neighbor's lily flowerbed. My eyes are red and swollen. My cheeks above my beard look shiny and greasy, not wet. I stop blubbering, embarrassed by the sight of myself. By the reality of myself.

As the credits roll, I'm betrayed by this movie, my first movie in months. Jim Carrey is just pretending. Kate Winslet isn't anything like Clementine. These are fake scenes. False reality. It's all a joke, and I'm a fool for believing it. They don't believe it. They love the paycheck. They believe the paycheck. Money talks, said AC/DC. The world agrees, says me.

When Trey wakes, I look at him. At his red eyes, his undefined chin. In his face, I don't see any of Pastor Bradley. I just see Trey. I think of Pastor, and I want to be mad at Trey. Instead, all I see is my friend . . . my friend that might have burnt all my possessions to ash. My friend that might *not* have burnt my possessions to crispy black outlines of what once was. My friend who's only supported me—a one-way relationship.

Has he ever done anything wrong to me?

More importantly, have I ever done anything right for him?

I ask, "Whatcha got going on today, guy?"

"Just, you know, living the dream," he says. His frazzled, static hair swoops across his face, and, thanks to Keri, I notice split ends curling near his bare, thick shoulders. *Time for a haircut*, her voice says. Trey's friend Caleb walks out of Trey's bedroom, rubbing his neck.

"Sheee-it," Caleb says. "Them blow-mattresses kill your neck."

Caleb's been crashing on that blow-mattress—named Queenie by Trey—for a few weeks. It feels like a relative staying with you; you have to be polite, courteous, generous, and all that unnatural bullshit. Seeing his close-cropped jet-black hair and tan Pop-eye arms against Trey's and my paleness and blondeness must be like seeing the dark of the night right before a flash of pale lightning.

Those two are in sync like Livi and Trey were. Two peas in a pod. Ernie and Bert. Peanut butter and jelly. Adam and Steve.

Pastor Bradley might appreciate that one.

Time is the all that gives Trey and me the advantage over Caleb and Trey's friendship. But while I'm out working, taking classes, going through the motions of my days, Caleb and Trey spend days clicking through the Internet, thumbing PS3 controllers and yelling into Turtle Beach headphones.

The days blend together as one continuous consciousness with no break. I rely on Trey for my medication, but the pills are kept under a close eye by the pharmacy; only so many prescription refills are allowed in a given time period, so I ration them out. Two, maybe three a week. That's it. Otherwise, I've built in my mind a list of options that assist me medically.

One wonderful advantage of Americans' fear of germs is the use of hand sanitizer. The smell is so common that I can leave a water bottle's cap off when it's filled with vodka and Sprite because people just assume the smell is hand sanitizer, not vodka being drunk in the middle of the day. So, even when I'm sitting two feet from a college dude-bro I'm tutoring, I can sip a mix drink from a plastic bottle and no one thinks twice. Or if they do, they don't say anything. Thank you, germophobic America.

2.

"Bush, man, that president," Trey tells Caleb and me. "His administration pushed fear more than anything. Terrorism," Trey says in his George Dubbya voice. "It can be anywhere, anything, or *anyone.*" Trey squints his eyes and points to the ceiling fan. "Terror!" he yells, and walks away into the bathroom, shutting the door behind him, leaving Caleb and I standing in the kitchen. "Terror!" we hear Trey yell from the bathroom, while pointing at the toilet, I imagine.

"Trey's always pitching old news," Caleb says pouring coffee grounds into Trey's Keurig. Trey's muffled, strained voice comes from the bathroom.

Trey's saying, "Germs and bacteria, it's all bullshit, too. Bush admin, man, they just made it all up to sell more—" Trey pauses and strains, his neck veins probably popping out, a sweaty thick forehead vein running down between his eyes. "Hand sanitizers and antibacterial soaps."

Caleb nods his head, pouring water into the coffee maker. "And Haliburton, man. *Shee-it*. Talk about some fucked-up B.S. going on within that nepotistic White House." He turns around to me, points at me as if he just remembered to ask, he says, "How'd you like *Eternal Sunshine*?"

From behind the wooden door, Trey says, "And my dad, man, he was all down on his knees for Bush. Heard he was even pitching Bush and hailing him in sermons. Talk about shady. And not just slim shady; we're talking like big, girthy, veiny shady behavior."

"I give it two thumbs up," I say while flipping two thumbs in the air. "*Eternal Sunshine*, I mean. But I kept thinking, actors have to be the most fucked up people on the planet to be manipulative and dishonest. So willing to pretend to know what it's like to have Downs or CP or an IQ hovering around room temperature. You know? Or they're willing to pretend to have experienced the Holocaust or something horrible. Or even for Jim Carrey to not act insane and twitchy and spastic—that's as crazy as anything."

"My dad," Trey says through the bathroom door, "he even met with a church member who was supporting some politician who supported free universal birth control for college students. Ma told me Dad claimed 'It's sinful, heinous, disgusting and irresponsible. Sex is for procreation.' And I told Ma, 'You guys have one kid. What, you only have sex once?'"

Caleb flips the switch on the Keurig, and it begins bubbling, the old-people smell of coffee filling the room. "Nah, man," Caleb says to me, ignoring Trey. "The way I see it, actors understand the human experience better than anyone. That's their job to understand what it's like to be someone else. To jump into the mindset of someone who's going through the genocide of her people, or to assume the identity of someone with a dinged-up brain, like in *I Am Sam*, that

flick where the fella has something wrong with his thinker and
somehow has a kid."

I nod, but think of Sean Penn, the "humanitarian" and
philanthropist who beat the shit out of Madonna.

"Fuck Sean Penn," I say.

"Hey, man, he's done plenty of good for plenty-a people," Caleb
says, noticing a faint red stain on his white T-shirt. He licks his
thumb and rubs it. "Pretty sure he's the ambassador of goodwill to
Haiti or some shit. That's good stuff, dude."

"Yeah, right. Real easy to preach it, to get sent overseas to meet
with some people over coffee with no risk to yourself. Easy to wear
the 'End Hunger' long-sleeve fleece while you beat your girlfriend
or cheat on your wife. Just like John Lennon, man." I point to the
cartoon version of Lennon's mug on Caleb's mug. "Dude was
hateful and abusive, yet he sang hippie-dippie songs about a world
with no religion and everyone just living for the day. Anarchy, man."

Trey's voice rises over the sound of running water in the
bathroom. He says, indifferent to whether or not we're listening:
"Dad asked me to fix his computer once. He had too much malware
and pop-ups making his mission work online impossible. Know
what his history was riddled with? Every Monday, he visited dirty
nurse websites. Sponge-bath hand jobs, semi-harmless stuff like that.
I tried not to look in too deep, but curiosity, you know? He had a
bookmark folder named *NORP*. 'Porn' scrambled into a different
arrangement. It looked like he actually paid for at least one of the
websites, too. As if not paying was a sin or something. *Stealing
porn! For shame!*"

Trey opens the door, drying his hands on his *Los Pollos
Hermanos* t-shirt, also stained faint red in splotches.

I say, "Spaghetti last night? Or lipsticked cross-dressing?"

They ignore me.

"Trey," Caleb says, pouring a steaming stream of black coffee
into his John Lennon mug. "Penn is the Haiti Goodwill-for-men-and-
peace-on-earth-embassador, right?"

"Fuck Sean Penn," Trey says. "You never go full retard."

And that makes me giggle and feel all warm, like I won a prize at
Six Flags and that prize is a big cuddly friend. Trey dressed like
Winnie the Pooh, a friend agreeing with me. *Trey* must *go as Winnie
the Pooh for Halloween.*

Caleb smiles, says, "Aww, look at you two. Great minds, huh?" He steps toward Trey, grabs his cheek and jiggles it like a grandma would. "You're just so totes adorbs!" Caleb says in a high-pitched lisp.

Trey stares at him blankly. "You touch me again, and I'll bang your sister and mother. One, then the other. Then your dad, just to make a point."

"My dad's dead," Caleb says, stopping the mug going to his mouth.

"Shut the fuck up," Trey says and gives him a purple-nurple.

3.

Days and nights evaporate like this. Some are memorable. But most, like this interaction, are forgettable and insignificant. These moments feel better with an altered mindset, one that breaks the crushing weight of time and reality.

A poem I once read pops into my mind as the vague wasteland of the afternoon settles in.

Charles Baudelaire. I have no idea how to say that name, but I look it up on the Internet and wish I could abide by his poem's advice. But without the wine:

Be Drunk

You have to be always drunk. That's all there is to it—it's the only way. So as not to feel the horrible burden of time that breaks your back and bends you to the earth, you have to be continually drunk.

But on what? Wine, poetry or virtue, as you wish. But be drunk.

And if sometimes, on the steps of a palace or the green grass of a ditch, in the mournful solitude of your room, you wake again, drunkenness already diminishing or gone, ask the wind, the wave, the star, the bird, the clock, everything that is flying, everything that is groaning, everything that is rolling, everything that is singing, everything that is speaking . . . ask what time it is. Wind, wave, star, bird, clock will answer you: "It is time to be drunk! So as not to be the martyred slaves of time, be drunk, be continually drunk! On wine, on poetry or on virtue as you wish."

4.

As an audio book of something by Nietzsche plays in the background, I ask Professor Nelson if I can audit (for free) a class he's teaching on Dostoevsky. I'm standing there in his office, trying not to breathe in the smell of corn-chip-sweaty socks dipped in cigarette ashes and urine. He whispers to me, his coffee-cigarette breath overpowering my hand-sanitizer-vodka breath: "Only if you speak up." He lights a cigarette and inhales. He exhales out the window cracked next to him. "You can come as much as you want. You can write and read as much as you want. You can do whatever you want, long as you gimme your two cents *once* a class. That's what it'll cost you."

The alternate option is filling out paperwork through Admin's bureaucratic cesspool, which will try to charge me $500 to simply sit and listen in a class and not get any credit. Pay to take up space, which is something I've done for free all my life.

I shake Professor's sweaty palm as he switches his cigarette hand, his eyes squinting behind those round John Lennon glasses. He says, "I'm glad you came back for this course. Fucking—" he yells just this word and glances at the ceiling light, "school only lets me teach a Dostoevsky course every three years. Not as important as *How to make a dollar profit off a cancer patient* business course. You know, those fucking," he yells the word again, glancing up to the harsh yellow fluorescent light panel, as if the administration is listening. "Those asshats, that chancellor. I can only imagine how many di—" he keeps rambling, unleashing his thoughts as we walk to his classroom where I take a seat in the back behind a room full of college students who clack on laptops and poke at phones.

"These asshats," he says, pointing to the PowerPoint picture of the chancellor projected onto the white pull-down screen. "They just want the cash flow, *riiiight?*" He bends to pick up his dropped purple marker, flashing his asscrack to the class. "They look at enrollment, graduation rates, GPA, professor-ranking websites produced by you dolt-dope dinkuses, and *that's* what they think determines value in academia. No! Learning should be painful, with emotional struggles and internal dialogue and debates. It isn't measured by reductive numbers and scores and multiple choice or agree-disagree bubbles. Pain, discomfort, uncertainty, questioning— these things mark true progress. It's all about the struggle, *riiight?* Those in power make the calls without any understanding of learning, of passion. No, they're empty. Dead." He pauses and cracks a window at the front of the room. He lights a cigarette despite the *No Smoking* sign hanging at the room's entrance. "Dead just like the buried they trod upon."

Students poke at their hidden cell phones as he continues. "They're making the real money," he says, pointing backward at the projection of the chancellor. "Isn't that right, Mr. Linley? One of my stars from days past, gone, like a distant star . . . but I still react to the delayed, dead light." No doubt, Nelson thinks of me in high school, and all the time I spent with his brilliant daughter, Marla. Marla and I—another relationship built up. I let it break down.

"Right on, Professor Nelson," I say, not sure what he meant, but still mentally prepared to speak. My head is too swimming to care what the class thinks. Most are on Myfacetagramingbook, and they don't care what Nelson and me think. I raise my BPA-coated plastic bottle, filled with Barton's plus 0 percent juice "orange juice" and regurgitate: "Society is filled with capitalistic pseudo-intellectuals who are propelled through the academic system by rich parents bent on the reduction of a dynamic, multidimensional academically oriented learning environment." I'm shaking my head, ashamed of those people in power, also a bit ashamed of my regurgitation of what I've read. What I've been told. No original thoughts bounce around this skull. Just echoes of smarter men and women's thoughts. My regurgitation is so unlike a bouncy ball whipped by Randy Johnson into a spiraling stairwell skyscraping the ozone layers.

I just act out the movies I've seen, the books I've read, the people I've watched. I am the amalgamation of clips, of behaviors. That's all I am.

Nelson knows this. How long has he known this?

Regardless, I finally fully feel and know it.

Nelson smiles, nods, and points his purple marker at me until he drops it again. He bends to pick it up, flashing his thick, hairy plumber's crack to class. I smile as the class averts its sedated gaze out the window to the idling green city bus, which reflects the scene back at them; the reflection offers them a flashing moment for reflection in which they see their faces lit blue by cellphones. But instead, I think they're reminded to check for updates.

It's the first time this semester they make eye contact with the bushy crevice, but I don't avert my eyes; I appreciate, even enjoy, that Grand Canyon-esque crack. Being here as Nelson challenges our limited, undeveloped understanding of the world—this is a privilege. So much of our lives flies by unchallenged, and here stands a man willing to challenge our thoughts with Sparknote versions of philosophers' thoughts. He has dumbed-down ideas for us. We, the reality-TV culture. So much of our time is spent eating free lunch-plan meals, driving a mommy-bought car, fucking using free condoms and reading subscriptions to *Cosmo*. I'm guilty, I know, but being here, I'm proud, like I'm Nelson's assistant, his hype-man, ready to jump into the conversation when the thought bubbles above the students are blank but for tumbleweeds rollin' on through. If just one student in the class starts to think, I can at least *feel* like I helped, regardless of how my mind's been muddled by my medications and escapes. I may be starting to understand why Livi is off in Peru.

5.

At the back of the classroom, I'm daydreaming a scene where Professor Nelson and I sit at a bar, knocking back straight whisky shots and chatting about the nature of being. His hand rests on my shoulder like a proud father. He catches me up on his daughter Marla—how she's off at an Ivy League school and is engaged to a med-school student. In the daydream, a Packer game is playing on a small black-and-white TV, the bartender is asking us by name if we'd like another, and Nelson bellows, "Put it on my tab!" slapping me on the back.

Breaking me from my momentary reality, I feel a thud on my temple. I exhale a dumb *Buh?* and a whiny fart ekes out onto the hard plastic chair.

My eyes dart around the room until they meet sky eyes outlined by flipping eyelashes, tips dabbed black. The girl smiles, shakes her head, and rubs her finger on her nose, mouthing the words *brownnoser*. Brushing her red bangs away from her face, her slipper feet are resting on the empty chair next to her, and a notebook rests on her yoga-pants legs. The notebook is filled with bubbly pink letters—her notes from the class. I feel a visceral surge of optimism.
How do I react? Totally unlike Ryan Gosling or George Clooney, maybe I could jump on the desk, a la Jim Carrey, tuck my head between my legs and squawk like a parrot, repeating *brownnoser, brownnoser,* all while letting out more whiny eking farts. It worked

for Jim Carrey and got him Jenny McCarthy, that *Walking Dead* chick, *and* that *Mad Men* chick. It got him the *Eternal Sunshine* gig, too.

Instead, I just smile, sip from my plastic bottle, shrug, and mouth the words, *What can I say*. She flips a notebook page, jots something down, and holds it up just below her chest, the low-cut white T-shirt catching my eye before the bubbly pink letters ask me if I work at the Writing Center.

I nod.

She nods and goes back to taking notes as Professor Nelson lights another Pall Mall near the cracked window. I finish my plastic bottle and pull a full one from my backpack. I wonder: with other girls, am I supposed to act like I do with Livi? Or will that get me slapped or arrested? Then it dawns on me: I'm not sure how to behave around females anymore. So, maybe I ought to hit the gym; it's best that I'm in good shape, because ripped and handsome dudes don't need the same personality as flabby or ugly dudes do. The gym will be my next stop.

Chapter Twenty-Two

Progression and Recession

I'm pedaling on a stationary bike as the TV in front of me plays an ad for a truck. A thick-shouldered quarterback stands in front of the chrome grill. He says, "You can't stop working, so neither should your truck." The scene cuts to the quarterback, shirtless, off-roading in a mud field. Brown goop sprays in slow motion as his veiny forearms flex and jerk the wheel. His abs—oiled and slick—stay tight the entire voice-over, in which the quarterback narrates: *It's good for fun, too.* He then explains the hemis and payloads and the gargantuan size of the truck's balls.

Two college-age girls in yoga pants ride bikes next to me, both gazing at the same channel, the same commercial, the same oiled six pack.

For me, or Livi, or Keri, the girls next to me, or that girl in Nelson's class—I want to get ripped. Toned. I want people to ask me if they could wash their clothes on my washboard abs. I'd let them, of course, and maybe I'd start charging, like a mobile laundromat. After I save some cash, I'd buy a truck that runs on bald-eagle carcasses and Native American tears—like a true American. In the nearest mud field, I'd off-road shirtless, oiled and tanned, with a bed of sexy lingerie models pillow fighting and giggling. On the sidelines, a horde of men would wish they were me. Their faces would contort in disappointment, their heads shaking.

A few weeks of going to the gym, careful eating with accompanying drinks, and I'm looking trim in the mirror. Still skinny, but the definition clearly shown because of a lack of fat.

One day, I chat with a body builder. He's a giant chest muscle with creatine-bloated tyrannosaurus-rex arms too big to rest on his sides. His legs are tiny and wobbly compared to his upper-body, and his little shiny head sits between two bulbous shoulders. He looks like a distended Stretch Armstrong. His raccoon eyes watch me, and one of his meaty nubs shakes a protein drink as he tells me his routine to stay *huuuge, bro.* Every two hours, he eats a chicken breast. His alarm buzzes at midnight, two A.M., four A.M., *and* six A.M., so he can roll over in bed to his nightstand mini fridge. Squeezing the peppered chicken out of the clear plastic bag like a candy bar, this guy chomps away, then rolls over, back to sleep. Every morning, instead of bacon, Reese's Puffs, a bagel, or coffee— instead of these things, he gulps nine egg whites from a glass. Rocky style. Montage style. Buff dude-bro style.

He says, "My man, building mass and keeping it is just like a relationship." He tells me this after he learns my girlfriend's been gone for a few months. "Gotta keep building it up, feeding it, changing up the routine so your muscles don't predict it. You gotta keep 'em on their toes. Except with working out, ain't no bitches to deal with, you hear?" He laughs a guttural *uh-ha-ha-ha* and points to the bench press next to us. "You need a spot?" And with his shrunken testicles hovering above my face, I push and grunt. All around the gym, I pull, sit up, sit down, yank, hover, oscillate, stretch, bend, thrust, and squat until I'm standing outside the shower, dripping wet. That after-workout feeling, endorphins flowing through the body, it's like a weak benzodiazepine. A healthier one.

Standing naked next to this meathead, I tell this chest-muscle man, "Working out is better than booze and pills."

He laughs, slaps me so hard I drool on myself. "Life's all choice, bro. Choose this." He flexes and gives me knucks. "See you tomorrow, my man."

I do this workout stuff again and again and again until I skip a few days. I've earned a break, right? I drink a bit. Lie around a bit. Read a few books. Stare at the white wall.

In the mirror, after only a couple days, I see the progress fade away like a time-lapse progression. Every week of work is lost in a day or two of not working out. Like Livi and I, our relationship. Every day I don't see her, I forget a bit more about her and how we were with each other. It fades away like water spilled on concrete beneath the sun. Each day I skip the workout, progress disappears. Popping muscles relax back to skinny, less-defined blobs. The whole workout process loses its appeal to me. Like dusting, it all feels futile, despite my desire to be positive. It's just in my genes. Like the people before me, dead, buried, rotted. They're in heaven, hell, purgatory, or just in the ground as worm food, decaying into what will eventually be something we eat. A decayed body, eventually nutrition in the soil for an apple tree to grow. The corpse processed into apple trees that we'll eat and digest to keep us going. We just feed on dead people's rotted bits. Who you were and what you believed—that determined where all these people ended up, Pastor Bradley had told me. But it seems they all just end up in a supermarket.

Before Mom died, after a kid ate a bottle's worth of pills, Pastor Bradley told me: "One of Paul's epistles to Corinth says, 'If any man defiles the temple of God, him shall God destroy; for the temple of God is holy, which temple you are.' Only suicide cannot be forgiven; it shows one has given up all faith in God. We can hope and pray for him, but his thoughts the moment of death are what hold his eternal life."

Hours later Pastor Bradley switched roles, to Coach Bradley. He stood behind me, adjusting my batting stance, propping my back elbow up. "Keep the elbow up so you don't drop your back shoulder and hit a pop-up, like last game. You've got the skill, the power." He made his hands into fists. "But keep that elbow up, just like *this*. 'Kay, T.W.?" He smiled, his straight-brim Pete's Radiator Service hat askew on his sunburnt forehead.

"Last-second forgiveness," Bradley—in his Pastor role—later said. "It's the only way a suicide could result in heaven. Like Judas, after he betrayed Christ for money. He went out into the field and hung himself from a thick tree. If, at the last moment, he begged for true forgiveness, he may have been saved. It is the moment between the leap from the bridge and the impact of the river beneath. Could have been that Judas was saved because he asked for forgiveness for betraying Jesus, thus allowing himself and all humankind to be saved . . . ." He laughed. "Judas's weakness saved us all."

Coach Bradley—wearing his red hat—would tell me, rubbing his cleated-toe into the dirt, "Squish the bug with your hind leg, just like *this*." I'd do it, looking up at him for approval. "Perfect, bud. Now, you want to work on flipping your wrist; flip your wrist, *just like this*, and you'll get speed behind the bat. That's where the speed comes from."

In the church narthex, I wore my little kid tux. Pastor told me, "Last-second forgiveness is possible, like with Riley Pancratz." As the funeral ended, the mourners shuffled out, and Pastor Bradley bent down to me and explained: Riley, who was too young for a license, drove his dad's camo Hummer 3 out into the dense woods beyond Stark's Marsh. Under his breath and beneath the classic rock radio, he repeated the steps of loading the gun, ensuring that the safety was off. Riley ranted how another back surgery, another year of that stilting, disfiguring Quasimodo back brace beneath his T-shirt—it wasn't worth it. Another medication, another reason for classmates to rip on him—*retard, arf-arf*—the kids'd say, mocking his impulsive twitch. Pastor Bradley explained: kids would mock his flailing arm movements, which were unpredictable to Riley. Riley repeated to himself how it all was godless, pointless, cruel, and without an end unless he made his own. "Riley Pancratz," Pastor told me, "he could have asked for forgiveness in that last moment."

I could see it in my mind's theatre: Riley, hyperventilating, with salty tears caked on his face, his throat swollen and dry. Riley, setting the 30-30's butt on the dusty dashboard, he was unsure how to reach the trigger. Adjusting a few times in the front seat, maybe he had set the butt on the foot mat. Maybe he decided to cut and pry away the trigger guard with an X-Acto knife and pliers. The arm-length ice scraper propped in the backseat caught his eye—glistening gold like an item of importance in a video game.

At least that's how I couldn't stop imagining it went.

Pastor told me, "They all could have asked for forgiveness. In that endless last moment, like a day-long dream, they could've said sorry for the one unforgivable sin. I have faith in this."

Standing behind me, Coach Bradley said, "Huge thing, T-Dubs: Get your legs and hips behind the swing. Let your legs do the work, just like lifting a heavy box." Coach placed his freckled arms on my striped baseball hips, and he twisted me. "Just . . . like . . . *this*," and my arms follow-through, propelled by the momentum created by my hips and legs. The bat snapped quickly around from the twist of my wrists. My wrists cracked, and in the follow-through, he pressed against me and it felt like a hug. Coach waited a long time before letting me go.

Trey sat at home playing *Tiberian Sun* on his computer. Meanwhile, I stood here with my pastor and coach, and I don't know what Pastor-Coach thought, but I know he wished something. He wished something were different.

I sat in my li'l kid tux across from his massive desk. He said, "You could lead ninety percent of a full life, completely pious, dedicated, and loving, but if you waver in the last moment, you may suffer endlessly."

After letting me go, Coach frowned in his straight-brim hat. "We, uh, should do some field work," he said to the team, all dressed in red Pete's Radiator Service practice uniforms. Our shirts tucked into our black-striped pants. The tops billowed over our belts. Our ears were tucked under our oversized hats.

Coach said, "First, though . . . go run the bases. I need a moment."

Think of it: Years of offering ten percent of your income and your Sunday mornings. One day, things start looking a bit bleak; you lose a job, your husband, you get rejected by your artsy-fartsy lover, so maybe you lean back in your car seat. Maybe you park in the garage and let the car warm up, the vents breathing hot air on you. The exhaust coughs and billows gray smoke that engulfs you. You get light-headed as the Eagles' "Hotel California" fights to be heard over the heater's blast. Don Henley sings, *You can checkout anytime you'd like, but you can never leave.*

Then, it is finished. All done. All that faithful work, undone.

But if, in that light-headed pre-death delusion, you say sorry. . .

Like Mom's dad, Rodney, who was ordered to run to the local shop to buy arsenic for the rats. Mom wouldn't tell me what happened to Grandpa. But Pastor Bradley did: "His wife had yelled at him from atop the kitchen counter, her knees quivering, just like in a '50s sitcom: 'You getchyour hiney in gear,' Grandma Raymond said, 'and kill these dagnab filth-mongers.'" Her lanky finger shook while pointing at cartoonish holes in the walls.

Pastor tells me Mom tucked her sleep pants into socks so rats didn't climb up her pants when she slept—something she still did when I was growing up. Grandpa Rodney—which is what I'd call him if I had ever met him—he bought three bottles of arsenic. He smiled and offered small talk to the pig-tailed teen running the check-out. He drank the bitter mixture of arsenic and gin. And there on the living room couch, my mom found him.

They buried him unmarked and only his wife and daughter showed up to the funeral. These details—none of them were told to me by my family. They were all relayed from my mom to Pastor to me. She never spoke a word of any of it to me. Yet I ended up in the same position she had with her father. Was that her plan?

Looking back, now I know why Pastor knew these specific details. Details Dad probably never knew. Details Mom had shared with a pastor during confession, at church, at home, in bed. She shared her life with a coach and lover and pastor and artist.

"Linley, coming your way," Coach Bradley yelled, tossing a ball in the air; he slapped a rocket grounder at me. I squatted, butt down, chest out, glove down, just like Coach said. Blazing, the hardball hit the pitcher's mound, took a goofy bounce, came flying at my face, the red laces blurring together like a spinning globe. At the last moment, before it crushed my face, I snow-coned the hot ball in the top of my leather mitt. I turned and side-armed it to our tubby first baseman.

"T.W., nice snag, buddy. Saved yourself at the last sec there, didn'tcha?" He laughed and slapped another ball at the next kid.

Chapter Twenty-Three

You Got What I Need

It's two in the morning. On my bedroom stereo, I hit play. Biz Markie's "Just a Friend" vibrates everything throughout the apartment.

"Girl, you got what I need, but you say he's just a friend!"

Every night, as we're about to crash, I play the song. Same Biz Markie song every night, just before bed. Today is day number ten of doing this.

The next night, after watching Trey and Caleb play Sega Genesis's *Golden Axe*, I'm in my bedroom. Trey and Caleb are in Trey's, doing whatever they do. I don't play the song tonight. After a few minutes of silence, I hear two toneless voices singing:

"Girl, you got what I need, but you say he's just a friend, say he's just a friend."

~ ~ ~

Next morning:

"Check it out, Ty," Trey says, clicking at his computer. "Photos from your lady-friend's trip." Trey and Caleb sit on a piano bench in front of the upgraded seventy-inch monitor.

I squeeze between them, suddenly wondering about the status of my breath and armpits.

"Oh, boy. That dude!" Caleb says, pointing at the screen where C.J. the Frat Boy stands in the foreground of a group picture. In the background, Peru's cool-colored Sacred Valley cascades down until it's out of the frame. C.J.'s arm is wrapped around Livi's shoulders. Livi is wedged between C.J. and Zeke. Her head is resting on Zeke's shoulder. Her brown curls are unraveled across his tank top.

Trey hovers the cursor over the Facebook tag of C.J. "That dude's real name is Marshal Morrison. Holy shit. He has a name. And a fucking nerdy one." Trey laughs, a derisive Nelson Muntz laugh, and I'm staring at the tan shoulder on which Livi's head rests. Her white smile and emerald eyes show legitimate happiness, as if this is where she has always belonged.

Caleb says, "Wow. I haven't seen him in forever." He pokes the screen, the pixels puddling. "Zeke and I played on an intramural ultimate Frisbee team. He wore that same damn tank top with the gray stripes running up and down. He said it was his lucky shirt for getting lucky." Caleb glances at me, his eyes inches from my face. "He meant, like, getting lucky in ultimate Frisbee, Ty." Caleb laughs, pats me on the back. "Your face got all white there, which is amazing. You went from polar-bear white to purgatory white."

Trey says, "Eggshell white to Antarctic snow. But truthfully, my God. That man is handsome. Look at that jaw line." Trey taps the screen, right on Zeke's face.

"Gotta admit that," Caleb says. "I've always told him he's mastered that thin, scraggly, I-don't-care hipster beard."

"Ch-ya, man. I bet he *loves* PBR," Trey says.

"He does," Caleb says. "He collected a whole deck of PBR bottle caps and hammered them into a wooden coffee table."

"What a cool, handsome guy." Trey looks at me, and I'm not amused. He pushes me and Caleb off the piano bench. "Lighten the fuck up, Ty. We're messing with you."

Caleb pushes me off him, and I yank Trey off the bench. His ass thuds against the linoleum, rumbling the house.

Trey says, "Don't worry, guy. Just because this Zeke guy is handsome with his chiseled jaw, interested in environmental issues, and he likes fashion and PBR—that doesn't mean anything. Ty, you're still, like, really, you know, cool and stuff or whatever." He pushes me and works my head into a headlock. He is not wearing deodorant.

"You guys are pricks," I struggle to say from within the headlock. I try to show that I'm bothered yet that I can play along; I want them to rip on me, just as I want to rip on them. It's part of being accepted and being normal. It's part of being the third wheel of this duo that'll never be a trio.

Caleb is back on the piano bench, clicking through the new Facebook trip pictures. All of them are new to me, a Facebook-less American.

He cycles through the pictures quickly, probably searching for more bikini and shirtless pics. I struggle to wriggle out of Trey's heavy headlock.

"You fat fuck," I say, as the huge monitor flips past a picture of Livi on Zeke's back. She's on his back, a piggy-back ride—a Zeke-back ride—with Machu Picchu's ledges and hills providing background for their giggling faces.

"I'm not fat," Trey groans in a Cartman voice. "I'm big-boned."

I knee him in his nads, and the next photo on screen cuts my breath off. At Zorritos' Beach, white sand all around, a circle of travelers recline in beach chairs under sporadic umbrellas and makeshift awning. Bikini tan lines, hairy chests, flower swimsuits, martini glasses, Speedos—it's all jumbled into the picture. But clear to me, Olivia's arm is entwined with Zeke's, the tan arms blending together as one, each hand holding a pink-tinted martini glass. Livi's bikini is one I've never seen. Her stomach looks flatter than I've seen. Her smile is whiter than I've ever seen, and it is spread from ear to ear.

I thought they were in Peru to build ovens out of buffalo poop and slap houses together, adhered with love and care.

I thought they were rescuing endangered animals. Feeding the starving. Saving the children. Slaying childhood obesity. Ending breast cancer. Reviving the dodo. Thickening the ozone. Toppling the fat-cat corporations. I thought I knew what is going on.

I'm an idiot.

1.

Each night is filled with a dream of either Livi and Lou or Livi and Zeke. As if each social media picture of Livi and Zeke was a seed, my dreams germinate and morph the photos into vivid nightmares. But with nudity . . . porn nightmares. Pornmares (which sounds too much like bestiality).

Livi cheats in the dreams. Videos and photos of her and Zeke and Lou circulate my friends and family; they are posted on websites, completely vivid, real, and I'm the last to know. When I confront her and whine at her, she's indifferent and annoyed that I'm bothered. The melatonin pills I swallow to sleep make the dreams lucid, more vivid and memorable than daily life, with its predictable routines and unremarkable events. These dreams, bit by bit, replace whatever Livi was to me. The real girlfriend that I once spent my days with is pushed to the back of my mind, where a noose lassoes the relationship and the floor falls out beneath. I'm forgetting her, and she's becoming the idle daydreams and night terrors that my pessimism brings to life.

Viscerally, I feel what she is doing.

2.

"Wait. You're going to share her?" I ask Trey and Caleb.

They look at each other for a moment. They nod in unison. They're sitting hip-to-hip on the piano bench in front of the huge monitor.

"Just click, click. Then they ship her to America?" I say.

"Sort of. Little more to it, but yeah. Then she's here to stay," Trey says.

"UPS? FedEx?" I say.

Trey says, "Whichever is cheaper." Caleb laughs.

"That's fucked up. She'll arrive here and be with both of you."

Caleb nods, says, "We're both clean, you know?"

"Eh, I don't know about you, Caleb," I say. "I've seen you with a wide range of males and females, and, once, I swear I saw you with a good-looking bulldog. But Trey, you're definitely clean."

"Sure am. Saving myself for the right one." He winks.

"You had so many chances in high school, man. It still baffles me," I say.

Caleb says, "I get it." He gestures something with his hand by his mouth.

"I don't," I say. "Girls loved you back then, but you shot 'em all down." I remember all the phases he had in high school where he claimed to be bisexual or gay or something—it seemed to change every few months. I assume it was just a phase, but, still, he turned down every chance he had with girl. And since living with him, I've never seen him with a guy or a girl. It's as if he's asexual, like an amoeba.

Trey smiles, blushes a bit. "Again, I'm waiting for the right one."

"For the right Russian mail-order bride," I say.

"Yup. The right one." Trey clicks on a new tab and types in a new mail-order spouse website.

"I have first dibs, though," Caleb says. "Because I'm older and more experienced with both teams."

"That's not fair, man," Trey says, and they launch into an argument. Caleb asserts he doesn't want Olga Putin to have her first taste of America ruined by a confused, big-boned vagina-virgin. Caleb makes air quotes with his fingers when he says the word "virgin."

"You know, one day you'll be at work, and she'll disappear with everything you've got," I say.

"That's pretty sexist and anti-Russian, Ty," Caleb says, finding a blue stain on his sweatpants. He licks his finger, scrubs it.

"Besides," Caleb says, "she isn't going to have a car or a license. She won't get far with both of us keeping a tab on things."

"She'll be your prisoner?"

"No," Trey says. "She'll fall in love with me. Love takes time."

"Sounds like a prisoner," I say. "Like a pet that you don't let outside."

Toki the Cat comes to mind.

"No," Trey says, clicking on profile pictures. "That's sexist, or something."

Caleb says, "This is going nowhere. Let's head to a bar, watch the Packers' game." Caleb grabs a Clay Matthews jersey from his duffel bag, which permanently sits next to the cushy couch.

Trey rolls his eyes. "Football is idiotic," he says.

"Jesus Christ. Here he goes," Caleb says, his head sliding through the mesh jersey.

"All these homophobic truck ads and the doltish meathead culture of the NFL make no sense. What's more manly and heterosexual than to dress up in colorfully designed skin-tight yoga pants? Every couple years, teams ask the red-blooded, pussy-lovin' fans to vote on new uniform colors and designs. *Do you guys like the pretty tiger mascot or should we change it to something with pizzazz?* Fans all over flings wads of cash at the NFL to get different fashionable apparel. *Ooh, you got the throwback jersey with another man's name on the back! Awesomely manly. I really like the manly, testosterone-y swooshy check-mark on the lapel. Really represents your brand awareness.* Chest-bump!"

Caleb rubs his index finger and thumb into his eyes, shaking his head.

"Then," Trey says, "after everyone has slipped on their designer performance gloves, they run out onto the field as colorful fireworks explode, and a fully grown man dances around in an animal outfit trying to stir up some cheer-tastic spirit. First down, the quarterback'll stick his hands under a fat guy's taint, keep 'em warm, maybe diddle a bit—*diddle diddle, tee-hee*—then run away from a bunch of men who are trying to catch him and pile on top."

"All right, enough, you fat windbag," Caleb says, grabbing and jingling his keys in his hands.

"Don't shoot the wise one bringing you the truth," Trey says, sounding like a wise Wond'ring Turtle. "But seriously, I swear, I was watching the cute Tigers versus the ferocious Kitty-Cats—*grr*—last game of last year. And I heard a dude yell, 'I gotchoo!' while he giggled to himself as he tried to tickle a running back into fumbling."

"Dude, shut up," Caleb says, opening the front door.

"Yeah," I add, detached from them, observing.

"For one," Caleb says, "you're just wrong about all that. Another, Trey, you're fucking obnoxious and stupid." Caleb pauses. Smiles. "No offense."

"None taken."

"So, you coming?" Caleb says to Trey.

"I'm bringing my 3DS."

"Pussy."

"My name is pronounced 'Trey.'"

Caleb stiff-arms Trey's face. Trey, muffled, says: "Be gentle. I don't want to lose my manly shampoo and facial lotion endorsements."

Chapter Twenty-Four

College Bar

Leaving the house means throwing on a mask and deciding who I want to be. So at the bar, I decide how I'll alter my behavior. *Whose persona to adopt tonight?* My belt itches against my lower stomach, and I'm rubbing it red-raw against the wooden bar ledge when I see Matthew McConaughey in a TV ad.

It's decided.

We're sitting at a round table on the bar's raised platform, yelling at each other over the thumping dance music. It's the type of bar where skin-tight Ed Hardy T-shirts are visible at every turn. Looking down from our table on the raised platform, we see the dance floor below. The floor lights flash blue, green, and neon pink, alternating. Fake-bake dude-bros clutter the dance floor. A small clump of girls dance together, clear plastic cups in their hands. My eyes meet one of the girl's, the outline of her fluttering eyelashes knocking me into a daze. Professor Nelson's classroom pops into my head like a thought bubble, and I feel the thud of this girl's eraser against my temple.

Brownnoser. You work at the Writing Center, right?

I glance at Caleb and his Matthews jersey tight around his chest. Trey's hunched over his 3DS, his mouth agape so I can see his tongue resting on his bottom teeth, wiggling slightly as he watches his screen. Every few minutes, he tries to find the straw in his drink, but he doesn't look away from *Zelda*, so he's moving his open mouth around trying to capture the straw as it slides away. My stomach is swollen, my side is aching and itchy; today, or maybe the last few years—it's become clear I've put too much into my body. In the morning, a calming pill, followed by afternoon cough syrup, then Skol with fresh squeezed O.J. along with muscle relaxers that Caleb takes for his back pain. He offered me a sample. One day, I rely on a muscle relaxer to alleviate the raw weight of reality. The next, a different pill. The next, alcohol. This way, I'm alternating and distributing the reliance as to avoid what Dr. Phil would call an addiction. I know—I'm ignoring the signs, but it's working right now. I'm highly functioning, right? Lately, though, it's odd: my urine is dark and pungent despite drinking lake's worth of water throughout the day. Sixteen-ounce gulps of water, then a mixed drink. Rinse, lather, and repeat.

"Look at these tools," Caleb says, nodding his head at the dance floor. A TV hangs above our heads showing the Packer kickoff underway. The bar roars as the game begins. "Just out there like drunken squids."

"Squids?" I say. I want to point out *his* fit physique. His body is nearly identical to the college kids meatheading-it-up out on the stand-and-gawk dance floor.

"Yeah, man. Like squids." He glances at me, his face saying *duh.*

Trey speaks up, still hunched over his 3DS, his face lit up purple. "Male squids fling sperm packets at females. They're shaped like arrows. The dude squids fling them at the lady squids."

"Splooge missiles," Caleb says.

"The sperm arrows break through the lady's skin, and—*bam!* Sex has been had."

"Gross," I say.

"And Squidward got laid," Caleb says. "That's all these dudes are here for. To try and fling a sperm packet at any *chick* willing to catch it. The more orange-skinned and meat-bloated you are, the more likely a female college girl will catch it."

"Creatine—that's what gives 'em that jiggly bloat," Trey says, his mouth searching for his straw. "It's just water retention, but ape-brained humans think it means *buff.* Really, it's more like SpongeBob chock-full of water."

I glance back at the girl from Nelson's class. She's grinding her ass into another girl's yoga pants' crotch. She's sipping from her plastic cup. The mob of male squids huddles on the other side of the dance floor. They ogle the girls. A top-heavy Ed Hardy-type wearing a Marines shirt high-fives his identical friend, and they chug their light beers without breaking gaze at the girls. In my gut, there's a primal urge to protect the girl from class—it's this flash of jealousy that doesn't belong. I don't even know her name.

I say, "Know what's weird? I can't remember how to act around gals that aren't Olivia. I can't remember much of her, either. Like every day, in my memory, a part of her flakes off and I forget her more. Chip by chip, piece by piece, she disappears."

"She's been gone for like, a few months, man. That's not that long," Caleb says, gazing at the guys on the dance floor. The tables around us suddenly burst into a cheer. One guy throws his cheese head into the air, and another knocks over a beer as he yells, "Interception."

"Yeah, but I can't remember all of her. Movie girls and novel ladies are more real that Livi now. All I can remember is how *I* acted, and if I act like I did with Livi with a different girl, would that get me punched? Or the cops called on me?"

"Yes," Trey says, his eyes glued to his screen. His mouth searches for the straw. "Yes to both stupid questions."

"Yeah, probably," Caleb says, absentmindedly, eyeing the dance-floor huddle of guys.

"The girl in the pink dress," I point, closing one eye and sighting her. "The one with the zipper running down the front. She's in Professor Nelson's class." I make a *pew pew* sound as I shoot my finger gun.

"The class you're auditing?" Trey says.

I nod, and explain how I'm a brownnoser according to Pink Dress Girl.

Trey says, "So what? You've a lady friend. Doesn't matter if she rips your pants off, chomps at your kibbles 'n' bits. You've got a lady." His mouth searches for the elusive straw. Pausing the game, he looks up, grabs the straw, and throws it anticlimactically. It floats like a feather to the dance floor below.

I say, "I'm just saying I don't know how to act. Like what jokes or attitude I'd adopt. You know—do I stay away from sarcasm, do I act detached, or do I pretend I'm interested in stupid shit like her GPA, or her cat's funny way of sleeping, or her grandma's sweet cherry pie. Am I going to be sullen, short, and overly confident? Do I carry a big stick but say little? Like a Hemingway. Or should I be a coked-up Jim Carrey? I could be any of those things; it's just an act."

"Just don't think. But don't get any ideas, bud," Trey says, unpausing his game, glancing toward the group of dude-bros, the corners of his mouth smiling.

Caleb and I finish our drinks, and he says, "Come on. I'm buying." We weave through the crowd, which is packed butts-to-nuts. Elbows peck my chest, my kidneys, and my itchy, bloated stomach—until we stand next to each other, my eyes reaching only to Caleb's hairy chin. His forearm next to mine, it's the size of my shoulder. His tan arm, stained wood; my pale arm, raw pine.

"Listen, man. I messaged Zeke. You know, to catch up with him. See how the trip is. He and I—we used to be closer than close, you know?" He pauses and gauges my reaction. "Those pics with your girl, they're unsettling. I know."

I look away as I get more uncomfortable and feel the need for a drink. My stomach gurgles, pressure pushing down from my stomach. My legs start to itch and then my back. Then my shoulders. Now my stomach.

Caleb says, "I asked Zeke directly about Olivia, saying that I noticed they looked a little more than just chummy. He just said, 'I'm just glad I brought my lucky tank, man,' and then he made one of those smiley emoticons. He's always using those fucking stupid emoticons, like he's so clever and hip and it's—" He stops, takes a breath. "He's never been clear with anything. So wishy-washy with what he wants, what he says." Caleb gauges my reaction.

He continues, yelling over the music. "Zeke went on about how cool she was, how caring she was for the environment, for people. 'Such an insightful, hip girl'—stuff like that. Made it sound like they had some plans when they came back. Something about a project. I don't know; he's always into some new form of expression. A dilettante in every sense."

I look back at him, sensing he's tiptoeing with his word choice, pausing every few words to not shatter the eggshells. To not hurt my feelings, to not reveal something.

I say, "Did they . . . you know?" I nudge my head forward, heart thumping, breath shallow like a hyperventilating dog. I look down at the floorboards, soaked with light beer. I watch all the feet standing in the beer puddles: the white Jordans, the high-top Chuck Taylors, the wobbling high heels, the brown slippers. My lower stomach itches again. As I'm scratching away where the belt rubs against my groin, I notice how bloated my abdomen in, causing the belt buckle to dig into my skin. Like a pregnant man. I feel the pressure in the stomach drop. I clench my entire lower-half of my body, afraid a shit anvil will drop out my ass.

Olivia. Pastor Bradley. Mom. They're all on my mind, spinning like a carousel.

"Man, I'm sorry," Caleb says. "I don't know . . . Zeke speaks in a weird way. Never direct, always implying things. I know he's good with the girls. And good with guys." Caleb shrugs. "I would know. But with Olivia, I don't know. I don't think that Olivia is like that. Doesn't seem like that type of girl. She's too dedicated and idealistic."

I'm about to squeeze my sardine body through the other sardines toward the can's restroom when a pink dress catches the corner of my eye. A soft hand rests on the back of my neck, brushing down the ridges of my spine softly, sending a chill through me. I turn toward her, clenching my entire body to keep gravity from yanking out my shit anvil.

"Tyler Linley. That's it, isn't it?" her voice rings in my ears like Natalie Portman's.

Her pink dress hugs her body, ending at her rear, so the bottom of her ass pokes out. A zipper bordered with silver starts at her pushed-up cleavage and runs down her front until it ends at the skirt of her dress. It's as if you could just unzip the whole thing and peel it off like a pink banana peel. The pink nearly glows under the lights. She says, "I knew I recognized you that first day in class. Nelson talked about you last semester, about how the failures in the class should go see you for help. At the tutor place."

I have never seen her at the Writing Center.

"You weren't one of the failures, I take it?" I say, unable to relax my body, my attention split two ways—her and my body. I channel a McConaughey drawl in my voice.

She laughs, a soft and coy exhalation. "I'm the 4.0 type of girl." Her lashes flutter, and she grabs my hand. "But sometimes, I like to have fun. Just like you. Guys aren't the only ones allowed to unwind, you know." She, like Caleb, gauges my reaction. "You like to have fun, right?"

Every move she makes feels calculated, like she understands how to manipulate.

I smile with my mouth, not my eyes. In my head, Livi is on a beach, sitting on a hipster's lap, whispering in his ear, biting at his neck—all those things she once did to me . . . months ago? It seems so far off. But now I imagine her doing those things to this new and improved partner in an improved place, Peru, a place with scenic and historical backdrops. A perfect place to begin a relationship. An ideal place to plant a seed of intimacy. My jaw is clenched and it cracks. The cartilage echoes down my ear canal. My teeth crush and grind against each other.

Do I like to have fun?

"You bet your ass I do," I say, a carefree drawl. I grab tight on her little hand, it now hidden in mine. Hers is lotioned. Soft. Different than my muscle memory recalls. *This is not Livi's hand,* a part of my ape brain flashes. *Not Olivia McDermott.* An angel appears on my right shoulder and a demon on my left. Their squeaking voices are drowned by the loud music.

"Let me get you a drink," Pink Dress Girl says, unfolding her pink purse. "You know, I normally hate pink, but it's one of those colors that reflect a mood. For me, at least." Looking at the line of people, as if she's too warm, she unzips the top of the dress a finger length and begins weaving between people, dragging me behind. Her hand is holding my wrist; her fingers are too small to wrap around it.

"Hey, I need to tell a buddy I'm staying for now. He, uh, wants to leave," I say.

"I'll come with."

"He's out," I say. "He's—he's in the restroom right now. Having some, you know, internal combustion issues," I say, rubbing my bloated abdomen in circles, nodding my head in implication, making a point to suck in my stomach to avoid looking bloated in addition to feeling it.

"The poops, huh?" she says, and in that moment, I remember I can be whoever I want, whatever persona fits the situation.

"Yup. Bit of the liquidation sale." Like the eight-year-old within, I pull my thumb out the bottom of my fist, making a squishy ker-plunk noise with my mouth.

"Go," she says, pushing me away, leaning over the bar to order us drinks. "But hurry."

I bust into the doorless restroom, pushing past a line of thick arms holding ultra-light ten-calorie water-beers.

"The fuck?"

"What're you doing, asshat?"

"You got a prob, bro?"

Each anthropomorphic protein glob yells something at me as I push my way to the one stall, which also has no door. Apparently, someone ripped it off in a post-defecation muscle-bound rage.

"I'm gonna blow, dude-bros," I grunt, pulling the peeing Ed Hardy away from the toilet, his weak stream arching in dotted lines over his sparkly designer jeans.

They all yell, toss homophobic insults. But it doesn't matter because I'm curled over, feeling the stabs within my stomach, my legs, my sides. My stomach is bloated, like I'm halfway through a pregnancy. Between my legs, it's red. Burning, itching, and red.

This cannot be good.

Not good. Not good.

I am going to die. Maybe it's for the best. Maybe it is how this should play out.

Chapter Twenty-Five

Heart Pink

I walk back into the crowd and her pink dress catches my eye like Waldo in a crowd of black. Up on the second floor, overhanging the dance floor, she sits at a round table with Caleb's white smile and Trey's purple-glowing face.

I slide onto the barstool, where a vodka lemonade sits in a clear plastic cup.

"Kristina here knows your tastes, Ty," Caleb says, nodding to the drink.

Kristina, the Pink Dress Girl, digs into her purse, producing a small clear Ziplock bag. She pulls a button pill from it and sets it in her mouth.

"Mr. Bradley the third here is quite the *Zelda* aficionado," she says, sipping her drink from a pink straw while looking up at me. "I'm almost jealous."

Trey tries to fight back a smile, but it grow across his face. A purple-lit Glasgow smile. "What can I say? I'm a wise man with a unique talent set. Don't ever steal my daughter," he says in a perfect Liam Neeson voice. He looks up at us for a second, then back to his glowing screen.

My ass wiggles on the wooden seat, trying to find a comfy position. The cheap bar TP rubbed raw the entire cushiony part of my buns. I can feel another round of blood stewing.

"Much as I enjoy venturing out to destroy Ganondorf, I'm in a dancing mood. It was nice meeting you both," Kristina says, sticking her small hand out to Caleb, who shakes her hand. I'm wondering whose hand is softer between the two when she says, "C'mon," yanking my hand again. Trey glances up from his screen, the lower-half of his face lit purple in the dark room, his head shaking. Caleb shrugs his shoulders. The bar roars again as the Packers score.

"I'm not really in the mood to dance," she says. "Those sluts," she points my hand at the dance floor. "They're just looking to be ogled to boost their self-esteem. I mean, look at the girl there, with the white-tank on. No bra. Thong slung over those wide, birthin' hips. Every guy's lizard brain is just looking to pass on their dumb, inbred genes. Gimme a break." She leads me toward the front door. "I've a ride coming to get us out of here." She gauges my reaction, which is blank and confused, torn between worrying about what's happening to my insides and what's going through this girl's mind.

I nod stupidly with my mouth half open.

"Stick your drink in your mouth. It'll make you look smarter," she says, laughing. Her tiny smooth hand pushes up on my hairy chin. She leans forward onto her tip-toes and kisses my neck. Warm, wet, a fruity air. Strawberries. She runs her hand through my hair until it hits a snarl, which she gently works out so she can run her fingers through again; this time it's smooth. I just stand there.

"I've been in a mood for a blond lately," she says, grabbing a fistful of hair and pulling me close to her face. Her nose touches mine, her eyes meet mine so close that I have to focus on one eye or the other; otherwise, my vision blurs her into a cyclops.

Next to us, near the door, in my peripheral, a muffin-topped bouncer watches us. I feel the scrutiny, as if he'd be relaying the scene to Livi via his headset at any moment. Or maybe he's seen the video/pictures of Livi online . . . but the Peruvian scene pops into my head. Kristina bites my bottom lip, and the pain sends a jolt of anger through me, directed at Livi, at that hipster she's with, at the dopey bouncer, and I bite back.

"Whoa-ho, tough guy," she says. "Be gentle. For now." She pulls my arm, and I'm simply watching the scene, being dragged along. I'm an observer, holding off moral judgment in favor of curiosity of how the scene will unfold. This is just entertainment.

I'm an observer. The man in a black trench coat from my stupors—somehow, he's given me what I've wanted. I am just watching. Observing.

She says, "Ride is here, Tyler Linley."

Outside, a silver BMW is idling. The driver is hidden behind tinted windows. Kristina leads me to the backseat door. The door locks click. Kristina the Pink Dress Girl yanks the door open and climbs in ahead of me. Out the bottom of her dress I can see her ass, a lacy black thong running down it. I climb in after and buckle up. The leather seat is cool against my body.

A wrinkly face turns from the driver seat, and a pair of slow-blinking eyes scan me.

"I love blonde hair, honey," the gravelly voice says as the engine purrs. The car lurches forward, bottoming out as we leave the bar's parking lot. "So fair, delicate, like a man I knew back when." She turns the radio up. A Dean Martin song plays. The driver lights a cigarette as the window slowly opens.

"Mimaw, we're just heading to my place," Kristina says as she slides next to me, her face leaning forward between the seats so her head is next to the older woman.

"Good. Jonathan and I, we're not in the mood for guests tonight. We're in the mood for *other* things," she says, laughing in a controlled, uptight manner. Her mouth exhales a cloud of gray.

"Linley," Kristina the Pink Dress Girl says. "This is my Grandma. Or Mimaw."

"Nice to meet—" I begin before getting cut off.

"Tina, you're wanting to be dropped off at the stacked complex, right?"

"Of course," Kristina says. She slides closer to me. Her hip is against mine, and her soft hand rubs my thigh.

"I must say," Mimaw says, "I'm delighted you went with the pink zip-down instead of that ultra-conservative aqua sundress." She turns her head toward me, revealing her face again. Crow's feet border her black-lined eyes, and her curly brown hair is French-braided and slung over her shoulder. Her face, maybe a few years more aged than Keri's. The way the two interact makes me wonder if all people are closer with family members than I am. How could anyone ever be comfortable asking a grandma for a ride with a possible one-night stand?

My stomach rumbles and groans as Kristina rubs my groin. The entire right side of my body itches—insanely—yet I bite my lip and ignore it.

"Be careful, Tina. Experience the world, as we say, but you don't know where some people have been," she says, glancing in the rearview, laughing coldly. "Of course, I'm kidding, Lyle."

Lyle? Not even close to Tyler or Linley.

The BMW pulls into a parking lot that looks familiar, but it has changed. A stacked apartment complex sits where my duplex once sat. The yard is now a parking lot. The building is lined with stained brick. A pool glimmers, bordered by a black fence. The sign at the entrance reads *West Haven Residency.*

Mimaw pulls into a handicapped stall, and Kristina leans over my lap, resting her breasts on my legs, and opens the door, as if I couldn't do it. She says to her Mimaw, "I love you."

"Still on for Victoria's Secret tomorrow?" Mimaw says.

"I *need* to stop there," Kristina says, unzipping her dress down to her bra. "The seams are popping on this thing."

"I think we *both* need to stop there," Mimaw says. "Jonathan ripped through my favorite lace the other day. Such a savage." She laughs, and Kristina joins me outside the car. The BMW glides away and Kristina waves to the window's tinted blackness. Grabbing my hand, she leads me to the glass door to the apartment building.

"This is where my old place was," I say. "Right *here*, where we're standing."

"Was. That's all gone and doesn't matter anymore. Now there's this monstrosity." She unlocks the entrance door. Inside, calm jazz plays from the Bose speakers mounted in the corners of the entryway. Walking ahead of me up the stairs, she pulls from her purse an airplane-size bottle of whiskey. "Thirsty?"

I nod, and she breaks the plastic seal without missing a stride up the white stairwell. She tosses it back to me, pulls another from her purse, cracks the seal, and says, "Cheers." We nudge the plastic together and we each take a swig.

I debate pretending to be like a raging alcoholic with my tiny bottle of booze, but instead I remain quiet. On the third-floor landing, she stops walking ahead of me. Turning around, she says, "You were looking up my dress just now, weren't you?"

I pause. I had been. But am I honest? Detached? Arrogant, cocky, respectable? No. I'm Matthew McConaughey: cool, laid-back, chill. And me, I'm not respectable. Neither is my girlfriend, off in Peru with a guy who sports a Pabst Blue Ribbon tattoo on his ankle but hates beer. Both of them wearing *Save the Polar Bears* T-shirts made of recycled diapers and condoms; yet they sit there on the beach, tanned and glistening. Stars of a Corona commercial.

"Maybe," I say.

"And when I crawled into the backseat. You were looking then, too?"

No more hesitation. "Yes."

"In front of my *mimaw*. My *grandmother* . . ." She pauses, watches me for a moment, studying something about me. "You're hesitant, aren't you? Why?"

"I'm not."

"Don't bullshit a bullshitting psych major, bud." She says this like a child bragging that her dad could beat up my dad.

"I'm not."

"Whatever you say, David Wooderson."

1.

Inside Kristina's apartment, dishes are piled in both sides of the sink. Near the door rests a stack of empty pizza boxes. Bottles of wine, name-brand vodka, whiskey, rum, and gin line the top of the kitchen cabinets. An L-shaped leather couch lines the living room wall. A wall-sized flat screen is mounted above a set of hip-height surround-sound speakers, which she turns on using a small remote pulled from her bottomless purse. Thumping bass vibrates the soft blue carpet, and she says, "I love the vibrations just jolting through me." She digs in her purse again, pulls out a bag, and takes a button pill out, swallowing it dry.

Standing at a book-size clean spot at the kitchen counter, she says, "Vodka and . . . let's say, lemonade? That's what you like in Nelson's class."

"What?"

"You think no one notices you downing those plastic bottles during class? Nelson's dull as shit—or he doesn't care—but we onlookers in the back, we notice things. I'll even throw in a few extra shots. You strike me as the type who needs it."

She leads me into what might be her bedroom. Or, I realize, more likely, her sex room. There is a coverless twin mattress plopped in the center of the room; a flower design covers the twin mattress. Body-length mirrors line the wall to the left of me, and I see my reflected image. My long sleeve Packers shirt, my jeans a little baggy where my ass should be. My shaggy blonde beard; ruffled hair; tired face and eyes—it all looks foreign and out of place next to this girl in a pink dress. Almost anachronistic, like seeing an ancient Mongolian playing Ping-Pong with a Chinese man.

"Maybe," I say, taking a drink. "Can I just get your number? You know, hold off for a night?"

"Don't make this awkward."

"I'm not."

"I'm not giving you my number; now, you're here. We don't need a phone to be involved."

She steps toward me and grabs the hairs under my chin while kissing me. Her eyes closed, mine wide open, I'm scanning the room. Dildos lean against the wall in the corner of the room like nubby baseball bats; one's tall up to my hip; another tan and veiny; another black with curly hair at the base; another bright blue like a battery-operated *Avatar* dong. On the wooden nightstand, a candy dish of colorful condoms sits—a cornucopia of condoms. Behind them hangs a Playboy pin-up of Marilyn Monroe spread on a red bed. In the closet, there are fuzzy handcuffs, hanging lingerie, and a black jump rope. Whip, I mean. Not jump rope.

Jesus Christ.

She pushes me onto the mattress. She yanks a gray tie from under the mattress like a magician and ties it loosely around her neck. The gray tie lying between her cleavage evokes in my mind the first porn I saw. Trey had shown it to me in fourth grade, just after his family got a Gateway computer. He giggled throughout. But I was speechless, exposed to a new world hidden beneath every adult's clothed body, like when you find out that buried in your pal's garage, under that dirty blue tarp, is some vehicular treasure . . . except you can masturbate to it.

She yanks out another tie, and Windsor knots it around my neck. "Ties are hot. They give me better leverage, and they're fucking classy," she says as she works my tie.

In her, I sense a dual personality, fluctuating depending on the context. One, a socially adept A-student with money-management skills. Ahead of her is a lucid career path. She's in close relationships with her family, her mimaw, and she's assertive and powerful in class and at work. Side two, a Hulk-like animal. Side two, she's a hedonistic explorer that purges any pent-up urges in a truncated weekend session. I doubt she spreads her addictions and vices out through every day. Maybe she'd be played by a young Helena Bonham Carter.

Sitting atop me, she unzips the front of her dress down to her belly button. Her breasts, double Livi's, hang over the pink dress and the tie falls between.

The details run together. At times, she's on top, the skirt of her dress pulled up over her ass to allow access. At other times, she's crawling, growling, clawing at the back of my neck, at my back.

In the corner of the room, I see the shadowy man. He mouths, *You are not here. Let this happen and just watch.* I blink rapidly until I can ignore him. My lower stomach begins to itch again, and my insides are gurgling. I can't focus on anything but soothing that itch and making peace within my intestines. I think: Livi. Keri. Family. My bleeding insides. That maddening itch. Livi, my girlfriend. Keri, my family.

These things compound and I burst out, "Are you clean?"

In the corner, the shadowy man shakes his head. *You fool.*

Kristina stops and death-stares me. She says, "There's a pile of condoms right there if you don't believe I am." In her stare, I can palpably feel she's offended. I'm calling her a whore. Yet somehow, as a man, I'm not a whore, which isn't fair, and her face says it. "Put one on if you need to. Otherwise, I'm close, so, *shh.*" Her thin, soft finger over my lips, our reflection in the wall mirrors is pale. My paleness against her, it just evokes the word "meatbag." Clueless meatbag. On my chest and neck, fresh hickies are visible. My burning insides, itching pubic area, dry mouth—these are all symptoms belonging to someone not meant to continue existing. These things are the makeup of someone unsustainable. The word wiggles its way into my head as Kristina the Pink Dress Girl is on all fours in front of me.

Unsustainable. A word I'd never used before Livi. I'm unsustainable, this moment is proof. Each day, a blast of abuses

string together. Without her, I have nothing. I've created nothing.
I've built no relationships, just escapes. Day in, day out, I just
alleviate the burden of time, tasks, dealing with other people through
pills and drinks. I dull any issues that arise, and without Livi, it's
clear I can't face reality alone. The pills, alcohol, they're a poor
stand-in for Olivia. For a family.

Kristina is still on all fours, moaning and mumbling something.
Even though her tie is held tightly in my fist, I've disappeared
completely. I'm watching, lingering next to the shadowy man.

2.

Months ago, I'd been tutoring, editing the local newspaper,
overseeing a poetry publication, and taking nineteen credits. I'd had
a panic attack in Livi's dorm room. The weight of too many options,
the burden of social interactions, and a growing sense of wasting my
life built up into an awful feeling: that feeling you sometimes get
where you feel like you aren't really there. Depersonalization or
derealization, my doctor, WebMD, said. You feel like you aren't
here, and you're aware of it. And being aware of it only makes you
more panicked. *Will this last forever? Where am I?* It's constant
confusion and anxiety, and it lasted for weeks, each day worse than
the previous. I thought it'd never go away, and I broke down. When
I did, Livi called in for work—food poisoning, she'd said. She
skipped classes—a family death, she'd said. The only times I've
factually known her to lie. Like a nurse, she went through everything
to soothe me. I, a pants-shitting child. She, my calm and collected
nurse. She read WebMD articles, emailed a nursing professor,
checked out books, flipped through medical magazines, laughed at
Dr. Oz's fad medical advice. I resisted her help at first; "I'm fine—
just swing by the gas station," I'd told her. "Pick up my usual and
I'll be fine."

She didn't. Instead, she gave back rubs while singing my favorite
Iron and Wine songs—calming and soothing. She defined love for
me, but I hadn't seen it or understood it at the time. I'd spent my life
looking for it, but when it was right in front of me, I didn't even
know what it was. It was as if a written masterpiece lay in front of
me, but I wasn't able to read. I just knew the book would burn
easily.

At first, part of me recoiled from her intimacy, the genuine concern. I cherished it, but it felt inappropriate that someone would show me such concern. I couldn't reproduce it for her. I couldn't create my own affection and show love. I just reflected sentiments and gestures like a mirror. I conjured an illusion learned from the Clooney's, the Gosling's—the masters of illusions. A mirror has no soul or ability to love—just the ability to reflect. I can only act. I can only pretend, and it seems obvious that no one should be sentenced to a partnership with that.

~ ~ ~

After, Kristina is lying butt-naked on the flower mattress. Face-down, she's asleep. I slide into my clothes, and in the bathroom, I rinse my naughty bits in scorching sink water. Hot as it can go. Red flesh. Painful. I'm scratching my legs, my crotchal region—everywhere. On the way out, I take a bottle of Oval vodka, a can of Sprite, and, with my hand hovering over the door knob, I hesitate. Pulling my wallet from my back pocket, I unfold two twenties and set them on top of a plate caked with desiccated pizza sauce.

I'm walking through the rain, as if the director of this cliché knew how to fill this moment with stock images and filler. I claw at my lower stomach, at the shaved area above my junk. It's itching worse than ever.

Is it raining in Peru?

3.

The next morning, Caleb and Trey sip coffees and rename common items with more literal names. See if you can guess them: Finger Pants. Spray Scream. Aroma Light. Horse Tornado. Raw Toast. Cat Puppies. Decorative Retainer.

I sip my drink, and I've continued on through since last night, unable to sleep. One day and the next are blurred together in constant consciousness. There is no punctuation.

I sit on the toilet seat in the bright bathroom, the fan whirring, trying to think of words to write. The blood's died down a bit, now just a twinge. But the itching is insanity now. My skin is yellow. My eyes are yellow. I am a *Simpsons* character.

"Livi," I begin on a notepad. Nothing comes. No small talk. No common recent history. *How's the weather?* Hers and my recent pasts are different. We've been diverging since that day I hit the deer. She's been growing, improving, expanding. I've been receding like a hairline. She hasn't checked her social media accounts since she disabled them, so I have no way of quickly contacting her. I'm glad I don't have a Facebook, because I'd be unable to fight the urge to check every hour whether Zeke had posted some new bikini pic of him and my girlfriend. Even if he'd never post another picture, I know I'd still stare at the ones Caleb showed me; I have little ability to fight off my desire to hold onto painful thoughts like they mean something to me. I choose to inflict it upon myself, as if it does something good for me; as if maybe I inflict enough pain, like self-flagellation, something good will have to happen to balance things out.

But that is one of my many illusions. Only I can balance things.

4.

I'm driving Trey's car. (R.I.P. Betsy the Buick.) The headlight beams light the blacktop ahead. The people walking down the street look aimless, wandering around. One woman pushes a stroller while poking at her glowing phone. A leashed dog yanks another lady, a plastic shopping bag in her hand; a man with hobo gloves clings to his shopping cart handles, a plastic bag set in the cart with crushed aluminum cans. I'm curious where they're going. I'm intrigued by what motivates them, what they fear, why they do the things they do. What causes this man to push his cart another step, as the cart's wheels bump-bump over cement cracks, one wheel sputtering.

I hit a bump in the road and my drink in the cup holder barely sloshes. No spills on my junk, no damp underwear for two hours. I love Trey's car. I love its cup holders.

On the Bose speakers, a local philharmonic orchestra plays a live rendition of Chopin's work: trudging arpeggios, dynamic volume. It's subtle, calm, and settling. Homes I pass are decorated with orange and purple lights; scarecrows pose on lawns; skeletons splay on the grass dressed in second-hand clothing; plastic tombstones are hammered into grass near porches; pumpkins are set beneath window sills where months ago a pie might have sat, cooling. Pumpkin faces melt and decay, drooping into themselves.

Just a few hours ago, Caleb, Trey and I cruised through the city collecting these rotting pumpkins, setting them on a tarp in the trunk.

They rolled around like heads. In the lot of our apartment, under the lot's lighting, we set up empty vodka bottles, one, two, three—until ten bottles sat ready to be toppled by rotting pumpkins. The first few pumpkins I tried rolling splattered because I wasn't gentle enough; I hadn't bent over far enough. Orange seeds littered the pavement like someone had punched out the pumpkin's teeth. The yellow parking lines served as our gutters, and spares proved most challenging, as the pumpkins sometimes unraveled, slinging orange goop, while rolling toward the remaining bottle-pins. The stems also fucked up the route of the roll.

Like a child, I was cheered up by this simple activity. It was Caleb and Trey's idea—pumpkin bowling. Like old times, when Trey and I used to steal gnomes from the neighborhood yards. We'd hide them in the woods where hunters set up their tree stands and ground blinds. Or we'd relocate the pointy-hatted gnomes in new yards, within eyesight of the gnomes' original homes, all in hope a credulous neighbor would believe the gnomes to be stealing their underwear and cavorting around the neighborhood in some *Willy Wonka* nighttime shenanigans.

But now, in Trey's car, the streetlights' orbs light my path to Kennedy's mom's duplex. The music, the foggy road ahead of me, my numbed mind—it all feels like a lucid dream. I'd last slept a couple of days ago. My sleepless mind's been wandering aimlessly. Then it stumbled upon the thought of Kennedy. My curiosity led me to cruise here, and I park across the road in front of his mom's duplex. I'd left Trey and Caleb at home, where I'd left to escape the familiarity and monotony.

I'm going to do something. I don't know what. I don't know whether to hate Trey or Kennedy for taking my life. My escapes. My everything.

Sitting here, though, I'm relaxed and comforted by the comforting placebo motion of glass-to-mouth. I'm comforted by the calm nighttime music of Chopin's live music. The car radio is set to play for one hour, and then it'll shut down.

In this car, it's easy to focus, like a cocoon for my mind. I run through the details of my duplex's fire. Kennedy or Trey? I run through it all. Before my closed eyes, colors mix and blur, forming shapes that morph into figures: Olivia, Keri, Toki the Cat, Mom, Kristina (bent over). Livi, her head rested in the nook of Zeke's tan neck, either a scene of friendship or a scene of betrayal. I know I betrayed Livi. My pessimism assured me of her guilt. I do all I can to push the two from my mind. Again Kristina the Pink Dress Girl pops into my thought bubble. I let her take over my mind along with Chopin and calmness dilutes into sleep.

I wake to the sound of brass tapping on glass. Contacts dried to my eyes, everything is blurry. I have cotton mouth, and my bladder is thumping and painful. The car smells like a vodka candle had burned all night. I force a yawn to wet my contacts. I look to the sound of tapping. At my window, a hand with brass knuckles taps on the glass. A few black hairs arch over the brass knuckles. My aching neck pulsates as my eyes meet his eyes. His yellow teeth flash, jagged canines overlapping his bottom lip. He keeps the rhythmic knocking. Another knocking joins from the passenger window where another guy stands, now blocking the sunlight that had been streaming into the car. Brass is also wrapped around his knuckles. I hit the automatic lock button and try to find the keys, but they're not in the ignition. Not on the floor. I tuck my head between my legs, running my fingers across the carpet—*where are the fucking keys*—when I hear glass shatter and feel shards landing on my back and neck. The door is yanked open from the inside. I jerk my head up, smack it on the bottom of the wheel.

By my belt, Kennedy yanks me from the driver's seat onto the cement, my hip smacking it while my head cracks against his knee. In my ears, my skull hitting his knee sounds like aluminum bat against hardball. The side of my head bursts into warmth. A liquid runs around my ear, warm through my beard, into my mouth. Metallic.

There are two of them standing over me. Ka and Kennedy.

I hear Kennedy's voice, quick and rushed. I don't register what he's saying, but the old scenes flash in succession:

Grade school, behind the softball bleachers, I held Jordan in a headlock, yelling, "Say uncle, say uncle," just like Grandpa Linley did to me. Insult my mom, you get beat up. After detention, parent meetings, my dad was never more proud. *Someone insults you, you protect your name.*

Grandpa Linley showed me WWF movies, boxing moves— "Hands up! Quick jab." Grandpa contorted my arms and legs into painful angles, saying between breaths: "Just . . . like . . . this."

Football practice, Coach taught swim and spin moves, bench-press max-outs, clean and jerk. It all means nothing now.

Kennedy's voice says, "Yeah, Ka. I like that idea." He's nodding his head. The two stand towering over me like tall trees. Ka yanks the hair on the back of my head, flips me over, and his heel thuds against my liver. Ka stomps his boot into my throat and unzips his fly, pressing more weight onto my throat, cutting off oxygen. His fly zipped down, he winds up and punches me in the gut. The brass knocks the wind out of me. My knees jerk up to my chest and burning acid shoots up my throat, out my mouth, over my face, and onto Ka's boot. A volcano of vomit.

Kennedy turns away and looks down the street. I swear he shudders and shakes his head. I swear Kennedy mumbles to tone it down, to chill. I swear, but my hearing is fading in and out.

"You fucker," Ka says. "Not on my goddamn boot." He lifts it from my throat and wipes his boot along my shirt. He takes a deep breath. He says, as a judge might: "You know, theft's a crime." He smiles, laughs. "And sure, you didn't take much. But it's the principle of the matter. You steal. You get punished." He kicks my ribs. "And, goddamn, fella. I must say it sure is creepy that you're postin' up outside my aunt's house. The fuck is wrong with you? You know how pathetic you look? With puke, drool, all of your mommy's puked-up spaghetti."

I realize it's blood in my vomit, not spaghetti. It'll be blood in my stool again, not juice dye.

My bladder is so full that all I can focus on is not pissing myself. Ka, his fly still down, stomps down on my stomach with his vomit boot, and I lose all control and piss myself.

Kennedy's back still faces me. His cousin is laughing as he says, "Kennedy, dude pissed himself." Kennedy says nothing. He's still looking away down the street, unable to watch. "Might as well shit yourself, too, bud," Ka says. "Try hitting for the cycle: piss, shit, up-chuck, bleed." He laughs, proud of his baseball analogy. He forgot cry, though. I'm not crying; I'm too dehydrated.

My breath is shallow and shaky. Blood trickles into my mouth. My groin is soaked with the stench of alcohol-piss. My face is layered with vomit and blood and spit.

I'm abandoned and helpless, like a gutter dog. I repeat it in my head. Like a gutter dog, a gutter dog, and I look up, helplessly, at

Kennedy's back. I stare up at Ka's boot as he mutters something about misery. My eyes meet the waffle-bottom of his boot and it all goes black.

Chapter Twenty-Six

A Coach, a Pastor, and Something Else

I woke up in the gutter, and now I'm sitting with my elbows propped on my knees, trying not to vomit. A cop is asking me questions while another is jotting notes about Trey's car.

"I didn't get a look at any of them," I say, trying to yawn to moisturize my eyes. "Do you have any eye Chapstick?" I ask the cop. He smiles and says the ambulance will bring eye drops.

"Can we not get an ambulance?" I say, rolling my tongue around in my mouth, poking at the open gap where my canine tooth used to be.

"Protocol. You look like you've taken some hits to the head, some blows elsewhere." He points at various spots on my body. The officer has noted the near-empty vodka bottle in the passenger seat, the glass of vodka sitting in the drink holder.

"Mr. Linley, you were drinking, I assume?" The officer holds my ID and my empty wallet.

I nod, staring at the cement where a splotch of red marks my impact spot. Next to it, I see a tiny jagged white rock. I lean and grab it, groaning as my *everything* aches. I try setting my canine tooth back in my mouth. It falls out. I slip it into my pocket.

"Hmm. The registered owner of this vehicle is also on his way. He said he'll pick you up from the hospital. A David Bradley. He knows you have this vehicle?"

I nod. Trey gave me permission.

"Good. Ambulance should be any minute."

1.

At the hospital, I'm wondering how I'll pay for this when a David Bradley walks in. Pastor Bradley. My mother's ex-lover.

Standing in front of the hospital bed, Pastor rolls up his sleeves. I prepare myself for a Sunday lecture. I imagine him asking the congregation to pray for the lost, like me, a prodigal son who's gone astray: *a boy who's lost control of his basic daily life. Pray! Pray for this infant who can't bear the pressures of simple life without the aides and escapes offered to him by the ephemeral world.*

Instead, he sits next to me and rests his hand on my shoulder.

"Are you ready to go home?" he says, his voice soft and calm. "I've got this all taken care of."

I nod. *What about insurance? The car? The booze?*

We go through the rigmarole to get me checked out with various painkillers and pharmaceutical pills, and Pastor drives me home without saying anything. Oldies play softly and he hums along, sometimes harmonizing.

As he pulls up to my apartment, he says, "Trey will be home soon. He knows already. He explained what probably happened. I understand. If you need anything, call me." He looks directly at me, calm, and unwavering. "It's okay to need someone." His voice lingers in the air. Standing at my front door, I watch his car shrink down the road, his rusted Camry sputtering and coughing an opaque cloud until it disappears into nothing.

2.

On the massive monitor, I log into Facebook. Trey's blue account pops up, and on the newsfeed is an update from Zeke:

To the things I'm seeing, the people I'm meeting: I'll never forget :)

I click through his pictures for anything with Livi. I haven't heard from her except for the few letters she's written, such as the coconut letter. She'd decided to deactivate her social media and cut herself off from all electronic communication so she could immerse herself in the Peruvian culture. So, now I'm searching through this guy's page looking for any sort of update.

I click, click, click, looking for anything to make me feel worse. I look for reminders of painful things—I'm back to self-flagellating. I see the same photos as before. Staring at the photos, I again have trouble remembering Livi's personality. It feels like looking at an actress I'd only seen on TV, but I had no idea what she'd be like in person. It's only been a few months, but I've lost so much of her in the evaporation of my memory.

I'm absentmindedly clicking through Trey's history when I stumble upon something I've never heard of before:

On a crudely designed website, there are clickable profiles of mail-order *husbands* (and not just from Russia). Trey and Caleb had been shopping for one. There's a Romanian. A racist from Missouri. A man from Southern Idaho whose caption is: "Ever drink paint thinner? Haha. Don't. I'm a fun guy, funny, too. Guy who knows a few card tricks." There's Jeb from Texas, with a forehead perfect for landing airplanes. There's a pinhead named Rueben from Nova Scotia; he enjoys slow, relaxing television. There's Earl, from West Virginia, who can "chop lots'a wood and climb a greased pole" and who "takes weekly baths after chasing chickens"; there's a man who wants love despite his "dead left arm." On the website's private messages, I can see that Trey or Caleb has even drafted a private message to one of the more appealing items, a tan European man named Pavel. The private message asks if Pavel would be interested in visiting—not as a husband—but just to get to know each other.

I don't even know my best friend.

Chapter Twenty-Seven

That Feeling When You Stand on a Ledge

My phone rings, and it's Keri again. She's called every day for a week, leaving messages each time, but I haven't returned a call. I listen to the voicemail:

"Momma Keri again. I'm worried about you. *Please* call me back, sweetie. I love you," the voicemail says, her voice affectionate and caring. Not trusting my ability to feign happiness, I don't call back. As I'm clicking through Trey's history, I hear the front door unlock, and I exit out of all the windows and lean back in the computer chair, closing my eyes, folding my hands behind my head, as if I'm deep in thought. As if I actually thought about things.

Caleb and Trey walk through the door carrying bags from BB's ComicLand.

"Look at this philosopher," Trey says. "Pondering the nature of existence—whether or not a man truly needs creamer in his coffee." He digs in the plastic bag and pulls out a box of popsicles. "Ty, you can eat these, or mush 'em on your swollen face."

"Trey told me what happened. Let's see the damage, you prizefighter," Caleb says, shadow boxing the air.

I turn to them and run through the impact, top to bottom. My brain's concussed, the proof being a squiggle of stitches on at the top of my jaw line. I try to widen my poofed eyes but can't because of the black bags beneath, which have swelled because of a broken nose. I stand straight on, facing Trey and Caleb to show my nose cocked to the right, and because each nostril is stuffed with gauze, my voice is nasally and whiny, like a nerdy child doing show and tell of his *My Little Pony* collection.

I lift my top lip while talking and tongue the vacant spot where my canine once resided. I point to a glass of milk where it chills. He mumbles *gross*, and I poke my pair of broken ribs and tell how the nurse wrapped my torso like a mummy and how Dr. Saiid suggested I should learn how to "throw smacks like a champ, you guy." I keep rambling, saying my upper-crotchal area has been itching, and I can't decide whether I have the clap or herpes or if my belt irritates me. WebMD says it could be caused by other ailments, but I ignore those. The more I say about my injuries, the harder my friends fight back smiles from bursting into laughs.

I tell them about my bloody poops, which I shouldn't have phrased as "bloody poops" because they both burst out laughing, hands on knees. I wear a stern face, 'cause it's not funny for me at the moment, but my distorted face can't be taken seriously. I burst into a laugh, one that a kid busts into after blubbering when he skins his knee and Dad makes a funny fart noise to lighten the mood.

"Oh, God, I'm sorry, man," Caleb says. "Who got ya? I mean, who beatcha up?" He pantomimes an uppercut, and I'm realizing Caleb should be in theater or should become a mime, with all his hand gesturing.

"Don't know," I say. "Seemed random."

Caleb nods, shrugs his shoulders.

Anger was my first response upon waking there in the street. *How could I get them back?* It was time for revenge. Time to even the scales. Then pity took over and I clung to that physical pain.

Caleb says, "Sometimes them motherfuckers get bored and gotta take out frustration on someone. That's why I keep at the gym. Every day, no matter what. When they come for me, I'll be ready." He puts up his fists in front of his face.

Trey eyes me. He knows what actually happened.

"Just a random attack?" Trey asks, slinging the plastic bag of comics onto the counter. "That only happens on the news."

"Yes, a random attack."

"You're a terrible liar."

Caleb says, "Let him be. He just got his ass beat. From the looks of it, they beat his ass with his own ass."

"That'd be a sight to see," I say, picturing a folded-over man being pummeled with his own ass like a ham.

"Why do you need to lie?" Trey says, ignoring Caleb.

"I'm not."

"You're a child, Ty. We're not the police or some fucking interrogation unit. We're your friends," he says.

"Chill, Trey," Caleb says. "You both need to let off some steam sometimes. And on that note, I'm out. Gym time for me so I'm not at people's throats . . . or getting my ass beat." He walks past me, grabs my tooth from the glass of milk. "Put this under your pillow. Get some quarters to fix your teeth." He tosses me the tooth. He smiles, good-natured, patting my shoulder as he walks toward Trey's room. "Hope you feel better, Ty. I can only imagine what that other guy looked like."

What did Pastor Bradley tell Trey? What did Trey tell Caleb?

Trey is staring at me as Caleb mashes his workout clothes into a *League of Legends* duffel bag. I'm avoiding Trey's stare by poking at my canine.

The tooth fairy. I recall those grade school days spent wiggling a dangling tooth with your tongue. It was painful but in a good way. That pain like a tickle, a loose tooth made class more bearable. After all my wiggle teeth fell out, I fought my first fight. Tyler William Linley versus Jordan Michael McDermott. Fisticuffs. My first suspension. My first and only win. Now I'm 1-1 in lifetime fights.

Grade school, back when I thought I had AIDS because of Olivia—all these memories come in flashes. It's funny to look back, because I realize how little I knew. But now, here, scratching my junkal region, an STD is less funny. It's more permanent now. Do I visit the doc or not? Even the idea of an STD scares me. Think about it: spending the rest of life working around some permanent burning, itching sexual leprosy that prevents any unhindered sexual intimacy. Condoms for all eternity, all for one night filled with bloody poops and swollen lips.

Caleb is heading out the front door when he says: "On the bright side, least you'll look super handsome when your face stops looking like you've been spending too much time with Sean Penn." He closes the door behind him and the door latches.

Trey says, "This have anything to do with why you stopped getting your relax pills from that inbred douche?"

"No."

"My dad called me, Ty. He never calls me. He told me where it happened. I know Kennedy, too. We all went to school together—at least for a bit—and I'm not an idiot."

I look out the window. A squirrel runs and down a tree. Then in a circle on the grass.

"I don't get you, man. You act like you've always got something to hide, but if you'd just tell your friends what the fuck is going on, we could help, even if it's just buying a box of fucking frozen sugar pops."

I look back at the tooth. Its roots make it look huge compared to the canine still stuck in my gums. When you see the canine in my mouth, you only see the tip of the iceberg.

Trey says, "Dad told me you got beat badly, just outside the duplex of one of his church members. Dad figured it out. Kennedy's ma is a member of Dad's church, and she's always asking him for help. For prayer, I should say. My dad knows about Kennedy's little drug deals. He knows about Kennedy's mom's dildo sex shows or whatever stuff she's got going on. He's known about your bouts with anxiety, and he didn't forget grade school—all the social anxiety stuff. Like that time you wandered off through the city and climbed the cell tower and got picked up by Officer Kaigo. We don't forget that stuff. And a pastor's job—I guess part of it—is to know people's Achilles heels. Their secrets."

I think of Mom.

"He should know his own damn weaknesses, too," I say.

"I'm sure he does. But he deals with it the best he can. And I don't know if he talks with people . . . or with God, but he doesn't do it alone."

I expected more of a fight from Pastor Bradley. I had prepared a cascade of insults to fling at the flawed religious leader, despite his constant attempts to help me.

"Of course he has flaws," I say. "And I'm talking about what happened with him and my mom—" I start, but I don't have the energy to unravel that mess, which has been so nicely swept under the rug.

"I'm not here to argue with you." Trey stares at me.

It's tough to judge if he knows what I'm implying, but he always knows more than he says. Always been that way. I'm always shocked to find out basic information that a well-balanced person would notice easily. Trey is a thoughtful and wise turtle. I'm more of a . . . the squirrel out the window catches my eye, its little whiskered face peering in through the window. It's standing on its hind legs.

Trey inhales, calming himself like his father.

"You know," Trey says, "he steals his mom's pills lots of times? Kennedy, I mean. Dad told me Kennedy pulls prescription pills right from the kitchen cabinet. Ken's mom came to Dad to ask for advice. Ken straight-up steals from his mom, but it's because Ka, his cousin, makes him."

I contort my face like Clooney might; a face to show disgust.

I say, "Aren't pastors supposed to keep those things a secret? Like a confidentiality clause?"

Trey shrugs. "I'm his kid. And Dad's got his flaws, too. He can hide them from a congregation, but family knows." Trey's look softens for a moment. "I told Caleb a different story than Dad told me. Caleb thinks you did some serious damage to one of the attackers. He actually thinks it was random."

"Yeah?"

"Yeah. You shattered another fella's face. That's what I told Caleb. Or maybe I said scrambled. It was definitely some comic book-style description that allowed Caleb's imagination to fill in the incorrect details. He probably pictured some *BLAM! KERPOW!* action bubble explosions. All I know is: you're fucking up a lot. I want to help. But I can't if you don't tell me anything." He stares at me. He wants me to feel that he's serious. "I am not only a wise comic book character, but I can try to help in real life, too."

I smile. "Thanks."

~ ~ ~

He's been a friend so long, yet I've forgotten what it means to be a friend, so I refer to the dictionary. According to Merriam-Webster, a friend is: (n) 1.) a person attached to another by feelings of affection or personal regard. 2.) a person who gives assistance; patron; supporter.

He's been a friend all along. I've neglected my part.

1.

Trey is drinking his coffee on the toilet because he's "all about efficiency. It all slides right through me." With the computer to myself, I fall into a Facebook Pit of Depression. I scroll and click through people's updates. All of them positive updates: Travel to Africa. Sexy date nights. Group trips to Packer games. Brewer games. Sexy food pics. People wearing bikinis and swimming trunks as they tube down rivers, lite beers in hands. Everyone's photos are sexy. Tan. Shirtless selfies where everyone has six or eight or ten packs. When did people start getting extra abs?

Everyone is having kids, adopting calendar-quality kittens and Air Buds and Shilohs. With every post I read, I feel shittier about myself and my Sean Penn-battered mug. I feel worse about my non-eight-pack abs. My childless, dogless, bikini-less, loser self. My stomach is still bloated, the redness above my pubic area has now formed into bumps—tiny red mountains of itchy, inextinguishable flames.

I see Zeke's update again, this time with sixty new pictures. I hold myself back from clicking.

2.

I hear Trey's snoring through the wooden door, which means his head is tipped back; he's probably drooling onto his chin, maybe sleep-apnea-ing, his pants around his ankles and his shirt on the ground. As it often happens, Trey has fallen asleep on the can with his coffee sitting on the counter next to him. He told me the best power nap you can have is immediately after drinking some coffee, before the caffeine's fully flown through your body. The nap plus caffeine is like a superhero power up, like two Mario mushrooms *whoop-whoop-whooping* you up 'til you can throw fireballs and fly. Pass on the Red Bull—just get coffee and a nap. The thought of Trey naked, snoring on the toilet—it makes me smile.

Trey being near gives me the illusion that these Facebook pictures won't bother me, as if we'd share and dilute any negativity. Half of the pictures are of the scenic views: the port city of Puno; the Nazca desert; the Sacred Valley; all the other Peru locales are like calendar photos. All these locations I've never seen other than in movies, books, and video game representations.

After these scenic shots, there's a new section of photos. Livi—with her brunette hair, now sun-bleached, braided into two pigtails—is sitting on Zeke's shoulders. Her small hands rest on his cheeks, smushing his smile and lips together. Happy—they look happy. Another photo is a candid shot of a group dancing on wooden planks tied together into a makeshift floor. In the background, a six-piece band plays. In the foreground, legs and arms are blurred all around except for the focused couple in the center. Perfectly still, Zeke's lanky arm twirls Livi. Her captured smile is caught at the center of the picture's frame.

Picture after picture, I feel worse. An addiction to feeling shitty, I can't pull myself from the computer. My gut just is pulled farther and farther down until I spin away in the computer chair. I look out the window where the squirrel scurries around a tree. This time, he's with a friend. Maybe a sexy lady squirrel with a six—no, an eight-pack; he's with a sexy lady squirrel who loves to travel and who owns a totes-adorbs apartment and just had cute squirrel twins and just scored a huge nut inheritance so he doesn't have to work at the nut-sorting factory. These two squirrels have the perfect life.

God, I need to talk to someone.

I pour a painkiller into my hand and swallow it dry. Pastor Bradley paid the entire medical bill, including the medications prescribed by Dr. Saiid. I should be more grateful, but instead I feel more like my mom than I'd imagined possible: general self-pity and self-loathing (but not in Las Vegas). Everything feels trite and laughable. I see value in what others are doing, but doing anything myself seems empty. So my faith is put in a pill to temporarily alter a mental and physical state.

Trey's snoring—with the occasional apnea breathing freak-out—serves as white noise as Mom fills my empty head. Once she became a mother, a life of possibilities died. No longer could she model or travel and paint or live a free life, youthful and unbounded. Birth control isn't perfect, and there are always those few that become the living manifestation of the "one to nine percent" of contraceptive that fail. That "failure" is simply a human being. A human being . . . a percentage.

According to the internet, pills are the second-most popular method to kill oneself. Like Mom. First is by gun, like Cobain and Budd Dwyer (on live TV; if you've never checked it out, the internet has the video). Third: hanging. Fourth: poisoning. Fifth: carbon monoxide poisoning, and so on. The website even provides what happens if you fail each of these methods. The website is a guidebook to suicide. It's a morbid informational guide. At the bottom of the website, in tiny font, it gives a disclaimer, encouraging people to live on, to get help, to visit these lists of websites and these lists of numbers that'll help you. I click on one. The website offers an online chat feature for instant support. I begin typing, the keys clacking.

"Hey. My name's Tyler. My mom's dead and so is Robin Williams."

The woman supporter who introduces herself as Sharon responds:

"Loss hurts, but time heals."

"Losing Robin Williams hurts the same as losing my mom," I type.

"I'm sorry to hear you've lost someone," Sharon the Online Counselor types.

"Because with Robin Williams, I can watch him in *Hook*, *Dead Poets Society*. All his movies show me a part of him."

"This is true," Sharon the Counselor types. "But you can never know an actor like you can a mother."

"But I've forgotten most of her. Sure, I've got a few videos from b-days and pictures. But I don't remember her voice. Robin Williams, though, I can do a perfect impression. Trust me, it's spot-on. Williams left something behind. I just have Mom's Precious Moments collection. My vague memories blend with movies and books I've read. She's no more real to me than an actor or actress." I punch enter and it sends.

The text box indicates Sharon the Online Counselor is typing, and as she does, I flip back to the other tab. Below the suicide disclaimer, there are a few notes about famous suicides. One of them is about poet and author Sylvia Plath's choice: head in the oven, wrapped in cloth, which I am surprised is not on the top-suicides list. But the note goes on to explain that this means of suicide is death by carbon monoxide poisoning—number five on the list. It's the same as running the car in the closed garage. A misremembered Plath line pops into my head: *it's as if a great muscular owl were sitting on my chest, its talons clenching and constricting my heart.*

The computer beeps, the tab blinking orange, indicating Sharon has responded, but morbid curiosity drags me across the room to the kitchen. I stand over the oven, reading the control panel to find the *ON/OFF* switch. I press it. The inside glows red. I look around for a cloth, but don't see one within reach. I listen for Trey's snoring, but it's stopped. No movement from the bathroom means he probably just adjusted his head during his toilet-time coffee nap.

I tip my head to the side, inching it into the oven, feeling the heat on the right side of my head. I'm careful not to make any sudden movements. I hold my head there, breathing steadily, just inches from the red heating coils. How long did Plath hold her head here? How long until she lost consciousness, her head falling limply onto the oven rack? The heat starts to make it difficult to breathe—too hot and stifling. I sense a presence behind me, and I roll my eyes to look down without moving my head.

"Sylvia?" I say. I see two bare feet standing behind me.

"You can't kill yourself that way," Trey says flatly.

"Sylvia did it."

"Yes, so did William Inge and Assia Wevill and Amy Levy. That was also a long time ago. We don't use the gramophone or the horse-powered buggy anymore. Ovens are different now. Natural gas isn't the same as what powered ovens when Sylvia Plath said, 'Later world.'" He pauses for a moment, watching me struggle to get my head out of the oven without searing the side of my face like a steak. "Also, Ty, *that's* an electric oven."

"Yeah." I say. "I know. I was curious what it felt like." I close the oven door and lean against the counter. "How was your toilet-time nap?"

"Supercharging. I feel like I could lift a . . . a big heavy thing." He shrugs and presses the *ON/OFF* switch on the oven. "You realize that if *anyone* else would have walked in on you like that, they would have freaked out? Called the cops, starting blubbering, reached out to save your unredeemable soul."

"Yeah," I say, standing next to the heating oven, leaned casually against the counter, my crooked nose blurring my right eye's vision as I focus on Trey. "They'd probably update their Twitter, Facebook, asking for prayers. *Keep him in your thoughts.*"

Trey nods. "I was thinking, during my nap."

"Yeah? That's called dreaming."

"For some people. I *think* when I sleep."

I roll my eyes.

"Right now," he says. "This moment—we're alive. Right?"

I nod like a kid being asked rhetorical questions by an adult. *Yes, I am alive. Do I get a gold star?*

"And we living people are only a few in comparison to all the corpses crushed beneath the grass and dirt. So, when we complain about little shit, like the fact that my *Walking Dead* comics aren't here yet even though I ordered them *four motherfucking weeks ago*, it's pretty damn ungrateful. Eventually, you and I'll be dead—probably not even lucky enough to be ambling around trying to eat people."

"We can only hope."

"I just mean," Trey says, "they're dead. *You're* alive." He says this slowly and deliberately, as if I need time to comprehend. "See the difference?"

Dead and alive. I get it. Do I get that gold star now?

I almost tell him to stop being so condescending.

Trey says, "I just say this because my power nap was filled with all the shitty, pouty things you've done since last year. It was a dream montage that should've been entitled *The Douchebaggery of Tyler Linley: The Ungrateful Living*."

I just stare at him.

"Pretty much," he says, "you've been douchey since the fire burnt our stuff."

"Yeah, well, I lost a lot more than you did," I say. "And it's not like I could've prevented it."

"It's just *stuff*, dude. It all gets old and thrown away." He pauses.

I want to say, no, it was more than just "stuff." Without my "stuff," I am stuck in my mind all the fucking time, alone with my own thoughts and personality. He says, "I'm still sorry about the Tokster, that little furball."

I really do miss Toki the Cat.

"But the fire didn't just end that day," I say. "It fucked with me. This whole thing with Kennedy would've never gotten bad if the fire wouldn't have happened." I stop and rub my nose. Inhaling, my crooked nose whistles. "I thought it was either him or you that burned the place down. I figured you couldn't be *that* much of an

incompetent failure with no job, no education, no girlfriend—
nothing."

"Hey, man, I choose my own life. I like it, and I'm not all wound
up and pretzel-gutted like you. I chose to take control of my shit,
without all the crutches like your little vodka-and-pill addictions."
He points to the recycling bin, which is topped with empty clear
bottles, all with a twist-off red cap. "I've been keeping track lately,"
Trey says. "Since Livi left, you've gone through forty-nine bottles.
Forty-nine. For pumpkin bowling, we almost had enough bottles to
set-up *five* lanes. We could've turned it into a block pumpkin-
bowling party."

I look at the bottles set near white recycling bin. Under my bed,
there are more. Enough to add another lane or two.

I'm avoiding eye contact now, looking back out the window, but
the squirrel and his friend are gone, off taking selfies atop the best
squirrel locations in the city, showing everyone how totally
awesome their lives are.

Trey waits an awkward moment. "I'm just being honest."

I nod. That sinking feeling is in my gut back again—a mix of
self-pity and the desire to curl up and disappear into nothingness like
dying Pac-Man.

"Now tell me," Trey says, his voice curious, curling into a
question mark. "How is this whole Kennedy thing *my* fault? I didn't
start anything with him."

I walk over to the couch, plop down. He does the same, and I tell
him the tedious details: Me getting fed up with Kennedy's free
tuition, his easy life. Me stealing the pills from Kennedy. Kennedy
threatening me (in poorly written text messages). Me narcing to a
cop about his pill sales because I thought he burnt the down the
duplex.

Trey's face shows disappointment, as if I'm telling him I
masturbated in church.

"Tyler, the fire was my fault. I left the candles burning. I was
stoned. I was off in my D&D world, lost in a thought bubble. Arson
guys knew right away. The insurance guys told me it was accidental.
Told me it was probably a cat knocking over a candle or brushing up
against one. I figured you knew it was accidental. Besides, Kennedy
isn't a bad guy, you know? He's just . . . a shitty off-brand Eminem-
slash-DJ Qualls."

At this point, *Oh, well,* is probably my best reaction.

"Ah." I say. I kick my feet up on the coffee table. Trey flips on the TV. On HBOGo, he starts a *Boardwalk Empire* episode and catches me up on the seasons I've missed. Even though I'd loved the show a year ago, now it all seems trivial and irrelevant. Nodding politely as Trey speaks, I watch the behavior of the characters on the TV series. Few escapes were available for the 1920s men and women. They faced more of reality than we do now, and the thought of living in a cabin, detached from the information-saturated society seems appealing. Alone, I'd be faced with just myself. Either I'd succumb to cowardice or I'd emerge stronger.

At the end of the episode, Trey asks, "How's the relationship with the lady friend?"

"I don't remember." I shrug. "I think I'm in love with her family—the idea of what comes with her more than Livi herself."

Trey nods and he rubs his hand on his chin—his philosophical pondering face. "You love her family, you say. But do you ever want to *make love* with them?"

"Oh, Jesus."

"Like her grandma and stuff? I mean, Liv is a *fox*, and so is her mom. I have seen Facebook pictures. So, I imagine her G-maw is probably a stone-cold GMILF with some tricks up her sleeve."

"She's dead."

"I'm not here to judge, brother." Trey begins to adopt a slower speech pattern, as if channeling the spirit of a wise turtle.

I say, "It's like Livi is more fun and enjoyable when we're with her family. The small irritations or problems are diluted by the family being there. With them around, I can ignore annoying things she says about the abuse of tuna, or the emotional impact on wolves during wolf-hunting season."

"Ah. I see," he says, nodding his head. He's leaned forward, resting his elbows on his knees.

"Even Jordan, whom I can barely stand, is fun to be around in the family setting. I love having that antagonist relationship with him"

"Nice use of *whom*."

"Thanks."

I say, "In a group, things are less predictable, dull, boring, monotonous. 'Cause after a while, I knew everything that Livi was going to say. Right after those first few words, I could tell where she was going."

"I hear that. It's how I felt after the first seasons of *Dexter*. The first few seasons—fucking awesome. But it got so repetitive and dull I could only watch it with other people."

"Yeah. Exact same thing." I roll my eyes.

"No, man. I hear you. Your family sucked and now you like hers. Pretty simple. Seen it in books, movies. You're not the only one, man. But it's weird. You and Liv don't really have the same shared pop-culture history, but you guys still mesh well. Growing up with no TV or video games puts her at a disadvantage in the relationship with you. You'd probably be best with a nerd like yourself, but, hey, I love Livi. She's great. No joke."

"So is her family."

"From what it sounds like, yeah, they must be cool, too."

"Quite."

"Indeed."

If Livi were here, she'd say, "Indubitably."

"Random thought," I say. Trey flips through HBOGo. "Has this ever happened to you? You're standing by a ledge of a high building, like the Sears tower or on top of the Ramada Inn. The closer you get to the edge, the more nervous you get. You have to back away. Part of it, you tell yourself, is because you're afraid of heights. But the real reason is because you think you'll jump. Like an inherent drive, a reptilian urge genetically passed down. So you just stay as far from the ledge as possible, because you don't know if you'll be able to stop yourself. You might have an involuntary muscle spasm, and *splat*. Over. Done with."

Trey stops flipping through HBOGo. He stares at me. "No. I've never had that happen."

"That's good. That's a really good thing, Trey."

3.

We sit in front in the glow of that huge TV for hours. We watch dancing shadows cast upon the dungeon's wall. We chat when episodes end. He catches me up on the things he's doing: writing a comic book series about a wise Turtle who travels the post-apocalyptic terrain helping those in need while searching for his ultimate purpose in life. In his bedroom, he's been building an old-school arcade cabinet with a computer-run emulator so he can get 3,000-plus old games all on one cabinet. Together in the garage, Caleb and Trey assembled an action figure replica of some battle from the Clone Wars.

"It's crazy how much time you two spend together," I say, my feet still on the coffee table. "Ever since he's been crashing here—I should say living here for free—you've been together twenty-four seven."

"It's not without its irritations, like you and Livi. Caleb can be . . . annoying. He makes things complicated for himself. You know, back and forth. All about the em, then all about the eff. Bee then gee."

"Why can't you ever just say something normally? I don't know what that means."

"Male then female. Boy then girl."

"No one knows that."

"I knew that."

"What does it mean?"

"Caleb bangs dudes and chicks."

Again the obvious needs to be spelled out for me.

"Lately, he's been talking about that Zeke hipster 24/7. Caleb complains that Zeke doesn't know what he wants and whatnot. Ever since he saw those stupid pictures with Livi, Caleb's been bringing Zeke up every day. I can tell it's on his mind more than he says, which is even more irritating."

"I bet."

Trey says, "I think Caleb hits the gym so much because he sees I'm not exactly a paradigm of athletic prowess, and he wants to distance himself from tubby me, even though he knows I'm better than Zeke in every way." He scoffs. "Vanity. And it's mostly for that hipster with his stupid summer beanies and bracelet-covered wrists and his 'Neuter the Whales You've Just Saved So We Can Feed the Children!' slogan T-shirts. Everything is so—"

"Illusory?" I say.

"Yeah. All in an attempt to appear philanthropic." He mumbles under his breath, "Zeke's a douchebag trend-follower. Everything is hidden under a layer of fake-baked irony."

There's a pause in the conversation.

"So you're not a fan of this guy, either, huh?" I ask, trying not to smile.

"No. And Caleb never does the best thing: ignore him."

"I can't seem to do that, either."

"Apparently. I see you've been flipping through pictures of him."

How does Trey know?

"I know because my phone has Chrome, and it has a history, showing me everything you've visited, even on the home computer."

"Yeah, right. I knew that."

I didn't know that.

"Man, you've got a lot to learn about shit in general."

I shrug.

Another moment of silence. This time it's awkward.

"This means," he says, "you probably saw the mail-order husband website, right?"

I nod. No use lying. I've been creeping through his history like an amateur gumshoe with no inklings or clue.

"Well, yeah." He pauses, searching for what to say. "There is a reason I haven't had a lady friend in forever."

I nod, "Yeah, I get it now."

"Took you a long time, huh?"

I nod. "I thought it was a phase. Then I stopped paying attention. I just remember all the girls in high school. I've just never thought about it."

Plus, I don't know, you've gained a lot of weight.

I say, "I've just . . . been busy. Movies. TV. Books. Livi."

Trey says, "You *really* gotta start learning about everything. Maybe start paying attention to things. I think you and my dad are the only ones who *didn't* think about it."

"Well, it's hard to tell. It's not like you've been butt-fucking Caleb on the couch."

"Whoa. Too far."

"Sorry. Just an image that popped into my head without my permission. You know," I say, "I've known it for a while—in my gut, like a feeling. But I just never really said it out loud."

Too caught up in my own minutiae.

"Well, good job, Mr. Marlowe. You've solved another already-solved case," Trey says.

"I'm sorry."

"Yeah," Trey says. "I'm just your best friend. Why would you notice obvious things like sexuality?"

"Yeah. I know. Again, I'm sorry. I just . . . I see, but I don't seem to observe."

~ ~ ~

I'm staring up at the ceiling. No appetite, restless, sweating, mind jumping to topic to topic—I can't sleep without a drink. I'm out of mixer, so I melt sherbet with my vodka. The cup rotates round and round in the microwave. As I wait, my heart beats in my ears and my hand twitch. I squirt liquid melatonin in with the sherbet vodka and wash down a sleeping pill. After the circus has come to town, I drift off.

4.

I wake. The moon's light paints my room blue. I grab a pen and paper and begin to write the dream. Lying on my stomach, my legs kick softly behind me like a schoolgirl writing in her diary. I don't want to forget this dream.

It took place here before my concrete apartment towered. Before paved streets ran between stacked buildings designed for paper-pushers and cubicle living spaces. Knee-high grassland stretched beyond the horizon in all directions. Little bubbles of poor villages sat here and there, all of them within eyesight of each other, but they were divided by some small disagreement: different interpretations of details in religious texts, or variant views of the roles of women or homosexuals or sexual relations with animals. You know, serious issues.

Off in the far distance from these village bubbles, two castles disappeared high into the clouds. A noble family owned each castle, and an intense power struggle raged between the two families. The origin of the feud was trivial, as both sides would admit. After weeks, it became apparent the origin of conflict didn't matter; what *did* matter? Both sides were pissed. They clung to that anger—it fueled all they did.

The two families attacked back and forth. First, subtle and petty: mudslinging and verbal attacks—political playground fights. But those amplified and morphed until stealthy assassinations left leaders bleeding to death in their beds. That exploded into public beheadings. Then suicides of honor or torture for information. Scene after scene, the families performed tortures for the poor villagers: Iron Maidens and Iron Chairs. Live flayings surrounded by thousands of gawkers. The Judas Cradle as family members watched. Rat and coffin torture as children stared, open-mouthed.

As the poor village people gathered to watch the punishments and bloodshed, they thought they were safe. They had no stake in the feud. They did not even understand it. Daily, one of the two noble families would hold public disembowelments or amputations. Nightly, rumors spread of fratricides, sororicides, parricides, patricides, matricides, filicides, dominicides, regicides, and genocides—these fabricated rumors spread among both the rulers and the peasants.

After years of daily killings, both castles ran out of room for body parts, so limbs began to litter the knee-high grasslands. The tall grass became matted down with twisted limbs, fingers, skulls, and scalps—all scattered like red confetti. The green grass dyed red, then black, as time took color of the remains.

Among the littered remains laid a young mother's corpse. Her blonde children huddled around her as if she were a warm fire. They didn't cry; they just stared blankly at all the death. As the feud grew worse, poor villages turned on each. *Which castle do you support?* They chanted mantras and choruses. To gain favor with their selected castle, villagers volunteered as guinea pigs so new medical techniques and knowledge could be gleaned. Some villagers were given various berries to test the results; others, the ingredients to what became identified as arsenic, ricin, and other poisons. Some lucky villager test subjects explored the world of psychedelics, before it drove them insane, leading them off to self-immolation to ward off creepy-crawly bugs; or the drugs compelled them to skydive from the tallest perch.

Only children remained off-limits. Until the age of ten, no one could do anything to a child. One day, a man tried strangling a child—a son of an enemy. To protest the nonsensical violence, an unknown man burnt himself alive. He withered away in flames as the slack-jawed villagers gawked. He protested, saying before dying:

"Let the past be. Let us move on." Yet people still killed because of the forgotten feud they clung to.

A day came when only children remained. In each of the village bubbles, children sat on their knees, huddled around their disfigured parents' and relatives' corpses. Like scattered Mr. Potato Heads. Bodies bloated, decayed, and settling into the ground. Some were buried, but most lay above ground. The children could not bury them all. Only those they knew were buried. Limb by limb. Like putting toys away in their proper places.

The children aged, and I learned I was one of them.

I saw a beautiful green field, a calm warm freeze filtering through the knee-high grass, which tickled at my bare legs. Beneath my feet, under a thin layer of grass, I felt the sediment shifting, like standing on an airport glide way. Beneath my feet, bloody corpses wriggled like worms, pushing the grass around like the wind itself. Beneath the apple trees and berry bushes, dead bodies were scattered. The plants' roots fed on what our ancestors left behind. I stood there—existing. I stood upon their downfall, just as it's always been. I live with the gifts they passed on, and this knowledge added a weight to my chest.

Someone had to test all the medicines I now gather from the local Walgreens to clog up a spell of diarrhea. I buy a pill to alleviate bloating. I think nothing of it, although someone once had to be the test subject. They suffered, died, and I benefit, living in this luxurious and accommodating society with instant everything: coffee, noodles, French dip, rice, soup, painkillers, anti-diarrhea meds, oatmeal, pudding, porn, hot chocolate, and, if you're a go-getter, death. We even know what'll kill us swiftly. Knowing all these obvious and simple things is a blessing and curse. To not make the most of this time is insulting, cruel, and irresponsible. To waste all this is a *fuck you* to the past.

It's this thought that makes my heart race. It's this dream that causes my pen to scribble across the notebook pages in a panic. This is a thought I cannot forget.

Each day, I am being drawn by horses, yanked in four directions, each direction an option for my life. I have this one-time blessing; this one-time life. Once I can't decide, I'm quartered. I need nine lives. One life to be a savior; one to help all in need. Another to lead. Another to teach. Write. Create music. Build beautiful carpentry that stands generations. Another to be a full-on crook, to understand a part of me (and Keri). Another to live among the poor, every day, in full survival mode. But I have one life, and then I pass the life on. Anything I haven't done, I pass the opportunity on. I become the ground on which apple trees feed.

It's elementary.

It's all *The Lion King*. The circle of life.

I'm writing this now with a throwaway pen, at age twenty-three, as if this is profound. As if the burden of choice and the weight of time are new. Everything is novel to me, the first time I've thought it, and I've done it. All of this is a movie never before shown to me.

Wasting this gift is despicable, I'd tell a psychiatrist. It makes me disgusted with myself, I'd tell that psychiatrist, his leg crossed at his ankle, his hand jotting notes. Maggie Ann Linley, my mother, she'd rather dump her last drops of water out in a desert than ration it out. The dream makes me disgusted with her, with Grandpa. Rat poison? Grandpa, you knew what it'd do, and that was your choice?

I tuck the notebook into my underwear drawer and stumble to the bathroom. Standing in front of the mirror, I stare at myself. My black and blue eyelids are split by my cocked, swollen nose. I stick my tongue through the tooth gap where a canine should be. Red lines spider-web over the whites of my eyes. I'm sleepless. Over nothing. I stare at myself like the scene from *The Royal Tenenbaums* in which Luke Wilson's character tells the mirror, himself, us, his audience— he is going to kill himself. Like Luke Wilson, I trim and shave my face. Those faint pockmarks show up again under the shave. Acne scars, fading with age. The ground below me is still and smooth, but the thought of all the dead I stand upon forces me, as Jordan McDermott might say, to man up.

The dead buried and planted like seeds in the ground. And I stand upon them, living their gift.

Chapter Twenty-Eight

Scene Not Found

Chapter Twenty-Nine

The ~~King~~ Girlfriend Has Returned

Keri lends me her Audi, her arrangement of '80s CDs, and a few cassettes (although there's no tape deck). Heading to the Chicago listening to shitty Poison and Van Halen, I weave through traffic at eighty miles an hour. I'm prepping what I'll say to Livi when I see her.

Our relationship is only a little over a year old, yet I've set a lot of weight upon it because of her family. Livi and I had spent nearly every day together. When I had free time, I thought first of running it by Livi, to see what she was up to. *Play* Metal Gear Solid *or see what Liv wants to do. Watch eight Wes Anderson movies or ask Livi to go for a bike ride.* If Livi was busy, Keri was my next thought. *Help Keri with her newest freelance article or watch sixteen episodes of* The Office. *Get drunk in a dark room or play Scrabble with Keri.*

I marked each holiday in bright colors on my calendar. I looked forward to seeing Keri, her grandpa, uncles, and nephews—even though most annoyed me and made my anxiety bubble, ready to pop like a pimple. I looked forward to Red Beard and his kids. I couldn't wait to get shat upon. The only family member of mine Livi's met was my Uncle Dave. He, upon first introduction, proceeded to lift his shirt and show her his non-existent belly-button. He said, "Lost it during 'Nam. Just kiddin'. Gallstones. Couldn't pass them because I got a narrow uree-tee. You know what a uree-tee is?" This same uncle wore a bungee cord the same day, the day of his son's wedding, while a nub cigarette hung out of his three-toothed mouth. Her family. It's more than Livi and my relationship. To me, it's more than the two of us.

~ ~ ~

I'm parked on the terminal ramp. In the rearview, I see my mushed-up face and prepare for Livi's reaction. She approaches, carrying her luggage. Behind her, Zeke follows. Livi's sun-bleached hair is braided over her shoulder, hanging between her breasts. She says, "Oh, my God. What happened, honey?" She sets her luggage down and runs her thin fingers over my face. Gently, she touches my swollen eyes, pulls my lip down to see my canine gap. Zeke steps to me and runs his thumb down my stitches. His touch shocks me— static electricity, maybe.

"You get in a bar fight, my man?" he says, genuinely concerned. His thin arms are suntanned and exposed in his sleeveless Peruvian coffee T-shirt. The curly chest hairs poking out of his shirt look like cursive writing. The whole car ride to the airport, I thought of strangling him or bludgeoning him with a whack-a-mole mallet, but now he's showing me concern. All my anger is gone. Poof.

I remember a scene from a movie or TV show, so I say, "Should see the other guy."

Zeke laughs and nudges me on the shoulder. Livi looks concerned, steps on my feet and kisses the side of my face. She smells like tanning and calamine lotion. Smells different. Not Livi. Different. And not Kristina the Pink Dress Girl, either.

"Honey," Livi says, "do you mind?" She points to Zeke and his luggage.

"A ride?" I ask, as if some part of me knew this was coming.

She nods and smiles. Stepping on my feet again, she kisses my swollen cheek, which throbs. I had imagined hundreds of conversations that'd occur at this exact moment. I had hundreds of ways I'd accuse her, how I'd work a confession out of her. I'd play good cop, bad cop, good cop, bad cop. All those fictional conversations disappear, and I'm quiet. I'm the silent driver. I am the chauffer.

In Keri's Audi, I'm focusing on navigating the rush-hour traffic: gas, break, honk. Gas, break, honk, flip the bird. Leaning back from the passenger seat, Livi is cracking up with Zeke. She's calling him Ezekiel, and they're impersonating someone from Peru. I turn up the radio, and Livi quickly turns it down.

"Don't stifle conversation with recorded history, *Tyler William.*" She turns to Zeke. "He's like this with movies, too."

After blocking out their inside jokes, I accelerate to ninety. Zeke leans forward and says, "I knew no one was picking me up. I never like planning that far ahead. Figured I could catch a ride with this gal's boy-toy." He pokes her arm. She pokes back. "Ty, you sounded like a great guy from what Livi's told me. I shouldn't have assumed you'd help me out. I'm sorry for that. But I figured you wouldn't mind."

Zeke, a grade-A freeloader. Me? A nice guy?

I laugh and smile with my mouth into the rearview.

He'd probably asked for travel money from his grandma and her church, which was filled with his grandma's friends. All of them wanting to pinch his cheek, saying how good-a boy he is; how he's so unselfish with his desire to travel to help those in need. Me, I'm a sap who'll nod his head, say, *Yes, I'll do whatever you say. Yes sir, I'll drive you around. Drop your tip in my cubby on the dashboard.*

I'll hold back anything I'd like to say. I'm not really here, anyways. I'm just the cabbie. I'm the observer, watching a few rows back in the theatre.

After the two giggle for a month, I can't push away the thoughts anymore. I say, "Can Livi and I get a minute? I haven't seen *my girlfriend* in four months."

He nods. "Sure thing. Anything you need, boss. Anything you need." Zeke puts massive headphones over his tan head. He lies down in the backseat, propping his legs on the luggage pile next to him.

Livi asks again, "Honey, what really happened to your face?"

I swear there's a bruise on her neck. A hickey like in grade school. Or is it a Peruvian punch-to-the-neck? A birthmark I never noticed?

Deep inhale, exhale.

"Olivia McDermott, what happened to your neck?"

She's looking out the window at the cows grazing in fields, the fences bordering clumps of towering trees. Maybe she misses Wisconsin's landscape. Maybe she can't look me in the eye.

"What do you mean?"

"I mean, look at your neck," I say, backhanding the rearview so it reflects her image.

She adjusts the rearview. Looks at her neck. She scoffs. "What's this, the third grade? No one gives or gets hickeys at our age. Why would I have a hickey?" She looks out the window. Poison's song about doing it behind the tool shed plays on the speakers.

"Why didn't you look at me when you said that?" I ask.

"You're driving a car. That's why. I don't particularly want to kill us by drawing your attention away from the road. Remember last time? The time you almost *did* kill us?" She looks at me now, scowling.

Yes, I do remember. I've felt shitty about it since you left, I don't say. I've felt shitty about what I could've done, should've done to show you what this all means to me. What you mean to me. I've thought about my crushed and ruined Betsy the Buick rusting away in some junk yard, scavengers picking her apart. I've thought how I neglected you.

But this guy in the backseat? He changes things.

Instead of saying anything I feel, I ask about her trip because the little boy carpooler in the back seat sits there, inhibiting my true thoughts.

She goes on about the details. I nod, look at her frequently. But she's just looking out the window, daydreaming and describing it all: she's reliving the scenery, the people, the feelings. Her mind is back in Peru. She's gone. She says, "And this little, adorable boy, he became, like, best friends with Ezekiel. It was so sweet. This little impoverished boy had lost his writing hand in a terrorist-motivated bombing. Ezekiel even gave the little boy his old iPod because the boy *loves* music, especially Carlos Santana."

If I take a sharp enough turn, Zeke—not buckled right now and dozing off—might go hurdling out the back door.

Only one way to find out.

After a while, Olivia realizes I've said nothing.

"I'm sorry, sweetie. I didn't even ask. How were things? Did you start any new TV series? Zeke told me Caleb and Trey have been watching *Boardwalk Empire* lately. I know you wanted to read that R.R. Martin fantasy-world series and the dead people comics."

I almost start. Instead, I say, "Good. Everything's been good. No TV shows. No movies. Nothing to report on. Just been doing nothing." I'm sarcastic, but she doesn't seem to notice or mind. She's still off somewhere else.

When I drop off Zeke, he leans between the seats, pecks Livi on the cheek, and reaches around my seats and hugs me. "I can't tell you how much I appreciate it, Ty. Olivia McDermott, I will never forget our time together."

She smiles, gets out of the car as he does. They hug. I stare forward at his apartment building.

The automatic locks click as she gets back in the car.

"Did you cheat?" I say.

She looks directly at me.

"You're being serious?"

I nod.

"No. I absolutely did not," she says, staring at me. She swallows hard. "You think I value a commitment so little that I'd cheat on you? Just because you don't know what I'm doing? That's what you think of me?"

I don't know why I busted out with that thought—too impulsive. Now I'm on the defensive. "I saw the pictures on Facebook and it made me think that—"

"Pictures on Facebook? Pictures of our tour group together, enjoying ourselves? *That's* what makes you think I'd break off a commitment? Random pictures on social media make you think that I'd go off and fuck someone just because I felt like it?"

"No, I just—"

"You don't know me very well, do you, Tyler? Maybe this epoch apart skewed your idea of who I am." Her body is entirely facing me now, her legs on the seat, her arms bracing the dashboard and headrest. "You think me saying 'I love you' means nothing? You think words are just words, empty and void? Hmm? Like an actor on screen?"

Now I'm looking out the window, watching the sedans and minivans reflect sunlight into my eyes. I want to jerk the wheel into the oncoming traffic.

Livi says, "Now you've got nothing to say. After accusing me, you've got nothing. Nothing." Her gaze is hot. The sun beams reflecting into my eyes spark an instant headache, and I don't know what to say.

"I'm sorry . . . ? I don't know why I assumed. I just haven't seen you in so long that, I guess, I don't know. I forgot who you are. You started to blend in with all my other ideas of people."

"I blended into your cynicism," she says, relaxing her pose now that I've responded. "You force your cookie-cutter interpretation onto everyone. *Everyone's doin' it for the glory. Everyone's selfish but trying to hide it. People go off to serve the nation, to do charity, but it's all self-serving.* I went to Peru to fulfill a desire I have. I want to help people. So I tried. What have you done?"

I almost mention my tutoring, but I know I do it only because it pays well. I do it only because it pads my résumé. Instead of lying, I just look at her—a deer in headlights.

She turns up the radio and we listen to terrible '80s stadium rock until we pull into Olivia's apartment. I'm helping her unload her luggage. I set it down, stop her, and hug her. I say, "I know I have nothing to offer. Maybe that makes me suspect of anyone who shows me affection. I'm sorry, and I love you." But it doesn't sound right.

She steps on my feet, kisses my cheek. "I love you. But you can't be this way forever."

1.

That night, I ask if I can stay over. She says yes, and when I show up with my little bag of toiletries, she's sitting at the kitchen table across from Zeke. They're playing Backgammon and laughing—at me, my gut feels.

"Tyler," Zeke says, standing and shaking my hand. He's wearing a tank that reveals his tattoos: a PBR symbol on his tiny bicep; below it is a *reduce, reuse, recycle* symbol. On his shoulder is a green wispy stem, sinewy like a snake with baby leaves sprouted. "It's good to see you again. Bought some PBR because I know you love your drinks." He laughs, pats me on the shoulder. "I also got you some vodka." He whispers, smiling.

"I didn't know you were here?" I say to Zeke while looking at Livi.

"Figured I'd swing by, say hi. I was in the neighborhood." He points to his bike, which is leaning against the white wall. "You're a lucky fella, Tyler. She's a blast to be around." He's looking at Livi and she's looking at him. I'm not even in the room as far as they're concerned. I've disappeared completely.

"Yes. I am lucky," I say. "Quite." I hope Livi says *indubitably.*

Zeke says, "We'll finish up here, and you two can finally be alone."

They finish their game and I sit on the couch, away from the two. Waiting.

When Zeke is finally leaving, he reaches over the couch and pats me on the chest. "Good seeing you again, boss."

I nod, and he leaves. Livi puts away backgammon and stands in front of me.

"Why can't you at least try to be social?"

I shrug. "I didn't think you'd be alone with him again."

"Again?"

"I figured you'd be here alone."

"I'm sorry for having friends."

"I have—" I cut myself off. "I'm just off today. I'm in a funk."

"Let me help you get out of that funk." She climbs atop me and says, "I've been counting."

"Counting what?"

"The days since the last time we . . . ." She undoes my belt, and I scratch at my lower stomach.

"*Ohhh,*" I say.

"One-hundred-twenty-eight days. I counted." She kisses my neck, but she smells so different. Sunburn and tanning lotion. Like a new person. Bit by bit, she gets closer to me until memories of her flood back. On her shoulder I notice something new: a wispy stem of a plant with leaves branching off.

2.

"Let's go out to breakfast," Livi says as the sun rises. I'm lying in bed, but she's already moving around the room, slipping into tights, pulling a dress over her head. She's detached and rushed. "I figure it's been such a long time. And I have something we should talk about. So, let's get breakfast at Bailey's."

Bailey's, our first and favorite breakfast date location.

"You going to get the usual?" I stretch and yawn.

"I'm not eating eggs anymore, so no more omelets." She stops rushing around the bedroom and says, "Do you know how some of these chickens are treated? It's horrible. I saw one video where a chicken gained so much so fast that its legs couldn't even support its weight. Every step it tried to take, it just plopped down on the ground. I cried. It was so sad." She pauses for a moment, and moves around the room again. I want to get up, but my head aches. I feel self-conscious being naked around her.

"Are you getting up and getting ready or are we just going to lie around all day?"

"I'm getting up."

"I'm sorry. I just—I only have so much time today. I have an interview this afternoon."

"An interview?"

She nods. "I told you last night."

"You didn't."

She pauses. "Oh. Okay. Maybe I forgot. Well, I have an interview today." As she leaves the room to make her morning coffee, I slip into whatever I find on the carpet. She explains how the job is in Milwaukee, that it's for a co-op trying to grow healthy food in the middle of a city. She can't wait to do the interview because it'd be such a great opportunity for . . . and I stop listening. A two hour drive from Ashgrove, I hate Milwaukee. It's filthy, sardine-packed, and everyone has a car despite there not being enough room for everyone to have a car.

"You'd move to Milwaukee?"

"*If* I get the job," she says. I could say a thousand things, but I just nod and climb into the shower, not thinking but scratching at my southern regions like an ape.

3.

Bailey's smells like mothballs and burnt coffee. Liver spots dot the elderly who gum their omelets. The couple next to us looks out the window, away from each other, as their shaky hands hold their coffee mugs. The droopy waitress approaches and greets us; she's the middle-age who is a pro at her job and will probably be such until she retires or wins the lottery. We order drinks, and Livi is poking at her phone—something she never did four months ago. The old man next to us starts mumbling and picking at his teeth. His wife looks at him, says, "The adhesive won't hold if you're always picking at them."

Just as I'm about to comment on Livi's phone usage, my phone vibrates, which scares me a bit—I'm used to *never* getting messages or phone calls. In fact, I should probably cancel my cell service. I'm wasting sixty bucks a month. No one ever contacts me except Keri or Livi. And Livi's certainly not texting me right now. My message reads:

Kennedy: Hey. Ka gets outta hand, and i been thinkin. He went to farr. Fucked you up good. nd yer a fuck no dout, and i hurd yur cat died. Sorry. But lets meet up, ill buy u a drink. on me. O'Malley's tonight? no more pills tho.

I tongue my absent canine. They should've just killed me. Could've eliminated many problems with one action. I text back:

Sure. By the gambling machine? 9 p.m.?

After all, I started all this. I caused the conflict. Yet he wants to buy me a drink? All I've done is be an asshole.

The waitress brings Livi orange juice and me chocolate milk. Livi thanks the waitress. Livi says to me, "You know there's high-fructose corn syrup in that, right?"

"I'm doing method-acting research on what it's like to have diabetes, so it's all good."

She pokes at her phone again. "I'm sorry I seem so distracted. On the trip, my God, my thoughts were running a mile a minute." She stops poking at her phone and looks at me. "It's like, seeing all that new terrain and all the beauty—it just overwhelmed me. I wanted to do *everything*. I filled a full notebook—no joke—with ideas and plans." She pauses, pokes at her phone. I refrain from telling her that *I* supplied almost four pumpkin bowling alleys with empty-vodka-bottle pins. *How's that for impressive?*

"So, this job," she says. "It would be an *amazing* start on my journey." She pulls her notebook out of her purse a bit. "This notebook has my future all planned out."

"And what does this future look like?" I say. Out of the corner of my eye, I see the old man picking at his teeth. He pulls them from his mouth and a long ribbon of drool droops as he plops his dentures into his water glass.

The old man mumbles, "Good thing I got the soup."

"Well," Livi says, dropping her phone into her purse, which—by the way—is made entirely out of hemp and love. "That's why I wanted us to come here."

It's when she says this that I'm glad I took my medicine this morning. On cue, my junkal area starts itching again, and I'm not wearing my belt today, so why all the itching? Is it because of last night? Sex with Livi for the first time in months? An STD? Did Olivia fucking McDermott give me the clap? Or did Kristina the Pink Dress give me the herps? The clap? The clam, the pox, the morning drip, crotch crickets, dysury, penis atrophy, crotchal canine madness, or the red card? Did she infect my naughty bits with her spoiled bologna curtains? How quickly do AIDS and herpes and crabs show up? Is it a morning-after explosion of festering itching? Is it a slow-burn surprise like a good ol' detective novel? My God, how I wish my Christian education included sexual education.

"Did you give me herpes?" I blurt.

Goddamnit.

She looks at me like I just shat out of my mouth, *South Park*-style. I rub my eyebrows. I say, "Just ignore my sudden Tourette's. Say what you were gonna say."

"Last night, I was talking with Zeke before you came over. He thought I needed to see if you and I still had our 'spark'."

The waitress returns and takes our order, interrupting Livi. The waitress's tired eyes sag. I order whatever Livi does.

The old couple next to us begins arguing when the old woman says, "I can't eat with those things floating in front of me." Her shaking hand points at the dentures.

The waitress leaves. Olivia sips her orange juice. "I'm sorry." She pauses and stares at me. "This can't work. We're fundamentally different."

I'm blinking rapidly, and her mouth moves like in an old silent film. On her shoulder, I imagine her new tattoo of a wispy stem of a plant with leaves branching off. It sprouts and grows off her shoulder. Leaves hang gently as she speaks.

"I love you," she says. "My family does. God, I mean, I loved you with my family, when my cousin pooped on you. Seeing you like a father—I adored that. But this isn't going to last forever. You and I—we'll never get to that point. We're branching off in two directions. You know it's true." She waits, looking at me. Her eyes are soft and caring. She's concerned. No longer hurried and frazzled like she'd been all morning. "See, I know you. You're so different than me. I bet you're comparing this situation, right now, to something you've read or watched. Am I right?"

She is right.

"But . . . I love you," I say. It sounds pathetic, and I'm too aware of it. I'd laugh if it were said in a movie. I'd pause the movie and make fun of it with Trey. *Look at this ass-hat.*

But I say it again.

She says, "I know. I guess I just needed a different perspective. In this new country, in Peru, I saw it all through a new lens." She pauses and sips from her orange juice. She tucks her hair behind her ear. Biting her lower lip, she says, "You know how you drive past something every day, and eventually, you just stop seeing it? It just becomes the norm. You never think about it anymore? You don't even notice the graffitied water tower or the police station anymore. Then one day, you stare at it. You see it with fresh eyes. And you can't stop looking at it. Things look out of place." She's watching my reaction, but I'm just blinking nonstop. It's all strobe lights.

She says, "Being too familiar with you blinded me. I couldn't see the whole picture." She pauses, sips, and then snaps her fingers. "It's like when you sit too close to the screen in the theater. You can't see everything. You miss the audience. You miss the corners of the screen. You can't see it all at once. Get too caught up with some chick's cleavage on one side of the screen." The waitress brings us our food. There's a leaf and some kibbles and bits on my plate.

Reaching to grab my hand, Livi says, "I truly do love you. But this is a step. My family loves you . . . in small doses. You love them, in small doses. But permanently, this'll never work. You have too much to fix, and I have too much to learn and explore. I really mean this. I adore parts of you. But it is unsustainable. This whole thing. You know it, even if you don't realize it yet."

That word again. Sustainable.

She says, "And it's just—none of us are the same as we were a moment ago. Change is all there is."

I stand, pushing my plate away from me. She did this in public, here among Old Man Dentures and Lucy the Lifer and the other calm citizens so I wouldn't make a scene. Like firing a longtime employee. Here in public, I won't throw a drunken fit of rage. She did this in the early morning, an hour or two before my habit starts. And—no—I won't make a scene. Not here. Not now. She knows this. She knows me. She loves me. Yet this is happening.

Standing among thirty round tables of gray-haired retirees, I ask Livi for one last kiss, one last feeling of those full lips.

"Yes," she says. "I'd like that." She stands up, walks to me, steps on my feet. I tuck her hair behind her ear, like I've seen in so many films before me. She kisses me, and I use all my mental power to capture that feeling, image, and moment—a snapshot. And that's it. She stays to eat. I drop cash on the table. Before I walk off, she asks me to burn her one last CD. Knee-jerk reaction, I ask *her* to burn one last CD. I say, "I love Iron and Wine. I'm sorry I ripped on it at first."

"It's okay. People hate new things at first." She sits back down at the table, sipping from her orange juice. I nod. I tell her I love her again, as if this will change something.

She repeats it back.

"Someday," she says, "we'll be at each other's weddings, and this'll be a funny story."

4.

I'm lying alone on Trey's loveseat with a glass balancing on my chest when my phone rings. Numbed by 'pam medications, horse tranqs, muscle relaxers, and cheap liquor, I answer it.

"You answered your phone!"

"My mistake. Goodbye," I say, pretending to hang up.

Keri laughs. "I had to call."

"I knew you would."

"Believe me, sweetie, I've talked with her. I can't convince her. She's made up her mind. She knows what she wants. I'm sorry. But she's my daughter."

I nod into my phone. "The other day, I was listening to that God-awful Poison CD in your sexy Audi when 'Every Rose Has Its Thorn' came on."

"I love that song," she says.

"It's terrible. But I thought, 'Is he talking about a whore? About some chick with VD?' I think he is."

"Well, yeah."

I scratch my junk like a monkey. "I can imagine what that's like," I say.

"What?"

I change the subject. "I wish I could keep you. Just you," I say. Quickly, I add: "And your family. Even Jordan. But I can't do anything. I can't balance this out. All I've got is my reaction. For a split second, Keri, I seriously thought of ways I could get back at Olivia. Ways I could even things out. Ways to get back at Zeke, that guy she's always with. But just the thought of hurting her, that hurt me. Maybe I'm a human," I say in my best robot voice. "I brought this upon myself." I sit up and do the robot, but she can't see me. Who am I trying to entertain?

"It is pretty robotic to hate Poison," Keri says.

"Does not compute," I say. "Hanging up cellular device."

"You know, I'm still going to call you. I care about you no matter what. When I said you're family, I didn't just mean temporarily. It'll be different, but I still want to know how you are and what you're doing . . . if that is okay."

"That is okay. You are wonderful." I let the words hang for a moment. I'm not embarrassed saying them. "But Bret Michaels and Poison still suck. Love you, Keri." I end the call and finish my drink. Not two minutes later, Jordan calls. His photo for caller ID is him in a camo sweatshirt. He's flipping the bird with one hand at me, saluting the flag with the other.

"Sorry to hear, man," Jordan says. "She told me before she told you. I'm in the know. But really, yeah, it sucks. I was just starting to like you, too. I mean, sort of."

I say, "Not that it matters anymore, but did she tell you about Zeke?"

"That dirty fucking hippie?"

I nod into my phone.

"Yeah. And I know what you're thinking. Chicks cheat. That's what they do. My old flame, while I was out fighting for her freedom, she was out with some dirty fuckin' douchewad. He was diddlin' her coochie while I'm out busting my ass. All so he has the freedom to fucking diddle *my* girlfriend's coochie. Can't trust 'em. Can't trust chicks, man." He pauses, as if running through it in his mind. His voice turns monotone. "But . . . I don't know. I've know my sis for my whole life. She's never been a liar, a cheat, or even . . . morally ambiguous."

Silence fills the air, and I let his comforting words settle over me.

"I feel for you, bud. Maybe she didn't cheat. I don't know," he says, distant. "In the end, nothing in the past matters. Keep plowin' forward." I keep my words short. I tell him good day, and that's that. I'll never speak to him again.

Chapter Thirty

Off Into the Sunset

"Mr. Bradley?" the receptionist says, looking up over her glasses.

"Yes," I say. I drink from my water bottle, washing down medicine.

"Birthdate, please." I rattle off David Bradley III's information. With his permission, I check myself in to see a doctor. I know Trey's social security number, mother's maiden name, father's middle name, his mother's stillborn sister's planned name, both parents' birthplace, where Pastor Bradley was ordained (*and much much more!*). But—spoiler alert—I never once acknowledged that Trey was gay. Since high school, he's mentioned it, and when people found out, it was a big hubbub at our Christian high school, but I've never seen him with anyone. I figured he was confused. Figured it was a phase. Figured wrong. I never paid it attention; too busy with my movies. Yet all the details were there. Caleb and Trey have been sharing a room for months. I never took the time to put it together. Why? I'm too caught up in my own neurotic solipsism. Rather than fading into an observer, I've been withdrawing into myself—the worst possible place to be. I do not see the shadowy man. I only see the nurse in front of me.

He asks about my face. Like a trained monkey, I repeat: "You should see the other guy." After waiting for an hour, the doctor asks about my face. I say, "I got the shit beat out of me. The other guys were exhausted from how much they beat my ass. And not just my ass. My ass-face, too."

The doc nods, smiles, and listens to my fears. I say, "So . . . my stomach is bloated. And I think I have the herp or the clap or the crabs or a collection of STDs." I don't mention that I'm worried I got it from my girlfriend who maybe cheated on me. I don't mention that I'm worried I got it from Kristina the Pink Dress Girl when I cheated on my girlfriend.

I drop my pants, and the doctor pokes around my naughty bits. I turn and cough—*Cough harder, please*—and she asks if the upper-crotchal area is the only area of concern. I nod. Affirmative.

"Do you wear a belt?"

"Yes."

"That," she says, pointing to my upper-crotchal region, "is just a rash—a reaction to the cheap metal. But we'll do all the tests, just to be sure, but it looks like your skin doesn't get along with your belt's cheap metal."

"I'm sorry for wasting your time," I say, pulling up my pants, feeling betrayed by my belt.

"It's no worry, David. Better safe than sorry," she says.

"Good point." She's about ready to shoo me from the room when I say, "I accused my girlfriend of giving me herpes."

"Well, you *could* have herpes. Often, people can have it and not show symptoms. We won't know until the tests come back. Nothing is showing, though."

"What kind of person accuses his girlfriend of giving him herpes?"

"David, I'm sorry, but if you need to work through this, I can refer you to a colleague of mine."

"Right. Sorry," I say, playing the role of David Bradley III.

1.

The real Trey picks me up from the clinic. He's laughing at me as he drives us to Barnes and Noble. "You had to tell them about your herpes? And it was just a rash because you're an idiot?"

"Pretty much," I say.

"You didn't just WebMD it?"

"WebMD didn't answer my questions. It's school's fault I'm stupid. At least all that STD stuff is under your name. You whore—out sleeping around, worried about your chode fallin' off."

Trey says, "Whatever. At least I can provide charity to those in need, such as my ungrateful friend." He rests one hand on my shoulder, his other hand at twelve on the wheel. "I'm glad your penis is okay."

"Thanks, Trey. Me, too."

Trey says, in a high-pitched voice, "Me, too," impersonating my penis.

"We're in our twenties, and this is how we speak," I say.

Trey answers, still in penis-voice: "Yes, much growing up we have to do."

2.

Inside Barnes and Noble, I'm flipping through the Self-Help section. Specifically, I'm looking for the section on how to improve: stop addiction; end depression and anxiety; cut down on being; end loneliness; how to foster a familial situation in which you love and are loved; how to develop an actual personality, one not derived from fictional characters.

I check the Dr. Phil and Joel Osteen sections. Jenny McCarthy. Dr. Oz. Even *Steven Seagal: How to Dominate With No Skill Set.* There's nothing that fits my specific needs. A sales associate asks if I need help. I explain what I'm looking for without taking a breath. She just laughs and says, "Call a doc, sir."

I laugh. I smile. I'm Ryan Gosling.

Maybe she'll be my next girlfriend.

When I'm ready to leave, Trey is still flipping through the comics section, irritated that I haven't allowed him several more hours to peruse. So I sit on a chair outside the restrooms. I stare at my phone for a bit. I dial the unfamiliar area code. I wait, staring at the phone. Part of me hates that I'm doing it, part is optimistic, but I poke the rest of the numbers.

"Son?"

Bruce, I almost say. Instead: "Dad." I fight off any negative Pavlovian reactions.

"Keri called. I heard about Livi," he says. I nod into the phone. "After she called, I've been thinking. What do you say—if you're up for it—a little trip out west? I'll pay for it all—flight and all."

Instinctively, I want to ask Livi. Then I remember that I need to retrain my mind—she is gone. But visiting Dad makes sense. The military has doctors. Dad's been in there for so long, maybe he can set something up with a shrink. Someone I can talk at. I've got nothing left. Not my plastic DVDs. Not my paperbacks. Not the family I'd clung to like a leech. I can't even feed like a parasite off my former ladyfriend. Like a sudden surge of energy, I'm hopeful. It's an odd feeling. Unfamiliar. Maybe it's what caffeine drinkers feel or religious people feel after singing and throwing their hands in the air. But maybe I've been wrong about Dad. Maybe he's got a baseball glove tucked away somewhere. Maybe a razor he could show me how to use. A Kodak moment: Bruce Linley showing his twenty-three-year-old son how to shave. Maybe it's time for a montage. Through a corrected lens, I see my dad has only loved me. He saved that stupid seal drawing; he kept Mom's infidelity a secret; he didn't even stay mad at me after I tried to pop his head off at my graduation party. And maybe, according to Dr. Phil-Oz-Osteen-Seagal, it might be time to love to someone else. At a certain point, I can't just keep receiving it. Gosling and Clooney—they don't give a shit. They aren't even real.

I say, "Yeah. It sounds like the right thing to do."

After silence, Dad says, "It's weird to lose somebody by their choice, isn't it?"

Mom.

There we find common ground. That seems like all we needed to do.

I ask Dad, "Do you mind if my best friend visits, too? He's gotten pretty chubby, so he might need two plane seats, but he'll love giving you shit for your military stuff."

"Oh, I've got plenty I could say to the pastor's kid."

A moment of silence.

The affair. Duh.

Reading my mind, Dad says, "Not about that. I mean about religion."

"Oh, right. But Trey's not religious."

"Too bad," Dad says. "Guess I'll have to give him shit for being fat."

"Big boned."

"Fat."

"Yeah, fat."

A moment of silence, and there's a voice is in the background.

"Hey, someone wants to talk to you," Dad says.

"Okay," I say. I hear sounds of the phone rustling and *SpongeBob* on a TV.

"Hi," the voice says.

"Hi."

"Are you Tyler?"

"Yes."

"You're my brother."

"I know."

"We've never talked before. And we're brothers."

Well, technically half brothers, I almost say. Instead: "Well, now we've said 'Hi' to each other. But you're right. Even at graduation, we didn't talk."

"How come?" he says.

"Because I'm selfish."

"You're shellfish? What?"

"You know what, Christopher? Can you ask your dad something?"

I can hear his face rub against the phone. He's nodding.

I say, "Ask him if I can visit next week. I'm going to order tickets today. I want to show you how to pumpkin bowl."

"It's not Halloween, though."

"We'll use watermelons instead."

He laughs. He nods his head against the phone. Dad's voice says, "Tyler can't hear you nod through the phone."

Christopher says, "That sounds funny and fun." Christopher drops the phone and asks Bruce *if Tyler can visit next week*. I hear Bruce's low voice. Christopher says, "Yes! Can we take him on the boat?"

After the phone fumbles between the two, Bruce says into the receiver: "You know how excited he is?"

I nod against the phone like Christopher. I hear Christopher running around the house, his feet pounding against the hardwood.

For the first time, I see it from the kid's point of view. I'd always wanted an older brother. He's technically had one for his whole life. Just an absent, disinterested one. Me, like father like son. My utter lack of empathy hits me like sunlight after days spent in a dark basement.

Dad says, "If I were younger, I'd probably be just as excited."

I don't know how to respond, so I just say, "Can you get me a military discount on one of the base's motels?"

"How 'bout this. We've got an extra room. It's yours as long as you want."

"A few days, I'm thinking?"

"Get a one-way ticket. We'll figure the rest out later," he says. "If we end up fighting again, I'll send you back to Wisconsin. If things go well, we'll take it from there."

Somehow he knows I have no job; no more college tutoring after graduation; no more local paper editing—that was an internship. Without a doubt, Keri told him. She's still looking out for me.

"Okay," I say.

"Yeah."

"Call me when you get the details," he says.

"I will," I say. "Dad?"

"Yeah?"

"I'm . . . uh," I say.

"I know you are. I am, too, son. Don't make this awkward."

"Bye."

"Yeah."

3.

On the plane, Trey's noise-cancelling headphones play "Hotel California," and I think of this place I've hated for years. The lifestyle, the mindset, their reductive view of non-coastal life . . . but then, it doesn't matter what I think. I've got nothing. No job, girlfriend, possessions. Well, I've got a degree in English-ing now, and I've been shitting blood, if those count.

Why didn't I bring that up at the doctor? The military doctor will take care of it.

He has to.

The thought of Livi and Zeke enters my mind. Vivid images materialize and animate. I wish I had an escape. But there's no on-flight film. I forgot a novel. All I want is to be emotionally manipulated. I'm rational enough to know that's what I'm looking for. For so long, I've been able to sit in the warm glow of escapism. I've been able to live vicariously—feeling anger, sadness, elation, loss, victory—a hit of any emotion. Instantly.

So often, I debated: Do I focus on the truth, or do I delude myself into happy ignorance? I want to be aware, but I want distance. I want to understanding truth, but I don't want to be swimming in it. I want to be sitting on the shore watching others doggy paddle, keeping their heads just above the water so they can breathe happiness and oxygen and not drown in pure, hopeless truth. But now I've decided. I can't allow the distance anymore. I need to be in it with everyone else.

Yet, I can't push the thoughts of Olivia and Zeke out of my mind. Logically, I can't imagine Livi being unfaithful . . . but the scenes still play until I'm thinking of the time I climbed a ladder up a reception tower in eighth grade. I'm thinking how I held onto the frozen ladder handles three stories above the ground. How I imagined the red splat I'd make when my body hit the snow-covered cement. I remember how Officer Kaigo coaxed me down and calmed me. A warm, muscular hug—he was not your typical officer. The jumping part—it seemed and seems so real, so easy. With one choice, in one moment, I could make that splat happen. It'd all be done. No more of these thoughts. No more being trapped in this mundane daily existence.

I rip out a page from the in-flight magazine and begin to write:

Livi, I lost a part of me because I was selfish. I'm sorry I wasn't what you deserved. I'm sorry I'm stuck in the past. I'm sorry I accused you. I'm sorry—

Trey taps me and I'm brought back to the reality of the airplane in which we sit. He mouths *Video Game Orchestral Music* as he points to his iPod. He gives two thumbs up, and he's smiling because he likes the CD I bought him when I invited him to California. He loves the Sonic theme song played by violins and other stringed instruments. He loves Zelda's theme song performed by a full ensemble. And I love having him here with me.

I smile back, and the suicidal thoughts evaporate like a wisp of smoke. I glance at my scrawled writing. The ink smears as I crumple the glossy sheet. It's over. Livi and I are the only ones who know what we had—that it ever existed, and I'm glad I had it. We both will always have it. But I'm only alive for a short time, and I want to experience something full and real. I need to move onto the next thing, whatever it is. I'm done with the past. I have to be.

Instead of Livi or Zeke or my melted DVDs, I think of Dad. My stepmom. My brother. My best friend.

I just need them—not delusion. Not Hollywood-filtered memories.

I switch my musical artist to Iron and Wine. Sam Beam's voice sings, "Poppa died while my girl Edith was born," and I start to panic about the missed time and events my family could've shared. I don't have any of those Kodak moments. These last eight years— just a fart in the wind. I've held onto anger and pain that long because I made it mean so much to me. Just like Olivia's grandpa, who clamped onto his wife's affair so many years ago.

An old man is boarding the plane. He wheels his oxygen tank behind him, and a flight attendant lugs his carry-on. She helps him sit down; she buckles him, adjusts the armrests. The flight attendant even opens a small bag for him. He rifles through the bag with his shaking hand and pulls out his medications. His chapped lips move, asking for water. He's helpless. He and I, we're the same, just different ages. I look down at my hands. They're shaking. I'm sweating, the withdrawals beginning. I gave all my pills to Kennedy because I want to face my family sober. Kennedy sincerely wished me luck.

I'll be mentally clear. For once, I am just *being*, nothing spiking my heart rate or sedating my mind. I vomit in the restroom as people board the airplane. The vomiting is so violent that I burst a blood vessel in my eye, and I glance in the mirror. In the reflection, I see that shadowy man towering behind me. *You can leave this all behind and just observe. You don't need to put yourself through these painful relationships. They always end badly. Everything ends in death. Why engage when you know the ending? Why—*

I rub my eyes and take deep breaths until he disappears. The stewardess knocks on the door, asking if I'm all right. I mumble, "Yes." I wipe my chin and the vomit-tears.

The next Iron and Wine song is more upbeat. Images pop into my head: Shaking Dad's hand; giving Christopher a noogie until he says "uncle"; pinning him down and tickling him, if he's ticklish. Maybe he'll poop-pee on me, just like Little Tyler at last Christmas.

I'll hug my stepmother and tell her I'm sorry for being an ass at their wedding. I'll tell them I've always been selfish. I'll ask her: *what's your favorite band? Do you use the Internet? What's your favorite TV show? Do you like sports? How 'bout them Cowboys?*

I'm running through all possible questions I could ask. On a napkin I'm jotting down all answers I should provide. Then I realize, if they're family, it doesn't matter how dumb I sound. I don't need to prep. If I'm an idiot to them, so be it. It is what it is, and I can't control everything. I'll wing it. I'll go with the flow. I'll call a quack and pay to talk to him. I'll meet up with other people in a local church's basement and explain how messed up I am. I'll tell them the fucked up things I've done. I'll join AA (but ignore that religious part). I'll collect my one-month chip, then six months, and I'll collect them until I'm normal. I'll do whatever works. I need to try it. I exist, standing upon all the dead, living this gift. I can't waste it any longer. I need to let it all play out without being in control. I'll let go. Admit defeat. And I hope it all works out. It will. It has to.

~~~

About the Author

D. W. Anderson's first release, *Mind the Gap* (2016), is a book-length collection of humor essays and stories. His writing can be found in publications such as *A & U Magazine*, *Cream City Review*, *Poetry Quarterly* and other periodicals. He teaches creative writing and English courses in Wisconsin. Equally important, he found his cat, Toki, in a plastic bag near a Redbox. They now live together in sitcom fashion.

DRUNK IN THE WARM GLOW
is also available as an e-book
for Kindle, Amazon Fire, iPad, Nook and
Android e-readers. Visit
creatorspublishing.com to learn more.

∘ ∘ ∘

CREATORS PUBLISHING

We publish books.
We find compelling storytellers and
help them craft their narrative,
distributing their novels and collections
worldwide.

∘ ∘ ∘

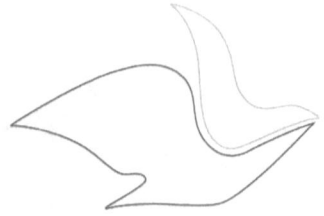